I
f
I
7
S
j
7
S

P

'S
ti
c
h

'I
re
w
pr
ab

'Unlike so many of the "writers" of her generation—those known as the literary brat pack—who spend their time describing in thinly disguised detail their own lives or the lives of people they know, or lives that they once led or hope to lead, Shriver creates a text, a̶   novel of depth an   ce'
orld News

'The quality and vividness of Errol's imagination is a tribute to Shriver's own; the pieces fall neatly and compellingly into place. This is a confident first novel, and a consuming one'

Publishers Weekly

'From beginning to end, *The Female of the Species* is intelligent, sensual, absolutely fascinating, and thoroughly extraordinary. And that's not half the praise it deserves'   *Richmond Times-Dispatch*

'Lionel Shriver is a remarkable new storyteller. These almost mythic characters and their exotic background are drawn with compelling imagination and verve . . . A daring beginning for a young novelist, bold in its choices and sometimes technically brilliant. Its sheer invention makes it a heady debut'

Cleveland Plain Dealer

ALSO BY LIONEL SHRIVER

Checker and The Derailleurs
Ordinary Decent Criminals
Game Control
A Perfectly Good Family
Double Fault
We Need to Talk About Kevin
The Post-Birthday World
So Much for That
The New Republic
Big Brother

THE
FEMALE
OF THE
SPECIES

LIONEL
SHRIVER

THE BOROUGH PRESS

The Borough Press
An imprint of HarperCollins*Publishers*
1 London Bridge Street
London SE1 9GF

www.harpercollins.co.uk

This paperback edition 2015
1

First published in Great Britain by Viking 1988

A catalogue record for this book is
available from the British Library

ISBN: 978 0 00 756401 9

Set in Adobe Garamond by Palimpsest Book Production Ltd,
Falkirk, Stirlingshire

Printed and bound in Great Britain by Clays Ltd, St Ives plc

To Jonathan Galassi, whom I owe not only for this novel, but for a life.

The envy of any housewife up to her ears in dish towels and phone bills, the women of the Lone-luk had their water carried, their children watched and wiped, their meals prepared and their plates cleaned, while they sat in judgment, sculpted and wove, led religious services, and oversaw the production of goods for trade. However, one could recognize in them, as in equivalent patriarchal oppressors, the cold boredom of domination.

GRAY KAISER,
Ladies of the Lone-luk, 1955

Il-Ororen thought they were it. Yet they did not have the celebratory abandon of a culture that saw itself as the pinnacle of creation; rather, they were a sour, even embittered lot. If these were all the people in the world, then people were not so impressive.

. . . I have wondered if they took Charles in as readily as they did because they were lonely.

GRAY KAISER,
Il-Ororen: Men without History, 1949

I remember, in a rare moment of simple dispassionate clarity toward the end with Ralph, she said to me, "You win and you lose; you lose and you lose; you lose."

"Some choice," I said.

She was a beautiful woman, and she was tired.

ERROL MCECHERN,
American Warrior: The Life of Gray Kaiser, 2032

chapter one

"Errol, I'm tired of being a character." Gray leaned back in her chair. "When I meet people they expect, you know, Gray Kaiser."

"You are Gray Kaiser."

"I'm telling you it's exhausting."

"Only today, Gray. Today is exhausting."

They both sat, breathing hard.

"You think I'm afraid of getting old?" asked Gray.

"Most people are."

"Well, you're wrong. I've planned on being a magnificent old lady since I was twelve. Katharine Hepburn: frank, arrogant, abusive. But I've been rehearsing that old lady for about fifty years, and now she bores me to death."

"When I first saw you in front of that seminar twenty-five years ago I didn't think, 'What a magnificent old lady.'"

"What did you think?"

Errol McEchern stroked his short beard and studied her

perched in her armchair: so tall and lean and angular, her neck long and arched, her gray-blond hair soft and fine as filaments, her narrow pointed feet held in pretty suede heels. Was it possible she'd hardly changed in twenty-five years, or could Errol no longer see her?

"That first afternoon," said Errol, "I didn't hear a word of your lecture. I just thought you were beautiful. Over and over again."

Gray blushed; she didn't usually do that. "Am I special, or do you do this for everyone's birthday?"

"No, you're special. You've always known that."

"Yes, Errol," said Gray, looking away. "I guess I always have."

They paused, gently.

"What did you think of me, Gray? When we first met?"

"Not much," she admitted. "I thought you were an intelligent, serious, handsome young man. I don't actually remember the first time I met you."

"Oh boy."

"You want me to lie?"

"Yes," said Errol. "Why not."

Errol found himself looking around the den nostalgically. Yet he'd be here again, surely. He was at Gray's house every day. His office was upstairs, with a desk full of important papers. And though he kept his own small apartment, he slept here most nights. Still, he seemed to be taking in the details of the room as if to mark them in his memory: the ebony masks and walking sticks and cowtail flyswitches on the walls, the totem pole in the corner, the little soapstone lion on the desk, and of course the wildebeest skeleton hung across the back of the room, leering with mortality. In fact, it was a cross between a den and a veldt.

The furniture was animate: the sofa's arms had sharp claws, its legs poised on wide paws; the heads of goats scrolled off the backs of chairs. In the paintings, leopards feasted. The carpet and upholstery were blood red. The lampshade by Gray's head was crimson glass and gave her skin a meaty cast. "I am an animal," Gray had said more than once. "Sometimes when I watch a herd of antelope streak over Tsavo I think I could take off with them and you'd never see me again."

Yet there was no danger of her taking off on the plains today. They were in Boston, and Gray did not look like an animal that was going anywhere. She'd been wounded. She was sixty years old. Though in fine shape for her age, she'd been sighted and caught in a hunter's cross hairs. He had shot her cleanly through the heart. Though she sat there still breathing and erect, Gray had never talked about being "exhausted" before, never in her life.

"I don't think—less of you," Errol stuttered, apropos of nothing.

"For what?"

"Ralph."

"Why should you think less of me?"

He'd meant to reassure her. It wasn't working. "Because it ended—so badly." Then Errol blurted, "I'm sorry!" with a surge of feeling.

"I am, too," she said quietly, but she didn't understand. He was sorry for everything—for her, for what he'd put off telling her all night, even, of all people, for Ralph. Jesus, he was certainly sorry for himself.

Pale with regret, Errol paced the den, trying to delay delivering his piece of news a few minutes more. And perhaps it is possible for parts of your life to flash before your eyes even if you're not about to die—because for a moment Errol remembered this last year of a piece, holding it in his hands like an object—a totem, a curio.

A year ago Gray had uneventfully turned fifty-nine. Errol had finally convinced her to do a follow-up documentary on *Il-Ororen: Men without History*. Her now classic book of 1949 had sidestepped her most interesting material: without a doubt, Lieutenant Charles Corgie. That February, then, they'd flown to the mountains of Kenya to the far-off village of Toroto, at long last to set the world straight on the infamous lieutenant. Though he'd struck the most compelling note in the story of her first anthropological expedition, until now Corgie had been peculiarly protected.

Shocked that Ol-Kai-zer was still alive, Il-Ororen were at first afraid of her. Yet no one could remember having seen her die. When she described how she'd escaped from Toroto, the natives dropped their supernatural explanations and soon decided to cooperate with Gray's film. They recalled that in '48 she'd taught them crop rotation; a few claimed she'd shot "only fifteen or twenty" Africans, which struck Il-Ororen as moderate, even restrained. The rest, of course, declared she'd shot "thousands," but then the whole story of Corgie had clearly gotten out of control. Il-Ororen lied fantastically. Charles Corgie had taught them how.

The first day Errol remembered as out of the ordinary was the afternoon they were hiking from the airstrip to Toroto, since some of their equipment had been flown in late. Always eager for exercise, Gray had refused help with their cargo, so the two of them were ambitiously lugging several tripods and two packs of supplies. Errol had been in a good mood, chattering away, imagining what their new graduate assistant would be like. Arabella West, who normally would have been with them for this project, was still ill in Boston, so B.U. was sending someone else. Errol could see her now: "'Yes, Dr. Kaiser! No, Dr. Kaiser!' Getting up early to fix breakfast, washing out our clothes. Gray, we'll have a sycophant again! Arabella is competent, but she passed out of the slavery phase last year. That was so disappointing, going back to making my own coffee and bunching my own socks."

What did they talk about then? Corgie, no doubt. It was a long hike, after all. Maybe Errol asked her to tell him the story again of how she found out about Toroto. Whatever happened to Hassatti? Did she still keep up with Richardson, that old fart?

She was not responding, but Errol knew the answers to most of his questions and filled them in himself. The air was dense; Errol enjoyed working up a sweat. For the first time he could remember, they were plowing up a mountain and Errol was in front, doing better time.

"Too bad Corgie isn't still alive," Errol speculated. "That would be a hell of an interview. 'Lieutenant Corgie, after all these years in Sing Sing, do you have any regrets? And, Lieutenant, how did you *do* it?'"

Errol turned and found Gray had stopped dead some distance behind him. Disconcerted, he hiked back down. There was an expression on her face he couldn't place—something like . . . terror. Errol looked around the jungle half expecting to see a ten-foot fire ant or extraterrestrial life. He found nothing but unusually large leaves. "Are you wanting to take a break? Are you tired?"

Gray shook her head once, rigidly.

"So should we get going?"

"Y-yes," she said slowly, her voice dry.

She could as well have said no. Errol made trailward motions; Gray remained frozen in exactly the same position as before.

"What's the problem?"

Her eyes darted without focus. "I don't feel right."

Errol was beginning to get alarmed. "You feel any pain? Nausea? Maybe you should sit down."

She did, abruptly, against a tree. Errol touched her forehead. "No." She waved him away. "Not like that."

"Then what is it?"

Gray opened her mouth, and shut it.

"Maybe we should get going, then. It'll be dark soon."

"You don't understand."

"I certainly don't."

"I can't keep going." She looked at Errol curiously. "That is the problem."

"You just can't."

"That's right. I have stopped." She said this with a queer, childlike wonder. And then she sat. Nothing.

Errol was dumbfounded. He felt the same queasy fear he would have had the earth ceased to rotate around the sun, for Errol depended as much on Gray Kaiser's stamina as on the orderly progress of planetary orbits.

"What brought this on?"

"I'm not sure. But I wish—" She seemed pained. "I wish you wouldn't talk about Charles. Ask so many questions."

"Don't talk about him? We're doing a documentary—"

"Nothing is mine." She looked away. "Everything belongs

to other people. I'm fifty-nine and I have nothing and I'm completely by myself."

"Thanks," said Errol, wounded. "All you have is professional *carte blanche*, a lot of money, an international reputation. And merely me with you on the trail. Of course you're lonely."

Gray picked at some moss. "I'm sorry. It's just—I think I imagined . . ."

"What?"

"That he'd be here." She seemed embarrassed.

"Who?"

"Charles."

"Gray!"

"Oh, I knew he was dead. But I don't enjoy studying him much. I did that plenty when he was alive."

It was about this time that Errol seemed to remember a prop plane whining overhead, as if carrying out surveillance, spotting her: see, down below? Weakness, desire. Snapping aerial photos for a later attack: nostalgia, emptiness. The propellers chopped the air with satisfaction. Hunting must be easy from an airplane.

"And lately the whole thing," she went on. "The interviews, the feasts . . . 'The meal was delicious!' 'That's a beautiful dress!' 'And how do you remember Il-Cor-gie?' As if I can't remember him perfectly well myself. 'No, you can't have my shirt, I only brought three.' Some*times*."

Gray let her head fall back on the tree trunk. "You're disappointed in me."

"It's a relief to see you let up once in a while, I guess. So you're not perfect. Lets the rest of us off the hook a little."

"You know, I'd love to be the woman you think I am."

"You are."

Gray sighed and rested her forehead on her knees.

Errol relaxed, and had a seat himself. It was a pretty spot. He enjoyed being with her.

They stayed that way. Errol's mind traveled around the world, back to Boston; he thought about Odinaye and Charles Corgie. Finally Gray's head rose again. She said, "I'm hungry." She stood up, pulling on her pack. Neither said anything more until they were hiking on at a good clip.

"Food," said Errol at last, deftly, "is an impermanent inspiration."

"Wrong. It's as permanent as they come. Gray Kaiser, anthropologist, is still sitting by that tree. Gray Kaiser, animal, keeps grazing."

"That really does comfort you, doesn't it?" Errol laughed. She was amazing.

Errol hoped Gray had gotten this eccentricity out of her system, but the following afternoon she proved otherwise. They were sitting in a circle of several women, all of whom had been girls between sixteen and twenty when Corgie ruled Il-Ororen. Now they were in their fifties like Gray, though Gray had weathered the years better than this group here—their skin had slackened, their breasts drooped, their spines curved. Still, as Errol watched these women through the camera lens while Gray prodded them about Charles, their eyes began to glimmer and they would shoot each other sly, racy smiles in a way that made them seem younger as the interview went on, until Errol could see clearly the smooth undulating hips and languorous side glances that must have characterized them as teenage girls.

"It was the men who believed he was a god," one of them claimed in that peculiar Masai dialect of theirs. "We weren't so fooled."

Another woman chided, with a brush of her hand, "He was your god and you know it! I remember that one afternoon, and you were dancing around, and you were singing—"

"I was always dancing and singing then—"

"Oh, especially after!"

"Now, why did you suspect him, though?" Gray pressed.

"Well." The first woman looked down, then back and forth at the others. "There were ways in which he was—very much the man." She smiled. "A big man."

The whole group broke down laughing, slapping the ground with the flats of their hands. "Very, very big!" said another. It took minutes for them to get over this good joke.

"Yes," said one woman. "But if that makes him the man and not the god, then you give me the man!"

The interview was going splendidly now, yet when Errol looked over at Gray she was scowling.

"No, no," another chimed in. "Now I have said years and years Il-Cor-gie was not ordinary. He was a god? I don't know, but not like these other lazy good-for-nothings who lie around and drink honey wine all day and at night can't even—"

"That's right, that's the truth," they agreed.

"I'm telling you," she went on, "that the next morning you *did* feel different. You could jump higher and run for many hills and you no longer needed food."

"Yes! I felt that way, too! And it was a proven fact he made you taller."

"What do you mean it was a proven fact?" asked Gray.

Errol looked over at her so abruptly that he bumped the camera and ruined the shot.

"Well, look at Ol-Kai-zer," said one of the women, smiling. "She is very, very tall, is she not?"

They all started to laugh again, but cut themselves short when Gray stood abruptly and left the circle. Errol followed her with the camera as she stalked off to a nearby woodpile. The whole group stared in silence as Ol-Kai-zer bore down on a log with long, full blows of an ax until the wood was reduced to kindling. Panting, staring down at the splinters at her feet, Gray let the ax drop from her hand. Her shoulders heaved up and down, and her face was filled with concentrated panic. Her cheeks shone red and glistened with sweat. She would not look at Errol or at the women, but at last looked up at the sky, her neck stretched tight. Then she walked away. This was Gray Kaiser in the middle of an interview and she just—walked away.

"Did we offend Ol-Kai-zer?" asked a woman.

"No, no," said Errol distractedly, still filming Gray's departure. "It's not you . . ." He turned back to them and asked sincerely, "Don't people ever do things that you absolutely *don't understand*?"

The women nodded vigorously. "Ol-Kai-zer," said one, "was always like that. Back in the time of Il-Cor-gie—we never understood her for the smallest time. Then—yes, she was always doing this kind of thing, taking the big angry strides away."

"I did not like her much then," confided one woman in a small voice. Her name was Elya; this was the first time she'd spoken.

"Why?" asked Errol.

Elya looked at the ground. She was the lightest and most

delicate of the group; her gestures retained the vanity of great beauty. "Back then—it was better before she came. Il-Cor-gie became funny. It was better before her. That is all."

"He did get very strange," another conceded.

"But you know why Elya didn't like her—"

Elya looked up sharply and the woman stopped.

"He did, during that time remember, have us come to him almost every night."

"Especially Elya—"

"Shush."

"But he was not the same," said Elya sulkily. The passing of so many years didn't seem to have made much difference in her disappointment.

"Yes, that is true," said the woman. "He was hard and not as fun and you did not jump as high in the morning."

"He was far away," said Elya sadly.

"Not so far, and you know it. You know where he was—"

"She bewitched him!"

"It is a fact," many murmured. "She took his big power away. That is why he ended so badly. It was all her fault."

Errol had this on film, and wondered how Gray would feel when she got this section back from the developers. She'd already confided to Errol that it was "all her fault," and might not enjoy being told so repeatedly as she edited this reel.

Meanwhile the hunter was stalking the trail Gray and Errol had just hiked down the day before. Perhaps he paused by the same tree where Gray had thrown down her pack, picking up flung bits of sod and finding them still fresh, to quickly walk on again, completely silent as he so often was, and dark enough to blend in with the mottled shadows of late afternoon.

A fter putting away the camera, Errol found Gray in the hut where they were staying.

"Why did you walk off like that?" asked Errol.

"I felt claustrophobic," said Gray.

"How can you feel claustrophobic in the middle of a field?"

She didn't answer him. Instead, she said after some silence, "I'd like to take a shower." She lay flat on her back, staring at the thatch ceiling. The hut smelled of sweet rotting grass and the smoke of old fires. It was a dark, crypt-like place, with a few shafts of gray light sifting from the door and the cracks in the walls. Gray's palms lay folded on her chest like a pharaoh in marble. Her expression was peaceful and grave, yet with the strange blankness of white stone.

"That's ridiculous," said Errol.

"I would like," she said, "to have warm water all over my body. I would like," she said, "at the very least, to hold my hands under a tap and cup them together and let the water collect until it spills over and bring it to my face and let it drip down my cheeks." She took a breath and sighed.

But Errol had never *worried* about her. "Gray?"

"I feel absolutely disgusted and tired and stupid," she said in one long breath, and with that she turned over on her side and curled into a small fetal ball, with her arms clasped around her chest, no longer looking like a pharaoh at all but more like a child who would still be wearing pajamas with sewn-in feet.

In a minute Gray had gone from an ageless Egyptian effigy, wise and harrowed and lost in secrets, to a girl of three. It was an oddly characteristic transition.

Errol wandered back outside, calm and relaxed. His eyes swept across the village of Toroto, the mud and dung caking off the walls, the goats trailing between the huts, the easy African timelessness ticking by, with its annoying Western intrusions— candy wrappers on the ground, chocolate on children's faces, gaudy floral-print blouses. In spite of these, Errol could imagine this place just after World War II, and it hadn't changed so much. It was good to see this valley at last, with the cliffs sheering up at the far end, and good to finally meet Il-Ororen, with their now muted arrogance and wildly mythologized memories. All this Errol had pictured from *Men without History*, but the actual place helped him put together the whole tale; so as the sun began to set behind the cliffs and the horizon burned like the coals of a dying fire around which you would tell a very good story, Errol imagined as best he could what had happened here thirty-seven years ago.

chapter two

It was fitting that Gray finally do a documentary about Toroto, for in some ways Errol had already made this film. Errol's great indulgence—it bordered on vice, or at least on nosiness— was a curious sort of mental home movie. His secret passion was piecing together other people's lives. Going far beyond the ordinary gossip, Errol pitched into history that was not his own like falling off a ledge, in a dizzying entrancement with being someone else that sometimes frightened him.

Naturally, Gray Kaiser's life was his pet project. Assembling the footage on Charles Corgie had been especially challenging, for whole reels of that material were classified. Twenty-four years is a long time, however, and with plenty of wine and late nights Errol had weaseled from Gray enough information to put together a damned good picture. In fact, for its completeness and accuracy, *Kaiser and Corgie* promised to be one of the highlights of his collection.

Errol could see her in 1948 at the age of twenty-two, holed

up in the back rooms of the Harvard anthropology department, gluing together some godawful pot. It was late, two in the morning maybe, with a single light, orange, the must of old books tingling her nostrils, the quiet like an afghan wrapped around her shoulders—those fine shoulders, wide, peaked at the ends. The light would fill her hair, a honey blond then, buoyant and in the way.

Gray would be telling herself that Dr. Richardson was a first-rate anthropologist and she was lucky to be his assistant, but Gray Kaiser would not like having a mentor, even at twenty-two. Richardson told her what to do. He did all the fieldwork, and she was desperately sick of this back room. She loved the smell of old books as much as the next academic, but she loved the smell of wood fires more, and of cooking bananas; she certainly yearned for the wild ululation of the Masai over this suffocating library quiet.

Padding dark and silent down the well-waxed linoleum halls of that building, a tall Masai warrior came to deliver her.

"I will see Richasan."

Gray started, and looked up to find a man in her doorway. He was wearing a gray suit which, though it fit him well, looked ridiculous. The *man* didn't look ridiculous; the suit did. His hair was plaited in many strands and bound together down his back.

"Dr. Richardson won't be in for six or seven hours." For God's sake, it was three in the morning. Then, an African's sense of time was peculiar. If you made an appointment with a Kikuyu for noon, he might show up at five with no apology for being late. With a Masai you did not make appointments. He came when he felt like it.

"I wait, then." The man came in and stood opposite Gray, balancing perfectly on one leg, with his other foot raised like a stork's. His long face high and impassive, he stood immobile, as he had no doubt poised many times for hours in a clump of trees, waiting for a cheetah to pass in range of his spear. Six or seven hours was nothing.

"Can I help you?"

"No."

"I am Dr. Richardson's assistant."

"You are his woman?"

"I am no man's woman."

The Masai looked down at her. "Pity."

"Not really. I don't need a man."

"You are silly fool, then, to shrivel and dry soon."

Gray couldn't bear his towering over her any longer. "Won't you sit down?"

"No."

"Then I'll stand." When she did so the Masai glanced at her with surprise. Gray was six feet tall, and looked him in the eye now. "Anything you want to say to Dr. Richardson will have to go through me first. You want him to do something for you, right?"

The Masai's eyes narrowed. "Yez . . . but I wait for Richasan."

"What is it?" Gray stood right next to him, close enough to make him uncomfortable. "An apartment? Or you want into Harvard?"

"I do not come for myself," he said with disgust. "For others. These, not even my people—"

"Who?"

The man turned away. "Richasan."

Gray was beginning to get curious. She tried polite conversation. "How long have you been in the U.S.?"

"One day."

"What are you here for, to study?"

"Yez . . ." he said carefully. "I learn this white people."

"What will you study?"

His eyes glimmered. "Your weakness."

"You're a spy, then."

"We want you out of my country."

Gray nodded. "I've done some work for Kenyan independence myself."

"The lady has not worked so hard, then," said the Masai dryly. "You are still there."

"Well, who in Kenya would listen to a woman?"

"Yez."

"We're not the same tribe, you know. As the English."

"No, you are the same. This becomes clear with Corgie."

"Who is Corgie?"

The Masai did not respond.

"How do you plan to get the whites out?"

"Masai—" He raised his chin high. "We like to put the man to sleep with steel, the woman with wood. But the gun . . . Kikuyu think we best fight with talk. Kikuyu talk so much, this is all Kikuyu know," said the Masai with disdain. "But this time Kikuyu right. I begin my study already. This white man smart with his gun, not so smart in his head."

"Don't underestimate your opponent," said Gray pointedly.

"We get most whites out with talk. Talk take time. One will not wait. I come to Richasan."

"*Whom* do you want to get rid of?"

The Masai folded his arms.

Gray released a tolerant sigh. She went back to her chair, settling in for the duration. "Where did you learn English?"

"Richasan. He come to my country. I save his life," said the warrior grandly.

"How?" Gray hadn't heard this story.

"Richasan make this picture. My people want to kill him with steel. They think this camera, it take the soul away. Ridiculous. I have worked this camera. Ridiculous to think a man could take your soul."

"Oh, I don't know," said Gray quietly, with a slight smile. "That's what I'm afraid of."

The Masai looked down at her with new interest, though he didn't press her to explain. "So I stop the killing of Richasan. I help with his work. He teach me English. My English *excellent*."

Gray shrugged. "It's all right."

"My English vedy, vedy excellent," he reasserted with feeling.

"Your English *is* very excellent."

"Yez."

"No, I mean you left out the verb. You said it wrong."

The Masai answered angrily in his own language.

"You're quite right," said Gray. "To outstrip a foreigner in one's home tongue is weak and easy. But you were being arrogant, and I don't think I deserved that kind of language."

The Masai stared at her and said nothing, as if doubting his ears. Gray had responded in Masai—correct, intelligible, and beautifully spoken. As he was silent, she went on, "If you were more comfortable in your own language, you should have said so."

The Masai stared, and she was concerned she'd angered him—Masai were easily offended. Still, she went on, enjoying the language she so rarely got to use, its lilting, playful, vowel-ridden sound: "And I don't think I bear the least resemblance to a hyena, in heat or not." Hyena, "*ol-ngyine*," she took care to pronounce just as he had.

The Masai began to laugh. He extended his hand over the table and clasped hers. "Good, Msabu." His grip was strong and dry. "Vedy, vedy good, Msabu. Hassatti. Pleasure, big pleasure." Hassatti took a seat opposite Gray. "How you learn Masai?"

"Richasan."

"Msabu must like my people," he said with satisfaction.

"You're a powerful and magnificent tribe. Straight. Angry. You bow to no one. I've studied and admired you a great deal."

"So why you treat Hassatti from so high? Change his English?"

"What I admire I also embrace. I also bow to no one, even Masai."

"Ah." Hassatti nodded. "Now tell Hassatti. In America United States, this woman is different thing? Yez?"

"I'm different. Yes."

Hassatti's brow rumpled. "Richasan, he do not warn me of this . . . Why Msabu has no husband? Your father ask too many cows?"

"I strike my own bargains."

Hassatti reached out and touched Gray's fine honey hair, pulling a strand toward him across the table and running it between his fingers with a smile. "Eight, ten. Beautiful fine strong cows. Barely bled."

"I'm very flattered, but why don't you just tell me why you're here?"

"It is man's business."

"I'll strain my brain."

"You want twelve?" asked Hassatti, incensed. "Twelve cuts Hassatti's herd in half—"

Gray held up her hand. "I don't judge by wealth but by what you consider a man's business."

That seemed to make sense to Hassatti. "I come in kindness," he said loftily. "These are not my people."

"That's admirable."

So encouraged, Hassatti stood and strode about the small room. Gray watched him with pleasure. There was nothing like the unabashed self-glorification of a Masai warrior, even in a gray suit. Hassatti switched completely to Masai, and told his story with style and drama, as he might have to a gathering in his own kraal. Gray could imagine the fire flashing up shadows against the mud-and-dung walls, the long faces row on row, huddled in their hides, baobabs creaking in the wind.

"When the sea washes forward over stones and withdraws again," he began, "sometimes cupfuls are caught between the rocks and the water remains. So the Masai washed long ago over the peaks of Kilimanjaro into the highest hills, the deepest creases. A small party got separated from their tribe and caught in a pocket, with the hills reaching steeply on all sides. Tired and lost and with no cattle, they erected their kraals and remained cut off like a puddle.

"As a puddle will grow scummy, dead, and dark with no stream to feed it, so did this people stagnate and grow stupid. Their minds blackened and clouded, and they no longer remembered their brother Masai. Caught in the crevices of Kilimanjaro, these warriors had sons who dismissed the talk of other tribes as superstition. They called themselves Il-Ororen, The People, as if there were no others. With no cows to tend, they scraped the soil like savages; the clay from the roots and insects on which they fed filled their heads, and their thoughts stuck together like feet against earth in the monsoons.

"Meanwhile, the Masai had forgotten about the Puddle, leaving this obscure tribe for dead. My people had greater troubles: a scourge of pale and crafty visitors infested the highlands. As we discussed, Msabu, they still do. Forgive, Msabu, but white like grubs, haired like beasts, they played many tricks, trying to trade silly games for the fine heifers of the Masai. These grubs tried to herd and fence my people as we do our cows, making rules against the raids on the Kikuyu with which a man becomes a warrior. The white people liked to show off their games like magic, but the wise of the Masai were not fooled. Hassatti has learned," he said archly, "to work the dryer of hair. Hassatti has flown in the airplane.

"Yet the Puddle was lucky for a long time. Your people, Msabu, did not discover them. The trees and hills obscured their muddy kraals. Arrogant and dull, Il-Ororen continued to think they were the only humans in the world. Imagine their surprise, then, Msabu, when one of your own warriors landed his small airplane in the thick of this crevice and emerged from its cockpit with his hat and his clothing, with all its zippers and pockets, and his face blanched like the sky before snow—"

"Hassatti, when was this? What year?"

Hassatti looked annoyed. To place the story within a particular time was somehow to make it tawdrier and more ordinary. "Nineteen hundred and forty-three, perhaps," said Hassatti, "though the boy from whom this story was taken is an idiot of the Puddle and cannot be trusted. Who knows if he can count seasons."

"Sorry to interrupt," said Gray. "Go on."

"Well, the wise Masai of the highlands always knew what your people were—clever, but often weak and fat; with no feeling for cows, but good with metal. Granted your women store their breasts in cups and your men grow fur, but you copulate and excrete; you bleed and die, though—excuse, Msabu—not often enough for Hassatti's tastes. All this my people could see. Yet Il-Ororen of the Puddle had grown superstitious and easily awed. With the constant looming of the cliffs on all sides, shadows played over their heads and made them fearful. When the white warrior stepped into their bush they quivered. They imagined he was a ghost or a god. They bowed down and cast away their spears, or ran into the forest. They had eaten clay for too long and their smiths made dull arrows, their women made pots with holes; their minds would hold no more cleverness than their pots would hold water. They had forgotten how to raid and be warriors, since there was no one from whom to steal cattle, and their boys were no longer circumcised."

"So what happened?"

"I will give Il-Ororen this much: the gun is a startling thing, and even the sharp arrows are not much good against it, and the man Corgie made this clear with great swiftness."

"How many people did he shoot?"

"We do not know. Yet this Corgie is of interest, Msabu, for in my studies the white man does plenty of foolish things, and Hassatti is amazed that the Corgie could fly into the crevice and set up a kingdom as a god and not soon disappoint his disciples, even if they were only Puddle people."

"Let me get this straight," said Gray, beginning to get excited, for if Hassatti was telling the truth—that there was a tribe out there that had never been in contact with Western civilization before—then he was talking about an anthropological gold mine. The discovery of the peoples of New Guinea in the twenties had made several careers, and that was supposed to be the last frontier . . . Gray was on the edge of her chair. "This man Corgie stayed? Didn't go back and tell anyone?"

"No, he still reigns there. He shoots those who disobey. Hassatti has no respect for such a tribe, superstitious and easily trapped, but they were once Masai and now they are servants to this ungentle visitor, so Hassatti has come to his old friend Richasan so that the Corgie may be flushed out of the crevice and brought to justice."

"How did you hear about Corgie?"

"There was a boy of the Puddle who had two brothers. They had been playing on a sacred square of dirt and made the Corgie angry. I know this seems ridiculous to you and me, but this boy spoke of some area of their compound that was worshipped and made perfectly flat, marked with mysterious lines he believed to be about the stars. His brothers disrupted the surface of this square and were killed; the boy, too, had been party to the gouging of the sacred flatness, and fled the village, climbed the cliffs, forded rivers, and finally wandered into my own kraal. It took him much time to talk at all, for he was frightened of the Masai, as he was of this Corgie—he supposed the Puddle to be all the world's people. I did not blame him, either, for fearing the Masai. We are a great and strong people raised on meat and blood, and he was weak and scratched dirt and ate ants. He huddled in the corner of my hut for some days and would not speak, and no one of us could say where he was from. He was stunted, and had none of the earrings, markings, or clothing of my people.

Though old enough, he was not circumcised. He would not eat the meat or milk we put before him, but when our backs were turned he would tear the insects from the ground and the roots from the trees.

"We thought he was a savage, but when he spoke at last he did not speak Swahili or Kikuyu, but a garbled tongue with words we recognized. With these and pictures, we pieced together his story. We might not have believed it but for the occasional rumor we Masai ourselves sometimes heard of a warrior who got lost in the far bush and returned telling tales of a gnomish clan in the wrinkles of the mountains who offered him no meat and no milk and no wife to share, but shut him out of their compound. And when this boy first saw white people in our midst, he screeched like a flamingo and hid in my hut. To this day I do not believe I have convinced him that your people are not gods. Forgive, Msabu, but the fallibility of your people seems so self-evident to me that I have to conclude the boy is a complete dwarf in the head."

"Why have you come to Richardson? Why didn't you go after Corgie yourselves?"

"Would that we could, Msabu. It pains Hassatti, but for the Masai to take action against a white man is dangerous. It is best for a tribe to discipline its own."

Gray nodded. Richardson would be salivating if he were here. He'd be on the phone already, chartering a plane to Nairobi.

"Hassatti . . ." said Gray slowly, "you know how it is customary for boys to go out on the plains and slaughter a lion that's been killing Masai cattle, and when he returns with the tail and paws he's considered a man?"

"Yez."

"Any man—or woman, Bwana—wants to pass such a test, Masai or not. I have yet to pass my test. I want to, desperately. Dr. Richardson has passed many. He is *ol-moruo*, an old man, now. Let me have Corgie, as you would send a young warrior to kill a beast when the elder has killed several."

Hassatti looked at her hard. "You? Go after Corgie?"

Gray's face flushed and her heart beat. "I am very tall," she said simply, "and very strong and very brilliant."

Errol could see it, hear it; he liked to play this moment over in his mind: I am very tall and very strong and very brilliant. Her ears scarlet, her eyes that piercing blue-gray.

Hassatti kept looking at her. "Perhaps—Richasan should decide."

"Dr. Richardson wouldn't trust me, and he never will. He will never believe I'm that grown up, just as your father will never believe you're a man."

"Ah." Hassatti nodded and smiled. Gray was only twenty-two, but she already understood how much psychology crossed cultures. Fathers condescended the world over.

"Richardson may never let me hunt my lion," said Gray. "Will you?"

Hassatti shook his head with incredulity, reached over, and touched her cheek. "*Ol-changito*," he said. "*'L-oo-lubo*."

He had called her a wild animal; an impala, though translated literally "*'l-oo-lubo*" means "that which is not satisfied."

Gray replied, "*Ol-murani*."

Hassatti shook his head. "*E-ngoroyoni*."

"*Ol-murani o-gol*," Gray reasserted.

Hassatti shook his head again and smiled. "*E-ngoroyoni na-nana*."

There was a conflict of interpretations here. Gray claimed to be a warrior, as Errol knew she saw herself. "*Ol-murani*" was an old joke with her, though they both knew it was no joke, not really. Yet Hassatti had called her something else, and wouldn't take it back.

"You have," said Hassatti, "a great deal to learn, *'l-oo-lubo*. And as long as Msabu claims she is *ol-murani o-gol* and not *e-ngoroyoni na-nana*, she will not understand what even such a clever antelope must master."

"And what is that?"

"To pour is to fill, Msabu. *Ol-changito*, to pour is to fill."

"I'll remember that," said Gray.

"No, you will not," he assured her. "This is to be understood, not remembered, fleet one. The words have already flown from your head like birds of different flocks to separate trees.

"However," said Hassatti. "Since *'l-oo-lubo* is such a costly creature, and she will not accept the twelve cows, perhaps Msabu will accept from Hassatti: one lion."

Gray smiled. "And you won't tell Richardson where I've gone?"

"No more," he said, "than I would show him the food in my mouth." Hassatti then wrote the name of his tribe and where it was currently located; he drew her a map and gave her the name of his family. "Now you will bring me the paws and tail of Corgie when you return?"

"You mean I should deliver the witch's slippers?"

"The Corgie wears slippers—?"

"Never mind. I'll bring you his gun, how's that?"

"Most of all for Hassatti *'l-oo-lubo* must go out and become wise. Then come back and we will talk of becoming Hassatti's wife."

"I don't know if I'll ever be that wise," said Gray.

"Neither do I," said Hassatti. "I tell you, Msabu, it will take you a long time, longer than most *e-ngoroyoni*. Know from Hassatti that this will cost you. It is like when a boy waits too long and becomes all grown before he is circumcised. There is much pain, and slow healing."

It was five in the morning. Hassatti said he would wait for his friend Richardson; Gray would find an airplane. They spoke in Masai.

"Well, I am about to go," said Gray.

"*Aiya naa, sere!* Goodbye. Pray to God, accost only the things which are safe, and meet no one but blind people."

"Lie down," said Gray, "with honey wine and milk."

"So be it."

Hassatti followed her out the door to watch that long, sweeping stride of hers, listening to the clean click of her heels against the linoleum like the clop of small hooves. Gray never seemed to be walking fast, but she covered ground quickly, like a languorous, leggy animal across the plain. Strange she was not Masai. She had the bones of his own people. Hassatti could see her ranging into the bush, standing spear-straight to meet this ghostlike white man and his many guns. Though he had just arrived in this new country and had much to study, Hassatti almost went after her down the hall, for this was a scene he would have given much to see.

G ray returned that morning to her apartment, having arranged her trip to Nairobi for the following day. She sat at her desk and composed three notes. First, to Richardson, she wrote: "On good advice I am off to become wise.—Gray Kaiser."

Second, she wrote the man she was dating. Most certainly he wanted to marry her, too. "Dear Dan," she jotted. "I've been called out of town. May be gone for a long time. Don't hold your breath. —G."

So you put a stamp on it, Gray, what was it, three cents then? That's how much it cost *you*. What did it cost him, though? You didn't even know. Set on the corner of your desk, it was one more of those easy dismissals of a man who adored you. Ever since she was fifteen, men had been proposing to her, and she'd learned early to whisk them away like so many flies. How many times had Errol himself watched her discard prostrate admirers? He'd enjoyed watching, yet it pained him a little. Errol truly believed she didn't understand how they felt, and for an anthropologist that was a failing.

The third letter she sent to her father, and it was the one note of consideration she struck all morning. Gray enclosed a copy of Hassatti's map, just in case she didn't return. Perhaps Gray feared as Errol did each time they returned to Kenya that *ol-changito*, let loose on those hard-packed plains, would lope across the white horizon to graze under acacia trees, to bolt between watering holes, to sniff the hard brilliant air and so give up on English and coffee and little efficient notes in the mail altogether.

More likely she knew the situation she was walking into was dangerous. Even Gray now admitted that going on this expedition by herself had been pigheaded. But *ol-murani* was planning on shouldering her pack and her spear and her wooden club and launching off into the sunset to find her lion . . . Gray had seen too many Westerns, and you knew she identified, not with the simpering prairie wives, but with the sharpshooters.

Gray took out her tent and began to reroll it to fit into its insanely small bag. So it was dangerous. So he had guns. Gray paused at the thought for one tiny, intelligent moment. She took a breath and kept on going. Fine. Here was a woman who had spent the better part of World War II thinking. Enough was enough. She was tired of having men tell stories about dragging their best friends for ten miles on their backs under fire, all the while Gray feeling abstracted and left out. It was time to begin a life in which actions could have consequences.

Besides. Gray shot a look up at the mirror that hung on her door and caught her own face looking keenly back at her. You didn't look at a face like that without staring for a second, even if it was yours. Not bad hair. Kind of strange the way that collarbone stood out, but interesting, too . . . No, he wouldn't shoot her. Not right away, she was sure. Gray wrapped the straps around the tent summarily; it fit in the bag.

Gray did own a handgun, and considered taking it. The gun had been a gift from an earlier suitor, the one he'd captured in the war. (It chilled Errol how often Gray was given weapons as presents, all over the world. As if she weren't destructive enough already.) Yet finally Gray decided to leave the gun behind. To prepare for a military encounter was to create one. As many movies as she might have seen, Gray knew she would not succeed in her mission by hiding behind a boulder and picking off the troops. That hair and collarbone would surely prove more powerful weapons than her German Luger.

Throwing the rest of her gear together through the day,

Gray thought about the Great White Corgie. She already had a strong sense of the man. He was arrogant. Ruthless. Racist. Brave, she conceded. But cruel and condescending.

And for some reason she decided he was handsome.

chapter three

Hassatti's mother also called Gray *'l-oo-lubo*, taking her into the family like a stray from the plains—isolated from the herd, difficult, but a fine specimen, and tamable.

The boy from the Land of Corgie, Osinga, was as terrified of Gray as Hassatti had predicted, but bent on his brothers' revenge; after repeated reassurances, Osinga agreed to guide her to Toroto. Hiking out, however, he insisted on walking behind her, which made it awkward for Gray to follow him.

Errol could easily imagine Gray on this trip. Many was the time he himself had hiked behind her while a voice screamed in his head, "Go ahead, Gray, say, 'I am tired.' Say, 'My muscles are killing me, Errol.'" But Gray would keep going silently in front of him, until finally Errol would growl in irascible defeat about needing a break, and Gray would answer smoothly, never out of breath, "Oh, would you like to stop, Errol? Of course. Maybe I'll do a few push-ups while you're resting . . ."

She was too goddamned much.

Toward dusk, Osinga speared mongooses and brought them to Gray like sacramental offerings. She skinned and gutted them quickly and without queasiness, for Gray enjoyed butchery. Errol had watched her take animals apart before. She liked to study the muscles glistening underneath the skin of a fresh kill, and move the joints in their sockets to see how they worked. She never called small prey "cute," and when the glazed eyes of a mongoose in her hands rolled up, her face never softened.

Nights Gray slept fitfully, dreaming of Corgie. The dreams flipped from terror to pleasure and back again. Corgie would reach for her in her sleep, and she wouldn't know if he meant to caress or strangle her until the moment his fingers wrapped around her neck.

The bush got thicker and more hazardous as they advanced. Through thorn trees Osinga stared at Gray's hands, surprised that they bled. Yet she didn't cry out or complain when the thorns stuck far into her flesh, so he assumed she felt no pain. All her life people had made this mistake with Gray.

When she stepped on a trail of fire ants and they swept up her legs, Osinga stood back and watched as she rapidly picked the insects off. At last she stamped angrily and shouted for him to help her, and he was surprised that these small animals could hurt such a thing. She seemed impregnable; she seemed that way to everyone.

There came a moment when Osinga looked up at a particular mountain and went wild-eyed. He wouldn't go any farther; he'd only point. Gray walked the last length alone.

Once she'd climbed to the top ridge, Gray looked down into a deep valley with cliffs shooting steeply up on all sides and waterfalls sweeping down in white rushes. Finding only trees below, she worried whether this was the right place. Yet as she inched down the steep cliff toward the valley, grabbing scraggly trees and sometimes crawling on all fours, Gray could gradually discern one odd structure jutting from the foliage below, a strange, towerlike thing in blond wood. When she was nearly down, manyatta after manyatta also appeared among the trees. Aside from these traditionally constructed mud-and-dung compounds, Gray could now see three other blond-wooded buildings, large and angular and queer even by Western standards.

The rest of her way to the village Gray walked slowly, with her head high, nose to the wind. Gone was the smell of curling pages. Smoke drifted from the huts, and colors flushed beside her. Gray Kaiser was alive and in Africa and something was happening at last. When she glided past the mud-packed walls, children fled before her; men and women swept into their compounds and posts cracked against the gates inside.

As Gray drew into view of the blond tower, natives stopped carrying wood, froze mid-circle as they lashed joints on the tower with vine, left off mid-sentence as they called in their gnarled Masai. In the stillness, one figure kept jabbing angrily from the ground at a man on the third story. He was the last to turn to her, following the line of the native's gaze as he might have tracked a fuse to dynamite.

"What doesn't belong in this picture?"

"I don't," said Gray. "You don't, either."

"You don't feel a little the lost sheep?" he asked. "Astray."

It was a big comedown from antelope to sheep. "On the contrary," said Gray, "I've found my way quite nicely. I have arrived."

"I was unaware we'd become a tourist attraction."

"Oh yes," said Gray. "I'm here to help you set up a hot-dog concession. I thought you'd want to get in on the ground floor."

The man smiled a little, perhaps in spite of himself. Gray took the moment to assess him more closely. Errol had seen several brownish photographs of Charles Corgie. He always wore a wide hat with a sloppy brim. His coloring was dark, his bearing sultry. His eyes flickered as if long ago someone had done something terrible to him for which he had planned a perfect revenge; when it came due he would laugh without sympathy or regret. In a few of these snapshots he was smiling, like now, though always with both humor and disdain, as if the two of you could have a high old time if he would only let you in on the joke. Of course, he was not about to.

Casually, Corgie pointed his rifle at Gray. Through their interchange he played with the gun distractedly, as people will toy with an object on a coffee table in a conversation that is sometimes awkward.

Gray nodded at his tattered khaki. "So you deserted."

"I got lost."

"And you still haven't found your way home? You must not have tried very hard."

"I tried clicking my heels together three times," he said congenially. "It didn't work." Corgie turned and said something in Il-Ororen to one of the natives. The man shrank back and shook his head. Corgie repeated himself in a steelier tone; it was a voice that made all present, even Gray, take a breath. The native approached Gray and frisked her sides with a gingerly touch. "Raise your hands over your head, would you?"

Gray did not. "I'm unarmed."

"If that's true, then you're very foolish. But it's not necessarily true. White people aren't to be trusted."

"I've found that people's generalizations are largely illuminating about themselves."

"So what kind of generalizations do you make?"

"I'm more inclined to see people as judicious and reasonable. Unless presented with evidence to the contrary." She raised her eyebrows at Corgie. "Which I sometimes am."

"Some woman who can see the human race as judicious and reasonable in light of World War II."

"What concerns me about World War II is that barbarity on such a scale seems to make smaller, everyday barbarity petty and unimportant. Actually, it's just as important. It's the same thing."

"You wouldn't be making any accusations, would you? Being our guest?"

"Oh no," said Gray mildly. "We're just being philosophical, aren't we, Mr. Corgie?"

"Lieutenant. But I'm sure I would have remembered meeting such a *lovely* woman. I could swear we haven't been introduced."

"Funny. I feel as if I know you incredibly well."

"Pretty and telepathic, too! Do you have any other special powers? They could come in useful here."

"Certainly. I can receive disembodied transmissions, produce mirages, steal voices. All that old stuff. I'm sure you've covered it. But I did bring one thing you could probably use."

"Decent tobacco."

"Moral sensibility."

"You remind me of aunts at Christmas who gave me *socks*."

Gray nodded at his threadbare clothing. "It looks as if you could use those, too."

Suddenly Corgie said with a smile, "Osinga!"

"Lieutenant, you of all people should have enough respect for magic not to spoil the trick."

"I respect tricks on other people. My tricks."

"Well, your tricks made quite an impression on the boy. He thinks quite a lot of you."

"I bet he does. I made a bigger impression on his brothers."

"About an inch wide and several inches deep. A cheap way to impress people."

"It works."

"It's not very elegant."

"You have far too many opinions."

Gray stopped and looked at him. "Yes." That's all she said. It was an awkward moment. It is always awkward when people have nothing else to add or refute; when they agree.

"What the hell are you doing here?" asked Corgie abruptly.

"I'm an anthropologist. I came to study these people."

"By yourself?"

Gray looked at the mouth of Corgie's gun. It would be wise to create troops in the rear. "Yes," said Gray defiantly.

"And who knows you're here?"

"A few Masai."

Corgie smiled. "You didn't have to admit that. Though even alone you do present something of a problem."

"How?"

"They think I'm the Ghost of Christmas Past or something. Jesus. Gary Cooper. One of a kind, anyway. Like Zeus. Now we are two."

"Even godheads come in two sexes. You're not up on your mythology."

"But of course Little Miss Anthropologist is. It is Miss?"

It would be wise to be Mrs. Anthropologist. "Yes, Miss," said Gray.

They glared in silence.

"Well, what are you going to do with me?" asked Gray.

Corgie stroked the stubble on his chin. "Charlie has to think about it."

"Charlie had better," said Gray. "If you shoot me they might figure out that thing would work on you. Rather blows the immortality business all to pieces."

Corgie's eyes sharpened.

"And if you keep me prisoner," she went on reasonably, "they might decide you couldn't walk through walls yourself. You see," she explained cheerfully, "I could be of some use to you. In anthropology I've learned a few things, Lieutenant. For instance, that human savvy runs across cultures. If my hallowed white flesh will bleed, won't yours?"

Corgie looked at her steadily. "You get yourself into a fix, you think you can just weasel your way out of it, don't you?"

"Charles. Wouldn't you do the same thing?"

"I did. Already."

"By deserting your brigade?"

Corgie worked his jaw back and forth. "Miss—?"

"Kaiser."

"Miss Kaiser. I left one war and walked right into another. In this one I'm president to private, the whole shebang. I've maintained my borders for five years now. I think that makes me quite the little soldier, with no R&R. 'On the seventh day he rested' is crap. Gods don't get a day off, ever."

"It must be exhausting, creating animals, deciding on the weather. Doling out floods and locusts—"

"It is exhausting. You'll see."

"Maybe I don't want to be a deity. Maybe I'm happier as an anthropologist."

"You'll be a god, all right. I may not be able to use this rifle on you, but I gave earlier exhibitions. My parishioners remember them. If they get the idea that Charlie has been, ah, misrepresenting his authority, then Charlie and even his cute little girlfriend might not stay too healthy. Are you getting the picture?"

Gray nodded. "Mutual ransom."

Corgie toured her around his buildings, explaining that he'd been an architect before the war. Each was blond, precise, and remarkable. In his cabin he showed her their scale models made from chips of wood and strips of bark. A child would have loved them, with the bits of furniture and rope swings and knitted hammocks. Dark figures in black clay strode across the plans, though in each scene there was one figure of a siltier soil, a paler concoction; it stood taller and straighter than the rest, and wore a hat.

In the first of these models, of this cabin, the figure in white mud was isolated from the black ones, but there were tiny manyattas on either side with whole families having meals and couples trysting in corners. In the second, though—of Corgie's gymnasium—there were fewer natives, and some of these were smashed or dismembered. There were no families or couples. The blacks still standing walked starkly and singly across the ground like Giacometti bronzes. In the third model, of Corgie's "cathedral," there were no more dark figures at all, only the white one; his clay was of a dimmer cast and had no head and face, only a hat. The architecture in this model was more beautiful and refined than ever, but the little white man in the middle of it looked squat; his limbs had shortened, his pose caved in. In the fourth and final model, of the tower, there were no figures at all, not even a white one. There was only a building. The progression of the projects themselves had gone from the lyrical or even quaint— a quality this cabin retained, with its small details and attention to comfort—to harsher angles and harder edges, until this last project was jagged to the point of cruelty and inventive to the point of desperation.

Returning to the unfortunate black clay splayed in the dirt of the gymnasium, Gray asked, "Do you consider yourself at all—disturbed?"

"No," said Corgie, not seeming to take offense. "Mostly bored. That was a bad time," he admitted, gesturing to the gym. "They didn't understand what I was doing. The equipment. The courts. Sports aren't big here. I think they found it intriguing in a useless, mystical sort of way, but the crops were bad that year, which was hard on the old religion. I kept telling them they didn't get rain because they weren't cooperating."

"You sound as if you believe that yourself."

"Maybe I do." Corgie shot her a quick, mysterious smile. "Anyway, I'd come back here at night after haggling with shoddy labor all day, and I'd smash one of those little clay men with my thumb: squash. Sometimes I'd do that instead of shooting one of them. I thought it was nicer. Don't you approve?"

"Oh, absolutely."

Charles smiled and added wryly, "Of course, it's just shy of voodoo. I've been here too long." He looked fondly down at the scene, wiping some dust off the gymnasium roof. "I always liked miniatures, even as a kid. I liked balsa airplanes and Erector sets. I had a terrific model train, with lights inside the caboose—"

"I bet you spent whole afternoons wrecking it to pieces."

"How did you guess? And I liked to put little signalmen on the tracks and run them over."

"I suppose the nice thing about miniatures is that they make you feel so big."

Charles turned to Gray and looked at her hard. "Have you always been like this?"

"Like what?"

"Running a fellow down all the time. Why don't you give a guy a break?"

"It doesn't seem to me that you need a break."

"Why the hell not? Who the hell doesn't?"

"Any man with a thousand loyal fans outside his door."

Charles waved his hand in dismissal. "Yeah. A thousand of my closest friends." He tapped the arm of his chair and stared at his models. "You know, I'll tell you," he began. "The funny thing is—" He stopped. He closed his mouth abruptly.

"What."

Charles sat.

"What is the funny thing?"

Charles licked his lips, and went on reluctantly. "When that feeling . . . the way you feel around these models. The little houses. The little people. The way you look down on them. Put them places. When—"

"What?"

"When you walk outside to the regular-size place? And it's no different. That's what funny. When you're around life-size shit and it all still feels like—toys." Charles couldn't look Gray in the eye. "Animals seem stuffed. People seem like dolls. My own house looks like the station in my train set. With spikes around it. Like Popsicle sticks." Charles cleared his throat and raised his eyebrows, looking up at Gray with an indefinite smile, as if maybe he was pulling her leg. He laughed an unsettling little laugh. "You are here, aren't you? Say something."

"Something," said Gray dully.

"An old kid's joke. Not very helpful. You're supposed to say something that makes me feel normal-sized. In the big village. With the actual people."

"Isn't that the trouble? That you're not sure they're actual people?"

Charles stood up. "I don't know what the hell we're talking about." Charles rang a homemade bell; its clacker scrabbled in the tin. A native appeared below, by the stilts of the cabin. Charles ordered dinner—with one more look at Gray to make sure she was still there—for two.

At the end of the meal, roasted game with mangoes and banana, Charles rang his dented tin bell and the native climbed up to his doorway to take the plates away. Once the servant had climbed back down, Charles pulled the ladder up and set it against the outside wall. Charles invited Gray to his veranda, which looked out on the cliffs. He lit an oil lantern on the porch. Gray climbed into a hammock and stared up; the stars were brighter and more numerous than she'd ever seen. She felt peculiarly content. When she glanced down, Gray noticed that the sides of the porch were covered with long, sharpened wooden spikes. Charles explained, "They help me sleep nights."

Corgie himself leaned back in a broad cane armchair, and they both sipped honey wine. Smoke rose from the manyattas on either side, and the lantern, which burned animal fat, gave off a meaty smell, like a barbecue. The hoot of night birds echoed between the cliffs. Gray relaxed into the netting of her hammock; it creaked gently when she moved. The wine was sweet and potent. The flame flickered beside Charles Corgie and lit his profile as he stared off into the black bush. He breathed deeply and held the wine in his mouth a long time before swallowing. It was impossible to tell what he was thinking.

"What's your name?" he asked at last. "Your first name."

"Gray."

"Soft, for you."

"It strikes most people as dour."

"No, soft. Gentle."

"That's surprising?"

Charles reached over and rapped against her outstretched leg with his knuckles. "Hear that? *Bong, bong, bong*. That's what it's like when you knock against the side of a tank." He went back to staring out into the forest. Gray stared, too. The foliage pulsed as her eyes fought to focus, to pick up any object however slight. The trees bloomed on the edges in explosions of black. There's nothing like African darkness. It eats your eyes.

"Are you insulting me?" asked Gray.

"I'm not sure."

Gray decided to change the subject. "I can't believe you haven't asked me about the war. Don't you care what happened?"

"Kaiser—I left."

"It's over."

"You don't say. Who won?"

"I don't know if you'll be disappointed or not. Whose side were you on?"

Charles considered, leaning farther back in his chair and setting his boots up on the railing. "Adolf isn't my style. I don't like the way he moves, know what I mean? The guy's too excitable."

"And maybe you didn't like like the way his uniform was tailored."

"Actually," said Charles, looking over at her with his black eyes gleaming quietly under the looming ridge of his brow, "the tie—with the shirt buttoned all the way up to the neck—I prefer a dictator with an open collar."

"Clearly," said Gray. Charles's own shirt was unbuttoned to the middle of his chest, where the hair was thick and black like his eyes, and gleamed just as defiantly in the lantern light, with drops of honey wine.

"You did use the past tense," Charles observed.

"Adolf isn't that excitable anymore."

"And Benito? Hirohito?" Gray shook her head. Charles shrugged. "Just as well. Me, I'm a Napoleon man."

"Why's that?"

"Those losers wouldn't know what to do with a joint once they'd got hold of it. Bonaparte had plans. I liked his projects. But that slouch Speer built some nasty, hulking places. What a no-talent. Everything he put together looked like a goddamned morgue."

Charles pulled out a packet and rolled himself a cigarette in a leaf, quickly and expertly into a long, tight spleef. "Tobacco ran out first week," he explained. "But I found a weed—sweet, but with an edge to it. Wasn't common, though, so I've got the flock growing some over there. Doing pretty well, too. They dry it and crush it and wrap it up in packets. I miss my tins of Prince Albert, but what can you do?" Charles lit up with the lamp, then exhaled in a long, slow whistle. "The laymen aren't supposed to smoke any, but they do. I'll let them get away with it, as long as it doesn't get out of hand. Catch one occasionally and make an example. See, they think this stuff gives them knowledge. Actually, it doesn't even get you doped up." Charles took another hit. "Besides," he said with a smile, "it suits me if they keep looking for knowing with smoke."

"So you have them growing weeds instead of crops they could eat."

Charles rolled his eyes. "Let's not talk about agriculture. I like you better as the voice of the free world than as an anthropologist. So," said Charles, leaning back with an imperial air, "did Franklin D. string our boy Adolf from the top of the Washington Monument?"

"Roosevelt is dead. Hitler killed himself. —This is like *Reader's Digest Condensed World Wars*," said Gray with frustration.

"Go on."

Gray decided to save the atomic bomb for later.

Then she realized she could leave it out altogether if she felt like it. She could even have told Charles that Hitler now ruled Eurasia, the United States, and South America, and then this would be the truth in Toroto. It was a curious little moment of power.

"A number of Nazis are on trial right now in Nuremberg

for war crimes," she continued, thinking it was a little late in the day for inventing a whole new ending to an awfully big story.

"On *trial?*"

"Why not?"

"Seems pretty feeble is all. Why not shoot the guys and be done with it?"

"Out of respect for legal process. To reinstitute order."

"Come on. Laws are just to give you an excuse for shooting somebody when you were going to shoot them anyway."

"That's ridiculous," said Gray.

"Nope. I know about laws. I make them."

"Is there anything you don't know about?"

"Not that I know about." He added, "Except. I don't know about you."

Whenever he turned the conversation to her, Gray got inexplicably nervous. They sat in silence again.

"Hitler—" she ventured.

"Hmm?"

"He killed six million Jews."

Charles looked up. "No shit," he said noncommittally.

"Not in battles. In factories."

"Huh," said Charles.

Gray watched his face. "What do you think of that project?"

"Well," said Charles, snuffing out his cigarette on the arm of his chair. "Seems like a real—waste of time, anyway." He shot Gray a shrug.

Gray looked back at him in stony silence until she couldn't take it anymore and started to laugh.

"I missed the joke," said Charles.

"You are the joke! You've been trying to impress me, haven't you?"

"How's that?"

"You think if you're blasé about six million Jews that's going to impress me."

"You figure that's what Adolf was trying to do?" he said gruffly, looking away. "Impress little Eva?"

"Seriously, Charles, you want me to admire that, don't you? I mean, that's twisted, even horrid, but it's sweet, too. Quaint." Gray kept chuckling in her hammock. Charles rose brusquely from his chair. Errol knew these moments—Gray could be nasty in a light, lovely way, and she could turn a situation on a dime. Surprise, Charles Corgie.

"I'm going to bed," he said coldly. "So are you." He towered over her hammock, giving her a moment of nervousness Gray for once richly deserved. She stopped laughing.

"Where?"

"In my house."

"Maybe I'll stay outside."

"No, you won't. You're a god now, Miss Kaiser, and you'll sleep in Olympus with the rest of us."

Gray got up cautiously from her hammock. "I'm sorry, I—"

"On the floor," he assured her. "Believe me, it will give me far more pleasure to have you up half the night beady-eyed with worry than to do what you will worry about." With that he blew out the lamp perfunctorily and strode inside, throwing her a hard, leathery skin for a blanket. "Good night, dear," said Charles, crawling inside his own soft bed stuffed with feathers and pulling the warm, woolly skin over his head.

As it happened, Gray was up half the night. While Charles

Corgie's thrashing and mumbling on the bed did keep her on edge, Gray's real problem was far more prosaic: she did not know what gods did with honey wine once they were through with it.

When Gray told this story it was very funny. She could get tablefuls of international guests rolling on the floor. On the floor of that stilted African cabin, however, Errol imagined she had not been so amused. She couldn't sleep. The ladder was pulled up from the ground and she didn't know how to replace it, nor whether there were too many natives about for such a mortal safari. And the situation was not, of course, improving. She'd enjoyed the wine and had drunk her share; Gray's abdomen gradually billowed higher, until—a magic moment in Gray Kaiser's life—she cared nothing for power and reserve; her fantasies slipped from huge tribal celebrations in her honor and lines of obsequious good-looking men at her feet to ordinary indoor plumbing. Love, humor, and courage fell away. Money and fame, art and human history fell away. World War II and six million Jews fell away. Even, at last, remaining aloof with Lieutenant Charles Corgie fell away, and Gray found herself numbly climbing up off the floor and standing by his bedside at four in the morning.

"Charles—" she said softly. "Lieutenant—"

He only grunted and turned away. She put a hand on his shoulder. Charles sprang upright and in a single motion had a rifle pointed a few inches from Gray's chest. His eyes were completely open and alert.

"Don't shoot!" Corgie's rifle had very nearly taken care of Gray's problem abruptly.

Charles did not put down the gun. He said something in garbled Masai that Gray didn't understand.

"Please," she said in a small voice. "I need your help."

Slowly he lowered the gun as he recognized her by the moonlight coming through the window. "If you were thinking you could get this gun—"

"No!"

Charles looked at her more closely. "Come here." He reached up and touched her cheek, then inspected his fingers. "No shit. You're crying."

Gray looked down. Tears fell on the bed frame.

Charles put the rifle aside and pulled her over to sit beside him. Her sharp shoulders were drawn to her head; she looked narrow. Charles put his hand on her cheek, turning her head to face him. "Having nightmares about terrible Charlie Corgie, who doesn't care about six million Jews?"

Gray shook her head and looked away again.

"You miss Mommy and Daddy?"

"Don't make fun of me," said Gray, wiping her nose on her sleeve.

Charles pulled the hair from her eyes strand by strand and tucked it behind her ear. "What's the trouble?"

"It's stupid."

Charles waited patiently.

"All this god business," she went on. "You didn't tell me what to do—" She stamped her foot and looked at the ceiling. "I'm not usually shy! Charles, I need the bathroom! I have for hours!"

It must have been hard not to laugh, but according to Gray he didn't; he barely smiled. Charles cocked his head. His eyes were as warm and soft as they were going to get in the hard cool light of the moon. "That isn't stupid, Miss Anthropologist. You're new to your field or you'd know better. For a god, taking a leak is a serious business. You have to be careful. Quiet." He led Gray to a corner, where she slid down a pole to the foliage below. When she returned Charles lifted her back up. He wasn't a massive man but could pull her whole weight with obvious ease. When she was up, Charles kept hold of her hand a moment, then with a funny annoyance let go and told her to get back to sleep. As she was settling back down on the slats this time, again with irritation, he tossed her his feather pillow before turning his back on her with a grunt and wrapping his arms fondly around the muzzle of his gun.

chapter four

I've decided what to do with you," said Charles cheerfully the next morning. He was shaving, with a sheet of polished aluminum from the siding of his airplane propped up for a mirror.

"Oh?" asked Gray warily, still groggy and on the floor.

"Yes." Charles raised his chin in the air to sweep the razor underneath. "I've decided to let you go."

The blade made a sheer scraping sound that raised the hair on Gray's arms. "I did not come here," said Gray, "to go."

"You shouldn't have come here at all," said Charles. "You made a mistake. Usually when we make mistakes, that's it. But: you are dealing with Little Jesus. You have your own personal fairy godfather. Click your heels together and in your case it will work."

Gray picked herself up in order to get a better view of his face. Charles did not look at her but scrutinized his chin more closely. There was a bullet hole in the siding, and his stubble distorted and rippled in the aluminum.

"Aren't you concerned that I'll tell?" asked Gray slowly. "About you? About Toroto?"

"Now, why would you do that? When I've been so gracious? And these people have someone to take care of them?"

Charles may not have been looking at Gray, but Gray was certainly looking at Charles now, very very carefully. "Because I'm an anthropologist. I'd want to come back with reinforcements."

"So military! And I thought we were friends."

"You're the one who sees this village as one more battle of World War II."

"Against them, not you, sweetheart."

"Sweetheart is on their side."

Charles clucked his tongue. "No racial loyalty."

"The point is, I'd have every reason to return here with company. You've murdered people here. This is a British colony. You could be arrested."

"Miss Kaiser, are you trying to convince me to shoot you?"

"I'm not telling you anything you haven't already thought about."

Charles said nothing. It seemed to Gray he should have finished shaving by now. His face looked smooth. Still, Charles picked at individual patches with great attention.

"What are you planning to do, turn me loose in the bush? I had a guide to get here. How would I find my way out?"

"You could have an escort partway. Why, maybe the Tooth Fairy himself would help you up the cliffs."

"Maybe I'll stay here."

"Sorry. No room at the inn. Booked for the season. Manger's filled, too. One Jesus per village. It's checkout time."

"When those Jews were gassed in the camps," said Gray softly, "they were told they were going to take a shower."

Charles turned toward her finally and looked her in the eye. He said nothing. His eyes were large and deep and black and hard to read. The muscles in his face did not move.

"All right," said Gray. "Maybe you hadn't decided. But it had occurred to you. There was a good chance."

Still, he said nothing.

"It makes you feel a little funny, doesn't it?" said Gray. "You think because I'm white, American, it's different. But you also know, deep down, that it's no different, and that you could do it."

It was a strange moment. Charles still wouldn't speak. There was nothing else for Gray to do but keep going. "I just feel we should discuss this, since I plan on staying here a while. For example, I find it pretty amazing that anyone could be so convinced of his own personal importance that no one's sacrifice is too great. I mean, how many people, Charles? Is there any limit? You and Adolf. You may not like him, but. How many, Lieutenant?"

Charles seemed almost to smile. He turned his head a few degrees and looked at Gray from an angle. He pointed his forefinger slowly at her chest. "I don't believe you," he said at last.

"What?"

"I don't believe you're amazed. That you don't under-stand." Charles took his rifle from against the wall and slid it onto the table in front of her. "There. If you thought you could get away with it. If there weren't several hundred religious fanatics outside that door. Would you use this? On me?"

This time it was Gray's turn to be quiet.

"See?" said Charles. "If you climbed out of your cockpit a little dazed from an insanely lucky crash landing and you were surrounded by crouching men with sharp poles, would you be willing to shoot just one of them to make a point?"

Gray said nothing.

"And if one, why not two, if that's what it took? And maybe, Miss Kaiser, over five years it would take *even more than two*."

Gray stared down at the gun. "So is everyone like this?"

Charles stroked his chin. He touched it with a certain surprise, as if he'd never felt it so smooth; he didn't seem to like it. He took his hand away. "Some women wouldn't pick up that rifle, would they? Even with Charlie Corgie ready to cart them off down the trail. But you would." Charles looked at her steadily. "We're not so different."

It was appalling. Gray found herself flattered. That was how she knew he was right.

"I know," said Charles, looking Gray up and down. "You think of yourself as some sort of warm, gooey-hearted darling. I don't buy it."

"How do you know what I'm like?"

"The way you move. That's the way I get everybody's number. I'm never wrong. For example, I've never met such a tall woman who walked around so straight."

"You can tell I would shoot you because I have good posture?"

"Sure. And more. You use your hands a lot when you talk.

They cut the air, slash, slash." Charles did a comic demonstration. Gray couldn't help but laugh. "Listen, I've made a study of this. I didn't know the language when I got here. We used sign language. The natives signed completely different for the same word. Some signed way out here." Charles flailed his hands on either side. "They're wide open. Trusting. *Crazy*. You operate from the center. You keep your hands close in, stab and parry. You'd be good with a knife. And," he went on, "you keep your chin up. You have an unnerving stare and a long stride. You're sarcastic and you obviously think you're so smart. In short, Miss Kaiser," said Charles, taking his gun back from the table, "you move like a real bitch."

Charles walked out the door, letting his hand graze her hip as he walked by. Gray let out a slow, controlled breath and ground her molars together. No one had warned her that anthropology was going to be so complicated.

G radually Gray and Charles worked out their truce. Charles would allow Gray to study Il-Ororen as long as she did her part in promoting his mythology. Gray cooperated, but she didn't understand how they got away with it. While they took the most obvious precautions with injury and excretion, they still sweated and coughed and laughed, ate and grew tired and slept long, heavy nights. There was a thin line between being improbable and being debunked altogether, and the two of them trod this line as precariously as she'd skirted the ledges to this village. It was a long way down.

The other abyss before them was their future. Gray would conclude her study, and then what? Likewise, Corgie's religious gadgetry was nearing its demise: the spare airplane batteries off which he ran his miraculous radio were finally running down. His stores of ammunition were running down.

"Do you ever think about going back to the U.S.?" asked Gray one day.

"I'm a god," said Charles. "Why should I go back and be a schmo?"

The trouble was, while when Gray arrived Charles had seemed beleaguered, he now seemed to be enjoying his life among Il-Ororen with great gusto.

While Corgie was working on his projects, Gray helped the natives with their spring planting. It was right before the rains, but the only crop Charles cared about was his ersatz tobacco, so Gray taught Il-Ororen about topsoil and terracing while Corgie milled wood. Their first conflicts were over allocation of labor. Gray wanted tillers; Corgie wanted lumberjacks. Finally, Gray asked in the middle of a ritual confrontation over a work crew, "Why are you building that stupid tower, anyway?"

"Because I'm going to put a restaurant on top, why do you think?" said Charles blackly. "Three stars, with a great view of the city lights."

"It seems about as useful—"

"Just the point, I don't care about useful. I will build a scale model of King Kong or a ten-foot wooden replica of the Great American Hamburger if that's what I feel like. Understand? And if I wake up one morning and decide that I can't live without an Egyptian pyramid in my back yard, then these poor bastards will spend the rest of their lives mining stone—"

"Until they starve to death, and you with them. That's all

very capricious, but without a few Egyptians growing bananas along the Nile, those pharaohs would never have gotten past the first story. *Alot-too-toni*," she said imperiously to the men, and looking confusedly from Gray to Corgie and back again, they followed Gray down the path to her fields, leaving Corgie by his half-built Babel furiously without lumber for the rest of the day.

Grudgingly, Charles walled off a portion of his one-room Olympus for Gray. It was thanks to this arrangement that she discovered the advantages of being a god extended well beyond architecture.

Lying in bed one night, Gray heard the ladder outside clatter and a woman's shy, nervous laughter. The ladder was withdrawn again, and set with a clack on the other side of Gray's bedroom wall. Fully awake now, Gray listened stiffly to the noises from Corgie's bed. She was used to his gruff, angry orders in the night; Corgie didn't sleep easily, as, she thought, he had no right to. She was used to the occasional clatter of his rifle when it fell from his arms; though it was terrifying to wake this way, she actually preferred those times the rifle fell and even went off to what she was hearing now: the rustling, a chuckle, a light feminine squeal. A growl and snuffling as if an animal were rummaging through his things. Then, worst of all, the sound of Charles Corgie peacefully, silently asleep for the first time Gray had ever heard.

Gray's toe cramped. She found she had a headache. Her eyes narrowed in the darkness. She rearranged herself loudly, sighed, and drummed the bedside with her fingertips. She was still awake when early that morning she heard the pad of small feet, a brusque grunt from Charles, and the ladder again, down and up. A great male sigh. Only then did Gray turn limply on her side and doze for a couple of hours.

"You slept soundly last night," said Gray as they peeled mangoes at breakfast.

"Yes," said Charles. "I feel refreshed." He was imbedded in his mango up to the second knuckle.

Gray only toyed with hers, listlessly pulling the gooey orange strings apart and then leaving them in a pulpy pile. "I think you and I need to have a religious conference."

"Convened," said Charles. "Shoot."

"Do you have to be so jaunty?"

"You're always badgering me for being surly at breakfast. For once I wake up in a good mood and you run me down for that, too. I can't win, Kaiser."

Gray squashed a piece of fruit between her fingers. "I want to discuss a point of catechism."

"Philosophy! So early, too. That brain of yours must start ticking away as soon as your feet hit the floor."

"Some mornings," said Gray. "But I don't want to talk theory. I want to talk practice."

"Which makes perfect, as I remember."

"That depends on what you're practicing."

Having finished off his mango, Charles started in on a banana with large, lunging mouthfuls. "Want one?"

Gray shook her head. "You've got quite an appetite today."

"I have quite an appetite, period," said Charles. "So what's our Sunday-school lesson for today?"

Gray crossed her arms. "Listen, I think we should discuss this, but not because I'm prim. We take so many precautions to avoid the appearance of mortality. But your adventure last night seemed perilously biological."

Charles put his feet up on the table. "Kaiser, sweetheart, it's great to hear you worry about keeping the old religion afloat. But believe me, when it comes to keeping an eye on my ass I am an expert—"

"Seems to me you had your eye on someone else's last night."

Corgie grinned. "They like it."

Gray stood up. "Well, I don't." She walked out the door, Charles laughing after her.

"They think it makes them powerful," said Charles, leaning over the ladder as Gray clipped rapidly down.

"That's precisely my point," said Gray. "I think it does."

Charles must have watched her brisk and unusually rigid stride to her precious furrows with a smile on his face and a satisfied gleam in his eye.

In the process of overseeing the planting, Gray also conducted informal interviews. Especially after she'd applied first aid to several farming injuries, Il-Ororen confided in her completely. At the end of the day Gray would go back to Corgie's cabin and take furious notes.

What fascinated Gray as she studied this tribe was that, on a scale of generations, they hadn't been separated from the Masai very long. It seems they'd deliberately purged themselves of their own history. Maliciously they insisted on having no ancestors but those they could remember, no larger culture to which they owed their ability to throw pots, to mine and forge metal tools. Their creation myths and cautionary tales were no longer traditional Masai ones. While they still built kraals, they gladly constructed new blond structures. Nor had they gradually distorted Masai music, ceremonies, and dances; they had dumped them. Il-Ororen had invented themselves.

Most surprising of all, Gray now had no doubt that, while they resented particular tyrannies and didn't understand the gymnasium, they cooperated willingly with Charles Corgie. She'd anticipated a gentle native population abused and manipulated by a cruel Western intruder. Instead, she found a ruthless people that had eagerly latched on to an appropriate sovereign. They liked Corgie's projects. They enjoyed his anger as long as it wasn't directed against them personally. They identified with his arrogance. They'd rooted Corgie deeply in their mythology, and told stories as if his arrival had been predicted for generations, like a messiah. Il-Ororen were the only people in the world, and they'd gotten themselves their own private god.

Gray's concern, however, was with the arrogance that Il-Ororen and Corgie shared. It had bound them; it could sever them, too. A truly arrogant people were easily dissatisfied and individually ambitious. They would have a high leadership turnover. Corgie had been among Il-Ororen for five years, and that struck Gray more and more as a long time.

S everal times a year Corgie had a church service.

"What if I don't want to go?" Gray asked that morning. All around them Il-Ororen were painting themselves with colored clay and plaiting braids; it reminded Gray too vividly of Sunday mornings when she would pull the covers over her head while her mother put on makeup and fixed her hair with grotesque cheerfulness.

"Gray, darling," said Charles as he prepared himself for the service, trying on his red baseball cap at different angles in his airplane mirror. "When you're the one giving the party, you don't get to decide whether or not to show. You're on the program. How's that?" He turned to her with the visor off to the back.

"Little Rascals."

"Perfect. Now, Kaiser, you old cow, what are you wearing?"

Gray spread her hands. As usual, she was in khaki work clothes.

"You have no sense of celebration," Charles chided.

"What's there to celebrate?"

"Nothing more nor less than ourselves, Gray dear." Charles was bouncing around the cabin so that the structure shook. "For you," he added, "a tie." He proceeded to tie a Windsor knot around his bare neck. In some wacky way, with the red cap, it was cute. Once Charles threw on his flight jacket, laced his boots over his pants, strapped on his Air Force goggles, and, the final touch, hung one of those long, hand-rolled cigarettes out the side of his mouth, he stood before Gray for inspection.

"You look—absolutely—insane," she said, laughing until she fell over on the bed.

Charles flicked an ash. "Excellent. Now for you."

"Not a chance," said Gray. "The dignified anthropologist will take notes sedately in the back."

"Don't be boring," said Charles. "What did you always secretly want to wear in church?"

"Khaki work clothes. I hated dresses."

"Think again."

Gray smiled. "Well. When I first got breasts, my mother used to foam at the mouth if I wore a low-cut blouse to church. So I'd walk out the door with my coat on, buttoned up to the chin. She'd find out about my neckline when we got there and take a scarf out of her purse, swathe it around my neck, and tuck it in the bodice. It would clash with my outfit, of course. I'd scream . . ." Gray laughed. "I tore it up once. Threw it down in the parking lot. I was like that."

"You still are."

"I don't throw tantrums anymore."

"You get what you want, though."

"Yes," said Gray, "everything." She said this simply and with certainty; it must have disconcerted her later, since there were a few things she didn't get—she was talking to one of them that morning.

"Then Gray will go to church in something plunging. Or how'd you like to go topless? It's in vogue here."

"Charles, I'd think you'd be bored by now with looking at women's breasts."

"Not by yours."

Gray looked at her hands.

"All right," said Charles with a clap. "I've got it." He rummaged around the cabin until he found a long scrap of cheetah skin. "Your shirt."

"No!" said Gray, but with Corgie's urging she went behind her partition and tied it around her chest. For her skirt he dragged out his old parachute and began to tear off a long swath of the silk.

"Are you sure you want to rip that up?"

"Now, what good is a parachute going to do me in Toroto?"

"You never know when you're going to have to bail out of here."

"You bring that up a lot," said Charles, tucking the chute around her hips, making a full, low-swung wrap, like a belly dancer's. "My leaving. You don't seem to get it, Kaiser. I'm gonna be buried here."

"That's what I'm afraid of."

"Ah-ah. No more morbid talk. Now, let's see." He patted her hip. "Step back." She did so; Charles let out a slow whistle. "Terrific."

Gray looked down at the thin band of animal skin around her breasts, the long flat expanse of her bare stomach, the blousy white silk draping down to her feet. She extended her leg between the folds and smiled. "It's slit practically up to my waist, Charles."

"Very sexy."

"Are you trying to humiliate me?"

"Couldn't if I tried. Whatever we put on you, the congregation will receive you with tragic seriousness."

Gray put her hair high on her head, slipped on her sunglasses, and billowed down the ladder.

"Hold it," said Charles. "Where's that camera of yours? I want a picture."

Gray told him, but by the time he returned with her camera she was disconcerted. "This will have to be developed, you know."

Charles posed her by the ladder. "Raise your arm. Chin in the air. Come on, you're a goddess! And let's see that leg through the slit. Right.—Come on, what's the problem? The pose is great, but your face looks like you're still fourteen and your mother's dragging you to church."

"I just wonder how you propose to get this photograph if you're going to be buried here."

"Mail it to me," said Charles, looking through the shutter. "Charles Corgie; The-Middle-of-Fucking-Nowhere; Africa. Or send a caravan. You'll think of something."

Gray managed to smile, though wistfully. Errol knew this. He'd seen the picture: the wind catching the white chute, which trailed off to the side, her leg streaking toward the camera, and the poignant expression of a woman who hadn't yet finished a story that gave every indication of ending badly.

On the way to Corgie's cathedral they processed arm in arm with Il-Ororen decked out and ululating behind them. Corgie held his rifle like a papal staff; Gray's camera swung from her hand like an incense burner. Charles led her into the cavernous interior, with its one huge, unadorned room. The great thatched ceiling let in an uneven mat of sunlight over the dirt floor. As Il-Ororen passed into the sanctuary they went silent, threading in neat rows before the dais. Charles pulled Gray up with him on the raised platform before the crowd and waited with gun in hand for the gathering to assemble. When as many as could fit in the room were seated and still, Charles stepped forward. A baby began to cry. Charles pulled the trigger on his rifle, and the shot vibrated up through Gray's feet. There was an echoing rumble through the crowd, though they quickly sat still again. The mother of the crying child pressed the baby to her breasts and cowered out the door. Gray looked up at the roof. There was a whole smattering of holes in the thatch the size of bullets, and when she looked down she saw they let in absurdly cheerful polka dots of sunlight at her feet.

Deeply Charles intoned his invocation. His manner was so serious, his voice so incantatory, that it took Gray several moments to realize he was chanting a Wrigley's spearmint-gum commercial.

Gray stared.

"Knock, knock!" boomed Corgie.

"Hooz dere!" the cry came back, with the solemnity of a responsive reading.

"Mm-mm, good!"

"Mm-mm, good!"

"That's what Campbell's soup is!"

"Mm-mm, good!"

Somehow Charles kept a straight face. Gray stuffed her fist in her mouth.

Corgie launched into a hearty version of "Whoopee tai-yai-yo, git along, little dogies," and rounded it off with a Kellogg's corn flakes jingle. He gave them tips on freshening their refrigerators with Arm and Hammer and painlessly removing corns. He exhorted the merits of Wombley's uncrushable ties. For his sermon, Charles pulled a tattered *Saturday Evening Post* out of his leather jacket and read a rousing portion of "We'll Have Fewer Cavities Now," the stirring story of Bobsie Johnson of Brockton, Mass., and her battle with bad teeth. After the sermon he led the congregation in a moving rendition of "Little Rabbit Foo-Foo." He had taught them the hand motions, so an expanse of several hundred African tribesmen bounced their fists up and down, "scoop-nup de field mice an' bop-num on de head." Every once in a while Charles would look over at Gray and smile. Gray shook her head. Listening to Corgie was like putting your ear to the crack in a playroom door.

Yet the gathering also functioned in a serious religious sense, perhaps to Corgie's dismay. His English rambling seemed no more sardonic to his parishioners in its untranslated state than Latin to uncomprehending Catholics or Hebrew to unschooled Jews, so that the feeling in that assembly built to true spiritual frenzy despite Campbell's soup. The audience swayed and clapped in the best revivalist tradition. Finally, when Corgie turned to the miraculous radio behind him and delicately tuned in the one broadcast he could barely pick up—a Swahili station that also played American music—the Il-Ororen were on their feet craning forward and at a pitch of silence. Gradually the grainy voices drifted in, then out, then in—Il-Ororen's ancestors, men from other planets, gods, fairies, whatever, until the talking stopped and Corgie smiled; the reception became exceptionally clear and loud and Louis Armstrong's "Ain't Misbehavin'" blasted across Corgie's cathedral. Charles reached for Gray's hand, and they danced across the dais.

"Kaiser!" said Charles quietly, "you're a great dancer."

Gray smiled. She *was* a great dancer. Errol had watched her join celebrations all over the world. And this must have been something. Gray at twenty-two and this handsome, outrageous man in his red baseball cap and goggles and little strip of a tie whipping across his bare chest, all in front of hundreds of Kenyans in a swoon. Whenever Charles twirled her around or swept her back until her hair brushed the floor, Il-Ororen whooped. Finally he spun her until her feet lifted off the floor, pulled her out and into a turn and a bow, and the song was over. Il-Ororen roared. At a nod from Corgie they poured happily out the door.

Gray and Charles stayed on the platform until the last churchgoer was gone. The expanse of the room was serene. "How much of that was for my benefit?" asked Gray softly. The question echoed.

"In a way, all of it. But I don't usually read Leviticus, if that's what you mean. Last time I read them 'The Other Woman Was My Best Friend' and made them sing 'One Hundred Bottles of Beer on the Wall' to the last verse."

"That's real despotism, Charles. So what's next?"

"Everyone eats a lot and gets drunk. Then I coach the football team."

"You're kidding."

"Hey, Sunday afternoon, right? I'm an American missionary. I'd bring them beer and pretzels and narrow-mindedness if I could, but as it is, we have to make do. I sewed my own leather ball. Works pretty well, too. And I've changed a few of the rules."

"Why?"

"Because I could," said Charles.

"It must be frustrating," said Gray, looking around the big empty hall.

"How?"

"Well, they don't know you've changed the rules, do they?"

"No. So?"

"When you make the rules you can't break them, can you? A funny sort of solipsistic hell."

"My, we are talking mighty fancy."

Gray settled her eyes on this strange dark man in his little red baseball cap. Poor Charlie had surely spent his Sunday mornings as a boy sending spitballs arcing between pews; yet now if he were to introduce spitballs into his services, the whole congregation would obediently wad and wet them, and little boys would grow to resent sopping them in their cheeks every bit as much as Charles had resented stale communion wafers on his tongue. Here was a heretic whose every blasphemy turned uncontrollably to creed. Adherence to his own religion must have followed Corgie like a loyal dog he couldn't shake. Gray pulled his visor affectionately over his face. "All I mean," Gray explained, "is it must be hard when no one gets your jokes."

"Were you amused?"

"Very."

Corgie smiled a little. He looked at her. "You're beautiful," said Charles.

"Thank you," said Gray.

There was an odd, fragile silence.

"You dance great," said Charles.

"You said that," said Gray. "But thanks again."

Corgie took off his red baseball cap and aviator goggles, stuffing them in his jacket. He had trouble fitting them in his pocket. "Eat something?"

"All right."

Corgie took her arm and they walked slowly toward the door. For two people on their way to a feast, they were awfully reluctant. Finally they ground to a mutual halt. In the wide quiet of Corgie's cathedral, the dust settled on its earthen floor. Spears of sunlight through the thatch lengthened and warmed as the afternoon sun grew lower and more orange.

"You must get lonely here," said Gray.

"Yes," said Charles.

They looked at each other. The smell of wildebeest dripping on coals wafted into the room. The smoke stung. Their eyeballs dried.

Gray smiled, with difficulty. She took an inward step. Corgie's head made a quizzical turn. It was hard to know what to do. It was hard enough for Gray anyway, in Africa, so young. Of course certain pictures had flashed before her since she'd first seen this man by his tower, heard his rich, sadistic laugh, caught the glitter of his dubious intentions. But it was different to think things than to do them. Thinking, you could look the man in the eye the next morning and he knew nothing and you could smile to yourself and ask him to pass the mangoes. Thinking was a smug and private business. Moving your real hand to his face was a drastic and public affair. You could not take it back. It was like chess, when you took your hand from a piece, having moved it a square.

Incredulously, Gray watched her own hand rise to Corgie's cheek. Stubble bristled at her fingertips. Raking into his hair, she found it thick and coarse. Why didn't he say something? His expression was opaque. Her fingers crawled over his ear, to the taut muscles on either side of his neck. Still his eyes were secret. Gray felt frightened and stupid. Yet, having been taught since she was small to finish what she started, Gray pulled his neck toward her and raised her lips to his.

Later she could pretend it didn't mean anything at all.

Suddenly it was as if she'd nibbled at a trap and it had sprung. His arms clenched her with the strength of a stiff spring; his sharp fingers sunk into her ribs like quick metal teeth. Gray felt her feet lift from the floor, and Charles Corgie carried her in his arms out the door.

Charles carted her through the compound, past Il-Ororen, who stopped and stared with their shanks of meat poised in midair. Gray curled against his jacket, resting her head in the hollow of his shoulder. Her feet dangled helplessly from his arms. Il-Ororen shouted behind them. Their cries rose and fell in waves, like the serenade of cicadas in pines, wild and demented. Gray nudged the leather aside for his skin underneath; his sweat stuck to her cheek.

Charles worked his hand under the band of her skirt at the small of her back; Gray could tell that the parachuting was now precariously tucked around her hips. When he reached the ladder he swung her over his shoulder. As he climbed she clutched at the skirt.

Inside, Charles slung her off and she felt herself free-fall to the mattress. She wondered if the parachute would open. Charles slipped his hand under the silk and cupped her hipbone, moving down to the inside of her thigh. With his other hand he traveled up her bare stomach to the tiny strip of cheetah skin, which had slipped dangerously low. Tiny rolls of dead skin gathered under his palm. Gray felt a little sick. Saliva squirted and pooled in her mouth; she had to keep swallowing. Corgie leaned over and took her earlobe in his mouth; hunger rustled at her ear. He moved to the cartilage and licked inside. The pressure in her head changed as he sucked the air out; she heard a splashing and yawning "ah-ah," like the roar of a conch.

Corgie let himself down slowly on top of her. He was heavy; though compact, his body was dense and buried her beneath him. Gray sunk into the bed so that the mattress rose on either side of her. Every part of this man's body was hard like wood. He closed over her like the lid of a coffin. She couldn't breathe.

Corgie worked the gathers from her hips. Fold by fold he pulled the parachuting from her body. The material collected in limp rumples beside her, thin and wan and white like funereal linen. He exposed the sweep of her thigh. With one hard pull he snapped the band of her underwear.

Gray's eyes shot wide. She jockeyed him across her until she slid his body off to her side. Gray lay panting as Corgie propped himself up on his elbow and looked down at her with a smile one might use after an excellent appetizer, when the meal to come promised to be even better. He took a deep breath and followed the indentations of her ribs with his fingertips as her chest rapidly rose and fell. Her cheetah skin had inched down still farther, and he trailed up to the swell of her slight breasts, up, over, down; up, over, down. Gray didn't imagine for a minute he had stopped. He was resting. He was restraining himself. That was his pleasure. For now.

"I was wondering when you'd come around," said Charles. Her ear was up against his chest, and the cavity amplified the sound, like a tomb.

"Oh?" Her voice was small.

"Yeah. You've been pretty funny, I gotta say."

Gray struggled up on her elbows. Trying to look casual about it, she shifted the parachute to cover between her legs. "How is that?" She didn't like the idea of amusing him just now.

"Sleeping in your corner; playing the anthropologist."

"Oh?" she said again, pulling a little farther up on the pillow. The crease between her eyes indented, just a little. Playing the anthropologist. Gray remembered the snuffling in the night. How many other women had lain here?

"But I figured pretty soon you couldn't stand it anymore. Really, watching you's been a riot."

Gray looked over at him, scanning for some sign that this

was any different for him than one more snuffling. "A riot," said Gray. The indentation between her eyes was discernibly deeper now.

"A one-woman amusement park." He licked his lips. He seemed pleased with himself.

Gray tugged at her cheetah skin, now threatening to slide off her breasts altogether. "And how else have I been entertaining you?"

"Tromping out in those fields of yours. Taking notes. It's cute. But it's been obvious from the first few days what you've really been doing here. Guess the study's gonna be real in-depth, right?"

Gray pulled herself to a sitting position. She rearranged the straggles of her hair. She felt her face tingle and her ears heat; she was sure they were red. How did she get here? What was she doing in this bed? She tucked the folds of her skirt one by one decisively into its band. "Well, I suppose it takes me a long time to do my work, Charles," she said quietly, "since I spend so much time daydreaming about when big handsome Charlie Corgie will finally kiss me good night." Gray swung her legs over the side of the bed. She looked down at her outfit, for the first time finding it regrettably ridiculous. She decided she did not want to cry. She looked down at her lap and decided this was very, very important to her, and asked herself not to cry, the way you would ask a favor of a friend of yours.

"Getting your back up?" Charles went on behind her, still leaning on his elbow. "You're not gonna tell me you don't lie behind that screen just eating your heart out. Those sighs that keep me awake at night? They've cracked me up. And that night I brought a bedwarmer up here? Next morning you went nuts. It was hysterical."

Gray slowly uncurled and brought her spine straight. Her eyes were sharpening. "Funny," said Gray. "I don't remember going nuts."

"Sure you did. But now's the time to look back on it and laugh, right?"

"So far only one of us is laughing." Gray rose from the bed. She was six feet tall.

"Come back here, toots, we're just getting started."

"No, we're finished," said Gray calmly, smoothing the billows of her parachute down her hips. "I'm going to hoe. I guess I've just looked forward to this with you so obsessively for so long, all the while pretending to be a professional at work on some silly study, that now the time has finally arrived and you deign to look my way, I just can't handle the excitement." Gray started out the door.

"Okay, you've made your little speech, now come back here."

Gray started down the ladder.

"Come on," said Corgie at the top, suddenly more serious. "Give me a kiss and forget it."

Gray paused mid-step.

Encouraged, Corgie continued: "We've wasted plenty of time already, right? All these weeks we could've been having a fine time. Get up here. You look great. You're driving me crazy."

Gray came back up the ladder.

"That's more like it," said Charles with a smile. He gave her a hand up, but when he put his arm around her she slipped away, angling past him through the doorway.

"I need my work clothes to hoe." She whisked back out with her khaki in a bundle and brushed coolly by again. In no time she tapped back down the ladder and strode off between the manyattas.

"You don't know what you're missing!" he shouted after her.

"I don't expect I ever will!" she shouted back.

"That's right, don't think you'll get a second chance!"

"Well, I guess I'll have to live with that terrible disappointment." Her parachuting swirled out on all sides, alive like white flames.

Corgie watched her go from his porch. No doubt he muttered something like "She'll be back," but, an intelligent man despite his recent behavior to the contrary, he wouldn't be so sure.

chapter five

These scenes have their satisfactions, but they cost you. In Toroto, everyone paid for this one. Something had gone wrong; the script was awry. No one was happy. No one got what he wanted. Errol decided this is what it was like:

Corgie had "bedwarmers" almost every night. He laughed a lot then. He was loud. Gray lay on the other side of the partition trying to keep her breathing slow and audibly even. Yet the more asleep she sounded, the more Corgie rocked the frame of his bed. When he reached his pitch Gray even tried snoring. Finally neither of them slept well, or woke jaunty.

More than ever, they threw themselves into their separate projects. They drew up separate crews. The tribe was split tacitly down the middle, like troop divisions.

The tower got higher. Corgie liked to climb to the top at sunset very far away from everything.

Corgie had another worship service and Gray didn't come. He hadn't invited her. He came back and said it went wonderfully, though Il-Ororen seemed sodden enough afterward and didn't fix much food; they mostly got drunk.

The rains made everything worse. Gray would record interviews, with irritation helping his cause with the miracle of her machine. Corgie would lope in long, hapless laps through the expanse of his gymnasium. But it was the tendency of the rainy-day mind to stay home. Gray would lie about in her corner craving a book to read, but in lieu of that, starting to write her own. This was no relief, though, as she wrote about Il-Ororen, and she was beginning to despise them—they all seemed just like Charles Corgie. For distraction she made herself a deck of cards from the stiff dividers in her notebooks. Refusing to play with Charles, though, Gray was left with solitaire. She hated solitaire. Gray tried drawing next, but she didn't draw very well, and disliked doing anything she did badly. She wanted to hear music. She wanted to read a newspaper. She wanted to have a conversation.

Instead, they gave each other directions, edicts; they informed each other of passing incidents with great economy of language, as if every word were being telegraphed overseas.

Charles cleaned his guns. He worked on a new model. For several days Gray wouldn't ask what the model was of. Yet the severe angular structure, with its jagged points and narrow corridors and tiny rooms with no doors, did not shape into anything recognizable. Finally Gray came up to Corgie in the midst of a torrential, desperately endless afternoon and asked, "What is that?"

"A monument."

"To what?"

"To whom."

"You decided the tower wasn't pointless enough?"

"I've passed beyond functionalism," said Charles mildly, "to pure form."

"Pure something," Gray muttered.

"What's that?" asked Charles nicely.

"Is that just a monument?" asked Gray. "Or your gravestone?"

Charles turned to her squarely. "Now, why do you care?"

Gray turned away. "It's a boring afternoon," she said flatly. "It's raining. It was something to say." Gray wandered back to her corner and pulled the curtain tightly shut.

During the rainy season Il-Ororen worked in clay, for it dried evenly in the moist air. Out of raving boredom rather than anthropological duty, Gray made water jugs on rainy afternoons. To satisfy her own sense of irony, Gray fashioned Grecian urns with Apollos and Zeuses curling from the handles and sending fire and lightning bolts down the sides of the bowls. The women were delighted, and fouled Gray's already limping study of their traditional vessel forms by immediately copying hers—one more eager betrayal of their fusty Masai inheritance. It didn't matter whether Gray's innovations were better so long as they were *new*. They imitated urns and Chinese vases and squat British teapots indiscriminately, though they did not make tea. Gray had never read of any African tribe so taken with modernity.

The kraal where Gray potted belonged to Elya's family, once, before Corgie, the richest and most powerful in the tribe. The father had been the chieftain before Corgie arrived; Charles had shot him early on. Yet the remaining wives did not seem to hate Il-Corgie, and took Gray into their homes with deference but no anger. Corgie's murder of their husband seemed to make sense to them. Unlike most of the Masai tribe, Il-Ororen had no problem with killing, as long as it worked to your advantage and you got away with it. The wives clearly admired Corgie for felling such an imposing man as their husband, and spoke of the scene of his death not with grief but with awe.

The sons, however, kept their distance. The oldest, Odinaye, regarded Gray with suspicion when she came to the hut. Even for a Masai he was tall and grave. His eyes smoldered before the fire while she built her vases. He would stare silently at Gray for hours through the smoky haze between them. Gray couldn't shake the feeling that he was waiting for her to make a mistake. She would sometimes try to make conversation with Odinaye, but he never responded with anything but even keener scrutiny.

Gray began to notice Odinaye in her vicinity too often. She would look down from the porch when she was eating lunch and find him staring up at her with steady, unblinking accusation. She would lose her appetite, and go inside.

With Odinaye so often a few paces away, Gray found it increasingly difficult to slip off into the bush alone to attend to her all too mortal toilet. When she and Corgie had their dry, cryptic tiffs in the middle of the compound, Gray would turn and find Odinaye watching from the sidelines. Gray found herself talking more softly; though they were using English, she had the eerie sensation of being overheard.

"I'm being followed," Gray finally told Charles. "By Odinaye. I dream about him now. He's there every time I turn around."

"Maybe he's in love," said Charles.

"This is serious."

"Isn't everything serious lately?"

"What should I do?"

"Why come to me? You've got a problem. So take care of it."

I t was an ordinary afternoon. Gray was struggling with a large water jug. She'd gotten the clay too wet; the sides were collapsing. Odinaye's presence on the other side of the hut, crouching and staring as usual, was especially irritating. She couldn't help suspecting—was it only the play of smoke between them?—that there was a wisp of a smile on his face today. She was sure he could see she was having trouble—well, any idiot could see that; the thing was falling apart.

Gray decided to take advantage of her role as the leader of the avant-garde and cave in the sides intentionally. She composed her expression. When one side fell in again, she looked down at it archly and revised a dent here and there, as if that was exactly what the goddess of modern pottery had in mind. Imperiously, she told Odinaye to give her the wooden paddle beside him; she would bat in the other side, too.

"Here it is," said Odinaye, handing her the paddle readily.

Gray accepted the paddle before she went white. Now that he was closer, his small grim smile was unmistakable.

The daring of the avant-garde potter left Gray entirely. Awkwardly she used the paddle to bat the collapsed side back out again. Using props inside the jar, she secured the sides and quickly put it aside to dry out. When she dipped her hands in a pot of water to rinse off the clay, she noticed they were shaking.

Not saying another word, she ducked out the doorway and went straight to Charles Corgie.

"What's going on?" asked Charles, leaning on his bed with a cigarette as Gray paced the room. "Why can't you sit still?"

"Would you stop worrying about the way I *move* for once and listen to me?" Gray whispered.

"I'll listen if you talk loudly enough for me to hear you—"

"Shsh! Talk more quietly."

"WHY?" Charles boomed.

"Shut up!"

Charles rolled his eyes. "Shoot."

"I was working on a pot that wasn't going very well—"

"So your pot didn't come out pretty and now you're mad?"

Gray looked at him; there must have been something in her face to make him sit up without quite the same sultry boredom and put out his cigarette.

"Odinaye was there, naturally," she went on in a low voice. "I said, 'Hand me that paddle,' and he picked it up and said, 'Here it is.'"

Charles waited. Gray didn't go on. "And?"

"That's it."

"Some story," said Charles.

"Yes," said Gray. "It is."

"I guess it's one of those subtle narratives that depends on *texture.*"

"Charles," said Gray. "He said 'Here it is' in *English.*"

Corgie sat up. "No."

"Yes."

Corgie stood and paced. "Well," he reasoned, taking out another cigarette, "one phrase. Big deal."

"No, he knows at least two, Charles. I made a mistake. I asked for the paddle in English, too. And I didn't point. He knew the word 'paddle.'"

"So? Here it is. Paddle. So?"

"How do we know how many other words he's picked up, Charles? *What else has he heard?*"

Charles grunted. He smoked fast, as if his cigarette were hard work to get over with. "Damn it." He paced some more. "Jesus, we're gonna have to be careful." He was speaking more softly now himself.

Gray sighed. "He obviously figured out the language by watching us interact."

"When have we been doing that?"

"We do still fight sometimes."

Charles sunk into a chair. "So—what? We're going to talk even less than we've been doing? I don't even know if that's possible."

"Do you know any other languages? French, German, Latin?"

"Nope. But you do, of course."

"That wouldn't do any good if you don't know them, too."

"Why not? We could have our own separate languages. You could walk around speaking German. I can definitely see it, Kaiser."

"Well, say. How's your English vocabulary?"

"Me? The poor uneducated architect? All I know is damn, fuck, and shit. Jane-loves-Puff. Go-Timmy-go. You know that."

"Stop it. We have to work on this. I mean, we have to— cogitate on our—contretemps."

"Say what?"

"Odinaye may have learned go-Timmy-go. But he hasn't learned perambulate-Timmy-perambulate."

"Let me get this straight. When I hit my thumb with a hammer, I'm supposed to yell, 'Oh, coitus!'?"

"Exactly."

"This is going to be disgusting, Kaiser."

"Or fun. As long as we can't be heard we can drop it, but if we have to talk to each other in public we should only *palaver, parley*, or *discourse*."

"Or lately, *harangue, wrangle*, or *contend*."

Gray laughed as Charles leaned back in his chair with a sigh. "Maybe their learning English is all for the best," said Gray softly. "Maybe they'll finally appreciate that your invocation is a Wrigley's spearmint-gum commercial." With a rare moment of affection, Gray reached out with a wistful smile and tousled his hair.

The plan seemed to work to a degree. When Gray and Charles were in earshot of Odinaye, they switched to their most professorial language, and Gray could tell by the light panic with which Odinaye's eyes followed the conversation that he was no longer picking much up.

The whole vocabulary scam might have issued in an era of reconciliation, but Gray's lexicon was considerably larger than Corgie's. When she used a word he didn't know, he would furiously stalk off in the middle of her definition. To her credit, Gray wasn't trying to impress him but simply to use an effective scramble on their broken code. To her these multisyllabic marathons were an entertainment, like crossword puzzles.

Charles had his eye on another sport they could share, though; he waited impatiently toward the end of the season for a few dry days in a row. Finally the rain did let up for a week, and the ground was hard enough for Corgie to introduce Gray to the pleasures of his tennis court.

Charles claimed to have played an excellent game back in New York before he was drafted, and told Gray it was tennis he missed more than any other element of Western civilization. After setting a full work crew to refurbishing his court, he walked Gray proudly around its hard-packed clay. He'd had the crew lay down the sacred white lines with ash and string up the heavy hemp net the women of the tribe had woven. He showed her two rackets—laminated strips, soaked and bent and bound at the bottom with a leather grip. Carved at their throats were antelopes on one, lions on the other. They'd been strung with wet gut; as the gut dried it tightened, so the tension on the strings was surprisingly high. The rackets were a little heavy, but lovingly made, and beautiful.

Corgie's most controversial achievements were his tennis balls. He'd scrounged rubber out of the carcass of his plane and bound it with hide. They were, Gray conceded, miraculously spherical, but the bounce was another matter. "But they do bounce," said Corgie, taking his ball back from her ungrateful hands. "You try to make a tennis ball."

Corgie led Gray happily to his court, swishing the air with his racket, the lions at its throat in a position of yowling victory. Charles stretched out before the game with large animal glee, like a predator who's been cooped up in his lair too long and is ready for a hunting spree.

Il-Ororen gathered around the court with enthusiasm, and Gray called Corgie's attention to Odinaye's presence in the front row. "Heed your vernacular."

Charles snorted and went to his side. He didn't know the word "vernacular."

"I attempted to—instruct this—population," said Corgie after a couple of rather handsome warm-up serves, "on this—pastime. They didn't—comprehend it. Every—primitive I—inculcated—played a lob game." He went on quickly, irritated with the vocabathon. "I like a good hard rally, Kaiser. This counts."

When she tried to return his serve, it thudded into the net. "You ever—indulge yourself in this—diversion before, Kaiser?"

"Once or twice," said Gray. That was all she said for the rest of their play.

On Corgie's second point he double-faulted, but on the third Gray socked the ball into the net again; Corgie looked archly sympathetic, though he should have noticed that she'd nearly gotten the ball across this time. "It takes time to—accustom yourself to the—facilities," said Charles. "First game's practice."

Gray did win one point in their practice game, and Corgie was elaborately congratulatory. Compliments can be far more insulting than criticism; she hadn't won on a very good shot. Still, Gray gathered her lips together and said nothing.

Later, Corgie no doubt regretted his concession on the first game as practice, for Gray "accustomed herself to the facilities" quite readily. And Gray didn't play a lob game.

Corgie stopped making conversation. He lay into the ball with his full weight, but consistently started driving it into the net. His eyes blackened; his stroke got more desperate; his game plummeted. In fact, the whole set was over in short order. Corgie strode with steely control past Gray, his grip on his racket tight and sweaty. The lions at its throat were whining.

"You don't desire to consummate the entire match?" asked Gray.

"No, I do not desire to consummate the entire match," Corgie mimicked her through his teeth. "You didn't tell me you were some kind of all-Africa tennis champion."

"You didn't inquire."

Charles started to walk away, and Gray called after him, "Il-Cor-gie!" He turned. "Would you have preferred that I feign a fraudulent ineptitude?" Gray was exasperated with having to talk this way; the words themselves made him angry.

"I don't need your condescension," said Corgie.

"And I don't need yours."

Corgie waved his hand and shook his head. "This is point-less," he said, and walked away.

It was pointless. Gray had just wiped the court with Charles Corgie and she couldn't understand why she didn't feel victorious. She looked down at the antelopes on her racket. They looked back up at her with their antlers at a sheepish angle and their soft wooden eyes forlorn.

I can't find my tape recorder," Gray told Corgie in the cabin the next afternoon.

"You mean you lost it?"

"No, I know where I left it. It's not there anymore."

"Someone took it?"

"If you didn't—I think so." Gray felt a funny sense of trepidation.

Charles reached for his gun.

"Charles—"

"Then we're going to find it. They have *never* taken anything from here before. We're going to nip this sport in the bud." He checked that the gun was loaded. "You think that asshole who knows the word 'paddle' knows the word 'tape recorder,' too?"

"Odinaye is a natural suspect."

"Good. We'll see if he knows the words 'Hand it over' and 'Say your prayers.'"

"Charles, it's only a tape recorder."

"When there's only one of them and it makes you a god, there's no such thing as only a tape recorder."

Gray followed Corgie warily down the ladder.

When they got to Odinaye's hut, sure enough they could hear from outside the snap of buttons and the whir of reels; snatches, too, of native conversation about funeral rites. "How appropriate," Corgie muttered as he ducked inside.

In the corner was a dark figure huddled over the machine. Corgie dragged the man outside by his arm and threw him down. In the light, though, the figure turned out to be Odinaye's younger brother Login, who was only fourteen. Login crumpled at Corgie's feet, with his face to the ground. The only sound the boy made was a high, raspy breath, which hit eerie harmonics. Corgie took the safety off his rifle.

The wives, including Login's mother, quickly gathered around the scene, not daring to interfere. They said nothing. Gray turned and found, with no surprise, Odinaye, tall and silent and glowering ten feet away.

"Okay, you son-of-a-bitch." Corgie addressed Odinaye in English. "You know those words, mister? You should. Son-of-a-bitch. Now you listening to me? I don't know for a fact that you took it, so I'm not going to shoot you. But you're going to watch."

"Charles—"

"Go get the recorder."

Gray retrieved the machine. Charles announced in Il-Ororen to the crowd that Login had stolen the sacred voice box. Then he picked the boy up and propped him against the wall of the hut.

Gray put her hand on Corgie's shoulder. "Charles, we've got it back now—"

Corgie brushed her hand off and, with astonishingly little ceremony for a god, took the rifle to his shoulder and shot the thief against the wall, right in the heart.

The shot echoed back and forth between the cliffs of the valley, but died quickly; so did Login. Corgie slung his gun back over his shoulder and left Il-Ororen behind him blithely, the way he might walk away from one of his models with the dark clay figures posed in their attitudes of worship or chagrin. With one glance at Odinaye, who looked back at her with a stiff, unfazed resolve that seemed oddly familiar, Gray trailed after Charles, carrying the hallowed tape recorder. That's right. That look, it was Corgie's.

W hen Gray walked into the cabin Corgie had his back to her and was looking out the window. "Go ahead," he said shortly, not turning around. "I'm ready."

Gray stood staring at Corgie's back, watching those broad shoulders heave up and down from the kind of breathing he might do before battle. For a time she said nothing. She wasn't ready. She hadn't rallied the disgust she would need now. It must have been disturbing to enter a room with a man whose gun was still warm, with a dead fourteen-year-old down below, and not feel sufficient revulsion. Gray was shaken, but right now her deepest wish was to sink her fingers into the bands of his neck and relax the muscles, to rearrange his frayed black hair. Gray must have been asking herself what Errol had always wondered, too: how could she overlook that Charles Corgie murdered people? Maybe she wasn't a "warm, gooey-hearted darling," but she had her limits and one of them had always been shooting a young boy at five paces. No, she didn't go for that. How could she go for that in Corgie? Was she actually attracted to a man who shot fourteen-year-olds for stealing tape recorders? Did that impress her? Or did she understand that he didn't know what he was doing? That Charles's vision was narrowed enough that for him firing at natives was no different from shooting down ducks at a county fair? Could she forgive that poor eyesight? Yet even if people are born a certain way and end up a certain way for reasons out of their control, aren't there actions you hold them accountable for, regardless? Wouldn't Charles be convicted posthaste at Nuremberg? Or would Gray Kaiser be the one stolid juror who would vote to let him off the hook?

Errol had never answered these questions to his satisfaction.

It was with reluctance, then, that Gray began now, though there was one long moment when she actually considered keeping quiet and massaging his neck; in that same moment she also understood that he was tired and upset and would have let her. Instead, she said for the second time, still from across the room, "Charles. It was only a tape recorder."

Corgie sighed at the window. His body slumped, as if he could feel the fingers withdrawing from his neck. So it was this again. They were both good soldiers, but there were days—Gray, why can't we shut up? It was hard enough to shoot that boy.

Why can't we drop it? But instead he said, "What was I supposed to do, Gray? Slap his hand and send him to his room? Or sit him down and ask him, If everybody did that, what kind of world would we live in?" He turned around. "Gray darling, we're not in school anymore. We're in the middle of Africa. Keeping up this immortality stuff isn't just a game."

"It is in a way," said Gray. "You set the rules. Didn't you choose to be immortal?"

"That's right, to save my ass. I saved it, I have to keep saving it. Haven't we been through this?" Their talk was still without heat. The argument was tired. "In Toroto religion is a matter of life and death. It is for me. So it is for them. It's only fair."

"All of which fails to explain why you had to shoot a fourteen-year-old boy—"

"All of which does explain it!" Corgie at last took a few steps toward her, at last gave his voice some edge, some pitch. "I swear, Kaiser, you just don't want to understand, do you? You just have to be against me. Have to be on the other side."

"Of this, yes."

"Of everything and you know it. Kaiser, the irony of this whole business is that I have never met a woman more like me in my life. Lady, you surpass me! I mean it! You bitch all the time, but you took to divinity like a fish to water!"

Gray's chin rose a little higher. The idea of massaging this man's neck was now out of the question. "I have done here," she said coldly, "what I had to do. For my work and for my own survival."

"Which is what I said, but it doesn't wash when I say it."

"I haven't killed people."

"You haven't had to! I do it for you! Why do you think they're afraid of you, Kaiser? Why do you think you're still alive? Why do you think nobody's stolen your lousy tape recorder before now? Darling, you've cashed in. Your ticket was already paid for."

Gray shut her mouth.

"But come on, Kaiser. It hasn't been so bad, has it? Ordering guys around? Being *revered*?"

"Actually," said Gray, "I've found it quite uncomfortable."

"You're so full of shit!" shouted Corgie. Gray took a step back. For all the reluctance with which this argument began, it was in full swing now; she'd never seen Corgie so angry. "You eat it up, don't you think I can see that? Oh, you're nicer than I am, I'll give you that, but that's because having them worship you isn't enough, is it? You have to get them to *like* you, too. You want them to worship and adore you. At least I have the humility to let them hate me as long as they bring me my supper every night."

Their voices were carrying. Outside, the sky started to rumble; after a moment it poured. "Convenient," said Gray. "The gods are fighting. Venting their wrath on Il-Ororen."

"If there is a real one," said Corgie, "He's on our side. We've been lucky. *You* are dangerous. You may have a good time playing Jesus Christ, but I've never met more of a human being in my life."

"That should be a compliment, but it doesn't sound like one."

"Oh, cut the humanism shit, will you? For a minute? I mean the reason you're dangerous is that you're so jealous. And that's one big giveaway. That's the most mortal emotion I know."

"Jealous of what?" asked Gray incredulously, raising her voice over the rain.

"You can't stand it that I got here first, can you? You can't stand not having this whole shebang to yourself, can you?"

"That is—" Gray turned red. "That is the most ridiculous accusation I have ever heard—"

"Miss Gray Kaiser, valiant, beloved anthropologist—everyone goes to you, bows down, asks for advice, but Miss Kaiser doesn't need anyone, no—"

"You mean I don't need *you*."

The two of them stood face to face. Perhaps they were gods now, at this moment, and this was omnipotence: to know exactly how little they cared. Glaring at each other silently, both Gray and Charles recited together their real credo: Who cares about you, or anyone? Who needs you, or anyone? I blink and you disappear. I turn my back on you and all I see is the door that I can walk out of, always. I am tall and smart and powerful without you. I can make jokes and laugh, and then they are funny. I can write down thoughts and read them back and nod, and then they are wise. I put my hands over my ears and hum, and the things you say that so upset me could be birdcalls or the radio or a fly. You think I want you, and sometimes even I think that, but you are wrong and that is weakness in me, for I am stronger than even I know. I am a god. I am making it rain now. So if I want you to evaporate like a shallow puddle in the bright heat of my brain, then you will shimmer in this room and dissolve into the heavy air and I will not care—I will be thinking about what I would like for dinner; I will be thinking about my import-ant work; I will sleep well at night and get up the next morning deciding what I want to wear. Goodbye, Charles Corgie; goodbye,

Gray Kaiser. Only someone outside of us will be able to remember we were ever standing in the same room, that we ever laughed at the same jokes. Since no one else was there, no one will remember that we ever held each other on that bed and kissed and ran our fingers through each other's hair.

Perhaps at the end of their litany both Gray and Charles looked around the room in confusion, wondering, To whom am I talking, anyway? I must be talking to myself. So, since there was no one else in the cabin, Gray did not need to excuse herself, but turned on her heel and walked out the door. It must have been disconcerting for a woman who could control the weather to step into a torrent and immediately be drenched to the skin.

Charles turned away and went back to building his model. Yet had Charles watched Gray a moment longer he would have seen her fall from grace most literally. Her foot slipped at the top of the ladder to pitch her ten feet through the air to the thick black mud below.

As she lay spitting mud out of her mouth, Gray was sure that her left arm had never been in precisely this position in its life. She thought, Get up, but for some reason she did not get up. All that rose were her eyes, and as she took them up from the ground, they met a pair of long, muddy, patient feet, and, at the top, other eyes, with great frightening whites and too much intelligence. Gray found herself thinking rather irrelevantly that Africans were lucky to have waterproof hair. As strands dripped into her face, she wished hers would bead like that, with smart gleaming droplets crowning her head. For the goddess was looking poorly; Odinaye, princely and serene.

"I help you?" asked Odinaye in English, extending his hand.

Gray didn't take it. She felt suddenly as if the arm under

her chest were a filthy secret she should keep to herself and protect. "I'll be fine," said Gray, pointedly in Il-Ororen. "Even a god must rest sometimes."

"*Kaiser*," he said, like Charles. "No rest in ground." There was that gleam in his eyes again, that slight smile at his mouth, as he grasped her right arm and started to pull her up. When Gray gasped on her knees he let go. It had been a small, dry cry, but it was unmistakably the sound of pain.

With his eyebrows high and a look of feigned solicitude and surprise, Odinaye looked down at Gray's left arm. Gray, too, couldn't resist discovering what was hanging on the other end of her elbow. The flesh was swelling and purpling as they watched. There was a foreign object poking into her arm. It took her a full moment to realize that the object was sticking not in but out—that it was her own bone. All of this was bad enough, but worst of all for the immortal on her knees was the other, that substance, and Gray kept wishing it would rain harder; but the rain could not wash down her arm fast enough to rinse away her bright-red secret winding its watery way in streams to the tip of her elbow and pooling in the crook of her arm.

"Oh my," said Gray, "look at that." She tried for a tone of mild, disinterested curiosity; to a surprising extent she succeeded, too. Yet the whites of Odinaye's eyes loomed large before her, and she was sure now that this man knew her every weakness, her every flaw—that he could see not only that her bones were fragile and her blood red as his, but that she had stolen a roll of Life Savers from a drugstore when she was ten.

"I call help," said Odinaye, and he was now unabashedly smiling, his teeth sharp, shining in the rain.

"No—" said Gray, but Odinaye was already shouting; four

other natives appeared around her. She thought clearly: They are witnesses. Coldly Gray requested a board. Refusing any other assistance, she placed the wood under her arm and stood, carefully holding her limb before her like a roast on a platter. All this while the natives stared, and not so much at her arm as at her face. Gray knew this and gave them a fine performance. Those muscles were a miracle of ordinariness and careless physical comfort. Standing straight as ever, Gray dismissed her parishioners and balanced herself elegantly rung by rung up to Corgie's cabin. It was a shame Charles missed this ascent—it was one of those moments he would have hated but also admired, the way he felt about most things she did, but maybe for once the admiration might have won out. It was hard, after all, to strike a fine figure covered in black mud, or to look that haughty and regal and unaffected when in the very process of being dethroned.

"I think we're in trouble," said Gray from behind Charles.

"Woman," said Charles, not looking up from his model, "we've been in trouble from day one." He may not have fallen at her feet for returning so soon after such a fight, but for once his woodchips would stay where he put them, and he bound the sticks with dry grass easily and with satisfaction.

"We're in extra-special trouble today."

There was a strain to her voice, but after such a scene he'd expect that. "So you came back," he said, still focused on his monument, "to admit you don't mind being a goddess. Why don't we have a drink on it, Kaiser?"

Charles put his knife and grasses down and turned around just as Gray was saying, "Maybe two." Though her vision was dancing, Gray did succeed in watching Corgie's face go through a transformation—all its cockiness sloughed off. Gray wondered if she'd ever seen Charles look—serious. "Jesus fucking Christ," said Charles, reaching immediately for the board on which Gray's arm was laid, and taking her swiftly to lie on his bed.

Gray kept trying to explain reasonably what had happened and to warn him about Odinaye while Charles cleaned her up, but he kept telling her to shut up, and finally she did. Gray did not protest when Charles took off all her clothes, which were caked with mud and soaked through; he undressed her tenderly, but also with a careful asexual air. She was surprised she didn't mind lying before him naked. Without embarrassment she let him sponge her clean. He covered her slim, shivering body with a blanket. At last he reached for her left arm, swabbing it delicately. Gray turned her head to the side and pressed her cheek into the pillow.

There seemed to be a commotion building outside.

"Don't worry about it," said Charles, pushing her back down.

The sound got more insistent. Waves of discontented murmuring washed through the room.

"You know, Kaiser," said Corgie softly, brushing the matted hair away from her forehead, "we're going to have to put that bone of yours back. You might need it someday."

Gray nodded, and tried to smile. "I had," she said, "grown rather attached—"

"Shut up," said Charles fondly.

Outside, there were shouts. For a few bars the crowd struck up a chorus. Its words were unmistakable: "White skin! Red blood!" Il-Ororen shouted. "White skin! Red blood!"

Charles acted as if he heard nothing. "I'm going to get you some honey wine. I'd give my right arm right now—if you'll forgive the expression—for a good bottle of brandy, but then it would also be nice to have morphine and a hospital and the entire faculty of Yale Medical School. Wine will have to do." Corgie started out the door, paused, turned back to take his gun. As he walked out of the cabin the crowd grew silent.

"Dugon." He spoke calmly in Il-Ororen to one of the natives in the front row. "Bring me two jugs of honey wine."

Dugon looked at the warriors on either side of him and then at the ground. He shifted his weight from foot to foot.

"Dugon," said Corgie with exaggerated patience, "did you hear me? I meant now."

"Il-Cor-gie," said Dugon, not looking Charles in the eye, "is it true about Ol-Kai-zer? That her bones break and her flesh bleeds?"

"Dugon," said Charles, bearing down on the warrior with those eyes of his that could do their work awfully well when they had to—even if Dugon was already convinced that Charles was a mere mortal, he was discovering it didn't make much difference. "You changed the subject. We were speaking of wine."

Yet Dugon was surrounded by warriors who made small motions of discouragement; Dugon looked up at Corgie with an expression of appeal.

Charles let his gun dangle down toward Dugon's head. "Remember this?" Dugon nodded. "Do you doubt my magic enough to test it? Because whether or not Ol-Kai-zer bleeds may be in question; whether or not you do is not."

Dugon bolted from the crowd. Corgie watched him go, and waited for his wine serenely, looking down at Il-Ororen as if holding court.

"Odinaye claims Ol-Kai-zer bleeds!" a native braved at last. "Show us the arm of Ol-Kai-zer!"

"Since when," said Corgie, "do *you* tell *me* to do anything?"

Since never. His eyes razed the crowd, rich and dangerous. Il-Ororen went silent, back in church. Corgie stood over them, his eyes rather than his gun poised, aimed at them, cocked, until Dugon ran back with a jug of wine sloshing in each hand. He stopped, breathing hard, and then lifted them reverently to Corgie on his porch. With one final freezing glance, Corgie turned his back on Il-Ororen and returned to Gray.

"Intimidation isn't going to hold them very long," said Gray dully from the bed.

"Why not? It's held them for five years. Now, drink this." Gray had several sips, then shook her head. "More." He poured it in her mouth until the wine dribbled down her chin.

"Just like a man," said Gray, wiping the wine away with her good arm. "Trying to get me drunk."

"That's right," said Charles, "this is what I should have done to you a long time ago." Charles leaned over and kissed her lightly between the eyes. "Now drink some more."

"No, Charles, I can't. It's just making me sick. Besides, it's not going to make that much difference and you know it."

Charles stood up and sighed; Gray realized that he was interested in getting her drunk partly in order to put off resetting her arm. Charles looked down at it, its temporary dressing beginning to show red; his face paled.

"You don't know what you're doing, do you?"

"I bluff with them all the time," said Corgie, gesturing outside. "This . . ."

"You're not in your train set anymore."

Charles looked up and down the length of Gray Kaiser, as if memorizing her hard. "You do seem life-size."

"Go ahead, Charles."

It was one thing to shoot a piece of clay in the chest; it was quite another to work the bone back into the skin of a woman who actually existed. Corgie took a long swig of wine.

Corgie picked up her arm and put it down again. Breathed. Tried again. Breathed.

Charles did it. He straightened her arm, and worked that horrible red thing back inside her limb, closing the folds of her flesh over the bone, burying the secret of her mortality back where it belonged. He took one of the sticks from his model monument as a splint and swathed the break with parachute silk. When he was finished, the sweat was pouring down his cheeks as freely as down Gray's. Breathing heavily, they wiped the moisture from each other's face.

The chant outside had changed. "Show the arm of Ol-Kaizer!"

"Maybe we should show it to them," said Charles. "They might be impressed. I did a good job." And Charles did seem more proud of this achievement than she had ever seen him be of his dominance over Il-Ororen, or even of his precious architecture.

The tone of the gathering outside was angrier now. It sounded like nothing less than a lynch mob. Once in a while a stone hit the side of the cabin.

Gray lay on the bed, trying to keep her mind steady, for she felt she'd need a clear head soon. She was right. Corgie began to clean his gun.

"I'm sorry," said Gray.

"For what?"

"For that uproar. It's my fault."

Corgie stopped oiling his trigger. "It's not your fault you

broke your goddamned arm. I mean, you're not a god, are you? Isn't that the whole goddamned problem? I swear, you get into this stuff too deep, you start believing it, and you look down at a cut on your arm and, sure, the natives are surprised you bleed, but the thing is, so are you. Well, we bleed. And it's hard enough to go around bleeding all over the goddamned place without feeling guilty about it. I mean, for Christ's sake, Kaiser, doesn't it *hurt*?"

Gray shrugged, winced, let her shoulders carefully back down.

Charles went back to cleaning his gun, ramming the rod down its barrel. "I'm telling you," he continued, thrusting the rod in and out, "you've seen too many real, real stupid movies, Kaiser. The old ones, maybe, without any sound. God, give me a woman who screams once in a while. Give me a woman who *cries* sometimes, and who throws her arms around your goddamned neck and begs for forgiveness—"

"Forgiveness!"

"Woman looks down at a broken arm as if she's some kind of robot with a few wires cut. Comes in here to be repaired. Practically took out my soldering iron by mistake, Kaiser."

A rain of stones pattered against the front wall of the cabin.

"Charles," Gray asked carefully, "have they ever gotten upset like this before?"

"No." He tried to sound casual.

"Charles," said Gray, "your airplane doesn't work, does it?"

Corgie laughed, beautifully. "I'd love to be in that movie of yours, Kaiser. The one where the two of us leave in a cloud of dust and turn into a speck in the sky. That's a nice ending."

"You mean it doesn't," said Gray heavily.

"Of course, then there's the helium balloon."

"What?"

"You know, when I give Odinaye an honorary degree for being so smart—and hell, a purple heart for bravery; the guy's first-rate, let's face it—and float off and leave the Emerald City behind."

"And I click my heels. We've made these jokes before."

"For once in my life I have more important things to think about than new jokes. We're going to have to make do with the old ones."

The whole cabin shook. Corgie checked out the window and shot over the head of a man grappling up a stilt; the warrior dropped back to the ground.

"Charles, what if they storm the cabin? Are the two of us just going to pick them off as fast as they come?"

"Us! Since when do you approve of shooting people?"

She looked down. "Since now, maybe."

"No, Gray," said Charles sadly. "We might squelch this for a little while, but one rifle is nothing. Here this gun is like a scepter. The kingdom's falling, Gray, and without a kingdom a scepter is a stick. Now, come here." She came over to the window wrapped in a blanket; keeping an eye outside, Corgie made her a sling. He told her while he tied the knot, "I've always wanted to be in a revolution. I'm just surprised to end up on this side of things is all." The cabin shook again; Charles turned away from his handiwork with tired irritation, to shoot once more over the head of a would-be visitor and have him drop to the ground. "Show the arm of Ol-Kai-zer!" rang through the room.

"Would it help if I went out to them?" asked Gray.

"They'd run you straight through," said Charles calmly.

"Christ-like, but still not very appealing. Now, go get dressed. Put together a little food and a knife and some water. Pronto." He gave her a pat on the ass, as if treating himself to a moment of pleasant masculine condescension.

"What for?"

"You're going on a trip. The back pole is still an exit they don't know about. The trail is covered in brush all the way to the cliffs, right? Now get going."

"Then," she said uncertainly, "I should put together enough food and water for two."

Charles fired another shot. When he turned around again he looked angry. "Don't just stand there," he said in the same tone he used with Il-Ororen. "Move it."

"But why—"

"Idiot! How are the two of us going to saunter off into the horizon? With the music playing and the sun setting and the credits rolling happily down the screen? Why don't you use your mind a little when we actually need it? They're *mad* at me, Kaiser. Haven't you noticed? They're *peeved*. They're peeved at you, too, gracious agricultural consultant that you might have been. Our friends have been had, darling. They want in here. No one is sliding down that back pole without someone else at this window with a gun. It may be only a scepter but it still packs a punch. Now pack up and get the hell out of here before it's too late, and we both end up skewered on the same spear like one big messianic brochette."

"But, Charles, why don't I take the gun and you slide down the pole?"

Charles looked at her squarely. "Is that an offer?"

"Yes," said Gray. She drew her blanket closer around her

and looked away from Charles, embarrassed. She didn't know what she was doing. She'd said yes because it sounded nice. That wasn't enough.

Charles said nothing until she looked back at him, at a face that was haggard and regretful. It was a face that knew what it was doing. "You couldn't," said Charles. "Your arm . . . Besides, I might be able to talk them out of this. You'd never swing that. You don't have the clout."

"But all those Kenyans you've shot. If one, why not two . . . Remember?"

"Your first morning here. You were *excellent*," said Charles with satisfaction. "You impressed me enormously that day."

"But you said there was no limit."

"And you said there was." Charles smiled philosophically, glancing out the window to find the natives were getting restless. Once more, though, he did not fire into the crowd but shot off a tree branch over their heads. It crackled and fell, scattering Africans beneath it. Charles turned back to Gray. "Well, *touché*. You were right."

"What's the limit, Charles?"

"You," he said readily.

"That's it?"

"Yep. Just you." The simplicity seemed to please him.

Gray would not understand this for a long time. Already projecting herself into this coming confusion, Gray asked Charles one more thing: "Even if I make it—later, how is this going to make me feel?"

"Alive, for one thing," said Charles. "Swell. And maybe lousy, too." Gray still didn't move, so Charles had to explain patiently, "You'll feel like you owe somebody something. And you will.

Just not me. Pass it on. Give him my regards." And then Charles looked out the window again, in a pang of jealousy over someone who, as it turns out, was not yet born.

G ray went to her corner, dressed, and packed her knapsack. It must have sickened her to remember to take the rolls of film, the tapes, all her notes—to even now be planning on cashing in on her "study" should she succeed in returning home. It would have been a relief then, when Corgie instructed her from the window, "Don't forget those notes of yours, Kaiser. You write all this up and you get this published, understand? I want to be immortal somehow."

When she finished packing, Charles carefully threaded the strap of her knapsack around the sling. A spear flew through the window and lodged in Corgie's mattress. They did not make a joke about it. Gray looked at the spear, deep in the bed. Feathers from the hole floated up through the air and caught in Gray's hair. Corgie picked them out one by one. All the sourness was gone from his face, the vengeful glimmer. There were a lot of things to say, but it was too late for all of them, so the two kept quiet and stones rattled against the door and Charles Corgie kissed Gray Kaiser, *ol-murani*, goodbye.

In the oddest way, Gray did not quite enjoy it. It was, simply, not the kiss of two people who had loved each other hard and had to part. It was the kiss of two people who had fought each other up until the very last minute. It was a reminder, in its unfamiliarity, of what they had not been doing.

Charles helped her down the pole from above. That hand extended, keeping her poised above the ground for a moment before it let go—the long, tired tendons, the skin still dark and oily from cleaning his gun—was the last she saw of him. Silently she crept through the brushy pathway to the forest, making her way to the trail she'd followed down the cliffs on the way here. Deftly, dutifully, quietly, she hiked the narrow switchbacks, while behind her the rhythm of Corgie's rifle increased steadily, like a final salute. Yet soon after she started up the mountain, the firing stopped altogether. Gray decided she was too high to hear anymore. Later, when she could no longer see into the valley, she was sure she heard an explosion she couldn't explain.

While the pain in her arm was keen, Gray was grateful for its steady distraction. It was despite the wound rather than because of it that Il-Ororen might have made out down her cheeks the tears which far more than blood proved her a human being.

T he trip back was grueling work, and Gray bore down on it. She slept poorly, with the snarl of cheetahs at the edge of her ear. Gray told Errol later that those days on the trail she was as close to being "an animal" as she'd ever come, in a compulsive, dead migration to the rest of her herd. The body persevered. The mind went numb, speaking only to say: Don't step there; avoid those ants; this branch is in your way.

She did make it to Hassatti's tribe. Though in a fever, she refused to rest more than a couple of hours and insisted on being taken to Nairobi right away. She wouldn't talk about what had happened, and made the bumpy trip in a pickup truck in silence. When she reached the city, she hired a man to take her in a small prop plane over the peaks of Kilimanjaro.

During most of this trip, too, she didn't speak, nor did she explain her purpose. She gave her pilot directions until she recognized the deep valley surrounded by the plunging cliffs she'd stared up at so often from the hammock on Corgie's veranda. She told the pilot to fly closer; circling, the plane drew lower. Trees obscured the muddy huts, but Gray was not looking for traditional architecture.

"Wait," she said, "this might not be the place." Gray scanned back and forth across the valley. "Closer."

The plane swept lower, and Gray wondered how Il-Ororen must feel, seeing another god fly by—were they ready for their next messiah? No, surely they'd made do with the old one. Charles was such a resourceful man, he had that way of talking to them— and they'd always listened to him in the end, always. Well, they enjoyed him, didn't they? He was a fun god. Most certainly he'd pulled something. And wouldn't Charles be surprised when they landed roughly between banana trees and Gray Kaiser stepped out of the cockpit, smiling, finally able to kiss him and take him up in the sky with the credits rolling?

Gray's eyes darted across the familiar valley, panicked. "This can't be right," she said. "Maybe these valleys look a lot the same, I don't know . . ."

There was no tower. There was no treehouse, no gym, no cathedral. The plane flew closer in, at Gray's insistence, to the pilot's distress, until, there—she got her bearings. Gray fell back in her seat.

"Msabu wish to land? There is not space—"

"No," said Gray. "Take it back up. Take me to Nairobi."

"If Msabu wish to more look—"

"No," said Gray. "I've seen enough."

The small plane soared back up, its passengers' ears popping.

Below, the long, narrow valley grew smaller, but Gray couldn't help but see even as the plane rose quite high the four black scars of charred flat earth and a few wisps of smoke trailing from these patches, like the last sad smoldering of crematory ash.

chapter six

Errol scanned the compound in the dying light. The sites of Corgie's projects had seeded nicely and were overgrown. Despite their disregard for history, none among Il-Ororen had yet dared plant his own manyatta in these clearings. The patches remained plush and tangled, like small city parks.

So far this return visit was going well, and Errol fought off his own wistfulness. Errol had a peculiar weakness for other people's nostalgia. This helped him as an anthropologist but confused him as himself. He wondered that he never found his own memories as compelling as those of other people. This was a gift, he supposed; there were certainly enough people walking around absorbed in their own lives. While his imagination was sometimes out of control, Errol preferred that to being trapped with his quiet father, his dominating older sister, and his attachment to Gray long past the age he should have been anyone's protégé. Errol's own life made him feel claustrophobic, and these departures relieved him, as the long breaths of cooling air did now while he watched the sun drain behind the cliffs. It was a romantic setting, he had to admit.

So far their return had unearthed a few interesting post-scripts. Odinaye had taken over the tribe after Corgie, but he'd made a mistake. When you institute a new regime, it mustn't look too much like the old one. Yet Odinaye had tried to become Corgie II. Before he burned it to the ground, he ransacked the cabin for mementos. When he rose to promin-ence, he donned the red baseball cap, leather flight jacket, and aviator goggles he had found there. He wrapped the remains of Corgie's parachute regally around him, and used many of the words he'd learned from listening to Gray and Charles: Here it is. Give me that paddle. Il-Ororen were impressed for a while, but they'd heard this before, and in better style.

Furthermore, Odinaye was no architect. Early in his reign he commanded a palace of his own, to be taller than Corgie's tower. Halfway through construction, the place crumpled into a heap. Corgie's true disciple, Odinaye blamed the workmen and had them executed; wisely, he didn't try another palace and stayed quietly in his own hut.

It was the radio that felled him. Odinaye had made sure to salvage the device before the arson, but in lugging it away, he must have disconnected a wire. When he staged his own service—remembering many of Corgie's ads for Campbell's soup and a couple of verses from "Liddle Rabid Foo-Foo"—he turned at its climax to the wondrous supernatural machine and—silence. There was a riot. The radio was destroyed, along with its inef-fectual new master.

Soon after, Gray's study hit the Western press, which not only sent her career hurtling to eventually overtake Richardson's—who was now only a fortunate footnote in Gray Kaiser's life—but also sent a phalanx of Western civilization down on Il-Ororen. Surprise, more airplanes; surprise, better radios; surprise, English. Surprise, just a lot of strange, pale primates—so many of them, as Hassatti might have warned, disappointments.

Il-Ororen revisited were a slightly defeated people, though nicer, as Gray herself had remarked. They had lost their existential edge, and in its place was an attractive relaxation with being unimportant. They smiled more. They sat more. There were more fat people.

And, boy, did they talk about Charles Corgie. Corgie stories were a local pastime. While Il-Ororen may have mellowed, they still had that malicious streak in them from way back—their favorites were about the fires. As they told these tales, their eyes flecked with yellow light. Best of all, they loved to tell of Corgie's last gesture. When the bullets had ceased their regular reproof overhead, Il-Ororen had finally climbed up the stilts of the cabin, suffering by now highly exaggerated injuries from the protective spikes skirting the porch, and bursting into the main room to find both Il-Cor-gie and Ol-Kai-zer no longer there. Nervous but inflamed, guerrilla parties scoured the area, though they needn't have; Gray was well up the cliffs by now, and Corgie sent up a flare. Standing on top of the carcass of his plane, Charles fired in the air. A large crowd gathered. In his most terrifying voice, he ordered them from the plane. Gradually they backed off, Corgie training his gun on the group until every villager had withdrawn. Only then did he shift the rifle from the crowd and point it at a tear in the tail of his plane. With one bullet, as if he'd rehearsed this before and knew where precisely to aim, he detonated a bomb he never dropped on the Germans, and Charles Corgie left Il-Ororen in a blaze.

It was Corgie's warning rather than the splendor of his departure that made an impression on Gray. Errol, too, was surprised that Charles urged the villagers away from the plane. It seemed out of character. In Errol's experience with egomaniacs, they liked to take as much of the world down with them as possible; in a time of nuclear weapons this was a chilling thought. Yet Charles, in a moment of peculiar humility, left by himself.

While Gray was relieved to hear of Corgie's consideration, she didn't have much of a taste for these stories. In fact, Errol had to admit she didn't have much of a taste for this whole project. Gray was still in her hut, no doubt flat on her mat, with eyes of stone. If this torpor of hers went on much longer, they would have to pack it in.

Yet the air tingled. Errol's breath quickened. In the indeterminate gray light Errol felt edgy and could not stand still. The story of Charles Corgie rooted and tangled in his mind, as if it were not quite over. His eyes darted across the compound; always something seemed to be moving in his periphery, but when he looked over he found only trees. The light was funny. It was still bright enough to see, but not, it seems, what was actually there. Errol felt a strange nervous grip under his rib cage; he had the unreasonable feeling he should be pacing before Gray's hut, standing guard.

Oh, Gray, Errol thought, looking back on this evening

much later. It had been too early to be asleep. Dusk is a time to be preyed upon. Wise herds are astir, on their feet with their heads high and eyes open, but Gray stayed in bed with her long, bony head at a forlorn angle against the mat, picking up the pattern of the tortured weave in her cheek. The brush outside the compound rustled. It was not the wind. Bare feet pattered across the hard-packed earth of Toroto. Old women spoke in low whispers. They'd been frightened before, and this was ridiculous. Weren't Il-Ororen savvy now? They ate Almond Joys and Pez candies. They complained in their own language about static and weak stations. They knew the word "tape recorder" and how little magic it really was, without money. Some even had guns, and no longer particularly admired them. Yet anthropology is not about nothing. There was a culture here, and it rose. It believed in ghosts, despite Pez candies. And here their protector slept with her head on the mat, as if, because Charles Corgie had been "just" a man, there were no more mysteries.

You couldn't blame them for being frightened, though once again they'd made a mistake. Il-Ororen needed no protection. He was coming for a woman "very tall and very strong and very brilliant," though a woman with her length reaching toward she didn't know what anymore, her strength turning to an irritation, her brilliance casting about in the dark until it shattered aimlessly into a disappointed dispersion across the night sky.

It was dark now. Errol was surrounded by whispers and running feet. When he felt a hand on his arm, he started.

"He is alive!" It was Elya, with her voice low. "He has returned!"

"What?"

"I tell you, he has come back! *And he has not grown older*."

"Who?"

"Il-Cor-gie!" she said breathlessly.

Errol's mouth twisted, and he was glad she couldn't see his face in the dark. Sometimes Errol was not a perfect anthropologist, and all this admirable myth and culture soured into native weirdness. It was late, and Errol had had a hard day. What in Christ's name was she talking about, anyway. "Maybe you'd better talk to Ol-Kai-zer," said Errol. He'd worked on this dialect before the trip, but maybe he wasn't understanding her right. Besides, this was annoying and Errol wasn't in the mood—he'd finished that interview himself, and Gray was just *lying* there. Do a little work, Kaiser. On your feet.

But another woman had already run into Gray's hut and was dragging her out the door. Gray, too, looked confused in the light of the woman's lantern. Several women clustered behind her as she approached Errol.

"What's all this about?" asked Gray, with the same un-anthropological annoyance.

"Damned if I know. Something about Corgie still being alive if I heard right."

The women tugged on Errol and Gray, with a strange combination of fear and excitement. "He is back!" they kept saying. "Il-Cor-gie has returned to us!"

As Errol and Gray went with the women, the natives pushing them toward the center of the village, Errol muttered quietly to Gray, "Why do I feel as if I'm in the middle of a New Testament reading?" Gray laughed.

It was getting chilly. Gray and Errol rubbed their arms.

Amid the chatter and the quickened air and the odd, unexplained secret they were approaching, the evening had an offbeat holiday atmosphere. There was a glow in the center of Toroto that proved to be a bonfire. Its light cast brilliantly on an unfamiliar figure with such intensity that the man with his hands held gently before the fire seemed to be aflame himself.

As they drew nearer, Gray slowed. The man in the flames looked straight at her. Gray stopped. Took a step. Stopped. The sound of her breathing at Errol's side cut off altogether, as if she'd forgotten to inhale. Finally she herself stepped into the surreal molten glow of the fire, and stood, once more a statue; stone.

Errol looked away from his mentor to the man on the other side of the fire. Flames licked across his line of vision; the face burned among the yellow tongues. Errol found it hard to swallow.

But Charles Corgie was dead. Charles Corgie had fired his gun at his own bomb and exploded. Or were Il-Ororen lying again? Had they allowed Corgie to escape and made up that final episode? Then how would they have known about bombs to make up such a story?

On the other side of the fire there was a tall, dark Caucasian with a hat. His hair was black, his stubble heavy and rising, his eyes sharp and unblinking, but *he could not be more than twenty-five*. Even if Corgie had slunk away to rule another tribe, or moved to Nairobi and sold car insurance for thirty-seven years, he would still be over sixty now.

Errol started to speak, but Gray shook her head. She smiled more sweetly than he'd ever seen. In the hiss of escaping steam and the pop of knots, Gray seemed lost in a dream from which she had little eagerness to wake.

"What is your name?" asked Gray at last.

"Sarasola," said the man. "Raphael Sarasola."

Now, thought Errol. Wrong name. The joke is over. But Errol did not sense the feeling in the air change.

"I was unaware," said Gray with evident pleasure, "we'd become a tourist attraction."

"You made it one," said Raphael.

"You read my book?"

"The parts that interested me," he answered coolly. It was something Charles would have said.

Several women crept up to Raphael and laid offerings of bananas and dried meat at his feet and scurried away. Raphael looked at them without enough surprise, as if he was used to being given things. He picked up a banana, and peeled it.

Gray could not take her eyes off him. "How did B.U. happen to send me an assistant who hasn't even read the whole book?"

"There are other ways of getting what you want besides spending a lot of time in the library."

"You'll have to explain those sometime."

"I won't have to. But I might." Errol thought distinctly, He doesn't behave like a graduate student. "Don't worry, though," said Raphael. "They sent you the right man, all right."

"Yes," said Gray. "I think they did."

There was more silence; the fire popped. Errol was beginning to feel something he'd never felt before. *Terror*.

"I've been traveling for two days," said Raphael. He threw the skin of his banana into the fire and watched it sizzle. "I'm tired."

Gray led Raphael to the hut where she and Errol were staying. Errol trailed after them.

"That's my mat," Errol mumbled when Gray showed the new assistant where to sleep. Gray didn't seem to hear. "That's my pillow," he said more loudly as Raphael unrolled his sleeping bag.

"You can live without it for the night," said Gray quietly. "He hasn't slept in days." She whispered good night and walked softly out of the hut, pulling Errol with her, as if leaving a sleeping child.

They ambled back toward the fire. "You didn't introduce me," said Errol after a time.

"Sorry," said Gray, not paying the slightest attention.

They sat down on the warm stones before the bonfire, and though she'd been in bed only an hour before, "absolutely disgusted and tired and stupid," Gray's eyes were alive now, and she sat on the edge of the stone rubbing her hands together. "You know, I'm getting a lot of ideas for this film," she said. "It could be exciting."

But Errol was an ordinary person. He had plenty of excitement already.

E rrol scared up another mat but didn't sleep well without a pillow. When he woke the next morning, Gray was already up and dressed and was spending longer than usual fixing her hair. Raphael was out cold. Gray kept shooting quick, incredulous looks at her new assistant.

She looked different this morning, as if those fatigues were new, but she was wearing the same clothes she'd worn the day before.

When Errol stretched, dressed, and walked outside, he found a cluster of natives at the door with trays of food. "You will take this to Il-Cor-gie and Ol-Kai-zer?" asked the woman, holding a tray out to Errol like a cook to a waiter.

"I will not," said Errol. He stalked away to make his own breakfast.

When he finished mopping up his fried bananas, which had come out too greasy, he glanced over to find two of Il-Ororen scouring away over pails of water. When he looked more closely, he recognized the fabric in their hands. Of course. They were washing the clothes of "Il-Cor-gie."

"Before he gets up we need to talk."

Errol turned to find no more torpor, no more stone. The mind behind those blue-gray eyes was going a mile a minute. "I've been thinking about this documentary all night," she went on. "About format. I think we should question the whole interview and voice-over decision. It's dreary. It's a PBS-change-the-channel sort of thing. I think that's why I've been so reluctant lately."

"Sure," said Errol. "Format has been the whole problem."

"Why don't we use a more narrative structure? Bring in a larger crew. Build some sets. Film it scene by scene. Il-Ororen love these stories; we'd have extras galore. I'm sure it would have more popular appeal."

"And what gave you this idea?"

"He's a dead ringer for Charles Corgie and you know it."

"That doesn't mean he can act."

"If I don't miss my guess, he won't have to."

"Well, who's going to play you?"

"What?"

"Gray, you're fifty-nine now. You can hardly play yourself at twenty-two."

"I hadn't thought of that."

"You forgot you were fifty-nine?"

"For a night, I suppose."

"Allow me to remind you."

"Thanks a lot, Errol." She didn't sound very grateful.

"I'm skeptical, Gray, of this whole concept."

"Somehow I knew you would be. How is it that I'm twelve years older than you are and you stick so much more frequently in the mud?"

"You mean, why don't I glom on to your every idea?"

"I do not mean that."

Raphael had walked out of the hut now and was blithely watching them fight. His shirt was off; with a basin and compact mirror, he began to shave.

"Gray," said Errol, "we just don't have the money, crew, or equipment to film an epic adventure movie."

"I didn't say it had to be *Lawrence of Arabia*. It could be done simply, but I don't want to do another one of those dour documentaries that Charles himself would never watch."

"You don't have to worry about what Charles would think of it. Charles is dead."

"Thanks so very much, Errol," said Gray, now furious. "You're really bringing in all my favorite data: I'm fifty-nine, and Charles is dead."

"Il-Cor-gie!" cried Elya down the road.

"Brother," said Errol, and went for a very long walk.

On his return Errol got a better look at Raphael Sarasola. Gray had told her assistant to spend the day getting to know

Toroto; Errol watched as Il-Ororen offered the man pottery and candy bars through the afternoon. Raphael had every reason to find these gifts disconcerting, but he accepted them without question. He declined only cigarettes, and Il-Ororen were surprised that he no longer smoked.

Well, if this was Charles Corgie incarnate, perhaps Errol had gotten Corgie wrong and the man hadn't been as broad, loud, and bawdy as Errol imagined. Raphael was contained, poised. He stood with a slight tremble, like a well-tuned sports car at a light. If this was Charles Corgie, then Corgie was quiet. Raphael would lick his lips, take a breath, raise his eyebrows, and—nothing. He seemed always about to say something and then to think better of it; sometimes he'd smile as if what he might have said amused him. Maybe what Errol had most failed to capture in his version of Charles Corgie—if this was, as Il-Ororen claimed, his ghost—was his precision. He wouldn't have made mistakes. He'd never have made a joke that fell flat, tripped, or stepped on a rock that proved unstable; he'd never have reached for the sleeve of his coat behind his back and missed the hole.

Errol could depend on a few points of distinction, though. There were photographs of Charles Corgie, and these were not, precisely, photographs of Raphael. At first crude glance the similarity was overwhelming—the long face, the dark coloring, the tall, tight build, the contour of the heavy brow; the two profiles would have matched like the sides of an ink blot. They both had black eyes. All right, there's no such thing as black eyes, but these were so brilliant and so protected that you couldn't tell what color they really were. Otherwise, the more Errol studied Raphael, the more the man distinguished himself from

Corgie. Corgie approximated Raphael as a rough-hewn sculpture
does the finished piece. The bones of Corgie's cheeks now rose
higher; below them was smoothed hollow; the lips were sanded
and narrowed. At every point the artist had peaked what was
once blunted, articulated what was once vague. Raphael's face
was worked over with fine files and the skin buffed to a high
polish. Corgie was handsome; Raphael was beautiful. His face
was warm and olive and obscure, lit on the high points, with
the rest sunk into soft, secretive shadow, like the portraits by
Rembrandt; like those portraits, too, it was inexplicably sad.
Corgie looked vengeful; Raphael, more tinged with regret. Like
Charles, Raphael looked as if someone had done something
terrible to him at one time, but not as if this were an offense
he was planning to redress. Not that he had no taste for revenge;
rather, he understood to his despair that there was no such thing.
It was never possible to do something back to someone that
would undo what he had done to you. Your only power was to
create more pain, if that was your pleasure. This was a peculiarly
mature perception for someone his age; it was certainly a peculiar
thing to *emanate*.

G ray got more money. Of course. And it turned out that
the question of format hadn't been a question at all.

Because Gray "hated actresses," when Arabella West wired
she was better, they agreed she should take Gray's part when she
arrived. In the meantime, Gray worked on the script; Errol drafted
set sketches. Raphael had brought some work with him, too; as
they were all working distractedly one afternoon, Gray inquired
what it was.

"A grant proposal," said Raphael.

"Which one?"

"For a Ford Fellowship."

Errol noted with a look over Raphael's shoulder that he was hard at work on a doodle of some ratlike little creature in the margin of his pad. "Ford?" said Errol. "I won a couple of those. It's good money, isn't it?"

"Forty-five thousand," said Raphael, now doodling "$45,000" across the top of his paper.

"That's higher than they used to be," said Errol. "Competition's pretty stiff for those things, though. Your proposal had better be in good shape."

"Oh," said Raphael, embellishing his dollar sign now, "I'm working on it."

"I'm chairing the board on that grant," said Gray.

"I know," said Raphael, not looking up from the page.

Gray put her pen down. "How did you know that?"

"Oh, I knew before I came here," said Raphael with a shrug. "It's common knowledge."

Gray looked a little unsettled, then picked up her pen again.

Gray ducked in the hut with Errol behind her, and stopped. The lantern was lit. Raphael was in front of it, studying a square of paper.

"Stay out of my things," said Gray.

"Yes, Dr. Kaiser," said Raphael, turning to look at her with an intensity that was impudent. He put the square down and left the hut. Gray tucked it back in her file folders.

"What was that?" asked Errol.

"A photograph." She straightened the papers with agitation.

"Of?"

"Charles." She put a stone on top of the folders, though they were hardly going to blow away in here.

"Had you told him?"

She shook her head.

"And you weren't going to."

"It would have been just as well if he thought he was Raphael Sarasola—period. In my experience so far, that's plenty of trouble already."

A nd what would you do with your grant money?"

"What I'd like to do," said Raphael, "is find a village in a valley and become a god."

"Ford would love that," said Errol.

"Ford isn't making the decision," said Raphael.

"You might not like that valley as much as you think," Gray warned softly.

"I might like it even more."

"Charles wasn't so fond of it. Not really."

"According to you," said Raphael. "But then, you're not Charles."

"No one here is," said Errol.

D id you know him well?" asked Raphael.

"Yes," said Gray.

"How well?"

"Sometimes," she said, "looking at his face was like looking in a mirror."

"How were you alike?"

"We were both pigheaded."

"About what?"

"Everything," she said vaguely, folding her laundry briskly in piles.

"Did he like you?"

"I think so." Socks.

"Very much?"

"After a while . . ." Gray rolled a mismatched pair and had to unbunch them.

"Did you sleep together?"

Gray froze, and turned a rare red. "What did you say?"

"You heard me."

Gray turned around. "You're my graduate assistant. What makes you think you can ask me that question?"

Raphael smiled. "So you didn't."

B ut you liked him." This was later.
        "Yes," said Gray. "With reservations."

"Which were?"

"He murdered people."

"That doesn't seem to have bothered you so much."

"It bothered me."

"But not that much."

Gray turned pages, jotted in the margins, bowed her head.

"How much did you like him?"

"Just fine . . ."

Raphael leaned forward. "But you made him very angry, didn't you?"

Gray slammed her notebook shut. "Now, why would I do that?"

"My next question."

She paused, then blurted impulsively, "Because he was arrogant."

"And you made him pay."

"Everyone paid."

"He must have hated you," said Raphael softly.

"Most of the time," Gray admitted. "There was nothing else for him to do."

Y ou were beautiful then, weren't you?"

Red again. That past tense.

"Like now," he amended.

"I was all right."

"And you drove him crazy."

"I did my work."

"You held out."

"What are you accusing me of, please?"

"No accusation. I admire it."

"You admire strange things."

"I admire," said Raphael, "what you admire."

They looked at each other. "One of the things I learned with Charles," said Gray carefully, "was that finding someone is like you does not necessarily mean that either of you should be that way."

* * *

So what were you like at twenty-two?"

"The way I am now," she said. "That was the problem."

"It's still a problem," Errol intruded.

I don't see," said Raphael, reading over Gray's script, "why he didn't think of something. In the end. Why he had to blow up with that plane. Why couldn't he get out of it?"

"I don't think he wanted to," said Gray.

I was serious before," said Gray. "About the Ford Fellowship. What are you proposing to study?"

"An obscure society in the Pacific. The Goji."

"I read something about them once," said Gray, tapping her fingers together. Then her color changed. "That's right. I remember now. The article was in a linguistics journal."

"The Goji," said Errol. "They're the ones who don't have a word for 'love,' isn't that right?"

"Yes," said Raphael. "Curious, isn't it?"

"Could be a depressing study," said Errol.

"Maybe," said Raphael. "Maybe not. That's the question, isn't it?"

"For you, maybe," said Errol.

"Yes. For me."

Why did you go into anthropology?" asked Gray.

Raphael didn't hesitate. "To travel."

"For Christ's sake," said Errol. "That's *it?*"

"Errol," Gray cut him off. "That's why I went into anthropology."

Errol shut up. Little by little he was learning to do that.

So their triad took shape. It formed less in these short parries—deft strokes, like line drawings, never filled in—than in silence. They arranged themselves in quiet like actors before the curtain. Raphael would put his feet up. Gray would scratch out lines and pace and scratch and sit with her back to the leading man, pointedly. Errol would listen, and leave. From his distance, Errol watched Raphael. What he saw was Raphael watching Gray. Her new assistant licked his lips. He yawned, like a lazy lion under an acacia on hot afternoons. He was in no hurry. He didn't seem concerned that his prey would get away—as if she were fated for him; as if she had nowhere else to go.

The camera crew arrived. All five had worked with Gray before, and treated her with warmth and deference. During the day they never argued. When they were building sets of Corgie's architecture and they too successfully evoked the originals, Gray sometimes went stone white again and walked away; they made no remarks. At night around the fire she told them myths from Ghana or described amusing cross-cultural misunderstandings, and they laughed; they adored her, carefully.

Raphael would watch her hold court from a few logs away. Errol couldn't tell if he enjoyed her performances or if they annoyed him. So often it was impossible to tell what the man was thinking. He seemed to watch in a pure way, without appraisal; his face soaked up information and gave nothing back. This made Errol nervous. Furthermore, Raphael was too relaxed.

Gray put most people on their toes. Raphael rested calmly on the full soles of his feet.

Since Arabella had not yet flown in, they began shooting a few scenes before the arrival of the "young anthropologist." Gray had been right: Raphael didn't have to do anything but say his lines normally. It would take another project to test his skills as an actor. Steelier and more underplayed than Errol had imagined Corgie, Raphael's Charles was more chilling. Gray found she had to cut a lot of lines, for he didn't have to say much to get his point across. This Charles was quiet, terrifying, and compelling. During takes, the crew and surrounding tribespeople were cold and silent, and Errol felt the hair rise on his arms. Listening to that low, even voice, Errol had a crawling sensation that, were he among Il-Ororen, he, too, would follow its orders.

Panting, her color high, Arabella West puffed into the village late one afternoon. "Errol!" she cried, throwing her pack off and scraping her thick red hair out of her face. "Save me. I am *wasted*." They hugged. Errol and Arabella liked each other. More calmly, Arabella nodded to Gray. "Dr. Kaiser. So sorry I couldn't make it earlier." Arabella plunked herself down on a rock. "That mountain is too much."

Gray shook her head slightly. Errol knew what she was thinking. Arabella was wearing eyeliner in the bush. Arabella had well-manicured nails.

Errol was thinking something else. He was thinking that Arabella was gorgeous. She had big green eyes and light skin. Her breasts were full, her hips wide. She had one of those lush bodies that in later years, without her losing weight and doing an awful lot of jogging, would run to cellulite, but just now, in her mid-twenties, it was holding up nicely. Errol found it comforting to be around her kind of beauty—plush, expansive, curved. Certainly Gray was beautiful in a more sustainingly interesting way, but Gray's whole body was tautly strung, and somehow to be around it for long stretches of time was tiring.

"Well," said Arabella when Errol introduced her to Raphael. "So you're my replacement."

"Don't worry," said Raphael. "You and I are after different prizes."

"I'm not after a prize," said Arabella warily. "I'm here to do a job."

Raphael shook his head. "Every nose has its carrot."

"Oh?" asked Arabella. "So what's yours?"

"The nature of a man's carrot," said Raphael, "is his biggest secret."

"Sounds phallic."

"Yes." Raphael smiled. "Doesn't it."

They started shooting with Arabella the next day. Mid-morning, Gray said quietly from the sidelines, "I'm not sure this is going to work out."

"Why?" asked Errol. "I think she's doing beautifully."

"She's too flighty."

"She seems vulnerable. I think that makes her more sympathetic."

"She seems helpless, you mean. And the way she looks at him all the time with those wet green eyes? It's off. It's coquettish."

"Gray!" said Errol in exasperation. "What do you want, that she should roll onto the set like a tank?"

"No, but she comes across as weak."

"She comes across as a *woman*."

"Are you implying—"

"I'm implying that maybe you should watch her and learn something."

Gray opened her mouth, and closed it.

"I'm sorry," said Errol.

Gray looked as if she wanted to walk away again, but she must have realized she was doing that an awful lot lately; she stayed. Her eyes curdled.

"Maybe you're right," Errol stammered. "Maybe she should be stronger—"

Gray shook her head and looked at the ground.

"Is there some problem?" asked Arabella, walking over to Errol and Gray when the take was finished.

"No," said Gray, her voice with a slight throttle to it. "You're doing a lovely job. You're quite—winning. Likable. Keep it up. Go on to the next scene." Gray tried to smile.

"Listen, I have a question, Dr. Kaiser."

"Arabella," said Errol, "maybe later—"

"Go ahead," said Gray.

"Is this a romance?"

She smiled wanly. "That depends on how you play it, I suppose."

"How do you want me to play it?"

". . . No," said Gray, thinking. "There's no going back and fixing things, is there?"

"What?"

"Arabella—" said Errol, hoping to urge her away.

"It's just the situation is a natural," Arabella went on. "And if you want to appeal to a popular audience—"

"It is not a romance," said Gray heavily. "You are here to work. He occasionally interferes. He makes you angry, or for you—a *little* angry. As for popular appeal, I wouldn't worry about it. Charles was a very interesting man."

T he evening after they filmed the worship service, Errol leaned back on his mat, hands behind his head. "I wonder what it would take to get Americans to go bonkers like that. To bow down in the middle of the common and offer up their Cuisinarts and frozen wieners."

"Exactly the same thing," said Raphael, with his aviator goggles still on his forehead and his red baseball cap on backward. "A man like Charles."

Errol's mouth twitched. He'd been asking Gray. "In Boston we'd recognize Corgie as the small-time opportunist he really was."

There was a funny tingling in the following silence. Errol looked back and forth from Raphael to Gray, at their coolness, their embarrassment.

"Il-Cor-gie!" a native called at the door. Raphael turned. Silently the Kenyan slid a tray into the hut, along with a stack of beautifully folded clothes, and crept away. Raphael put the laundry by his mat, sipped the drink he'd been given, and wrapped the hot towel lying beside it around his neck.

"Gray," said Errol with annoyance, "you're the brand-name anthropologist. Do Il-Ororen understand about actors?"

"The concept, yes. But not about Raphael."

"Or maybe they do," said Raphael.

Errol was tired of these enigmatic quips. He sat up. "Are you a ghost? Is that what you mean? Or is it a god?"

Raphael looked back at Errol, his eyes dancing.

"It is odd," said Gray, with anthropological diplomacy, "that they've debunked white people. But Charles was exempt. I was always afraid for him that they'd find out. But they never did."

"There was nothing to find out," said Raphael. "They always knew who he was."

"You're evading my question," said Errol. "How do you think you know so goddamned much about Charles Corgie?"

"You're the sort who's done his homework," said Raphael, barely smiling. "How many societies believe in reincarnation?"

"So you were Charles Corgie in a past life?" asked Errol squarely.

"Now, how would I know?"

"Well, if you were," said Errol, "that's not much to be proud of, is it?"

Raphael shrugged.

"Gray?" Errol pushed. "*Is* it?"

Gray turned her back. Errol pulled the sleeping bag over his head.

The whole next day Errol watched the filming with a different eye. They shot the scene with Login that afternoon; Errol watched Raphael fire a blank into a young boy's chest and shuddered as the sound rippled through his own body. Yet when they filmed the scene in which Gray broke her arm, with the ensuing unrest, the fall of the house of Corgie was shot as a tragedy. Errol took a long look at the script after dinner.

"Gray," said Errol, "what's the angle on this project, anyway?"

"What do you mean?"

"The point of view. On Charles Corgie."

"Mixed . . ." she said, taking a step back from him.

"By mixed, do you mean critical?"

"In a sophisticated portrait," she hedged, "a man is neither hero nor villain."

"So you don't see him as a hero?"

"Not exactly."

"Gray."

"What." She busied herself with some papers.

"He enslaved a thousand Africans and murdered God knows how many of them—what do you mean you don't see him as *exactly* a hero?"

"His actions," she said steadily, "were morally dubious—"

"Dubious!"

"But he was a complicated man and he had his reasons and he had many admirable qualities."

"Like what?"

She spoke quietly. "He was powerful."

"And he used that power to do what? I'm warning you, if this film turns out as some rhapsodic elegy about dear old Charles, I'm taking my name off it." It pained Errol as he said this that in the eyes of the world, as long as Gray Kaiser's name was still attached, Errol's withdrawal would have no effect whatsoever.

"I would hate for you to do that, Errol. That would hurt me."

Before he left, she stopped him and added, "You're a very nice man. We're not the same."

"You're not nice?"

She shook her head, once. "I don't think so."

Errol wondered as he walked out of their hut how difficult

it had been for her to admit this—whether she was ashamed of not being nice or proud of it. Errol was convinced as he grew older that niceness was a much underrated quality.

When they filmed the fire, everyone else's color rose; Gray went pale. She couldn't eat dinner. When in an extension of the day's pyromania the village lit a bonfire that night, Gray went to bed early.

The following day was the last scene, with the plane, the bomb. They needed a take of Corgie surrounded by smoke and flames. Errol was close to Raphael when they shot these frames, and would long remember his glimpse of that face. Raphael had all along seemed in sync with the production; as aggravated as Errol got with Raphael's remarks about reincarnation, the man did seem to understand Corgie with an uncanny intuition. In this last scene, then, Errol was curious how Raphael would play it. He was surprised. Astride the plane, the man ordered Il-Ororen away with a remarkable kindness. Swinging his gun from the crowd to the back of his plane, Raphael swept toward the bomb and squeezed the trigger with an odd lyricism, even grace, like a dancer, and in the midst of the explosion the face the camera zoomed in on was not pained or regretful but ecstatic; relieved.

The movie was shot. They packed up and said goodbye to Il-Ororen. The chieftain had been eyeing the film crew's bullhorn; Gray left it as a gift. Raphael had grown fond of the red baseball cap and aviator goggles, and she said he could keep them. Il-Ororen presented Gray with a parting gift of pottery. Errol and Gray exchanged glances. Il-Ororen were still imitating Gray's Grecian urns and collapsed "modern" vessels from thirty-seven years before.

* * *

O n the plane from Nairobi Raphael inquired conversationally about Gray's next project.

"Are you familiar with my other work?"

"Not really." He didn't seem embarrassed.

Errol found this incredible. Gray was covered even in most introductory syllabuses. "And you've been in anthropology how long?"

"I don't read much."

"How do you manage that?" asked Gray.

"I do well. In school. For some reason I always read what I have to. Though I may have read nothing else in the book, I will always have read the one passage covered on the exam. Uncanny," he observed.

"That uncanniness may fall out from under you one day," said Errol.

"We'll see. Things have a way of working out for me."

Errol had taken offense at Raphael's reading lapses, but Gray, it seems, had chosen not to.

"Had you read my work," she went on, "you'd know I've done considerable research on matriarchies. One of them, in Ghana, is the Lone-luk. I've followed their society for thirty-five years. We plan to spend several months with the Lone-luk next year, starting in February."

"Why?"

"Matriarchies are important to me," she said simply.

"Politically?"

"Personally. It's personally important to me that they exist. I don't feel—incapable. I never have. Lesser. I'm not talking about political movements at all, opinions. I mean the way I feel."

Raphael nodded. "It has nothing to do with groups. With anthropology."

"That's right." She smiled; they seemed to understand each other.

"Do you have," she asked with unusual delicacy, "opinions? On sexual politics? On—supremacy?"

"None. I don't care. Men mean nothing to me. I am—" He seemed about to complete a statement, but it turned out he was finished. Raphael himself seemed surprised. "I am." That was it.

"The matriarchy is still politically useful," Errol horned in. "It's of obvious importance in dispelling biological assumptions of natural male dominance."

Raphael looked over at Errol with, he thought, the most inappropriate disdain.

Gray sighed. "That's true, of course. Except the Lone-luk haven't been dogmatically—tidy. Few things in anthropology are. Messiness is the field's annoyance, also its appeal. You know, the whole concept is a lie, in a way," she mused. "Defining 'cultures,' the way people are. Construct the 'typical American,' you'll have put together the one person in the country who doesn't exist. I find people behave as much in resistance to their culture as in cooperation with it. No one embraces his inheritance completely, just as no one absolutely obeys the law."

"I like that," said Raphael.

"What?"

"I like that you said that. You're intelligent."

Gray laughed. "I'm so relieved you finally decided that."

"I know you are."

Gray shot him an odd look, then went on, adjusting the tilt of her seatback. "Anyway, the Lone-luk. When I first studied them they did make near-perfect dogma. The stuff of pamphlets. A lovely, smooth society. Artistic and prosperous. As far back as I've been able to ascertain, this tribe has been led by women. The women were the acknowledged heads of household, and held all positions of power. They did prestige work; the men did brute labor. The firstborn daughter inherited. Et cetera. However . . ." She proceeded with some pain; the Lone-luk had become a sore spot with her from way back, which was why she'd finally put a definitive update at the top of her agenda. For some reason, perhaps because she'd first lived with them when she was so young, she took their fate personally. "Unlike Toroto, their villages aren't cut off. They've been exposed to both Western civilization and other tribes in Ghana, largely patriarchal. The men of the Lone-luk got the idea that elsewhere men were king of the mountain. Shortly after my first visit there, the men grew resentful, sullen, and uncooperative."

"You can hardly blame them," said Errol. "They really were treated like oxen, you know."

"True." Gray chewed her lip. "The women weren't about to abdicate, though. So the most peculiar thing happened. There was a rift, a split. The men actually moved to separate villages. For years now the schism has done nothing but get more hostile and more entrenched. There's never talk of compromise, of parity. Both sides want the upper hand. For thirty years the Lone-luk have been in a state of war. Marriage even more than sex has become taboo. Occasional intercourse has become fast and ugly and often aggressive; a high percentage of pregnancies are the result of rape. An entire generation of women has passed through its reproductive cycle largely without offspring. Huge numbers of middle-aged women are single and barren. The population has plummeted. The age structure of the society has shifted, gotten older. The children that are born, boys and girls alike, are raised by the women, but the boys are treated badly, like runts. Once they're about thirteen, the boys either run away or are kidnapped to the other side. And that's not all . . ." Gray's eyes gazed out the window forlornly. They were in a cloud; there was nothing but lost gray air outside.

"What?" asked Raphael.

"Well." She sighed. "Any society is an elaborate system of interdependencies, not just sexual ones. Somehow the lack of trust between the sexes of the Lone-luk has spread to other things. They won't cooperate intrasexually now. Each man or woman keeps a tiny separate garden. They won't help each other build houses or effect repairs. They won't take care of each other's children or sit with the sick. In many ways they're reminiscent of the Ik."

"Colin Turnbull," Errol interjected helpfully for the ill-read.

"Thank you," said Raphael coldly.

"The economy has fallen apart," said Gray. "Barter is limited and suspicious and full of fraud. Other tribes now refuse to trade with them. Their culture has become more racist. Crime, which was nonexistent when I first went there, has skyrocketed."

"The original crime-free state was intellectually convenient," said Errol.

"That's true. But, Errol, crime isn't on the rise just with men, but with women. Maybe because they've been used to an aggressive role, but even violent attacks among women aren't uncommon."

A stewardess asked if they wanted drinks, and Gray glared; she didn't like to be interrupted.

"It used to be so beautiful!" she lamented once the woman was gone. "Their villages were peaceful and well kept and just. It was a warm, even idyllic community."

"You were young," said Raphael.

"I was young, but I wasn't blind. It's not just my ancient cynicism warping my perspective now. I am not talking about a subtle shift. Those villages are squalid now. Ugly, littered, impoverished, covered in feces. Full of flies and starving animals. And the people aren't nice."

"Sounds as if you should stay home," said Raphael.

"No. I have to go. It's my lot, I suppose."

"Is it dangerous?"

"Quite. It's like an inner-city slum."

"Actually, this worries me, Gray," said Errol. "Since you and I are going to have to live in separate camps, there's not going to be anyone to look out for you."

"There's me to look out for me," said Gray. "As usual."

"Maybe you should bring someone—"

"That doesn't concern me," she cut him off.

"You haven't changed since you were twenty-two," Errol muttered.

"And I don't plan on changing, either," she snapped.

"You may have to," said Raphael.

"Why?"

Raphael said nothing.

"At any rate," she continued gruffly, "in the meantime I'll be doing a parallel study in the U.S. while I pull together this documentary about Charles. The one truly matriarchal element of our own society is urban black culture. Most households are headed, even supported financially, by women. So I've targeted an area of the South Bronx in New York. We'll be putting together family histories and doing interviews on attitudes about sex and marriage and power. As far as I can tell, the situation there has degenerated to a similar state of siege. It should be interesting."

But Gray didn't sound interested. She sounded depressed.

chapter seven

I t was a relief to be back in Boston, and a disappointment—as usual.

But then Errol liked usualness. Much as he thrived on the excitement in other people's lives, in his own he liked predictable routines. One of the most distressing aspects of this whole next year was to be its constant sense of disruption.

Errol had hopes that Charles Corgie would die back down into history. They'd troubled his brittle bones, but that wasn't to say they couldn't be buried again. Yet ghosts, once disturbed, don't settle so easily, especially when they are twenty-five and in good health and have found their "carrot."

Still, when Gray announced the week following their return that she was going to play Raphael at tennis, Errol had to smile. In the film they'd skipped over the game between Gray and Charles, and this was a scene Errol would particularly enjoy seeing replayed.

"I bought you a cheesecake for the big day," said Errol over breakfast. "The good kind. Third shelf." Gray was a nutritionist's nightmare; she lived mostly on sugar.

"Big day?"

"Aren't you playing the reincarnate this afternoon?"

"Oh, that's right," she said quickly, gulping down her coffee so that it must have hurt her throat. "I'd forgotten." A drip of coffee trickled down her chin; she wiped it away with the back of her hand. Gray got up and washed the stray dishes in the sink.

"I thought you hated washing dishes in the morning."

"Big piles," said Gray. "Crusty food. But a few water glasses and teaspoons can be relaxing. Warm water on your hands. Clean clear glass. Round metal."

"Why would you need relaxing?" asked Errol. "You'd forgotten."

"Forgotten what?"

Errol didn't bother. "You're really not going to eat that cheesecake?"

"I'm not hungry."

Errol got up and plunked the whole two pounds of solid cream cheese in the middle of the table. "Gray, it's not enough that you win. You have to do it with style. For that you need energy. I have no interest in wasting my time watching a routine victory. I want to see him weep."

"That seems unlikely, don't you think? Can you picture it? Raphael weeping?"

Errol thought a moment. "You know, it's rather odd. I can." For just as she said that, an image flashed into Errol's head that he'd never seen: the long chin pointed up, the head tilted back, and the eyes wide and unblinking. There were tears marking an even, steady track down both cheeks, a drop every few seconds, with the precision of an IV. The face itself was set in its usual relaxation, as if the tears were part of its natural state. As always with his images of Raphael, there was no sound—just the faint flap of his glottis, swallowing, with the Adam's apple lurching up and down.

Gray paused at the sink and looked over at Errol, and slowly nodded. "You're right. I can, too. Isn't that peculiar?"

"No sound," said Errol.

"Completely still," said Gray. "And in terrible pain."

Errol felt his scalp shift over his skull. They were seeing the same thing. They'd been together too long.

Gray turned away and wiped the counters briskly, though they were clean. "I don't think we'll get him to cry over a tennis game."

"No, I'm sure that wasn't it."

"It?"

"What was making him cry."

Gray didn't like this anymore. "What are you talking about, Errol?"

"An image. Which you saw, too, and can't pretend you didn't. I'd pay money to know what gets to a guy like that."

"Spoiling his own happiness deliberately," said Gray right away.

"He told you that?"

Gray stopped whisking the sponge across the table and laughed. "Raphael would never tell me something like *that*. I don't know why I said that. It just came to me."

"So why would he spoil his own—"

"Errol, this whole conversation is getting ridiculous." Gray squeezed out the sponge and strode out of the room, leaving the cheesecake untouched in the middle of the table.

S he walked down the stairs at three in her usual tennis dress. She'd worn this outfit to play ever since Errol could remember. The material was soft and gauzy, like cheesecloth; though once white, it was now the color of muslin. Gray wouldn't buy a new tennis dress, because she wore her wide amber sweat stains with pride, like old war wounds. Like Gray herself, the material had lost some of its body, but made up for it in grace and texture. She'd wear this dress until its threads dissolved on her back, for she held on tight to all that aged well.

Once at the courts, Errol realized he'd expected Raphael to show up in dazzling boxer shorts with smartly turned cuffs and a blazing Ban-Lon polo—the untrammeled overstarched look Gray so detested in a tennis partner. Catching sight of Raphael leaning against a bench, with his racket cocked behind his shoulder, Errol was disappointed. His faded cutoffs certainly weren't starched, and his broken-down T-shirt had the same amber mottling as Gray's dress. He took off his sunglasses as Gray approached. As imposing as he looked in their reflective chrome lenses, they were no match for Sarasola's naked eyes. Today these were insanely open and a wide confessional brown—Raphael seemed to breathe through his pupils.

Raphael reached for Gray's hand and kissed her deftly on the cheek. "Nice weather," he said.

"Lovely weather," said Gray.

They were talking about the weather, and Errol already felt left out. "Heat is good for suffering," said Errol to Raphael.

Ignoring Errol completely, Raphael swung his racket languidly off his shoulder and strode to the court with Gray. Errol thought about leaving, seriously, but instead found himself following behind them to a green bench that would surely give him splinters. He wished he had a book. No, forget the book. He wished a beautiful blond woman in a short, flouncy tennis dress would sit beside him and complain to him about arrogant young men, how she wanted someone for once who was considerate and intelligent and responsible. Then Errol thought about these adjectives that described him and felt drab.

Raphael and Gray were warming up with a rally. Their play was careful and polite. Gray could return balls like that in her sleep—an inch above the net, but still with a slope, and when the balls hit Raphael's court they actually bounced above the surface. Errol smiled and forgot about the girl in the flouncy dress who was obviously just looking for a father. This was going to be good.

Yet Raphael's shots were solid and evidently easy for him. He never seemed to have to run very far. For the first five minutes neither player was sweating. Each was toying with the other. They were smiling. It was a joke.

Slowly, though, Gray drew her racket farther back behind her for a wider stroke. Slowly she took a deeper breath below the amber folds of her old tennis dress. Gradually the arc on the ball straightened and the yellow fur began to blur across the net. Gray leaned slightly more forward and crouched farther down. Her hand tightened around the tattered leather grip as her shots angled toward the corners and skittered in sickly curves off to the side.

But in dull horror Errol watched Raphael's game respond

in kind. Sarasola's weight shifted fully onto the balls of his feet; the long muscles in his thighs rose over his knees to ripple under his cutoff jeans. His calves expanded above the rumpled cotton socks, and the tendons in his forearm caught the summer sun. His skin, already a deep brown in June, went liquid until his neck glistened and his forehead beaded like a tall glass of beer. The strings dangling from the fringe of his jeans moistened and matted and clung to his thighs. Errol shuddered and looked down at his lap. His own thighs were white. His shorts were beige and a little too long. He knew his legs were strong, but they didn't, somehow, assemble in that way, and they'd certainly never carried him around the court with that loping, buoyant alacrity.

Errol tried to keep his eyes off Raphael, and looked back to Gray in time to catch a forehand that she snapped just over the net and straight down. Raphael stood motionless in the back court, watching the ball skim its way over the next two courts. He laughed, and his teeth were brilliant, as if they, too, were sweating.

"All right," he said, "let's play."

They collected the balls. As Errol would have expected, Raphael was stylish in picking up balls, tipping them against the side of his tennis shoe or bouncing them quickly from the court with his racket from a stationary position. (Errol had never been able to do that, though he'd tried plenty of times when Gray wasn't looking. He'd hit the ball with the face of his racket, and it would just sit there. He would hit it harder until the racket struck it at an angle and the ball would roll into the next court. Lately Errol just picked the damned things up with his hand.)

The rally for serve lasted a long time. Finally Raphael got her off in a corner and smashed it to the other side. Gray's eyebrows shot up, and she looked keenly at Raphael for a good ten seconds before she nodded and centered herself to receive his serve.

Raphael stood behind the line very straight. He inhaled. Once he exhaled this breath, there wasn't a trace of tension in his face. His eyelids looked heavy. He tilted his head backward as if the muscles in his neck were no longer stiff enough to support it. His limbs went limp. Once, he bounced the ball in front of him, until in one rising motion like drawing himself out of bed he tossed the ball and fell into it in a gesture so complete, so full and uncontemplative, it brought tears to Errol's eyes. Raphael was alive. The serve was in, and Errol was actually surprised that Gray returned it. Through the point, too, Raphael responded to the ball in one continuous liquid ripple. Sarasola plays tennis, Gray, like an *animal*.

Gray's response was competent. She did not fall apart, and Errol had to admit that she was playing as well as she did with him. That wasn't good enough. There was a dogged quality to her play that was new. She didn't fall apart; neither did she win. She survived well into each point, and did put a few of her usual untouchables across, but she lost the whole first set without even making it to deuce.

In the second set, Gray's head was cocked a little to the side. Between points she walked more slowly than usual; sometimes she forgot the score or went to the wrong side of the court to deliver a serve. Her eyes were fenced in, and Errol's every effort to meet them and to somehow encourage her she pointedly closed off. Again, doggedly, she lost the next game, and the next.

"Gray!" Errol shouted after a game point. "Get over here!"

Gray rigidly shook her head. "Don't interrupt me, Errol."

The third game was a shutout. Switching sides, Gray didn't look Errol in the eye as she crossed right in front of him. Errol stared down at his feet, drawing aimlessly in the green powder with the tip of his sneaker. Gray lost the whole fourth game without Errol looking up once.

Now it was just a matter of waiting out the rest of the match. Dully Errol leaned back and watched the next game, sighing, sighing again; somehow it was hard to get enough breath or, once it was taken, to get rid of it. Gray looked smaller than usual, shorter even. Her legs didn't look so taut anymore, simply thin. Her movements were abrupt, and there was an odd delay in her response to each of Raphael's shots; with Sarasola's game you didn't have the luxury of that hesitation. Errol made himself look at Gray's face. He had never seen her defeated; he presumed that to observe this was good for his education. She'd taught him so much, but this was one lesson Errol wished he could have picked up somewhere else.

But where was the defeat? Errol looked hard at Gray's face, watching for a clenched jaw, pain. Instead, he seemed to be observing the latest IBM computer running through its paces for prospective buyers. Her eyes weren't glazed or flat but insanely busy, digesting information, filing each shot. The pong of each ball hitting the racket had the solid sound of a card falling into place, chocking into its assigned slot, and soon it made sense, though she missed them, that, yes, the shot would go there and nowhere else. Increasingly the game made sense, and it made sense that she was losing it. Now in this fifth game Gray lost perfectly, she lost more perfectly than she had lost any game, and at the game point she stopped and watched his last shot slam into its proper corner. She took a breath. She nodded her head.

She smiled.

Errol looked hard. That's right, she was smiling. And the smile was real; she wasn't just being a sport. Raphael, too, paused and stared. Gray looked different. She was losing, fantastically; she had one more game to go and the whole match was over, but she stood behind the back line leaning lightly on her racket like a cane, looking dapper, arch, amused; tall, spare, relieved. When she took the racket back in her grip to serve, it seemed to weigh nothing. As the ball rose and poised at its midpoint, there was a moment of complete stillness, Gray's arm bent behind her back; Raphael crouched, frozen, on the other side; Errol balanced on the very last board of his bench. There was no breeze. The clouds above them were round and turfy and still, like the tennis ball over Gray's head. In the adjoining courts, no one was finishing a point or retrieving a ball. There were no airplanes overhead, no children with scraped knees by the backboard, no birds—only Gray Kaiser and the pretty yellow target poised, tempting, waiting for her, until the moment broke and Gray was still smiling grimly as the racket cracked forward and Errol wondered seriously whether some women did not reach their prime until the age of fifty-nine. Singing across the net went the most exquisite serve that Errol had ever seen. Raphael barely managed to whip his racket back by the time the ball was well behind him, flipping up from the fence and tripping back to the net.

Raphael whistled lightly between his teeth. Errol decided that even if this were the only such moment in the match, this last serve redeemed the entire humiliation; he leaned back on his bench to enjoy the rest of the game. Gray herself looked not smug or ecstatic or surprised but simply content. She walked quietly to the other side and did it again.

Gray aced this game on her serve alone, but later Raphael mastered jabbing his racket out in time for the ball to ricochet halfheartedly over the net, and Gray had to actually play the point. However, the data were in. The program had been run. The cards had all, chock, chock, chock, fallen into their proper slots. Each shot Raphael sent over, Gray was there, and there, and there again—simply: input, output, as if her coordinates came tapping out on fanpaper. Raphael played like an animal, but Gray played Raphael like someone who had studied animals.

After Gray had won the second set and was into the third, their court began to collect an audience. The fact was, Raphael had not suddenly begun to play badly. Rather, he brilliantly and at great cost put each ball where he was supposed to. The two of them played like instruments in a duet with narrow harmonies. While the balance of the chord was precarious, neither was a half step off. The games were composed, though, so that at the end of each phrase Gray hit the last note.

Up until the final game of the match Errol was so caught up with Gray's computation that he neglected to scrutinize Raphael. When at last he turned to the other side of the court, Errol expected a red face with eyes constricted and grudging— after all, this twenty-five-year-old man with a splendid tennis game was now tied with an old lady. How happy could he be?

Very happy, it seemed.

Errol found when he faced Raphael not a blotch, not a rumple, not a single grimace of frustration. Raphael's hair flamed ecstatically out over his headband. His skin flushed with the blood not of anger but of excitement. His face shone smooth and bright with open pores. Dilated and wide, his eyes consumed Gray's every move. At length he stalked rather than returned her shots, licking his red lips, crouching behind the net, padding across the turf. Raphael prowled over the court with the gleam of a lithe and clever creature to whom hunting came so easily that slaughter had become a bore. At last, now, something faster and worthy of this predator.

The match point went back and forth for a long time. Raphael returned the ball with a meatier twist than he had all afternoon. Still, Errol didn't imagine that Raphael was actually trying to win. Rather, he was losing with abandon. Finally, with a wrenching downward slam, he threw himself on one of Gray's neat slicing shots; the ball smacked the top tape of the net and dropped, bounced, stopped. Still carried a few steps by his follow-through, Raphael continued to lope over to Gray's side of the court. In front of her he breathed, watched, nodded. He took her tennis racket from her, reached for her hand, and kissed it.

"You lost," said Gray. "Why do you look so pleased with yourself?"

"I'm not," said Raphael. "I'm pleased with you." His eyes were massive and fixed. He had not relinquished her hand. He turned it and ran his finger over the palm. "You have beautiful calluses."

Gray took her hand and her racket back. "You really know what gets to a woman, Mr. Sarasola," she said, and strode over toward Errol.

Errol kissed Gray's cheek, congratulating her on her game. She thanked him with the attention she paid strangers in reception lines.

"Rapha-*el*!" They all turned to find a pretty young brunette clutching Sarasola's arm. She was out of breath. "Long time no see!" The girl raked her hair out of her eyes with her fingers so that it flipped attractively back. Raphael stared at her hand on his arm and said nothing until she laughed nervously and removed it. "So what are you doing here?"

Raphael glanced down at his racket. "Playing soccer."

She laughed quickly and raked her hair out of her eyes again. "Right, sure." She turned to Errol. "So didn't anyone warn you not to play with Raphael Sarasola?"

Errol cocked his head and watched her shift her weight back and forth and smooth down her tennis dress and rake her hair back again, though it wasn't in her eyes this time. "No," said Errol, "but no one warned *you* not to play with him either, did they?"

She laughed again. "Oh, I learned my lesson."

"If you'd really learned your lesson, Pamela," said Raphael quietly, "you wouldn't be here."

Pamela blinked, decisively. In this small, strange silence it was if she'd just batted the remark away, like a bad ball. "Listen," she said, "I was wondering if—next week—I could borrow the car. You see, my father's going to be in town, and he thinks he bought it for me."

"Tell him," said Raphael, his eyebrows raised, "you lost it." Pamela's head bobbed dully. "I lost it."

"Yes," Raphael instructed. "Just like that."

Silence. Pamela didn't leave.

"So how was your game?" she asked brightly.

"Superior," said Raphael, looking at Gray.

"You mean you killed him," said Pamela.

Raphael sat on the bench and began zipping up his racket cover. "You assume a good game for me is one in which I trammel my opponent. Actually, I dislike that kind of game enormously."

"So it was a close game?"

Raphael pulled off his sopping T-shirt and completely ignored her. The silence got longer and longer, and still Pamela waited. Finally someone said, "Yes," softly. It was Gray.

"What was the score? Did you guys play a whole match?"

Raphael compressed his lips, swabbing the sweat from his neck. Pamela followed the towel as it traveled down Raphael's dark, tight, neatly haired chest. As he reached for a fresh shirt from his bag, Pamela looked regretful. She turned to Errol. "You must be pretty good to give him competition."

"I'm quite mediocre," said Errol, feeling sorry for her. "Dr. Kaiser gave your friend a good run around the court."

Pamela noticed Gray for the first time. She looked quizzically at Raphael and tried to catch his eye.

Raphael looked stonily back. "She's better than I am."

The two women looked at each other. "Gray Kaiser." Gray extended her hand.

"Pamela Rose.—Didn't you used to be in sociology or something?"

"Anthropology. I still dabble in it occasionally."

"I suppose it's good to stay active," said Pamela. "It keeps your mind alert."

"Why certainly," said Gray mildly. "I find that with anthropology, a little knitting, and charity work I can still remember the names of all my great-grandchildren."

"Don't believe a word of it," said Errol. "Gray has never done charity work in her life. So what do you say, old lady? How about a beer?"

"I'd love one," said Gray. "But I think we could buy Pamela something a little stronger."

"No." Raphael swung his bag over his shoulder, ready to go.

"Excuse me?" said Gray.

"No," he repeated.

"No, what?"

"No, Pamela doesn't feel up to it." He turned to the girl. "Your behavior is unattractive, Pamela. Please stay away from me. Go home." He spoke with the sternness one has to muster to discourage a dog that has followed one too far for its own good.

"I believe," said Gray, "that I invited your friend for a drink. That *I* did."

"I believe," said Raphael, "that I just uninvited her."

"I believe," said Gray, and they were facing each other squarely now, "that you can't do that."

Raphael shrugged. "Then have a nice time." With that he strode toward the parking lot, leaving Gray, Errol, and this woman an absurd threesome. They all watched Raphael walk away in silence until Errol turned his attention to Pamela Rose. All the remarks that Pamela had successfully batted away came pelting back at her. Pamela withered like a blow-up doll someone had pulled the plug on. The lines in her face curdled. Her stiffly held spine and firmly set shoulders collapsed. Her hair wilted strand by strand back into her face.

"This is silly," said Pamela weakly. "I don't know you. I'm sorry about . . ." She fluttered her fingers toward Raphael and looked off in a direction where there was nothing to see.

"Are you going to be all right?" asked Gray.

"Oh, just fine," said Pamela, with an unsettling little laugh. "He's always like that, you know. Kind of—funny."

"If you find that funny," said Errol, "then you have one sick sense of humor."

"I mean just a little insensitive. Some people," she said bravely, "like to spar. In conversation."

"You were sparring?" asked Errol.

"I'm—well. I'm real nice. I don't even know you, I'll tell you I'm sorry, right?" Pamela swallowed and shook her head, wafting her fingers behind her as she walked toward an open field, dragging her racket behind her along the pavement.

As they walked through the parking lot they found Raphael waiting for them, leaning against Gray's car.

chapter eight

Pamela Rose was the first evidence, but there was more. Errol didn't need to hire any private agencies; information came to him as if he were being warned or led. Yet in a way these clues were wasted, for Errol did not need to be warned; it was not Errol who was in danger.

A colleague, Ellen Friedman, stopped by one afternoon. It was a lovely day, so the two sat out on the swing on Gray's porch.

"I spent a lot of time on porch swings as a kid," said Ellen, moving the swing listlessly with her foot. It made a high-pitched *ee* sound. "Sitting around with friends on a Saturday afternoon. We'd put up someone's hair . . ."

"Talk about *relationships*."

"Mm," said Ellen. "Which at the time were fairly simple."

"Were they, though?"

"Jane loves Mark; next week: Jane hates Mark. None of this Jane loves Mark but also hates him at the same time. That's adult stuff."

"Well, no," Errol reflected. "I seem to remember even from when I was very young that when you loved someone you also hated them for making you love them, since loving someone is so incredibly humiliating."

Ellen laughed. "That's a dismal point of view."

"It goes way back."

"I can see why you never married."

"No," said Errol pleasantly, "you probably can't."

Ellen looked down at her hands. "Sorry. You're quite right. I have no idea why."

Her sudden embarrassment made her appealing, and Errol found himself watching Ellen Friedman move the swing back and forth with her heel and play with the ratty pillow at her side with real fondness for a moment. She was trim and short and had little feet. Her hair was dark and neatly styled close to her head; he imagined she'd once been pretty, and now—at Errol's age? a little younger?—would be considered "smart." She could have been his wife. Errol could have met her at twenty-five and gone to movies and agreed with her on everything she had to say about them; he could have been charmed by her idiosyncrasies and married her. This might be their house, with the porch swing to remind her of her adolescence; they'd be in the same field and recommend books to each other and have children and dinners and she would still be "smart." They could have dinners and once in a while invite Gray Kaiser and be nervous about what to have, since Gray was so bored by gourmet cooking. Yet he couldn't necessarily know that, since he wouldn't really know Gray Kaiser, and that was the end of that fantasy.

"I think I resist generalizations about age," said Errol. "Maybe if you learned more over the years, getting older would mean something, but I don't have the feeling that I understand things much better than I did when I was twenty-five. My tendency is more to see myself in a big mess that I've always been in. Know what I mean?"

"Not really."

"That's all right."

"Are you always this abstract?"

"It's safer."

She smiled. Gray's weimaraner, Bwana, nuzzled at Ellen's knee. She stroked his head diffidently. Bwana was a reserved dog and demanded a certain deference. "What a beautiful animal. How old is he?"

"Twelve. Feeble, for a dog."

"I envy the way dogs age, don't you? They get a little slower. They sit more. But physically they hardly show it. People fall apart."

"Not all of us."

Ellen smiled and shook her head. "You mean Gray. I know. I must have met her, oh, twenty years ago. Since then, well, her hair's turned, her face is a little more drawn. Otherwise she hasn't changed."

"No doubt there's a portrait up in the attic somewhere that looks terrible."

Ellen chuckled.

"Go for a walk?"

They climbed down the steps and strolled onto the street. Ellen was quiet for a while.

"I saw a friend of mine this afternoon," she began reluctantly. "We used to be quite close. Seeing her was upsetting."

"Why?"

"She was up for tenure in the history department last year. She had a good shot at it. Now she's a word processor at an insurance company."

"How did that happen?"

"She got into something over her head," said Ellen vaguely.

"You make it sound like a narcotics ring or something."

Ellen smiled. "She did have an addiction, at that."

"Pretty mysterious, Ellen."

She sighed. "It was an affair, of course. And instead of tenure, they fired her. Capsule version."

"Ellen, if everyone in the United States who had an affair lost their jobs, five people in this country would be working."

"He was a student, that didn't help."

"That's not so unusual."

"No. But she started acting inexplicably irresponsible. Not showing up for classes. Sometimes he'd come and sit in the hall where she was lecturing and stare at her until she forgot what she was saying and stuttered and dropped the chalk and scattered her notes. After he'd gotten her to really fall apart in the middle of the period, he'd get up and leave, looking disgusted. She'd make it about five more minutes and then dismiss the class. She used to come and see me afterward in tears."

"She should have told him in no uncertain terms to stay out of her classroom."

"You keep missing the point, Errol. She'd sacrifice her lecture just to have laid eyes on him that day."

"Sounds pretty adolescent."

"You mean you've never been so in love with someone that you organized every choice in your life around her? Ever?"

Errol grunted and shut up.

"Well, people began to report her, in droves. Meanwhile, he used her to the hilt. I'm sure it was largely her pressure that got him funding in graduate school. After that it was just fun and games, the way you play with a small trapped animal in a malicious mood." Ellen sank down on a bench and leaned back. "I'm sorry to get so worked up, Errol. It's just this came to a head only a few months ago, so it's still fresh. Anita—I didn't know people got like that, Errol. I wish I still didn't. And all over this stupid kid. I don't understand it."

"Or you do," Errol speculated. "As far as I can tell, that's what disturbs you, isn't it? That you understand it all too well."

Ellen sat up. "If you mean that I've been in that situation, I certainly have not—"

"Oh no," said Errol. "You and I, we're too solid, right? Feet on the ground. Charting our careers. We're sensible and responsible, and we make our decisions on the basis of what needs doing. We make everyone else feel better, because they know that at least someone will be paying bills on time and making airline reservations well in advance, showing up for work and sending routine correspondence, while they fly off the handle with these attachments of theirs. We grind away and make all their histrionics possible. Isn't that right, Ellen? We're the rational workhorses of the world."

"That's exactly what I meant, of course. I have no emotions. I'm a cold, efficient machine."

"Me too," said Errol. "What a relief."

They both laughed. Errol put his hands in his pockets and the two of them strolled down the street in silence.

"Sometimes—" said Ellen quietly, after a few minutes. "Don't get me wrong, Errol. I've enjoyed talking to you, even telling that story, but—sometimes I get tired of relationships. Just people and other people and their problems. Do you know what I mean? It's so wearying: the phone and the fights and the divorces. Friends and enemies, both of them."

"I know," said Errol. "It never stops: endless shifting alliances."

"Yes," said Ellen. "I get tired. And anthropology is no distraction: how people marry and bury each other. Who steps on whom and why. It's the same stuff, Errol. Sometimes I wish I'd gone into manufacturing. So I could talk about how two gears weren't interlocking and how to fix them."

"Sounds metaphorical. For a relationship."

"See, you can't get away! I just like something else sometimes. I like cleaning, even. Dirt here, a dried spot of jam to get rid of. For once a task rather than a gesture."

"Yes," said Errol, feeling in this last part of their conversation somehow lighter, sensing the air around him, hearing each silence between her words, walking with more spring.

"I'm divorced," she went on. "I live alone now. Once in a while I do miss living with a man. I do. Sleeping with someone warm, talking. All right, even fighting, having a problem. But lately it's more the case that I've been reading and it's midnight and I stop. I brush my teeth. I take off my clothes and fold them on the chair. I pull back the sheet and crawl in and it's cool, Errol. In five minutes, I'm asleep. It's so sweet, Errol. It's so simple. Such a relief."

They walked a few more minutes in silence, watching the trees now leafed out and deep green bend in the breeze. Errol thought of Ellen Friedman lying straight and easily between those sheets, her small body quietly living its life there, dreaming of objects, of gears and cleaners and these trees, with the sound of smooth breathing and the clock ticking on the dresser, for hours. He knew she didn't toss back and forth or sweat or snore or grind her teeth. Errol would have imagined himself with her, but that would have ruined the picture—the air would be thicker then; limbs would have to be woven together; there would be conflicts and competitions and things to say. No, just Ellen Friedman, there in the bed. The image made Errol feel rested and clear.

H e has an interesting history," said Gray out of the silence of the interstate. They were headed for New York, where Gray was a consultant for an exhibit at the American Museum of Natural History. The sweetness of Ellen's vision had completely worn off. Errol was in a mood.

"Don't tell me," said Errol. "He was raised by wolves in the wilderness, and that explains everything."

"Errol," said Gray, tapping the steering wheel testily, "these remarks of yours are beginning to accumulate."

"Remarks?"

"About Raphael. What is your problem?"

"My problem." That was a tall order. Errol tapped his own counter-rhythm against the car door. He measured his syllables with care into the small space of the coupe. "My problems," he amended. "I have two. One: Sarasola is an egomaniac, but with nothing to back it up. Two: he's a sadist."

Gray readjusted herself behind the wheel angularly. The muscles in her jaw tensed visibly in and out. "All right," she said. "One at a time. Ego. Did he have something to back it up on the tennis court?"

"Yes, Gray, he plays much better than I do."

Gray shot Errol a look. "But did he brag about his game?"

"Of course not. He lost."

"But how did he lose? Was he annoyed? Upset?"

"No, I got the impression he enjoyed it." Errol stroked his beard and read billboards. "It's his attitude toward you that gripes me, Gray. How can he be so blasé? As if he's in his element or something. As if he'd give Henry Kissinger a call tomorrow but he just doesn't have the time."

"You mean why isn't he obsequious."

"Fine. So he knows you would hate that. So he's clever."

"But why is he a sadist?"

"Because he tortures *me*," Errol wanted to say; instead he told her, "Pamela Rose was the clincher, obviously."

Gray sighed. "Granted, he wasn't overly kind—"

"Overly kind! 'Your behavior is unattractive, Pamela. Go home.' My God, I'm nicer to infestations of silverfish—"

"Errol, all right—"

"That was not just a tired tennis partner in a bad mood, Gray. That was the kind of man you don't want to run into on the T late at night—"

"Listen. Have you ever had a woman interested in you who wouldn't leave you alone?"

"Errol the Eunuch have a woman interested in him? Never."

"I tell you, lately this moping and baiting of yours all the time, Errol, it's—"

"Unattractive?"

Though they were riding along at sixty-five, Gray and Errol looked each other in the eye.

"I think the word we use in the United States is 'stupid,'" she said, looking back at the roads.

"Good." Errol turned back to the billboards. "That's a better word. Less chilling."

They rode the rest of the way in silence.

Y et working together at the museum on case arrangements and slide order, they jockeyed back to Old Errol and Old Gray: usualness. They were a team. She smiled and hit him lightly on the shoulder and made jokes about pottery. By the time they were driving back two days later, Errol was in good enough humor that he could actually listen to stories about Raphael Sarasola without getting a headache.

"You believe this stuff?" asked Errol halfway through. "This sounds like Walt Disney to me."

"Why would he make it up?"

"To impress you."

"He probably thinks he can impress me without going to any lengths."

"No doubt. Go on."

While Gray tried to draw the narrative out for as much of the drive as she could, the story didn't take long to tell, as Raphael's version had been quick and dry. Errol, however, was used to making home movies on scanty material, so in his mind filled it out quite nicely.

chapter nine

North Adams, Massachusetts, is a dark industrial town in the western part of the state that has not, unlike the eastern half, gotten the word about electrodes and microcircuits, the boom of high technology. North Adams invested in low technology, so is overshadowed not just by the foothills of the Berkshires but by long, brick textile mills, boarded, broken into, boarded again. On top of every hill these monuments loom; they've given the last two generations of fathers something to say. "Stay out of those old factories, boy. There's rats there bigger than you. Big as me, even. You think I'm scary? How'd you like a big old rat with whiskers and sharp teeth to tell you to finish your supper?"

But for Raphael Sarasola, imagining his father as a large and dangerous animal must not have been so difficult. Errol could see Frank Sarasola as a wide, hairy man who beat his child, as his father had beaten him, with a kind of sociological dutifulness, as if he'd read articles. What did he do for a living? Gray didn't know. Surely like everyone in that town he was professionally *disappointed*. Errol had driven through North Adams before, and he imagined the place as a mecca for bleak, disillusioned personalities who'd been romantic in their youth. Errol suspected the entire population sat at home listening to the radiator hiss day after day (it would be winter—it must always be winter in North Adams), listening to the wind shaft its way through the cracks in the window frame, always cold, always lonely, no matter who else was in the room, always put upon and grudging, and of course disappointed. On Fridays they probably passed out checks for the diligent disappointment the people had worked on all week, and there were bonuses for overtime, for those who made flat, eventless dreams in their sleep, full of dust and broken things and boarded-up brick.

Now, what did Frank do? Was he the mailman that children were afraid of, who never delivered any news? Errol liked that: Frank putting one more catalogue in the box, shoddy correspondence courses, death announcements of distant relations, last month's magazines.

It was his mother who'd named the boy Raphael, and you can bet Frank hated the name. "Ralph," he might say, "Ralph, you don't get that garbage carted off to the dump, you're going with it, understand? You can just move there. You could lie down on that mattress that caught fire over at Mrs. Willis's when she fell asleep smoking in bed. You saw that thing, all black and springy? Sound comfy, *honey, sweetie, lover boy*—" He imitated Raphael's mother by spitting these endearments like a string of profanities.

Raphael had to come by his looks from somewhere, so his mother must have been pretty. A little cringing; she was married to Frank. (What was her name? Errol made one up with care. Elise, Camille, Gabrielle . . . No, something simple. Dora. Nora. Nora would do.) But even given the occasional lucky throw of genetics and the unattractive cowering with which Nora must have buried her looks, for Raphael to have turned out with those long, sallow, carved features, his mother must have been something to see. Then how did she end up with Frank? All right, Frank the Inventive, Frank the Strong, but also Frank the Violent, Frank the Mongoloid? For Errol imagined Frank as a man of colossal thickness in every respect.

Errol had several theories. The first, pregnancy, he discarded as dull. It too patly explained why Frank would resent his son, and it did not explain how Frank would ever be in a position to get Nora pregnant in the first place. Why would she even share a Coke with a man like that? Pretty Nora, with all those ideas of hers, all her pictures? For Nora wanted to be an artist. When she first married she could only finagle enough money from her husband for cheap, chalky watercolors, though she yearned for oils. She used to explain to Raphael when he was young that the pale pink in her pictures was really "naphthol crimson," that a wash of leaves should really have been "peacock green," and she would search the house for the right color to show him, scrounging around scraps of material and the bright printing on ten-cent coupons and the quick-sale vegetables darkening in the hydrator until she found the sample she was looking for.

No, Errol had to get back to this: Frank and Nora. Nasty Old Frank and Lovely Nora. Explain this, Errol told himself. You're an anthropologist. Put some of those theories to work for once.

It made sense that for a whole town to make its living being disappointed, each citizen had to do an initial internship in expectation. Errol figured this precious period of enchantment hit at about seventeen. That was the age that Nora had hung a bedspread down the middle of the room she shared with her sister to create her "studio," with an old bulletin board for an easel and the chair swiped from her mother's vanity as a stool. Nora did portraits of people she'd never met and landscapes of places she'd never been. In the faces there wasn't a line or a sag, in the landscapes not a board or a brick.

Now, Frank had been seventeen himself. Frank had not always been so wide. Perhaps, too, the beatings he'd endured as a child had given him resilience, power, energy. No doubt he'd learned to hit back. No doubt he had plans, Frank did. Frank was going to "get out." (Surely planning to get out was a major pastime in North Adams—and judging from the number of digits dropping off the population sign every time Errol drove through town, an occasionally successful one. Errol knew that pastime well, though. Getting out always meant getting back in somewhere else. When you were born breathing that kind of bleakness in the air, it got into your lungs. You developed a taste for it, as for nicotine. Tarry and dangerous, bleakness was easy to pick up elsewhere—there were a lot of nasty boarded-up little towns in New England to absorb refugees from North Adams and make them feel at home.)

That's right. Nora, in this illness that struck the residents of the town in the prime of their young adulthood, could paint landscapes but could also have remained indefinitely in the room with the 60-watt overhead light and the bedspread beginning to tear on the nails that held it to each wall and the hairs falling out of her cheap brushes one by one and sticking into the paint.

She wanted privacy, and she was pretty, with amazing thick dark hair and tall bushy eyebrows that mingled sweetly above her nose, but she didn't have a fire under her; she needed Frank to "get out." And it was the oddest thing. In the end he did help her do just that. But by staying where he was.

So it wasn't hard to picture. The illness subsided. Frank layered in thickness like a candle being dipped once, twice, three times in a vat of hot wax. Nora at least had her pictures; nothing presented itself, as nothing ever presents itself, and there was always a living to be made being disappointed in North Adams.

Frank might have made it suddenly through with an occasional housewife on his route who asked him in for coffee on a cold day, with hot fresh bread and solid sleep, with one child who waved and wasn't afraid of him—Frank might have anchored himself to these minor satisfactions like a rock climber pulling from chink to chink, but what fouled Frank's steady, dutiful climb through his life was prettiness. Nora cowered, but in the morning when she was still asleep, the cringing wouldn't have been squeezing her face together yet, so Frank would wake up to her hair wide on the pillow, her lips full and parted, her small brown nipples hard from the cold when Frank took too much blanket. Now, you might suggest that Frank use Nora's hair on the pillow as one more chink to lift himself through the rest of his day, that he, all right, love her; you might also suggest, since there were many mornings when Frank looked over to find her lips fuller than usual and purpling, her eyes webbed in blue veins and swollen to thin slits, her nostrils encrusted with red crystals clinging to the hairs inside, that he did not. Yet to imagine that because Frank pulverized his wife he didn't love her would be to misunderstand prettiness—or at least Frank and prettiness. Surely

Frank felt that ache next to her in the morning, that yearning for what, presumably, he already had, that drawing as if even in her sleep she'd gotten hold of string in his gut and was tugging from a point just under his rib cage and could at any time pull out a stream of his insides through a little hole she had drilled there. What was a man like Frank to do with prettiness? When he'd already entered it, married it, even? Frank, not a sophisticated or a subtle man, had done all he knew to do. There it was, always pulling and tugging on the pillow, and Frank didn't like wanting something, especially wanting something he already had. What good was marrying the bitch, for God's sake, if he still had to get her somehow, do something?

So Frank came up with his own private therapy. To hit her was to do something, and to punish her for making him feel funny in the morning, not as a man should. And if he hit her long enough and hard enough, the next day he didn't feel funny or drawn or aching at all, because Nora no longer had a problem with prettiness.

If it were only Nora, Frank might have been able to keep this doing something under control. But there was the other prettiness, harder to suppress. There were her pictures, outside him, of places he couldn't recognize, of faces that made him jealous. There were strange men in his house with high cheekbones and dark complexions and heads of hair like the one he was losing. They had wide-open eyes without any disappointment glazing over the pupils like cataracts. He began to suspect her of seeing someone else, someone dark and quiet and somehow terrible, until he looked hard at his own son.

That was the way the boy always looked, even when Frank beat him, or especially then, with that stoic set of his mouth, stupidly relaxed, with the wide cavern of his eyes, stupidly trusting. Unlike Nora, his son grew more beautiful with violence: his color rose, his lips deepened, his eyes drove farther to the back of his head. Frank tried hard to teach the boy fear, hatred, and dishonesty—anything unattractive—but Raphael simply seemed to take in the beatings of his childhood like so much information, like part of the way the world was put together that he had better understand early. Frank got the impression as the boy watched him step by step take down the leather strap and call him over that his son was grateful for the instructions he got on his father's knee, the way other children were glad to learn about birds and flowers and trees. So Frank taught him about violence, and he taught him about beauty and about power: that is, by the frustrated look in his father's eye, even after the most drastic afternoons, with Frank finally off at the kitchen table slumped and picking at his food and his son red but erect and standing in the opposite corner of the room, Raphael understood that his father had beaten him, but the son had won. They both knew that; Frank would beat him again for winning and so lose once more, and again after that, and again.

Frank lost always and everything, out of love. If Frank had cared nothing for beauty and promise, he would have left the boy alone. If Frank had cared nothing for his wife, he wouldn't have staged a scene so carefully, so perfectly, to lose her. If he hadn't loved her, he wouldn't have known so well what to do to make her leave.

Raphael had told Gray of coming home from school one day to find the house in a shambles which, even for the Sarasolas, was impressive. Errol assumed that, as in most violent households, fighting was ritualized: we can break this, we don't break this;

we stay out of this room; we say these things, we do not say these other things, ever. In this case the rules had evidently been broken, along with a lot of furniture.

"You waiting for some professor to walk in off the street and discover you, Nora? 'Oh, what *genius, mad*-ame! This one picture is worth a *mil*-lion dollars!'"

"Stop it, Frank," said Nora. She would have been standing straight. She would have spoken quietly. She would have looked pretty today.

"Grow up, will you?" Frank went on. "When a kid brings home his scribbling, you put it on the wall, but at some point you gotta put the crayons away. It's today, Nora. Today's your graduation, Nora. You're thirty-five fucking years old, with little lines around your eyes and your tits down to your elbows—kindergarten is *over*."

"It's not a good idea to do this, Frank," said Nora. "Maybe you should stop now." She might have warned him then almost kindly.

"I've humored you, Nora, but that picture's pathetic, babe. That looks no way in hell like my face, darling. You just don't have it."

"I think, Frank, that it captures something—"

"Bull-fucking-shit, Nora!" Frank screamed. "That thing looks like some fantasy, some cartoon! You ever look at my face, Nora? Since you're an *artiste*, you're supposed to observe, right? Look at me, Nora. Look at the real fucking McCoy."

For a moment the living room froze. Raphael remained where he'd come in by the door, searching the wreckage for the offending catalyst of this event. Somewhere behind a shattered lamp or crumpled chair he'd spotted it: Nora's first portrait of her husband. True, it didn't look too much like him. She'd made him thinner, shorn off the layers of wax, the heavy jowls, the width of his neck. She'd drilled his eyes out and cleaned the whites clear. He looked younger and not like a postman. He was focusing on something far away. He looked smart. He looked pretty.

Yet Nora did as she was instructed and looked at the real fucking McCoy. "I see you, Frank," she said quietly, and walked upstairs.

There must have been some younger part of him, the Frank in the portrait, that wanted to bolt up the stairs and weep and throw himself over her suitcases. Instead, older Frank grabbed the portrait out of the shards of glass and flung it against the wall. The stretcher cracked, and the canvas folded; the eyes narrowed; the expression soured and twisted on the floor.

"What are you looking at?" he shot at Raphael. Raphael said nothing.

Hangers clattered one by one above the ceiling; drawers of the dresser opened and closed; bags bumped stair by stair down from the attic. Frank's stomach churned from a bilious satisfaction: no more desire, no more hole under his rib cage. Frank could get up in the morning and decipher incomplete addresses and misspelled names and bad handwriting, wrestle with packages a quarter inch too big for the box—that was the *story*, Nora. But no, Nora had to live in her own little world, and Frank couldn't take it anymore. Frank imagined this sounded very good. He would have to practice: "Her own little world. I couldn't take it anymore."

Errol had to tear himself away from Frank. Frank Sarasola was not the hero of this story. Frank would have to be left in that house, the clapboard in need of paint, the porch screen door coming off its hinges, the front yard with only patches of crab-grass. Errol would have to leave Frank with the dishes piling and breaking in the kitchen, stains permeating the enamel on the counters, Frank getting tired of frozen fried chicken.

It must have been a strange moment, and Errol was attracted to constructing it: the mother at the door with the bags announcing she was taking the car, the son right there, her son in the doorway; perhaps he'd even helped her carry the suitcases down the stairs; perhaps they loaded the car together. Frank and Nora not talking. Just Nora and her son, hurtling toward that moment when the key would turn in the ignition and one or both of them would never see that clapboard again, never pick at the flakes of paint while sitting in the porch chair, never listen to the door squeal and rattle on its one and a half hinges. One or both of them. The mother would take the son, or not. Take, or not. Or not.

The car packed, Nora ran a comb through her hair and didn't cry. Deftly she and Raphael positioned themselves on the porch, the son careful not to be any closer to the house, to Frank, to her whole past life with the swollen lips and Frank's peculiar hatred of his own desire, than she was. They faced each other equidistant from the broken porch door. A long time. Until Nora made a gesture toward him, but one which looked less like the kind of motion of enclosure that people make toward each other when they are about to take a long trip together than the gesture of despair and regret that a woman makes when she leaves by herself. So Raphael took a step toward the screen door; Nora was now nearer the stoop. Nearer the car. Nearer wherever she was going.

The boy shrugged. "How would you support us? Me?"

Nora shrugged back.

"How will you support yourself?"

Nora laughed a little. "Portrait painting."

Raphael was Frank's child, too. "Sure," he said. "You mean you'll waitress in a diner a couple towns away from here."

"Farther," Nora shot back.

He could have cried; he was only thirteen, and that would have been fine. He could have run to her. He could have held her and they would have gone together. But some people don't do that. Frank didn't do that. Raphael didn't do that, not that afternoon and not once since then, Errol was sure.

"Maybe," said Nora, her eyes flooded in a panic as she saw her son standing too straight against the doorway, searing black eyes dry and lips together and still and cheeks sucked in against his teeth. "Maybe we could work something out—later—"

"Don't say that," said Raphael coldly. "I'm supposed to sit here and wait for you? *Mother?*"

Nora took a step backward.

"I have school," said Raphael. "I don't want it interrupted. I want out of this ugly town, Mother. But if I go with you now, I'll just end up in another one. Won't I?"

"I thought Boston—"

"Come on! You know what the rents are like in Boston."

"Are they bad—?"

Raphael stamped his foot. "Mother! Like Dad said, grow *up*." Ah, thought Errol. He meant, Mother, you're supposed to be saying this. You're supposed to tell me about rents; you're supposed to tell me why I can't go with you. Why are you making me do this for you, come up with your excuses?

Nora looked down at the steps. "All right," she said quietly. "I don't have much money. I'll come back for you when I have a job. Understand?"

"I understand, Mother. That I can live without you. That you can live without me. So, good luck with your little paintings, Mother. I'll be *fine*."

"Sweetheart," she might have said after he closed the door in her face. "Everyone can live without everyone else." And the sad thing is, she would have been right.

D id she ever come back?" asked Errol.

"Raphael claims she might have, but she wouldn't have been able to find him. That seems unlikely, though. Even in his situation a lot of people in town must have known where he was."

"So Ralphie has illusions like the rest of us."

"At least on this point. It's rather encouraging."

"Did he tell you much about the next few years? The hole he moved to?"

"Only what I told you. Why, are you interested?"

"Sure. I was a movie fiend as a kid."

"Then I'll find out more. He does seem almost proud of it."

Errol waited, then, for the background research before he filmed the next reel.

chapter ten

By the time Gray turned the knob of the front door, Errol had strode quickly away from the window and was sitting in one of the armchairs on the opposite side of the den. He'd managed to find a book and pose himself as if in great concentration, loudly turning a page as she walked in.

Errol looked up to find Gray closing the door behind her with exaggerated care, the way preachers close their Bibles. It was a sentimental scene he wished desperately to deface. Had someone handed him a shaving-cream pie, Errol would have thrown it.

"What are you reading, Errol?" she asked vaguely.

With irritation he found himself holding *Il-Ororen: Men without History*. "Nothing important," said Errol, throwing the book down. "Have a nice ride home with Ralphie?"

"He has an amazing car." Her voice sounded different. Soft. "A Porsche." Gray leaned against the wall and tilted her head back. "White, with black interior. Leather. He has windshield wipers for his headlights." She laughed.

"You sound like a sixteen-year-old."

"Yes, that car brings it out in me. But when I was really sixteen—let's see, it was the end of the Depression—no one had Porsches, Errol."

"So you're reliving the youth you never had? And that explains it?"

Gray cocked her head. "Explains what?"

"Your perfectly normal behavior this evening."

She looked at Errol with curiosity, but let the barb go by. "As I was saying, it will do 130. Without even breathing hard."

"Please don't tell me that you drove from Tom's to here at 130 miles an hour. Please don't."

"All right, I won't."

Gray distractedly collected magazines on the table in front of him and looked down to find Errol's heel rising rapidly up and down. Errol found he couldn't make it stop. His leg shook the floor, and a vase on the coffee table rattled on its protective glass.

"We are either having a small earthquake," she said carefully, "or you are annoyed."

"Well," said Errol.

"Yes?"

"I didn't want to drive the coupe back for you, Gray. I'd planned to go home from the party."

"That's what you said, so—oh, you meant your own apartment. I'm sorry. You haven't been there in a couple of months. I just assumed—"

"Don't assume."

"Fine." She was impossible to perturb this evening. "Next time, though, be a little more demonstrative. I would have driven you home if I'd known that's what you wanted. However, if you know ahead of time that you're going to make yourself suffer in that cardboard box for the night, it might be better to take your own car."

"Of course," said Errol coldly. To keep his leg from shaking, Errol stood up and faced away.

G ray and Errol were accomplished partygoers. Like most things they did, parties were a team effort. Errol would pull Gray away from climbers; Gray would save Errol from divorcées. Gray would be eccentric and even insulting; she'd tell stories and try to draw lots of attention and then get it and be bored. Errol would be lower-key but surprise people with his sense of humor, though most of his jokes would be at his own expense. They were a pair.

But this evening at Tom Argon's they had gone once more from pair to trio. As Errol walked into the dining room with Gray, there, squarely positioned by the rum balls and fudge pies—all Gray's favorites—was the inevitable Mr. Sarasola. At each elbow Raphael had collected a beautiful woman: a tall underweight blonde with a fistful of carrot sticks, and—Errol cringed—Arabella. Both women were chattering away, the sharp shoulders on one side and the high, lightly freckled breasts on the other, both rising and falling with excitement, over a movie, a book—it obviously didn't matter. Raphael himself stood between them, nodding his head once or twice and meticulously taking apart a heart-shaped strawberry tart. While he did seem to be cocking an ear, most of his concentration was going into this tart. Most people at stand-up gatherings eat quickly and with embarrassment; Raphael ate slowly and with precision. Flake by flake he dissected the pastry. Delicately he edged his fingernail between the slices of strawberry to separate it into discrete cross sections. Lightly he swabbed the gelatinous cornstarch binding from around the fruit, taking the red filling drop by drop to his lip on the tip of his forefinger. Gradually he laid the specimen bare, nudging the raw red tissue out of its shell. At last, in the middle of the china lay four flaps of clean wet fruit. Raphael looked down at them with the satisfaction of a surgeon, as if he expected the slices, like ventricles, to beat on his plate.

Raphael looked up between the two women, his eyes flushing like torches; Errol stepped back from the heat. Color rose in the sallow cheeks. The lips filled and darkened, like fruit before fire.

"Mr. Sarasola," said Gray.

He collected the slices on his plate and held them out to Gray. But he had licked them! Errol wanted to warn her, But it has his saliva on it! Gray walked forward and took the strawberry in her mouth. Her lips touched his fingers.

An hour passed, and Gray disappeared. Searching for her through Tom's sprawling Tudor house, Errol felt inarticulate and short. When guests tried to talk to him he mumbled and wriggled away. Errol had to remind himself that he was an adult and he knew these people. Still, an odd little-brother feeling was overtaking him in every room. Errol felt lost and deserted and sad. How many times had she done this to him? Not Gray. His sister Kyle.

Four years older, pretty and popular, Kyle had naturally gathered groups. Wherever the brother and sister went, Kyle would have a band behind her after only a few hours. As young as ten, Kyle collected mostly boys, whom she would order about. They obeyed gratefully, and so did Errol. Kyle was physically strong, and up to sixteen was still able to beat boys her age at races and arm wrestling.

Kyle had been inventive, Errol had to concede. He could have played by himself, after all, or made his own friends. But it was more fun with Kyle; she had better ideas and older friends. She directed plays with intricate plots and created wild injuries after fights, wrapping swaths of torn sheet around Errol's arms and legs until he could hardly walk. Yet for all those ideas, all that energy, Errol had paid plenty. Like most petty tyrants, Kyle had been fickle, and her loyalty, fierce one day, dissolved the next. You couldn't trust her; that was part of the excitement. Kyle was on your side, "Kyle and I," but one false move and it was Kyle and somebody else. All this had been entirely instructive. As an adult Errol had often used his experience with his sister in understanding manipulative tribal leaders and dangerous Central American dictators.

Yes, that was how she kept her command from being boring, with "endless shifting alliances." Still, there were single incidents for which Errol had yet—for Christ's sake, at forty-eight—to forgive her. Somehow, isolated and confused and removed from his escort in this party full of people he knew who seemed like strangers, Errol remembered being eight years old more vividly than he wished to and felt bitter.

"The Lowry Boys will be here in a few minutes," Kyle had told him. "You're going to listen to their conversation and find out where they hid the secret tapes. Then, when they're not looking, you spring out of the cabinet and capture them. I'll be behind this door, and I'll help you tie them up." Kyle laughed and looked with a sidelong glance at two other band members. Everyone laughed, but in a slightly odd way. When Errol joined their laughing, they stopped, and Errol found he was hee-hee-heeing by himself.

"Okay, Kyle," said Errol soberly. "Can we leave them tied up to the table for hours and hours, like last time?"

"Errol," said Kyle slyly, towering tall and thin and clever above him, "whenever I capture somebody I leave them for quite a while. You know that." Laughter again. Errol joined in. They stopped. "Ready?"

Errol faced the built-in corner cabinet in the dining room. Kyle had removed one of the shelves so that there was just enough room for Errol to crawl in. Scrabbling up on a chair, Errol found he could fit in only by burying his head in his shoulders and drawing his knees tightly to his chest. Even then Kyle had trouble getting the double doors completely closed.

"Get all the way into the corner, Errol."

"Kyle—"

"Sh-sh. You have to be quiet and wait, Errol. Wait and wait."

Errol bunched up even more and moaned faintly as he heard the latch click. Through the panes of glass he could see his sister grin and stride away.

After a few minutes Errol's neck began to hurt and he yearned to unbend his legs. It was getting hot. His breath fogged up the glass, and Errol could no longer see whether the Lowry Boys had entered or not. Errol hummed a little tune. He wrote his name in condensation on the pane. He tried another position but found he hadn't enough leeway. Soon small shooting pains ran up and down his back. Errol pressed his head against the shelf above him, but this one was nailed in. Gently he tested the double doors, though hoping not to open them all the way because that would make Kyle angry. There was no danger of that, though. The doors gave slightly and stopped fast. Errol pressed harder, taking rapid shallow breaths. The doors still stuck. Gradually it dawned on Errol that the latch closed on the outside, so there was no way for him to "spring" out of the cabinet, Lowry Boys or no Lowry Boys.

"Ky-le!" cried Errol softly. For some reason, even though she'd fooled him about the doors, Errol still imagined she was stationed in the next room as she'd promised. "Kyle, I can't get out!"

Nothing. The glass buzzed from the vibration of his voice. Errol cried louder, until the sound of his sister's name hurt his ears in that small space. He rapped his knuckles loudly against the panes. His grandparents weren't home; Kyle was babysitting. No one came. When Errol stopped shouting for a moment, the compartment was deathly quiet.

Finally, Errol remembered, he'd lost control, and that was what saved him. Errol felt his knees and elbows ram up against the doors. His lungs filled and his shoulders widened, until, his voice hoarse and his knees bruising, Errol heard a long, high crack and the latch splintered free. Gracefully the door swung open.

Panting, Errol had to pick up his legs with his hands to swing them off the edge. He was alive; he could breathe; he was going to kill Kyle.

He'd found them at last in the basement. On an odd impulse, then, Errol found the door to Tom's basement and ambled downstairs. He heard laughter. He had heard laughter. Kyle and the boys of the neighborhood were clustered on the Ping-Pong table, conspiring.

"You ditched me," said Errol in the middle of the stairs. "Why didn't you just say you didn't want to play with me today?" Errol began to cry, and all the boys were silent. "Why did you lock me in the cabinet?"

"'Cause I couldn't just tell you that, Errol," said Kyle clearly. "You wouldn't get the message, would you? You tag along with everything I do. How else was I going to get rid of you?"

"Who's there?" asked Gray from below. Errol had remained halfway down the stairs. He walked down a few more steps to find Gray and Raphael playing pool by themselves.

"It's Errol," he said stiffly. "Don't let me disturb your game, though. I was just exploring the house." Errol began to walk back up.

"No, don't go!" Gray called back. "You can play the loser. Which will be me, I assure you."

"Is that Gray Kaiser?" asked someone from the top of the stairs. "In flight again?" Five or six anthropologists-at-large came trooping down the stairs, and Errol had no choice but to go down with them to get out of their way. "There's no getting away from fame, Gray," said their leader, a rangy guy of about forty whom Errol had run into before. Bob Something. His face was waxy and tan, for he'd done a lot of fieldwork in New Guinea, and handsome in that ageless American Western way.

In no time fifteen people gathered in the basement, so there was no longer an intimate duo to interrupt; Errol stayed.

Raphael and Gray had only been practicing shots; Raphael racked the balls for the upcoming game. Now, Errol asked himself as Raphael arranged the balls quickly and in order, how well do you think Sarasola plays pool? How well exactly? Tell me, Errol begged of whoever controls these things, tell me he is awkward. Tell me he talks a big line, but when his turn comes around he bounces the cue ball onto the floor. Tell me that in the middle of the game he frequently ruins the table by digging his stick into the felt, tell me this will happen tonight and we will *all be embarrassed*. Tell me, Errol pleaded as Raphael removed the rack and lined up the cue ball, that when he breaks the cue goes *puh* and meanders into a corner pocket and we will laugh—*tell me*, Errol heard screaming in his head as Raphael's stick pumped quickly behind him, *this guy can't play pool*.

The cue whacked hard and fast just to the side of the one and bounced back. The balls sprang over the table. Two sank, and they were both solids. Errol sat down heavily. Big surprise. It was going to be a long night.

The entire basement began to watch. Raphael went about the table, *pock, pock, pock*, simple and direct. No consideration, no angling, no figuring of dots. His game was fast and easy and sweet. The balls cracked against one another and followed mathematically perfect trajectories toward their pockets.

"Looks to me like this guy grew up with a table in his parents' den, Gray," said Bob. "You've been suckered."

"No," said Raphael coldly.

Gray hadn't taken her eyes off Raphael since he first chalked his stick. "Where did you pick this up?"

"Rudy's Blue Tip Billiards Parlor, North Adams, Mass."

"Played a lot of hooky, huh?" said Bob.

"I went to school every day," said Raphael, not looking up

from the table. "Played pool late—three, four in the morning. In the winter." He nicked a ball into a side pocket.

"So that was where the guys hung out when you were a kid?" asked Bob.

"The guys"—Raphael shrugged—"were a bunch of old drunks. Never brushed their teeth. Breathed in my face. Put their hands on me."

"But you were willing to sacrifice anything to finagle their pool secrets?"

"I was willing to sacrifice a lot, Mr. Anthropologist"—finally Raphael looked up at Bob—"to keep warm."

That shut Bob up. He didn't understand, and he wasn't going to.

Raphael sank one more ball and turned gently to Gray. "This must be boring you."

"Not at all. You're terrific."

Raphael leaned over and hit the cue into a beautiful setup for stripes. He handed Gray her stick. "All yours."

When she took the stick, her hand touched his. Errol was watching.

This was not like the tennis game. Gray would not now tower over the table and shatter balls into the corners two at a time. Gray may have played pool twice in her life. She did sink this setup—who wouldn't?—but she scratched.

"When you want the cue to bounce back rather than follow the ball," Raphael told her, "hit it a little below the center."

Raphael brushed her arm; their hairs intermingled. A light sweat broke out on Errol's forehead.

Again Raphael set Gray up. When she started to shoot he stopped her with a hand on her bare shoulder. "More over here."

Three fingers on her waist. "Lean over a little more." Shoulder again. "And you might find it easier to rest the stick in this cradle here—" He traced the valley between the tendons of Gray's forefinger and thumb.

Errol watched as Raphael molded Gray's game, arranging her body, taking her arm to show her the length of the stroke, standing behind her to help her position the bridge so that the tips of his nipples touched her back through his white shirt. Gradually her accuracy improved as he set up more sophisticated shots, but Errol paid less and less attention to the game itself. Instead, he watched Gray's shoulders round out of her sleeveless dress, as folds of white silk traced the curves of her body. Errol might even have enjoyed this game if it weren't for the frequent obstruction of his view: a hand on her back, an arm against her dress—the insistent eclipse of Mr. Helpful.

Errol noticed that the rest of the basement was following, like Errol, the progress of those hands: placed, removed, placed again, lightly, a finger—so deliberate, these moves, more like chess than like pool, deft, here, again, here, again, square to square. It was incredible to see: Gray Kaiser, tall and piercing and white like the icicle they all knew her to be, Gray the Snow Queen, who had sliced them all, swish, to the quick at one time or another, can you imagine, touched like *that*—Who is this guy?

Errol started.

"I said, who is this guy? Do you know him?" Bob repeated, sidling up beside Errol.

"A grad student," said Errol.

Raphael stepped back to watch Gray shoot. "You've already got a nice stroke," he told her. "Sharp, quick. Not timid. You play like a man."

"And that's the ultimate compliment?"

"If all women were like you, it wouldn't be," said Raphael. "But most of them aren't. So it is."

"You know, McEchern," Bob muttered, "there's something intensely irritating about that guy."

"What exactly?"

"For one, the way he shoots pool."

"You mean, because he's so good."

"No, it's the *way* he's good," said Bob. "Smooth. It's creepy."

What's creepy, you son-of-a-bitch, is that his little fingers are padding all over that white dress and that you've been after Gray Kaiser off and on for ten years yourself—that's what's creepy, cowboy. But Errol only replied blandly, "I don't know what you mean, Bob. He seems like a perfectly nice kid to me."

Seething, Bob went to find a more sympathetic audience and another drink.

A few minutes later, as Raphael leaned over Gray to explain a difficult shot, Bob and his friends laughed; something in their tone made Raphael turn abruptly toward them.

"Care to share the joke, gentlemen?"

"Don't trouble yourself, young man," said one of them. "I guess you just had to be there."

"I *am* there," said Raphael.

The basement grew quiet.

"We were just wondering," said Bob, "how your Ford Fellowship proposal was coming."

"Quite well," said Raphael.

"That was the joke."

No one spoke.

"But that isn't a funny joke," said Raphael distinctly. "Do you notice? No one is laughing."

Bob squared his chin and tugged his belt down on his hips with a Shootout at the OK Corral posture sufficiently ridiculous to make you swear off alcohol for the rest of your life. "I just couldn't help but wonder if you know who you are playing with," Bob slurred. "Who exactly."

"We've been introduced," said Raphael.

"Well, that's nice," said Bob. "But do you realize you're playing games with a mature woman?"

"Excuse me," said Raphael, smiling. "I don't quite know what you're getting at. Please explain."

"Bob," said someone next to him, "maybe you'd better—"

"I'll explain," said Bob. "I'll explain that this lady is old enough to be your mother, and while we think it's pretty funny when we make jokes at your expense, what is *not* funny is your screwing around for fun or profit with a woman who has friends. A lot of friends."

"So many, it seems," said Gray at last, exhaling, "that I can afford to lose one this evening." Quietly she set her cue on its rack. "Mr. Sarasola, would you care to escort the Ancient One to her car? Then maybe you can manipulate this declining moron into funding your own irresponsible projects. Errol?"

In a line the three of them filed up the stairs, and Errol had the strange sensation of himself as a member of a trio of cartoon superheroes.

When they got outside Gray shook her head. "I could have sworn Robert Johanas was smarter than that."

"I felt sorry for him, Gray," said Errol. "He was drunk, and besides, he was defending you."

"From what?" Gray looked from Errol to Raphael.

"Pool sharks," said Raphael.

"Mister, after tonight I'm going to become one."

They laughed and walked toward the street, and again Errol had a flash of TV, though this time, with Gray's hair loose in the night breeze as she strode between the two men, of old *Mod Squad* reruns.

"Honestly, Errol," said Gray, "do I really seem so gullible, so fragile? What's there to be afraid of?" She handed Errol the keys to the coupe. "Would you take the car home? Thanks." With that the two of them disappeared, and Errol was left with the keys dangling in his hand and her questions still unanswered; Errol considered them as he drove back, unexpectedly, by himself.

Well, did she seem fragile? Errol didn't hesitate: absolutely. Gray was a walking *Titanic*, coolly and permanently afloat. She would not watch out. She would not send out regular sonar to test for cold and dangerous diversions, but would slide along the surface of her life as if, unlike mere mortals, her prow did not plow into any deep sea. Certainly if Gray were a vessel she would be a great ship. But great ships sank big. That was a matter of historical record.

And what's there to be afraid of?

Suddenly one of those images again. Errol had to remind himself to keep his eye on the road. Of Gray. She was sitting in that big leather chair in the den, small and thin. She looked as if her face had been tacked up for years and someone had finally pulled the pins out. Her shoulders drooped; her skin was slack. This was an image of Gray Kaiser that Errol didn't want in his life. Don't ever, Gray, sit in that chair that way. Call me, anything. Just keep the pins in. Keep those eyes flecked and darting and elusive. Remain, though I know I tire of it, amused. Play games with me and keep me in my place. Humiliate your peers. Be busy. Be easily bored and impatient and make single deadly remarks. Whisk across the floorboards of that manse of yours, and hurry. Be late, make people wait. Sear the courts of this city with serves in the far corner of the square. Fly to foreign countries and let me watch you carefully explain to tribal leaders you cannot marry them, not this trip. Errol drove a little faster. He didn't want her to be rammed in the hull, sink, fill, and grow cold. He didn't want her to grow old.

Errol arrived at the house in a protective mood. He swung out of the coupe and slammed the door, eager to stay up late, have another drink. Gray wasn't back yet, so Errol switched on the lamp by the walkway, went into the den, and rummaged through the cabinet for glasses. Through the window beside him he heard a powerful motor surge and die; he pushed the curtain back to see Gray and Raphael pull themselves out of a gleaming, low-lying car. Their steps lingered. Raphael said something; they laughed and stopped, turned to one another and stared. Each was wearing white; they glowed in the light of the lantern. Raphael's cheeks rose high and bleached like raw bone. His eyes fell to black shadow. The stray ends of his hair shone in a faint halo around his head. Gray walked toward him. The folds of her dress rippled. There was a quiver to her profile, a tremor, a bending like a straight line seen through curved glass.

Errol saw something long, white, and shining rise in the night.

Quietly Errol switched off the light in the den so he couldn't be seen. Was this masochism? he wondered. No, he decided. He wished to live in the world as it actually existed. Out of some sad loyalty to exterior reality, then, he pushed the curtain back aside.

That left hand was still where Errol had seen it last, or perhaps a little farther into her hair. Their bodies were closer. The other hand (he'd watched these all night, hadn't he? Why stop now?) was at the small of her back. Up the left fingers crept into her scalp. Errol could see awfully well. Nice of them to stand right by the lamp.

Their lips met so gently that the lamp shone in the diamond space left between them. Raphael turned her toward the light. Gray went white, Raphael to shadow. Errol could see her expression now. She looked terrified. Her body seemed to crumple. Raphael pulled her so that his back rested against the lamppost. So braced, he assumed the full weight of her body against him.

Gray grew smaller and smaller. Errol couldn't rid himself of the image of an animal gorging itself on the veldt, feeding from the open wound of a formerly fleet and delicate creature. Why did she look so slight? Why did her dress blend so terribly into the folds of his shirt? The picture in front of him began to blotch and purple, as if Errol were rubbing his eyes. The white figures receded into the trees and disappeared. Black flowers bloomed in Errol's peripheral vision. The scope of his vision itself narrowed and rounded and withdrew like the last blue spot on a picture tube.

Errol blinked and shook his head. They were back, but separated, holding each other at arm's length. Letting go reluctantly, Gray turned toward the house. That was when Errol wiped his cheeks quickly and bolted to the other side of the room.

W hat took you so long?" asked Errol as Gray continued straightening the room with little efficiency.

"We got lost," said Gray.

"I guess at 130 miles an hour you got pretty far out of your way. You're getting old, Gray."

"I don't think that was the problem," she snapped, with the first irritation she'd shown since she walked in. "Anyway, it was a small detour. I'm back."

No. She was not all back. Errol watched her closely. A morsel had been gnawed off, a trickle of liquid sucked away. She stood a degree off the perpendicular. Her body was barely narrower. Her veins ran with several fewer drops.

Errol was suddenly exhausted and sagged in his chair. He felt his face blanch and his anger rise to his skin in a light sweat and evaporate into the late-night air. "Gray," he said with effort, "be careful, will you?"

Gray looked him in the eye. "I've been careful all my life."

"I wouldn't say that. The projects in the bush—"

"That's not what I mean. That kind of danger is easy."

"Yes," Errol admitted. "It's just—maybe it's good, being careful. Maybe that's the way you need to be."

"I'm not sure. I wonder."

They continued to look at each other, and with every passing second Errol grew wearier. "Are we going to use names?"

"Eventually. But not tonight." Lightly she put her hands on either side of Errol's face, kissed his forehead, and left for bed. Errol reached up and turned out the light, but remained in the den with the curtain of the front window fluttering in the breeze. The outside lamp was still on, and its rays fell on Errol's chair in long, pale shafts. The shadows of the trees shifted over the wall behind him, playing over the wildebeest skeleton as the branches whispered outside. Errol warily eyed the bones at his back, waiting for the wind to die and the shadows to settle before he walked heavily up to bed, stair by stair.

chapter eleven

The sounds at breakfast were unusually loud: the gurgle of the coffeemaker, the clump of the refrigerator door, the insistent click of Gray's heels. No one spoke. The clatter of a spoon in the sink was deafening.

"Maybe we should talk," Errol ventured at last.

"I really don't need you to lecture me."

"I didn't say—"

"You will, too; you'll lecture me and tell me how old I am and insult him—"

"It's nice to know, Gray, that I'm such a constant comfort to you." Errol gulped his last swallow of orange juice and slid his glass down the counter so that it slipped on the ridge of the sink and rolled around the trap. Disappointed the glass hadn't broken, Errol strode toward the door.

"Errol McEchern, come back here this instant."

Errol stopped, but kept his back to her. He folded his arms and looked at the ceiling.

"It's just—I want to enjoy this."

"Lecture!" Errol turned around. "Who do you think I am? Daddy?"

Gray sat down, spread her fingers on the table, and studied them. "I'm sorry. But sometimes around you I'm afraid I seem pathetic."

Errol leaned against the doorway and watched her, her head bowed, the arch of her neck sweeping long and sadly toward the table.

"You feel pathetic?"

"No! Errol! I feel—I'm no good at this."

"Go ahead."

"As if I'm in an airplane. One of those narrow military jets, a new design that hasn't been tested. Something slick and shiny and supersonic. *Sh-sh-shsh.*" Gray's hand took off from the table and soared in circles.

"Ever talk to one of those test pilots? It's a dangerous job. Sometimes there's something wrong with those planes. Sometimes they get up speed and start cracking apart. Pieces fall off. Engines cut out." Errol whistled and sent his own hand into a dive.

"Stop it. I find my metaphor and you wreck it. Literally. It's malicious."

Errol looked at her eyes, contracted now, with the pupils so drawn into their blue-gray fields that the aperture looked as if it might disappear completely. They asked: Will he call today? It *was* pathetic.

Through the morning, Errol read, as usual, about matri-archies. In preparation for the Lone-luk project, they were going through the literature on similar societies. Or at least Errol was. Gray's progress through the stack of books on her desk had not been impressive. She spent most of her time editing the Corgie documentary—splicing footage and ticking through reel after reel of Raphael. All morning he listened to the click of the projector from behind her closed door.

That afternoon Gray had a meeting with the Ford Fellowship Board. Arabella was at the library, so Errol answered the phone.

"Gray Kaiser, please."

The dryness of this request was of a rare and particular brand. "Sorry, she's out."

"No doubt this is Dr. McEchern."

"No doubt. Ralph, isn't it?"

A pause, a tiny, audible grimace. "Tell your master I called, would you?"

Errol clenched his jaw. "Why, sho, boss, I'll tell massa straight off."

"—You will tell her I called, will you not?"

"Of course. Is that all?"

Errol could hear Raphael smiling on the other end. "You are too much, McEchern, you know that? I can't believe you." Gently the phone clicked in Errol's ear.

"Ralph called," Errol informed Gray on her return. "He was rude."

"To you, Errol? I'm sorry."

She was not sorry. She had just taken off in her supersonic transport again, with the top down. Her eyes glazed from the wind; her hair streaked backward; her cheeks shone from the slap of the upper stratosphere. She began breathing more deeply, as if the air were thin up there. "I'll return his call, then." Her eyes flamed as she walked past Errol, reflecting the twin jets of her plane as she veered toward the phone.

"We're to expect a delivery," she said when she returned.

"Don't tell me," said Errol. "A bouquet of poison ivy. A corsage of thistles for your hair."

But Ralph sent worse. Errol was appalled. A UPS truck arrived. The box it delivered was large and full of holes. When Gray pulled out the cage inside, a little ratlike creature bit at her finger.

"What a beastly animal," said Errol.

Gray stared at the long brown body as it darted from wall to wall, jabbing at the bars with tiny gleaming teeth. "A ferret," she determined.

"They used them for hunting in the Middle Ages, didn't they? If I remember right, these little bastards are lethal."

Gray didn't take her eyes off the new pet. "There's one of these stuffed in the Museum of Natural History. It has a mouse in its mouth. Have you seen it?"

"I don't like them," said Errol point-blank. "I don't spend a lot of time in the rat section because I don't like them."

"It's so sleek. And conniving."

"Quite."

"And better without glass eyes. Look at them." She stooped and stared into the cage. The ferret glared back at her, clutching the bars with sharp, hooked paws. "So bright. As if he knows something."

"What does he know, Gray?"

"Too much for his own good."

"Or too much for yours."

"Look. So lithe. So charged. And the way it moves. Quick but graceful. I wonder if you can touch it."

"I wouldn't risk it."

Just then Bwana ticked into the foyer behind Errol and stopped dead, ten feet from his new companion. He let off a throaty growl, but when the ferret scrabbled toward the dog, the growl turned to a whine. Bwana stepped backward and barked once. The ferret hissed, and reached a claw through an interstice. Bwana stood stiffly in the doorway, sleek and striking as ever, but his pink-gray eyes were stricken. Braced away from the ferret, the dog began to bark uncontrollably, a rasping, panicky sound that filled all three floors of that tall Victorian house.

"Sh-sh, Bwana, Bwana," Gray crooned, but the dog was not getting any calmer. Nor did Bwana's fit soothe the ferret, which was now throwing itself against the side of the cage with its long, thin claws extended and its brilliant teeth bared.

Gray left the new pet to take Bwana's head between her hands and smooth the short gray hair. "Sh-sh, Bwana, he's not going to hurt you. So sweet, isn't he, Bwana, so pretty, Bwana, with pretty little teeth. With those long claws, I know, Bwana, he's scary, but he's our friend, Bwana. Our friends don't hurt us, now, do they? No, no, no. They don't, Bwana. No, they don't."

Bwana didn't believe her.

"Sh-sh . . ." She stroked the animal as it trembled under her hand. Gently she led the dog away.

"I think we should get rid of it," said Errol when she came back.

"No."

"Another pet? With travel—"

"There's Bwana, anyway—"

"This is a nasty, dangerous creature."

To bring the argument to a close, Gray took the ferret and locked it in the den away from the dog. Errol didn't pursue it.

Clearly this strange, hostile animal had already been insinuated into the household for the duration.

They were practically out the door the next morning before Gray informed Errol that they were not driving to New York, just the two of them. Raphael was going, too; in fact, he was driving. She liked his car.

So Errol found himself in the cramped back seat of the white Porsche. Gray's door shut with a clump like the refrigerator, airtight. Errol had to yawn to correct the pressure in his ears.

"Nice machine, Sarasola," said Errol gruffly. "Cost something, didn't it?"

"It cost someone something, yes." As Raphael pulled away from the house, he spun the wheel with three fingers. Errol's back pressed into the black leather as the car accelerated, to stop just in time at the next corner.

"I suppose Gray told you she received the token of your esteem."

"I thought it looked like an interesting animal. Unpredictable."

"I can predict it. Given the opportunity, it will do something unpleasant."

"I haven't named it yet," said Gray.

"How about a practical name?" said Errol helpfully. "Fur Collar. Coat Trimming. Muff Lining—"

"The ferret's name is Solo," said Raphael. The discussion was over.

Raphael slipped his arm over the back of Gray's seat and ran a fingernail lightly up and down her neck. Behind her, Errol could see the hairs rise at his touch. Errol felt embarrassed and forced himself to look out the side window, past which the scenery was whisking with appalling rapidity.

"We don't have to be at the museum by any particular time, do we?" asked Errol.

"No," said Gray.

They were on a secondary road that wouldn't reach the interstate for some miles. The road was hilly and full of blind turns. The speed limit was forty, yet Errol couldn't imagine they were moving that slowly. He edged toward the middle of the back seat to eye the speedometer. Raphael was holding the wheel with his three fingers, leaning languorously back in his seat. The wind from the corner window blew the driver's hair back and his collar open—why, you would never guess from this carefree figure that the car was doing sixty-five.

"We certainly are going to make good time, aren't we?"

"Yes," said Raphael.

"But I don't suppose we're really in a hurry, are we, Gray?"

"It never hurts to make the trip expeditiously," said Gray.

"It doesn't usually . . ." said Errol.

"But sometimes it hurts . . ." said Errol.

"Sometimes it hurts a whole lot . . ." said Errol.

He could as well have been shouting into the wind of the open window. Neither Gray nor Raphael looked around. Errol leaned forward and found that the speedometer now read seventy. On the next turn Errol was thrown to the side of the car. The road wasn't graded for this speed. Still, Raphael leaned back. Still, he kept one hand on Gray's neck. Still, he swept the steering wheel with three fingers. The air through Raphael's window began to roar.

"Don't you think we're moving a little rapidly?" said Errol.

Raphael rolled up the window at his side. Once the car was quiet, he replied in a level voice, "Excuse me, Dr. McEchern, I didn't make out what you said."

"Don't you think we're moving a little fast for this road?"

"Not really." They struck a straightaway and Raphael hit the accelerator.

"As one of your passengers, Sarasola, I'd like to request you stop speeding."

"When you're driving, McEchern, you can putter along however you like. Today I'm driving."

"I'm painfully aware of that."

The Porsche did hug the road admirably on the next turn, but Errol could feel that the vehicle was right at the point just before it would flip up on two wheels. Errol was gripping the rim of the seat so hard that the leather piping was tearing loose. Still, Raphael's three fingers draped languidly over the wheel.

"Sarasola," said Errol through his teeth, "of course I'm concerned for myself, like any other normal human being in extreme danger. But I realize putting the life of Errol McEchern in peril isn't likely to send you into throes. It's clear you have leanings toward self-destruction, so I won't appeal to you on the grounds of your own preservation. But if you have *any* feelings for the woman next to you, please slow this car down to a tenable speed."

"Gray K.," said Raphael, "do you want me to slow down?"

Errol turned to find Gray with her head back, her hands resting one on the other in her lap, her ankles crossed, and her expression impassive. "Drive as you wish," she said quietly.

"Gray, please!"

"Raphael is a good driver. I'd think you could see that."

"Good drivers don't do eighty-five in a forty-mile-an-hour zone."

"Good drivers have control, Errol. At any speed."

They took another turn, and Errol could feel the wheels on

the inside begin to lift and the back end of the car begin to shift—until they were around, and the car leveled and centered and surged off again. It took a moment, though, for the adrenaline to pump into Errol's system, so he felt his heart accelerate and his face drain only as they straightened out.

"Goddamn it," said Errol. "I was a teenager already, and once was enough. I'm grown-up now. Please let me out of this car."

Raphael lifted his foot from the gas. "You mean that?"

"I do."

"Fine," said Raphael, pulling up short and over to the side of the road. He got out and pulled the front seat forward.

As Errol stepped out of the car, he found his legs would barely support his weight. "It's obvious," said Errol, relieved to be able to look Raphael in the face when he spoke to him, "that you don't give a damn about Gray Kaiser or you wouldn't put her in this position for the sake of juvenile bravado. But the rest of the world does, understand? Me, I'll get a little write-up; you'll be two lines on the obituary page, in tiny print. But Gray is front-page material. Anything happens to her, you're going to remember, and so is everyone else."

"Are you through? We're going to New York."

"No, I'd like to consult my colleague, please. Take down any last requests. Check if I'm in the will. That sort of thing."

"Be my guest."

Errol went over to Gray and opened her door. "I imagine you can handle the exhibit on your own. I'll get back to Boston somehow."

"Errol, do you have to do this?" Gray looked pained and tired.

"Do *you* have to do this?"

"Do what?"

"Come with me. He's irresponsible. I like you. Don't kill yourself as a favor to me."

"You're making far too much of this."

"Too much! Jesus, why am I wasting my time? Look at the two of you. Cooler than thou. Who can be more imperturbable, what a contest. Cool at eighty, cooler at ninety, coolest at a hundred, until, cool as you've ever been in your lives, you go plowing through a guardrail and plant yourselves, Porsche and all, so far into the embankment that no one needs to bury you. Even Ralph is too old for this. But you, Gray, you—" Errol was so angry that he was on the verge of incoherence. "You who make fun of machismo—"

"You're the one who makes fun of machismo. I have a great deal of respect for it."

"Right," said Errol, slamming the door. He couldn't think of a parting line; he'd said all he had to say, so Errol stalked off down the road, hoping, in one terrible little flash, that they would redeem his gesture by having an accident. It was at that moment that Errol resented Raphael more than he ever had, not for speeding, for risking his life or Gray's, not even for forcing Errol to hitchhike back to Boston, but for making Errol so conscious of style and of power that he would take leave of the woman he cared for more than anyone else in the world and actually wish her ill for his own pride.

chapter twelve

Errol tromped for a couple of miles back down the road, kicking cans out of the way and stepping on wildflowers with satisfaction. However, it was hard to maintain this high quality of anger in the face of such a day. It was warm but not yet hot, and a light breeze held Errol in its breath and whispered that no one would have an accident on a morning like this one. The trees at his side listed and blurred, their leaves splashed in brushstrokes like Van Gogh's. There was hardly a car on the road, but once Errol stuck out his thumb, a pickup truck pulled over right away. Errol was forced to allow a finely tuned headache to ease into the summer air as he swung into the front seat and was sent so easily careening back toward Boston.

Errol placed the driver in his early thirties; from his dirty hands, leathered skin, and billowing arm muscles, Errol guessed he did manual labor. Errol prepared himself for a long ride of silence and taxes and weather.

"Don't tell me," said the driver. "You were a boring, screwed-up kid, and now you're making up for it."

"What?"

"I haven't seen anyone your age hitching since I had a fight with my dad by the side of the road when I was sixteen and swiped the car out from under him. There was Dad out there on the road, stranded, a regular Jack Kerouac in double knits.—I tried on a double-knit jacket once at a yard sale. Those things are *hot*, boy. Ever worn that stuff? Oh, I bet you have."

"You've got me wrong. I'm more the tweed and rumpled-cottons type. Patched elbows. Corduroys. Work shirts and painter's pants on weekends."

"Professor."

"No, but close. Go on with your story, though. Did you go back and pick him up?"

"I looped around. Passed by. My father red in the face, his chest bulging at his buttons, not sure whether to hold his thumb out, up, or down. Hysterical, really. He pointed his thumb toward the ground, looked like he was saying, 'Down with everything.' Poor Daddy. I tooted and waved and hit the gas."

"Did he get a ride?"

"'Course not. He walked a few miles to a gas station, nearly keeling over from the grueling journey. Called a fucking taxi, can you believe it? From forty miles away. Cost a fucking fortune, like, a hundred, hundred-fifty dollars. Which he tried to charge me. That was a laugh."

"He didn't get any money out of you?"

"How's the guy gonna get me to give him money if he can't even keep hold of his goddamned car?" The driver extended his hand. "Gabriel Menaker. Call me Gabe."

"Errol McEchern. And I was a strange kid, you were right there."

"I got an eye for them."

"I was actually headed toward normality when I was eighteen, until my older sister got married. That threw me for a loop."

"How's that, Aaron?"

"Errol. I was—close to her."

"You fucked her?"

"*No.*"

"Hey, don't act so shocked. Like, it happens all the time. I fucked my sister."

"Is that so," said Errol quietly.

"Sure. The younger one. No big deal. She loved it."

"Really?" asked Errol skeptically. "How much younger?"

"Four years. She was twelve. I helped her out, you know? That was no time in this country to be a virgin."

"You're quite an altruist."

"Hey, I'm giving you a ride. So don't come down like it was so terrible that I had a sick relationship with my sister."

"I didn't say that."

"You didn't have to. Come on. You probably wanted to fuck your sister blind, right?"

"Oh sure," said Errol with a sigh. "Everyone wants to sleep with everyone else, isn't that right? In the end? Isn't that the revelation we're all hurtling toward?"

Gabe leaned back, with his arms braced straight against the steering wheel and his eyes narrowed. "I guess you're right. It's pretty simplistic."

"And then eventually," Errol went on, "when we come to our realization, we can in fact have sex with everyone and with our pets and our doorknobs and our tennis rackets and all the other things we've secretly desired all our lives. And then everything will be different, I suppose. The planets will align in some special way."

Gabe smiled and nodded. "That's good. That's good, you're not some dumb guy. Maybe I'll take you all the way to Boston, after all."

"Don't go out of your way. Where are you headed?"

"I'm building this house in Boxford. Gotta deliver these two-by-fours in the back, but the rest of the crew is off today, so I'm loose after I unload. But what you said, that's good. See, you're right—I wasn't that close to my sister. I fucked her and I still wasn't that close. It didn't—uh—make so much difference."

"Well, maybe, with or without sex, all that's important is how someone feels about you, really. How you feel about them. Do you leave them beside the road and take their car or not? Can they make you pay for their taxi, or not?"

"Except no," said Gabe. "Getting back to this. Okay, I lied a little. We're in the truck, right? And I don't know you. I said she loved it. Well, it turns out she didn't. She wrote me this long letter a couple years ago—out of the blue, you know? Out of nowhere. I hadn't seen her in, like, five years. Shit, she must have been seeing some shrink or something. Anyway, typed, single-spaced, like, seven pages, all about how she hated it when she was a kid and I'd come into her room when my parents weren't home. Jesus. It was something. I mean, she *lost* it in that letter. So, what I'm getting at: it did make some difference, after all, my fucking her. Damnedest thing. I thought she liked it."

"You did not," said Errol.

Gabe's head whipped around. "How's that?"

"You did not think she liked it," said Errol calmly.

Gabe said nothing and rapped his fingers against the steering wheel. "All right," he said grudgingly, "I guess I knew she wasn't too hot on it. But, so, what I said still stands: fucking her made a big difference. She was pissed as all hell. She put this trip over on me like she was scarred for life or something."

"I believe it," said Errol. "But if you hadn't made her sleep with you, you would have done something else."

"Why?"

"You wanted to have power over her."

Gabe didn't say anything.

"And that," Errol speculated, "was why she was angry. She figured out what you were about."

"You mean she found out I was a son-of-a-bitch."

Errol shrugged, worried he'd gone too far.

Gabe laughed. "Well, good for her. She's right." He hit the steering wheel. "I'll have to write her back, then: 'Dear Glenda: You're right. Love, Gabe.' Think she'd get it?"

Errol laughed. "Maybe not. I'm sorry about butting in. I'm left alone a lot lately. I think too much."

"No problem. Long as I'm not bored, you can say whatever you want. But you never explained why you were hitching. Your car break down?"

Suddenly the whole ordeal with Raphael and the Porsche seemed a long time ago, and stupid at that. "I was with two friends of mine in a smart little sports car. The driver took this road at eighty-five, and I asked him to let me out. He obliged. Here I am."

Gabe scrutinized the road. "Eighty-five. I can see that. A good car?"

"Porsche. Handsome. Shiny. He takes great care of it. He's a pretty cold customer otherwise, so I suppose all his tremendous affection for the world at large has to go somewhere. I think it goes into lubrication and hard wax; pistons and valve jobs."

"Sounds pretty sexual."

Errol smiled, because they were already beginning to develop a joke between them, a good one, and they were strangers. "Oh yes. All imagery is sexual. Gets exhausting, interpreting all the time. Never being able to look at the Washington Monument without making a remark."

"So, is this guy a good driver?"

"I suppose. I don't know. He's very graceful," Errol remembered. "Smooth. He handles the car with connectedness, if you know what I mean."

"I think so, yeah."

"He's a good-looking man," Errol conceded. "He makes a pretty picture in that car. He drives like—" Errol stopped and smiled, because so often the same images recurred. "Like an animal. He and the machine together. When he shifts it's as if he's inhaling." Errol was surprised he could be so generous, but as they drove in the opposite direction he seemed to see Gray, Raphael, and the Porsche more and more in perspective, drifting off to the horizon, less and less involved with his life and more just a spot, something to see. He felt calm. The windows of the pickup were open and his shirt fluttered; the air was warm; the sun was high. Errol felt young and easily amused.

"So if he was such a hot driver in such a hot car, why did you get out? I mean, eighty-five is pushing it for this road, but it's not impossible. Give me a tight machine and I could—"

"To make a point."

"What point?"

"You know, I'm not sure."

"Seems like an asshole thing to do is all."

"It was," said Errol mildly. "So was going eighty-five. So was my best friend of twenty-five years not backing me up for the sake of a man she's known for five months."

"We're all assholes, right?"

Errol laughed. "Right. Everyone wants to have sex with everyone. And everyone is an 'asshole.' This is a big day for truth, I must say."

Errol found himself in a state of mind he had rarely experienced. All that he considered important had inexplicably dwarfed. Major dramas had shrunk to squabbles. His career was now a job. There was only this man beside him and the road as it sped underneath Errol's feet and the trees out the window. Houses. Small failing stores and pumps with overpriced gas. This sign. That fence. The expansion of his own lungs, the texture of the tattered serape covering the front seat. Errol felt as if he had cast aside everything: anthropology, newspapers, Boston; political opinions, his tastes in music and food; certainly Gray. With absurdly little prompting, he could go with Gabe to the house the man was building and hire himself out for light carpentry, rent a room nearby, and eat in diners and truck stops for the rest of his life. He could pick up a little plumbing and use coarser language and watch more TV. And this didn't sound so terrible. It sounded comforting and easy.

"Can I give you a hand with those boards?" asked Errol.

"It's not really in the same direction you're going."

"I don't care. I'm taking the day off. Two-by-fours appeal to me."

Gabe built houses, so he understood that.

When they arrived at the building site, Errol deliberately took more boards at a time than he could comfortably handle. With his jacket and tie off and his shirt-sleeves rolled up, he felt more relaxed around Gabe. Errol wished oddly that he, too, could tell stories of leaving his father by the side of the road, though his own father was a quiet, obsessive physicist with whom Errol had always gotten along appallingly well.

By the time they were finished, it was hot, and Gabe asked if Errol would join him at a nearby swimming hole where some of his construction crew were taking the day off. Errol easily agreed to go.

When Gabe finally asked Errol what he did for a living, as they drove over, Errol had to think for a minute before he answered, "I'm a social anthropologist." Errol had already so clearly imagined his little apartment in his carpenter's life that his real profession and Gray's Victorian house had grown dim. Errol now believed he lived in the back of someone's clapboard, with a cheap, small-screen, black-and-white TV that was always losing its vertical hold, mismatched dishes with only enough plates to have two guests over at a time, and sparse furniture: a metal table and two aluminum chairs, the kind with padded plastic seats with rips in the upholstery that he played with through breakfast; one ugly but amazingly comfortable armchair in which he often fell asleep at night, a beer at his side, a detective novel in his lap; a rack for stacks of newspapers, bad ones but entertaining, full of scandal, advice columns, comics, and raking editorials. Perhaps the bed folded into a couch to save space, and on the nights he didn't fall asleep in the armchair Errol went through a careful and satisfying ritual of laying out the mattress and tucking in the bedding and folding back the sheet, tossing two springy pillows out of the closet.

Errol remembered Ellen Friedman's description of going to bed, "so sweet, Errol . . . so simple. Such a relief," and had to smile. There had been such a smooth, freshly laundered feel to her picture. He felt it in her presence, too, a cleanliness. Perhaps when she'd been married she'd been as entangled and stained as anyone else, but now there was a clarity to her life, a well-ironed, cottony feel to it with sharp, straight creases. Errol realized sadly as he rode toward the swimming hole that he'd lived with a bentness and a festering for many years.

It was clearly worse than it had ever been. When Errol walked into that Victorian foyer now, the air was thick enough to clog his breath; his tie hung crooked; his shoulders rose and took a strange, hurtling curve. Errol yearned for the simple straight-backed chairs, for two tiny rooms, and a kitchenette kept scrupulously neat, for stacks of identical work shirts folded methodically in his drawers, for bare floors, for day after day of ordinary hard work and uninteresting friends. Errol would talk about taxes and weather.

If such a life was boring, so be it; that would be Errol's fault. Boredom was a personal failing; he believed that. If Errol would be bored in his little apartment, making instant coffee in the morning and sleeping late on Saturdays and meeting the rest of the crew at the swimming hole in the afternoon, then it would be only from his own corruption. The complications, the festering, got into your blood. You developed a taste for it; being busy and having screwed-up relationships with other people had their compensations. There was always something to think about. You could wonder, What are they doing now? or What are they saying about me? or What did she mean by that remark? because you would not have relationships with these people simple and direct enough that you could ask them what they said and did and thought and they would tell you. There were advantages to being lost in labyrinthine intrigue; there was always somewhere to go because you could never get there.

What was Errol really thinking? Really? This: Why couldn't he just tell Gray, say to Gray, "Listen—" Why couldn't he just ask her, "Gray, listen—Listen, I—Gray, I—Gray—" Ask her, "Why, Gray, why don't we—" No, more direct: "Gray, I would like to—" No, harder, fewer and fewer words, "Gray, I—Gray!" That was what always happened in Errol's fantasies: he said things—with the smallest words—and Gray said things back, not only what he wanted to hear but with short, terrifying clarity, with no bentness, with no wryness or irony or bite. "Yes, Errol, I—" "Gray, could we—"

It was no good. It would never happen. It was no good. They were at the museum now. Errol wondered what they were doing. Where they would go for lunch. What they were saying. He would never know for sure.

Gabe and Errol wound their way down amid a cropping of rocks to a pool where the river collected clear and deep. Errol leaned over and dipped his finger in the pool and felt the coolness cut through his complicated life and its problems. On the small grassy patch beside the hole there were two naked men stretched out asleep, the tan lines from their Levi's drawn across from hipbone to hipbone, as with a ruler. They were handsome bodies, on the whole, but each with its comforting imperfections.

Errol stripped off his own clothes and dived into the water, then dried off beside Gabe.

Gabe introduced Errol to the two men, Dave and Nathan, when they woke. The four of them drank beer from the cooler and assessed one another's body furtively. While the crew told Hunter Thompson-style drug adventures, Errol glanced down at his own body with pleasure for the first time in months. Not too shabby, he thought. It could handle a good many two-by-fours in an afternoon. And Errol certainly had less of a gut than Gabe. True, there was a soft place right under Errol's navel, about exactly a handful, for Errol had often inspected it with exasperation in the mirror of Gray's upstairs bathroom. However, even if he did skip Gray's desserts, the main part of the meal, for weeks, his limbs lost their brawn but the little bulge remained. Yet today Errol could be content at last to be well into middle age and still be able to hold his imperfection entirely in one hand.

When the other men told stories of acid, hashish, and cocaine, Errol returned with stories of hallucinogens they hadn't heard of—in Ghana, New Guinea, or Ethiopia; stories of whole tribes high for days, snorting green powder, so that when you entered the village the entire town was scattered along the edges of the road with mucus running in globs down their faces, the whole population glazed and oblivious—and no one was arrested and no one shot other people to get more. The men were entranced by everything but the snot, and Errol conceded that it wasn't a pretty picture, though if you snorted the powder yourself it didn't bother you anymore . . .

Their stories came faster, about joining rock bands and convincing psychiatrists they were too crazy to be drafted and bombing public high schools. They were young, but they'd worked on having stories from an early age. Once they got onto women, Errol knew he had a couple of good ones up his sleeve, and after a few beers he had no reason to save them. That was one thing you could say for a life of complications: it made for good stories, though someone had always suffered for them.

chapter thirteen

S o Errol told the crew about Nora and Frank; he used different voices. He told them about North Adams and the textile mills. They liked Nora. They weren't sure about the little boy.

Yet at this juncture in the story there was no point in liking Nora. Nora was gone. Raphael had turned his back on his mother at thirteen, leaving the screen door to creak and waver in the wind behind him. He stood there just inside the door, poised at the entrance of the living room now in shambles, long after he heard the car start and stutter and lurch away.

Methodically he picked up his father's portrait and worked the staples one by one out of the broken stretcher. From there he moved to his mother's studio, where he found her canvases strewn around the floor; there were footprints on the landscapes. He'd broken his fingernails on those first staples, so with a palette knife he started taking out the stays from her other paintings, all his favorites. His father had left the house, but could return any time, and Raphael must have known what Frank would do to these canvases once he returned, for he worked quickly, stacking the loose paintings, rolling them up, and wrapping them with rubber bands.

"What'd you do with them?"

The boy said nothing. His lips remained full and relaxed and inexpressive. He didn't even shrug. He looked at his father.

"Where'd you hide the pictures, Ralph?" Frank was almost patient. "You're makin me tired, Ralphie. This is gonna get real boring if I have to keep asking the same question and you just stand there. You never know what I might have to do to keep myself entertained."

Raphael stood, his shoulders low and back, his hands limp at his side, his feet comfortably apart, his chin high. Frank pulled his arm back and smacked his son on the jaw with the back of his hand, with methodical patience. Raphael's head turned squarely to the side, remained there a moment, and returned to the front, waiting. "Ralph." There it was, to the other side of the jaw, so Raphael looked in the other direction, his eyes open and keen and trusting. Raphael could trust his father to do what his father would do now. Though they both must have been tired and confused, since there was no dinner tonight, nor would there be again, they would each persevere this evening, in the mood or not. Father and son, real troopers.

The back of the hand again, again. Frank hit his son with boredom. At last Raphael's head took longer to face frontward, and at length lolled a little toward the floor. Encouraged by this flagging, Frank hit him harder, and began to knock Raphael off balance. His son staggered once to the left, once to the right, like a dance.

"Ralph," said Frank, "I'm warnin you, Mommy's not here to rescue you anymore, so you're gonna have to hang this bullshit up, understand? The party's over. Time to pay attention to dear old Dad, okay? Now, where's those lousy pictures, Ralph?"

Raphael breathed unsteadily. His nose was bleeding in a drizzle. His mouth tasted salty.

Somewhere along the line it must have occurred to Frank that Nora had left him. Maybe he told himself that she'd be back, but a voice deeper down inside him must also have replied, No, Frank, she's gone and you know it. The bitch. The bitch had left. And here was his son, looking insolently like her.

The rhythm of Frank's blows speeded up. Raphael could not remain standing, though each time he fell he rose up, dutifully maintaining his position, staying at attention, like a good soldier under fire. Yet at some point Raphael must have looked at his father and noticed something different. No doubt Raphael felt like any intelligent soldier left too long at his post, who sees that there are no other troops on his side left around him, that the flak is coming faster and harder than before, that he is suddenly alone and at such a strategic disadvantage that he is beyond duty and is left simply with survival versus pointless suicide. In short, he realized that Nora was gone and Frank was not going to stop.

The boy's eyes sharpened. He no longer tried to stand but crouched in a ready position—Raphael was down in the trenches. No more fife blowing or flag waving. He had leaped in the course of a minute from the Napoleonic Wars to World War I. When Frank came after him now, he fled. They stalked each other around fallen furniture. When the boy bolted for the kitchen Frank belted him in the kidney, but even doubled over, Raphael knew his new stronghold was worth the price. There were munitions in kitchens. Rolling pins, glass, knives—

"Stop there." For the first time since Nora had left, Raphael spoke. Frank had been about to make another lunge, but thought better of it. His son was pointing a ten-inch carving blade at a point just below his chest. The bevel had recently been sharpened.

"You little son-of-a-bitch, put that down." But Frank didn't move.

"You aren't hitting me anymore," said Raphael distinctly. "You know that, don't you?"

"Boy, you got any idea what they do to a kid who runs through his own father? It don't look good, Ralph. You don't just get a slap on the wrist and a pat on the ass." Still, Frank didn't move.

"You aren't hitting me *anymore*," Raphael repeated. "Go upstairs. Don't come down."

Now, Frank had read his share of tabloids, and this scene in the kitchen must have looked like eerily familiar front-page material. When Raphael took a step forward then, leading with the tip of the blade, Frank took a step back, though this kid was only thirteen and half his size. Frank had never in his life threatened his son with a punishment he hadn't carried out. Frank had set a good example. Raphael didn't know what an empty threat *was*.

"Okay, Ralphie," said Frank evenly. "I'm tired, I'll go up and lie down. You stay down here and cool off, understand? 'Cause that thing is for roasts and slicing cabbage for slaw. That's *all*. Don't you forget it." Strangely relieved that this scene had been resolved in some way, any way, Frank backed up to his bedroom and locked the door.

Keeping the knife in his right hand, Raphael collected provisions with his left—not the cookies and potato chips with which most children would run off to a tree and sulk, but a serious stock for several days: bread, frozen steak, and anything that would keep—dried beef, hard cheese, crackers. At no time did he put the knife down to make this process easier, nor would he go upstairs, so he was stuck with the few clothes of his in the laundry room. It pained him that these were still unwashed. Raphael was an excruciatingly clean child, so he took a new toothbrush, toothpaste, and a generous quantity of soap. All this he wedged tightly into his backpack. He looked around. Flashlight. Matches. Sleeping bag. And there was a jar in the kitchen where Nora threw the change that collected in the bottom of her pocketbook. Nora had always considered this "free" money, since there was no accounting for it, and usually spent it on paints. He knew she was generous with dimes and quarters for this reason, so he took the whole jar and set it on top of his load. Lastly he pulled the roll of Nora's canvases out of its hiding place, set it across his pack, and pulled the flap tight.

At the front door, Raphael took the key to the house off his chain and laid it pointedly on the table beside him.

Errol spared his audience this detail, and many others; the boys were just swapping stories by the swimming hole, after all. Yet for his own home movie Errol slipped this one in. Leaving the key was so like Raphael, even now. It made such a fine gesture; but he surely had another copy, and had every intention of sneaking back while Frank was at work once in a while rather than go too long without a shower.

Raphael knew where he was going. Perhaps he'd known early he would need such a resort; in any case, he'd never obeyed his father's edicts about the mills, surely handed down more to frighten than to protect him. There was little to do in North Adams, and he knew these places well. Cleveland Cottons was his favorite.

So Raphael Sarasola hiked through the streets of North Adams at midnight by the light of dim stars, listening to Nora's paint change jingle in its jar. At a side entrance to the plant, he pulled back the boards he'd loosened years before and stepped carefully into the cavernous ruin with his flashlight. With each step he could hear rustling on either side of him, and he shuddered. Curled up in his sleeping bag that night, he kept the knife at his side, reaching for it from time to time when he heard a scamper too near his corner, sometimes frightening animals away by shouting clearly into the factory's first floor, "Go upstairs. Don't come down." Down. Down. It echoed.

The crew were surprised that Raphael went to school the next day. "High school, too," Errol told them. "And college. He's a grad student now."

"That seems weird to me," said Gabe. "This guy doesn't seem like a company man. Is he smart?"

"He's clever. I don't know if he's smart. He hasn't needed to be. He's pretty."

"He couldn't have gotten by on his face at thirteen, though."

Errol shook his head and smiled. "I thought I made it clear, Nathan. We're not slouches, are we? None of us looks too bad?"

"Nah. We're a fine, healthy group of boys."

"And you don't have much trouble dating women."

"'Course not. I've had my dry periods, but—"

"Sarasola never had a dry period with women since he was

three years old. Nathan, you don't understand. By thirteen this
boy was a knockout. And *now*—"

"Now, what?"

Errol laughed. "He makes us look like poster kids."

"Sounds kind of sickening."

"Yes," said Errol quietly. "You feel it in the pit of your stomach,
a face like that." He smiled wryly. "Women feel it elsewhere."

It was March when Raphael left home. He discovered that,
with his sleeping bag and an oil-drum fire on which he
cooked the steak from his pack the first evening, he could stay
warm; warm enough. However, one steak and even crackers and
hard cheese wouldn't keep him well fed through the week. He
had just enough food to think out his dilemma, well or poorly.
Well, and he remained at Cleveland Cottons. Poorly, and he
inevitably returned home, where the knife would be taken from
him and there was no telling. Raphael didn't know for sure that
his father would kill him, but now that his mother had walked
out the door and driven away to work in diners there was no
telling.

At school Raphael Sarasola was a mystery. He was not
exactly popular, but he attracted a lot of attention. The boy
wasn't quiet but *silent*; there was a difference, and his classmates
were aware of that. He wasn't shy, but spoke to few people. He
never extended himself to make a friend, though when students
approached him, they found him surprisingly personable, even
amusing. Yet when they left him alone he kept to himself, and
no one had the sense that doing so caused him any displeasure.

Had the boy looked different, his peers might have grown

tired or suspicious of his standoffishness, labeled him "strange," and had done with him. However, Errol knew beauty to be as powerful for children as for adults; chances were they maintained a distance from him more out of awe than out of disdain.

Teachers, too, developed an odd deference toward him sooner or later. Raphael would never raise his hand in class but, whenever he was called on, smoothly delivered the correct answer, in a full, clear voice, lower and less piping than other children's. Yet they learned not to call on him too often, for when they did, a grit of irritation would grind into his voice, a steely patience would level his tone. His teachers would shiver, and leave the boy alone.

In the course of this particular March week of eighth grade, however, his behavior subtly changed. Each day he made a deliberate foray into the unknown world of social relationships. Unfamiliar with the traditional give-and-take of friendship, Raphael just asked for things. Point-blank. While his classmates were disconcerted when he made these requests, they were far more so when they gave him all he asked for.

The day after he fried his first and only steak, Raphael walked directly up to the boy who sat in front of him in Language Arts, while students were lingering on the field after lunch. "I have a problem," said Raphael. "I need something to eat."

"What?" asked the boy dully.

"I need something to eat," he repeated evenly. "I can't explain now. I've only got crackers and cheese. They won't last long."

"Is this some kind of joke?"

"You think it's funny?"

"Nope."

"Have you heard me make a lot of bad jokes?"

"I haven't heard you say much of anything." The boy, Louis, was beginning to enjoy this. "You forgot your lunch money or something?"

"I have a little money, but I have to save that for emergencies."

"You're not gonna tell me what this is all about?"

"Later."

Louis scrutinized his classmate, who was now discovering the power of secrets. Louis gave him a dollar. This was not a loan but a down payment. Raphael was being paid for his *story*. Accepting the money, he nodded and walked away. After all, his story was worth a dollar. Maybe two.

The next day Raphael learned another lesson. He tried the same approach on the student who sat behind him in Language Arts. The transaction took even less time, and rather than one, he got five dollars and a candy bar. But the student behind him in Language Arts was a *girl*.

After school he renovated Cleveland Cottons. Steeling himself, he methodically swept out rat turds and infestations of cave crickets. He pulled boards off the windows, picked out shards of broken glass left in the frames, and stretched clear plastic neatly over the rectangles without a wrinkle, fixing the edges with a staple gun, whose purchase he had given priority over food. He dragged out a cabinet, which he weighted with bricks to keep his food away from animals. Gradually he picked up cast-off furniture and cable spools until a couple of rooms downstairs looked habitable.

Yet cleanliness and even civilization were not enough, ingenuity was not enough. Raphael was an aesthete, his mother's son. Having picked up four bags of white sheets for a small price at the Salvation Army, Raphael went to work with his staple gun. Over the windows he draped elaborate white curtains, swept back and luxuriously folded. He upholstered in the same way, stapling pleat after pleat, trapping material into cushions over wooden chairs, skirting his spool tables, covering his rusty cabinet until the light grew dim and Raphael went out to pace the streets, munching what he had scavenged at lunch that day, planning under the moon. When he returned at night and ducked once more under the boards, the cavernous interior of the textile mill was lit up with blue light and the drapery over the windows shone; the newly upholstered furniture glowed and floated over the black floor. Still, the skirts of white shifted and fluttered, and Raphael kept his knife by his sleeping bag, listening to the scuttering as he fell uneasily to sleep. Later that week Raphael may have been the only boy in the history of that town to shoplift not soda or candy or water pistols but rat poison.

In the mornings Raphael woke early and bathed in the river that ran by the mill. Shivering, he'd build a fire in the oil can and do his homework. Raphael understood that his performance in school shouldn't falter. Raphael knew a lot of things, he was never sure from where. As mysteriously as he knew about rents in Boston, he also knew about social agencies. Frank wouldn't alert anyone to look for him—Raphael wasn't sure that Frank actually hated his son, but without Nora there he simply wouldn't want one anymore. Teachers, however, had to be kept in the dark, and the student body was going to be a major project.

He experimented again on Louis. Living in secret wouldn't work. Too many kids played in the mills. Too many kids would notice boards were missing from the windows. And he needed allies. While secrecy was winning, confidence was more so. Silently Raphael led his classmate to his hideaway.

Louis was thrilled. To him Cleveland Cottons was paradise, for Louis didn't have to wash at five in the morning in cold water or wear the same clothes all the time or eat stale leftover sandwiches from the school cafeteria for dinner day after day. Louis had a doctor, a dentist, electric lights, and a TV. Yet Raphael didn't try to disillusion the boy about his life here.

"God, you could bring girls here, have parties—"

"Only," Raphael warned, "if I can stay here."

"So what's the scam?"

"The authorities can't know about this. And I'm going to need help with some things. More than food. I want to put this place into shape."

"Looks pretty good to me already."

"I'm not talking about putting little dried-flower arrangements on the coffee table, Louis. You don't understand. There are animals that live here, Louis. I want them out."

"Animals?" Louis lived in a sweet little house with shutters and a kitchen with new linoleum. It took him a minute. "Oh," he said, and paled as he looked quickly around.

"Relax. They come out at night. While I sleep."

"Heh-heh," said Louis. "Sweet dreams."

"Exactly. So I plan to gut this place. When I'm through you'll be able to invite your grandmother here for coffee and pecan sandies, but I'm going to need help."

"What do I get out of it?"

Raphael responded with no hesitation. "Nothing."

Louis shook his head incredulously and smiled. "You got balls, Sarasola."

Raphael shrugged.

"So what do you need?"

"Alcohol."

Louis laughed. "So you can get so wasted you don't care about rats, right?"

"I need to be able to work at night. I've designed some lamps out of jars with cotton wicks, and alcohol burns clean. I need several gallons of methyl alcohol. It's cheap. Your father runs a drugstore."

"You got it, then."

So, Raphael mulled over after Louis had gone: Tell the truth. Ask point-blank. Promise nothing. Raphael smiled. It was *amazing*.

Errol skipped over much of this by the swimming hole in order to get to the upcoming part of the story, which would interest his audience more. The whole movie, though, line by line, frame by frame, was coming at him in a rush. It intrigued Errol the way he heard the boy speak at thirteen. So precise. So controlled. So correct. The way he spoke now, of course. Yet Errol didn't believe this speech was a failure of his imagination. Style like Raphael's didn't develop overnight. Frank was a slob, but Nora must have taught her son to speak well; Frank had taught him to speak little. It was a striking combination.

Raphael had no intention of turning Cleveland Cottons into the local clubhouse. Boys would make appointments, and sometimes were denied entrance even then and would have to try another time. Whenever visitors arrived they brought offerings—food, wine, and poison, like polite dinner guests— which he accepted with a nod of his head and no embarrassment. In fact, it was the boys themselves who felt grateful; if he suggested that what they'd brought would be useful to him, they glowed.

His conversations with the boys were terse and spread with silences that his friends enjoyed because they seemed so manly. It didn't take long for his classmates to notice that Raphael had little taste for loud, rambunctious, knee-slapping evenings, with pranks and dirty jokes and shows of physical bravado. No, these boys had to steel themselves for evenings of terrifying maturity. A visit with Sarasola was not a relaxing social occasion; it was a test they could not goof their way through. They would talk about serious things, school and politics, but not for too long, because Raphael had no qualms about telling them in the middle of a diatribe on the Vietnam War that he was quite bored. The savvy found he had a weakness for stories—stories, Errol smiled, like this one. He liked to listen. He liked to take things in and store them away for later. He loved small bits of information—he liked knowing that strong winds often preceded a temperature change; that there was a solvent which glued plexiglass in such a way that the molecules actually bound together like one piece of plastic; that doughnuts were good if you dunked them in hot coffee and then whipped them right back out again before they got too soggy. Raphael was never bored by information, however trivial.

Yet the best bet with Sarasola was to work. Raphael had ambitions for the whole structure of Cleveland Cottons, not just his original corner. As long as the two upper floors were infested, he would continue to hear long scuttering diagonals cut across his ceiling as he went to sleep. These former tenants had to go, and that meant dragging out all the boards and refuse, shoring up supports and holes in the floor, and laying out poison generously along the edges of every room. When Raphael worked he said no more than he had to, delivering cursory instructions which his friends had better get right the first time. Yet the boys enjoyed the delicious seriousness of it all—moving boards far too big for them, and saying nothing, just as Errol had enjoyed moving those two-by-fours with Gabe; tersely noting close calls with rotten floorboards and leaping broken steps on the dark way upstairs; coolly removing rotting rodent carcasses and flinging them in a long arc out the windows to bloop in the river below; getting small injuries, which Raphael would tend neatly and professionally with the medical supplies they brought him on their regular visits.

"But you're not going to tell me," said Gabe, "that this guy built his whole little empire with *boys*, are you?"

"No," said Errol. "I'm not going to tell you that."

"I can see it," said Gabe. "The entire school of blond German darlings and dark Italian sweethearts, in love with him. Out of control. Am I right?"

"Uncannily."

"We had a guy like that in my school," said Nathan. "Unbearable. But I stuck around him. Hang around the hoop, you can pick up the rebounds, right? I let them cry on my shoulder. After a while they got tired of crying, if you know what I mean."

"Likewise in North Adams," said Errol. "Boys would hint they were in Ralph's inner circle and, bang, they had a date for Friday night."

But they told Raphael everything. The secrets girls confided in his friends all arrived at Cleveland Cottons, so he knew which girls to hit up for his next meal and which girls to lay off because they were getting too frustrated. It was a great game, which all the boys enjoyed, for he generously left the girls for their own pickings.

The extent of Raphael's sexual exploits was entirely unknown. He collected information but didn't deliver much back. The aura of secrecy he first generated in eighth grade did nothing but expand. In fact, he kept his hands largely to himself. Girls would knock on his boarded entrance late at night, with pies, flowers, or, if they'd done their homework, nails and caulking and a new Phillips screwdriver. He'd give them a tour of the place by lamp-light, warning them of stairs not yet repaired and leading them through high-ceilinged rooms, showing them the polished machinery that once wound thread. He led them across his dance floor-in-progress so that they could later imagine themselves rocking into the night with Raphael as they went to sleep that same evening. At the end of the tour, to be described over the phone several times by morning, he would sometimes take the trembling face between his hands and kiss it once, carefully. Raphael's kisses were kind and sensual and deep, but overly defined, cut clearly at the end, resolved in a way that would not get reported over the phone but which the girls understood at once: they made no promises.

As the entire adolescent population of North Adams supported him, Raphael did his part in return. He never disillusioned them. Only when one of his followers decided to run away and join his idyllic life at the mill would he tell about the winters, about the poolroom and the lechers with bad breath. Then he would describe how older men sometimes walked along the riverbank drinking cheap Scotch and so discovered his lair, how he'd have to run them out at knife point, a fifteen- or sixteen-year-old boy against several irate drunks, so that it was only the look in his eyes of someone who had used a knife before, and effectively, that kept him safe on these late nights. Finally, Raphael would confide that his mother had left him and his father was dangerous and *that* was why he lived at Cleveland Cottons, not because he'd read *The Swiss Family Robinson* too many times.

Unless pressed, though, Raphael kept his mouth shut and didn't complain. His classmates imagined he lived in exhilarating Pippi Longstocking independence, and Raphael allowed them to believe that, to feel their own freedom through his surprisingly difficult, even restrictive life.

"Now, hold it. This went on for *years*?"

"Five, I think."

"And no adults knew about it?"

"No, I'm sure people figured it out. But Raphael pulled himself off as a phenomenon. People are tolerant of phenomena in small towns. Probably the owner of the mill didn't even live in town anymore, and no one in North Adams was going to turn it into a shopping mall.

"Anyway," said Errol, taking a breath, "there was a woman."

"I figured," said Gabe.

"An older woman," said Errol.

"I even figured that, too."

"Pretty—"

"Check."

"Dark—"

"Check."

"*Married.*"

The men on the bank laughed.

"Son-of-a-bitch," said Dave. "Every girl in town he can

have, and he picks some old married lady. God, how stupid can a kid be."

"Very stupid," said Errol. "But people pretty much get what they want. He must have wanted a challenge."

"Come on," said Nathan. "He didn't want a challenge, he wanted Mommy."

Errol inhaled and leaned back in the grass, staring at the blue sky and tapping his fingers against his ribs with a slight annoyance. "I think," he said at last, "that we've all been raised with too much watered-down Freudian psychology."

"What, are you trying to tell me I'm off the mark? This guy doesn't have some kind of mother thing?"

"I'm telling you," said Errol, "that I don't care. All right, he wanted his mother. He missed his mother, can you blame him? She was gorgeous and loved him and left him when he was only thirteen. But. He also wanted this other woman, Ida. She existed in the world and they had an actual relationship. Not a mother–son one, either."

"You mean, so he wanted his mother, who gives a flying fuck," said Gabe.

"Yes," said Errol. "Fine. We can say he was *transferring*. But then what do we know that we didn't know before? What use is looking at it that way? It's not even interesting anymore."

"Errol buddy," said Gabe, stretching, "I like the way you think, boy. You guys should listen to him."

"I don't know what the hell he's talking about," said Dave. "But I do want to know what happened with this Ida woman. Skip the philosophy. Did he fuck her?"

"Dave, you sure know how to kill a story, don't you?" said Nathan. "Right to the punchline."

"Nate, come on, you know how Dave tells a story. 'I met this girl. We ate. We fucked. We broke up.' Whoosh, it's over."

"I like to get to the stuff that's interesting," said Dave.

"You call that interesting?"

"Sure."

"And you probably thought in high school," said Errol, "that the Monarch Notes were better than the book."

"I wouldn't know." Dave shrugged. "I never read the books. The notes went on forever."

The crew laughed and everyone got another beer, settling down for the Monarch Notes of Raphael Sarasola's first affair.

chapter fourteen

Ida O'Donnell lived across the street from Cleveland Cottons in a sprawling, two-story, New England clapboard, painted white with dark-green trim. While the house was in dilapidated condition, it still retained its original latticework, garden trellis, and lovely diamond-shaped windowpanes, at which Raphael would stare jealously through plastic until he began himself to replace it window by window with real glass. Her clothesline was in the front yard, and she would saunter out with a basket in the warmer seasons and slowly pin a line of white shirts and boxer shorts next to a line of black slips and red nightgowns and dark-blue lingerie.

Raphael first really noticed her when he was just fifteen. It was summer, and he'd been in the textile mill for a year and a half. Ida would bring out a huge black towel and lie out in the front yard to tan. She wore a solid black bikini that blended in with her towel, so that from across the street her body was laid out for him in three discrete sections. Her face was sharp.

She had an insolent pointed chin, a short but severe little nose. Her black hair was boyishly cropped and tousled, and abruptly stood on end. This peakedness extended to her whole body— her shoulders came to points; her collarbone jutted forward; her rib cage hurtled upward, then plunged to her waist. Ida's stomach was the only part of her body that looked soft and whose shape was gentle, though two military hipbones rose on either side of her belly to protect it. Her flanks were lean, though with one endearing bulge of fat at each top inside, just about a mouthful. The rims of her kneecaps looked as if they could slice your finger; her shins gleamed like the bevel of a knife. She had long feet with high arches. At least Raphael knew she had high arches by the end of the summer, because he got one of the girls in the neighborhood to bring him binoculars.

Ida was not known in North Adams as a particular beauty. She was a little bony, too tall, and besides, she had an attitude. There was something about the way she carried herself, the way those bones of hers protruded so insistently forward, something arrogant and aggressive and fenced-in. Her neck was too long; it held her head too high. And she didn't talk to people. She didn't buy chocolate from kids trying to raise money for the football team; she didn't buy Girl Scout cookies. She didn't join committees. She had no children. She didn't shop much, and when she did, she didn't compare brands or look at unit-pricing stickers but walked listlessly through the aisles throwing a stray box or two into her cart. Raphael had seen her in the grocery and openly stared. He loved what she bought, stupid things: smoked abalone at five dollars a can, but store-brand saltines; candied kumquats and brandied apricots, but long, two-pound loaves of white bread, too, and American cheese. She was no gourmet, but she played. Sometimes she'd pick a jar off a shelf, look at the label, and laugh out loud, tossing it in the cart without looking at the price. When she stood in line at the checkout, people would stare at her groceries; Ida would take a look at tabloid headlines and then focus somewhere off to the side—on what, Raphael couldn't see, some point in the middle of the air maybe—and someone would have to nudge her to put her food on the belt.

She liked olives. They were always in her cart. Raphael had never had an olive in his life, but somehow he liked the idea of Ida popping them compulsively in that house. He liked it a great deal.

However, she wasn't in the store very often; no one knew what she did. Raphael had a better idea than anyone. She took thick books out with her towel and scowled over them, starting about noon. (He yearned to know the titles, but his binoculars weren't that good.) She spent the better part of the afternoon that way, and she might have been extremely well read if the same thing didn't happen on the towel as in the grocery store: Ida would gradually focus on a point *beside* the book. He often trained his lenses on her gaze. He'd watch it blacken and glimmer once it left the page. One time she looked right into Raphael's binoculars. He dropped them quickly to his waist, his heart racing.

Walking home, he deliberately remained on her side of the street, strolling by her lawn and taking in her body casually before he crossed to Cleveland Cottons. Sometimes she looked back at him, with the same cool assessment, with impudence, actually, like a dare.

Yet Raphael was fifteen and Ida must have been thirty, so he tried to put her out of his mind, working on the mill with his crew full-time now, taking his occasional satisfaction in the small shaky pairs of lips offered up to him evenings at the entrance to his castle. He knew, though, that there was something thin about those tiny mouths, something too simple, for their saliva didn't have the viscosity he was looking for; their spit ran down his throat like water and left no trail. Their tongues were eager but nervous, fluttering in and out of his mouth. It was easy to kiss these girls; it was also easy to stop. It would have been easier still not to kiss them at all, and sometimes, from sheer boredom, he left them at his entranceway, with their lips bright red and parted; he would nod farewell. They stumbled off bewildered, their eyes hot. Surely he'd lost a nice dinner or two, a pie, a new shirt, but sometimes it was worth the sacrifice just to keep his body whole and untouched and held cleanly by the air around it.

The winter was a hard one, cold. Though by this time Raphael had both a fireplace and an oil-drum wood stove, fuel was hard to come by, and the mill was too cavernous to heat. He slept little, usually during the day after school. His pool game improved enormously. Weekends and evenings he often spent in movie theaters, where his friends were ushers and let him in free. He dozed there, listening to the same movie over and over again, Bogart or Hepburn intruding on his dreams. He noticed that Ida often turned up at the movies alone, too. She also stayed through more than one showing, though she didn't have to keep warm. Sometimes he sat behind her, and smiled when he saw those eyes gradually shift from the screen to somewhere in the curtains and remain there, catching the light of the projection, flecking, going white, black. She laughed in the wrong places. Even tragedies amused her, and in moments of crisis suddenly a jagged little laugh would cut through the theater; other moviegoers would turn and clear their throats.

Toward the end of that winter Raphael grew thin and pale and was often lightheaded. There were times he couldn't answer his teachers' questions; often during lunch he slipped so quickly into a comatose sleep that he didn't manage to scavenge leftovers in the cafeteria and returned to the mill with nothing to eat. Louis and the boys brought him hot meatballs and cartons of soup, but not every day, and they didn't stay long; it was too cold. They slapped him on the back with a familiarity they'd never before have dared.

Then came March, April, May; Raphael was still alive, and more. When the color returned to his lips they were a keener scarlet than ever before. His cheeks had sunken in the cold and remained that way, but in the sun the mound of his cheekbones warmed and darkened, and his face was no longer waiflike but more striking, more aggressively defined. In that year he'd grown astonishingly tall, so that by spring he could see over Ida's head when he sat behind her in the theater.

So Raphael turned sixteen and school ended and Ida was back in her black bikini. Yet winter had made him harder-edged. He didn't watch her through binoculars or keep track of her from behind his drapes. Afternoons he leaned against the brick face of his fortress and stared at her squarely for an hour, with the same insolence she'd taught him the year before. She didn't seem uncomfortable. She'd glance up from her book to make it clear she knew he was there, and then go on reading or staring at a spot of towel. She seemed to enjoy being watched. He enjoyed watching. It was a good deal.

In July Raphael sat himself down. He knew what she looked like; those three sections of by now well-tanned flesh were burned permanently on his retinas. Watching was no longer enough, or even enjoyable; it was a torment. Much more of this and he'd start to hate her. But he liked having someone in his life he didn't disdain and who didn't bore him. Here he was, sixteen, and he could pass for twenty. She was married, but he never saw her husband much; he assumed the marriage was bad. Besides, who was she? A housewife. Big deal.

Still, his stomach grew heavy and drew together like a fist as he approached her house in mid-July. She's a housewife, he repeated. Big deal. For the first time Raphael walked straight across the lawn to her towel. She rose on her elbows; her shoulders charged forward. Her eyes glittered; she looked amused but not surprised.

"Your name is Ida," said Raphael.

"I know that," said Ida. "You came over here to tell me what my name is?"

"You like olives," he said, unfazed. He handed her a jar, and she took it as if picking it off a grocery shelf, with that much surprise, with that much gratitude. Raphael admired this. It was the way he himself accepted presents.

She looked at the label and nodded. "Oil-cured."

"What are you reading?"

"*Anna Karenina.*"

"Is it good?"

"I don't have the vaguest idea."

"You don't understand it?"

"If I didn't, who would tell me? I mean I'm not a discriminating reader. I don't know if it's good. And I don't care."

"Sometimes you don't pay attention," said Raphael.

"To what?"

"Your book. Sometimes you stop reading."

She shrugged. "So?"

"So nothing."

"So you're an observant little boy."

"So I'm not so little."

"That's right," she said, looking him up and down. "You've grown . . . How old are you?"

"Sixteen."

She laughed the way she did in theaters. "You're the vagabond, aren't you? Across the street."

"You don't have to ask. You know that."

She smiled. So she liked to be called on things. "Quite a playhouse you've got there."

"I live there. I work there. I have yet to play. I don't have time."

"Oh, sensitive! But it must get chilly. In winter."

"I do," he said, "wear a sweater evenings."

"I used to watch you," she conceded. "I felt sorry for you. Sometimes I thought about asking you in for the night. But I figured, Ah, Walter wouldn't like that so much."

"What might I do that 'Walter' wouldn't like?"

She smiled. "If you don't know that," she said, stretching down on her towel so that her rib cage rose toward him, "then you really *are* a little boy."

He nodded and looked at her body frankly. "We'll see," he said, "how little." He turned on his heel and returned to his factory, realizing as his heart whomped against his chest that he had, for the first time, made a *promise*.

R aphael checked out *Anna Karenina*. When he found out what the book was about, he laughed out loud.

He didn't finish the novel. He liked Vronsky. He was angry when he saw the author turning on his favorite character, making the man look mean and small.

Raphael strode up to Ida's towel and threw the book beside her. She jumped.

"I quit," said Raphael.

"Quit what?"

"That book. The writer has no respect."

"For?"

"The count. Starts to treat him like a jerk."

"Who does?"

"Tolstoy!"

"You think Vronsky's so great?"

Raphael shrugged. "He's all right."

"I think," said Ida, "he's petty and arrogant. I think he's just a dumb, pretty boy."

For some reason this made him bristle. He had to remind himself that he didn't care about books, and take a breath. "He's better than what's-his-name. Levin. Vronsky has something. Levin is mush. Levin is like mashed potatoes. And Kitty is a bimbo."

"A bimbo? That's your literary analysis?"

"Just my analysis."

Ida looked up at him through her eyelashes. "But you like Anna."

"She's all right."

Ida rolled her eyes. "You're just aglow with enthusiasm."

He paused, and licked his lips so that they shone red in the summer sun. "No, I like her *enormously*." Then Raphael tried out something he'd rarely tested: he smiled. A small smile; deft, even; the pilot versions must have been mere models of the commercial lines to come, yet even in its experimental phase that smile must have had something—a gentleness, a grace, a terror. Raphael spread out those clean white teeth like wings, and the thing lifted off the ground. Ida took a breath; and sat up straighter.

"My," she said. "We could start a regular book club, couldn't we?"

"With regular meetings. I'd like that."

Ida slowly shook her head in amazement. "*Sixteen*."

"That can be a lot of years," said Raphael. "A lot of winters."

Ida stared up at him from her towel. He seemed taller than ever, foreshortening into the periwinkle sky; his eyes flashed like jet sides catching the light overhead. "How did you get like this?"

"I've always been like this."

She looked at him a long time, and said at last, "You know, I think you're right," and laughed.

Errol knew that at that moment both she and Raphael understood something about character: yes, there were reasons, there were winters, as Raphael had said; there was Cleveland Cottons, there was Frank, and certainly Nora—you could point to all these factors and still have nothing. How did you get like this? We have always been like this. There was something before. How did you get like this? We have always been like this. That was the mystery. There was no explaining. Raphael Sarasola was a certain way and he had always been, even when Nora was still there; in his crib his eyes had shone like that, like the metal on airplanes in the sun, and there was nothing to say about that, no explanation. They shone like airplane siding in the summer sun. That was all there was to say. He was like this. Raphael was like this, and the only reason to say anything else at all was that you were bored and needed to pass the time by the swimming hole as the afternoon got later and more and more orange.

Walter was out of town the following weekend, so Raphael invited Ida to the mill for the evening. That afternoon he didn't know what to do. His preparations had been made. He peeked out the window and there was Ida on her towel, darker than ever, actually reading this time. Slowly he made his way out to the front of the mill, leaned against the brick, and stared. She smiled and kept on reading. He'd said seven. It was only three. It was hot, but he stayed against the brick, feeling the smooth, warm clay with his fingers, the rough rivulets of mortar, pressing his body up against the big, hot building, resting his cheek against the brick, feeling its redness, its pores. Now it was three-thirty. He would wait. The air was thick and humid and oxygen-poor, like breath under blankets. The three sections of Ida's body floated above her lawn. He smiled. She was actually turning pages. He wondered if she understood anything she read. But then she was older. Maybe at thirty you could actually read on afternoons like this.

Gradually the shade of her oak tree crept across the grass, and Ida picked up her towel to follow the sun. At five the patch of yellow was no longer large enough for her whole body, and she stood, stretched, and yawned in the spotlight left there. Methodically she marked her book, folded her towel, and swayed in the front door, without a wave or a nod.

Raphael returned to the mill, where brilliant orange rectangles shafted into the room. The walls and drapes blended in yellows and grays. He lay on the couch, and the sheet over it was cool and smelled bright. The hours were long and rich. He tried to think of as little as possible. The lean spears of light lengthened and flushed, cutting clean diagonals across the couch. He extended his legs into the sun and looked at them, as if for the first time. There were long muscles in his calves like unopened tiger lilies, soft and smooth and oily to the touch. He'd never really seen these muscles before. The hair on his legs was darker and thicker than he remembered. When he lay down, his legs would no longer fit entirely on the couch. He set them gently on the arm of the sofa as if they were an expensive present he'd just been given and he wanted to show the donor with what care he would treat them for the rest of his life.

At six-thirty, he reached over and put his bottle of French white wine in a cooler filled with ice, and leaned back on the pillow. Fifteen minutes later he reached back and pulled out two wineglasses, setting them on the table to scrutinize them carefully. They weren't entirely to his taste, but he'd worked them out of a box of unsold garage-sale merchandise that had been thrown out; he could hardly complain. Besides, they rather suited him right now—tall and fluted, with rippled rims, the glasses were thin and tinted a delicate pink. He decided to give Ida the one with the chip.

At just seven he heard a hollow rap at his entrance and let

her in, taking her hand as she stooped through the hole. She handed him a spray of tiger lilies from her yard. Raphael put the flowers down on the table by the wine. She was wearing a short black kimono over the same black bikini and a string of tiny pearls around her neck. Ida went straight to the wine, opened it, and poured two glasses. They toasted, to nothing. The mill was fantastically quiet. Neither had yet said a word. Sipping her wine, Ida lingered around the room, looking out the front windows to note the view of her lawn. Raphael watched her legs, the crook of her elbow at her waist, her slow but wide stride, the sway of the black silk as she swung from window to window.

"The concrete," she said, nodding at her feet, "is nice and cold." She smiled.

Raphael said nothing. He stood where he'd been standing, and she circled back to him at last; her glass empty, she put it down. He did the same, and refilled them, not because he was going to drink any more but because they looked nicer with the wine, the small bubbles forming on the inside of the glass and gliding occasionally to the top, to float, to pop. He set them in the light, and the wine caught shards of sun.

Slowly Ida unbuttoned his blousy white shirt until it hung open. He looked down at his own chest, again with a feeling of newness and revelation, a sense of finally having been given something—not a pie or nails or a caulking gun—for which he was grateful. His chest was still hairless, though with a fine dark down between his pectorals that Ida smoothed with the pads of her fingers. She trailed her fingers between the halves of his rib cage, then swept her palm around his side and smoothed up and down the furrows of his ribs. With the most pastoral look on her face, a kind of simplicity and lack of conniving he'd never seen in her before, she slid this same hand down the flat left side of his stomach, down behind the waist of his cutoffs to the hollow of his hipbone, until she moved subtly toward his middle and ran the length of her hand along the round of his prick.

Raphael did nothing but breathe. He knew he should be tense, that he probably even was, but he felt as relaxed as if he'd been drugged, and stood on his feet with a slight sway. He would have to lie down soon. His head was light, his balance precarious, for suddenly it seemed that two feet were far too few to stand on.

Ida unbuttoned his Levi's and unzipped his fly; the cutoffs slid to the floor. With great concentration Raphael lifted one foot, then the other, out of the legs of his jeans. He didn't want to fall. Not because it would make him look stupid; he just didn't want to fall.

Ida seemed to understand the delicacy of his balance now, for she led him by the hand to the long trunk opposite the couch. It was only three steps, but he felt so appallingly tall by now that the floor seemed far away; though the ceilings in the mill were vaulted, he wondered if he might graze his hair against the roof-beams. As if on stilts, he tottered slowly on his new legs and let himself down; it was a long way, and took a long time to get there. Ida pushed him gently back until he was stretched out along the length of the trunk, which had cool white sheets tucked around it like the rest of his curbside furniture. His shirt fell to either side.

When Ida leaned over him a moment later, she was still wearing the black kimono, but the bikini was gone. Ida

O'Donnell was no longer edited, and with relief he saw her as a unified body, not the three pieces he'd grown so used to. He looked at her small conical breasts, with the nipples sharp and angular and protruding like the rest of her. Between her legs was a severe, well-defined triangle; he had to smile. She was so consistent.

Ida drew herself over his pelvis, nestling one knee up against his ribs, letting her other leg extend between his, and together they held his prick tight between their stomachs. Ida looked down at him and smiled; she seemed pleased with what she saw. She took one of his hands in each of hers and pulled his arms over his head, over the edge of the trunk. Again he was conscious of his own span, and as Ida moved up his body until the tips of her pubic hairs tickled the head of his prick, he felt his whole body pull taut and lengthen, lengthen, until when she pushed back down on him it was as if he weren't three-dimensional at all, just a vector shooting from one end of the room to the other.

Raphael had expected his vision to blur, for the shapes in the room to go fuzzy as in soft-focus PG sex scenes; instead, their lines went sharp and hard. Perspective exaggerated, as the far end of the couch hurtled away from him and its closer end loomed large. The shafts of sun from the windows were at their longest and most narrow, and drew keen, even parallels across the floor. The wineglasses on the table were fully lit and glowed with a strange super-reality—not *un*reality, but an existence and dimension so startling that Raphael imagined he'd never perceived any two objects as so clearly present in his life. The whole room took on this quality, an exactitude, a definition, a clarity of edge, so that each piece of furniture was placed perfectly where it was and each chair was in the precise relation to the next one that it *was*, those folds fell *that way* and that shadow cut deeply *there*. The yellows and grays of the room were suffused with pigment, and textures rose from the cement; Raphael was sure he could see each thread and each interstice in the sheets on the windows and over the bed.

When he looked at Ida above him he could see it was from her that the clarity was emanating. The edges of her body were drafted with a square, the angles with a protractor, and she was really on top of him, until, fully alive at the age of sixteen, Raphael Sarasola came into a woman for the first time.

chapter fifteen

I can feel your heart beating," said Ida. "Here." She pressed her hand on his pelvic bone. She raised herself up on her arms, but he was still inside her.

"I've still never kissed you."

"That's not what you wanted," she said. "To kiss me."

"That's right. I've done that before."

"I'm surprised," said Ida. "I see pretty little girls sneak in and out of here at all hours."

"Why do you think they come back? I don't give them what they want."

"I got what I wanted," said Ida, "and I'll come back."

Raphael flushed with relaxation and relief. He stretched his feet and arms over the edges of the trunk and felt something he had never felt before and so could not name. He was already getting hard again; she smiled.

"You're a natural for this stuff, you know that? You've got a future."

"Do you do this all the time? With boys?"

"You know, sometimes I can't tell what I've done and what I haven't."

"How's that?"

"I think about a lot of things," she said vaguely. "I do a few of them. It's hard to keep straight after a while is all. What actually happened; what I read; what I dreamed; what I saw someone else do. It gets to be—all the same."

"You mean you're a nut."

"I don't care what you call it," she said, rolling off him.

Raphael felt the air hit his prick with disappointment. It seemed lost dangling over his stomach, lonely and blinded. Ida bound the kimono closed with its belt, and he felt punished.

"I'm sorry." He wasn't used to apologizing for anything, and the words sounded funny coming out of his mouth. "It's just I asked you a question and you didn't answer it."

"That's right," said Ida. "Some people think that asking a question gives them a right to know the answer somehow. Well, it's not true. You've no right to anything. I'll tell you what I want to. I don't care what you ask."

"Do you lie?" he asked on impulse.

"If I feel like it."

"So I can't believe you when you tell me something?"

"I don't care if you believe me. That's your business, what you want to believe. I don't owe you or anyone anything. If someone doesn't like that and they still stay around me, then they're just stupid. 'Cause they can leave."

"I find the truth very useful."

"No," said Ida. "I don't believe in it. I think the truth is a lie."

Raphael smiled and sat up. "You have one twisted little mind."

"It may be twisted, but it's mine," said Ida. "People are always trying to get at it, but they can't. It's mine."

"People like 'Walter'?"

"Of course," she said. "He thought he got me. He didn't. But he knows better now. He leaves me alone."

"Sounds like a great marriage."

"It is, actually," said Ida, with a warning in her voice. "It suits me just fine."

Raphael showed her the rest of the mill by lantern light, for the sun had set now. He led her around with a strange apprehension, for he realized he wanted to impress her. Annoyed with himself for this weakness, he went through his precious upper floors quickly and casually. It didn't end up mattering. At last Ida broke down laughing and admitted that she'd come in here several times while he'd been out; she'd seen all this before. Raphael felt resentful, and pleased.

When they returned to the living room, he lit the line of lanterns in their sconces, and the room flamed on all sides with the white, clean glow of alcohol. They finished the wine. Both were still only in shirts. Raphael pulled Ida down on the couch and fucked her—even Errol had to admit there was no other word—fucked her hard. His position over her felt so natural he was surprised it was new to him. The gnashing of their pelvic bones felt so familiar, the withdrawal, the attack: it was his life—thrust, retreat; drive forward, deny; press, pull away; take, take back; take, take back. He liked it. It was his life.

He fell asleep with Ida on his arm. When he awoke it was light and the lanterns on the walls were out and dry. She was gone. Be that way, thought Raphael. He proceeded upstairs to work on some broken steps and polish textile machinery; with concentration he refused to look out the front windows to her lawn, on which she'd surely be lying. He got a good deal of work done that day, almost too much in an odd sort of way. There was an edge on his life now that he wasn't sure he liked. No matter how brightly the metal shone on the spindles, levers, and wires, the shine gave him only the thinnest satisfaction, and he was sure that if he hadn't fixed the steps he could have jumped over the broken ones without much trouble.

Raphael worked late that night, went to sleep, which was boring, and set back to work the next morning. Still, in everything he did he felt oddly undercut, as if while he built his supports for the second-floor ceiling someone were digging underneath him, tunneling out below his mill to make the whole foundation shaky. He kept changing tasks that day, assuming if he could hit on the right job he'd feel whole and stable and sufficient again. Nothing worked, though, and he quit early to forage for food. He went out the back door and down the path by the river to avoid her house. The detour pained him, and he tried to hike a good distance. As he drew away from her neighborhood, though, he was overcome by malaise and wandered into the theater to score some half-eaten buckets of popcorn. Of course, he knew she sometimes came here on Sunday afternoons, and Raphael hated himself for staying through two showings of a movie he had seen and disliked. At dusk he scuffled home, passing in front of her house. She wasn't out, and her husband's car was back. He returned heavily to the mill, fidgeted restlessly around all three floors, and finally jerked off. It was no fun. This, too, had been undercut. The fucking had been fine, but he was none too keen on this erosion.

The week wore on, lapping at his projects, crumbling his ambitions. It was hard to pursue food with vigor, and he got hungry. He would now pass in front of Ida's yard as before, and she'd be lying there, all right, and she'd even nod at him or shoot him a compressed, wry smile and go on reading. He puzzled over that smile back at the mill. What was the joke? It had been a week. Damn it, she said she'd come back.

As firmly as Raphael tried to persuade himself that it didn't matter—that Ida didn't matter, that there were these other girls or even no girls, no girls and no boys and no Frank and no Nora and that was all just perfectly *fine*—he had to concede that Ida mattered. This information so startled him that he observed himself walk through the day, feeling different, doing things in different ways, with an almost clinical curiosity.

It was the following Sunday before he got it. She'd said she'd come back. However: he would have to *ask* her. It was that simple. That was the smile. It meant that though he might successfully walk over and pull her across the street, she would not herself call him over to her towel in the next hundred million years. He was so used to girls showing up at the mill with food, with tools, with pairs of lips, that he hadn't been refusing to ask Ida over; it simply hadn't occurred to him. Here was one more new experience, then: pursuit. He learned quickly. From that moment on, he pursued Ida O'Donnell with a vengeance.

"I want to fuck you again," said Raphael, having marched straight across the street after his epiphany that afternoon.

Ida laughed. "You want to announce that a little louder? Walter might have missed a word or two."

"I don't care about 'Walter,'" said Raphael, who had from the start put her husband in quotation marks, as if "Walter" were her imaginary friend and he was humoring her by referring to the man by name like a real person. "I don't care about 'Walter.' He's your problem."

"Walter isn't a problem," said Ida.

"I told you I don't want to hear about him. I want to know when you can stop by. I'm asking you to stop by."

She looked at him curiously. Perhaps she expected a game, a dance. "You are big on truth, aren't you?"

"Ida, I asked you," said Raphael. "I asked you a question. I know you don't owe me an answer. But it would be nice, Ida. It would be swell. If you answered me. I want to kiss you, which I still haven't ever done. I want you as soon as possible. I want you to tell me yes or no. When or why not. Right now."

"The question is," Ida mused, "have you just seen too many movies, or are you the most amazing little sixteen-year-old I've ever met?"

"No," said Raphael, hitting harder now, refusing to be flattered, "that's not the question."

"Then what is the question?" She smiled.

"I thought I was clear."

"You've noticed it yourself: sometimes I don't pay attention."

"I asked you," he said with elaborate patience, "to fuck me."

"What's that?" She was still smiling.

"I want to fuck you."

Ida leaned toward him. "Ask me again."

"I want to fuck you."

She laughed. "And when do you want to fuck me?" Her eyes were gleaming.

"Right now."

"When?"

"Right now."

"When?"

"*Right now.*" Raphael, too, had to smile. "You like sets of three."

"I like," she said, "*you.*"

"Can I make you say that three times?"

"You can't make me do anything."

"You'd be surprised."

"Surprise me, then. Make me do it on the lawn."

"Why, you think 'Walter' would like to watch?"

"I'm sure he would."

"Then we can't fuck on the lawn. I don't want to do anything 'Walter' would like." He pulled her up. "Come with me."

"You have an erection," she said casually, walking with him away from her towel.

"Yes, I do. It came in handy last time." He led her across the street by the hand. He hoped Walter wasn't a violent man, but he didn't hope this very strongly. Ida didn't believe in truth; Raphael didn't believe in Walter. He had to concentrate: Her husband is in that house, because it was painful not to slip his hands around her tight, narrow, little hips, all dark brown and shining with a light sweat, around her even narrower waist, with the long muscles springing on either side of her spine as she sauntered across the asphalt.

"The pavement must hurt your feet."

"Oh yes," she said, still taking slow, deliberate steps on the street. "It burns. It hurts, even. I like it. Then I'll step on your concrete. It'll be cold. I'll like that, too."

"You like all kinds of things."

"That's right. I'm not a discriminating reader. I'm not a discriminating anything."

"Terrific," said Raphael. "That makes me feel so special."

"I don't care," she said, "how it makes you feel."

She said this sort of thing a lot. She kept saying it for years. Raphael didn't hear her.

Raphael and Ida carried on. He told no one. He didn't know whether their affair remained a secret or was common knowledge through the whole town.

In the next couple of years Cleveland Cottons came into its own. The second-floor dance hall was complete, and on weekend nights Raphael would quietly string an extension cord for his stereo over the street between telephone poles and tiptoe to the side of Ida's house to plug the cord into her outdoor outlet. He'd warn her ahead of time, and she'd keep Walter inside. Late into the night the cream of his class would show up at his door, lining up, hoping to gain entrance with the same anxiety they'd feel later at Area in New York. The floor upstairs was polished and shook with rock and roll. Raphael oversaw things and kicked people out when they got too drunk, and often had a fine time himself, until it got so late that the sky was turning light and he was reminded of that first time waking up at this hour with Ida missing from his arms. Tired and bored by his classmates, he would stare out the front windows and wonder what exactly she did to keep Walter inside nights. He yearned to have her here at these parties—she'd even helped him with the floor—but she was married and then everyone would know and that wasn't the deal.

Ida kept her lover on his toes. Her personality changed drastically depending on what she was reading, what movie she'd seen. When she read *Madame Bovary* she was dramatic, but would also pull back and dismiss their relationship as flimsy and cheap; she referred to it several times as a pathetic, manufactured illusion. When she came back from seeing *Candida* in Stockbridge with Walter, she was arch and condescending and "larger than life," and Raphael stayed away from her for a week waiting for it to wear off. When she read *The Wild Palms*, she took on a Faulknerian fatalism; she was wan and dour and developed a strange bleak little laugh, which she used when nothing was funny. During this time she enjoyed short, dense conversations and awkwardness and silence. He found he had to read bits of what she was reading or see the movie she'd last watched in order to know how to play the next scene.

When Raphael was seventeen he was smitten with the same spell that hit his father at this age, and he'd talk with Ida for hours about places he planned to go. It was unclear how he'd finance these departures, but Cleveland Cottons would be practically perfect within a year, and that meant, somehow, that he'd have to move on. Ida knew a lot about different places, and sometimes instead of fucking she'd tell him stories that she made up as she went along, stealing bits and pieces willy-nilly from movies and books to fill out what she couldn't invent. Often in these tales Raphael and Ida were the main characters, and they got away with things all over the world.

There was just one little problem, which he had to admit grew intrusive. That was Walter. Even in quotation marks Walter seemed gradually to exist. Raphael would see him walk out of Ida's house in a surprisingly convincing imitation of a regular person, and the man would get into his car and drive to a plant in the next town where he was supposedly some sort of manager, and the car would be there, then gone—awfully persuasive evidence that an agent had moved the machine from one place to another. Also, unlike an imaginary friend, Walter was handsome, though in a manly, grown-up way, with a beard and decisive lines in his face and a substantial build. Were Raphael to imagine Walter, he would have a limp and a stutter and a hunched back. He would have no teeth, and even if he could stand up straight would reach only about four foot eight. Yes, Ida's imaginary friend would be a grotesque little gnome. Walter, it seemed, was her real husband.

At no point was this made clearer than one Friday night his senior year in high school.

As usual, Raphael strung his extension cord over the spikes of the telephone poles and crept noiselessly over Ida's beloved front lawn to plug it into the side outlet. He had to keep low, because the light was on in the den, a window of which opened right over the socket. It was an unusually warm fall night and the window was cracked open, the curtain partially back; he couldn't help but linger when he found he could hear their conversation.

"So are you going to run off and screw that kid, or are you in for the night?" asked Walter. His voice was grainy and low, and reminded Raphael of his father's.

Ida stretched. "No, he's having one of his Friday-night parties. I avoid those."

"Why, Ida, my dear. You're only thirty-two. Already reluctant to spend your weekends with a bunch of drunken teenagers? I'm surprised at you."

"Eat it, Walt."

"Well, if you're willing to screw little kids, why not go to their little parties?"

"Walt, you sound jealous. I'm impressed."

"I'm not jealous. I just wish you'd move on. I'm getting bored. Same old stories."

"I'll move on. When I feel like it."

"If you want a son, Ida, why don't you just get pregnant?"

"By whom?"

"You're such a bitch." But Walter sounded less angry than amused. "This guy's still all in love with you, right? It hasn't let up?"

"Nope."

"It's, like, this galumphing adolescent passion."

"Sure," she said, with distraction. She was drawing pictures with a set of Magic Markers.

Walter shook his head. "God, I'd hate to be that kid. I really feel sorry for him."

"I don't."

"You don't feel sorry for anybody, Ida."

"Why should I? People put themselves in the situations they put themselves. I didn't make him fuck me. Nobody put a knife to his throat. I didn't make him keep fucking me. It's not my problem."

"Yeah, you don't have any problems, do you, Ida?"

"That's right. And I mean to keep it that way."

Ida concentrated on her pictures and Walter flipped through

the paper. Raphael slipped back to his mill. It was a big party, but he didn't dance, and he made everyone go home astonishingly early.

Y ou didn't tell me Walter knew we were fucking."
             Ida didn't seem interested in how he'd found out. "So?"

"So you told me all the lies you've told him. The cover-ups. You've been pretty explicit."

"It happens I didn't tell the lies to Walter. I told them to you."

"I guess the two of you find this funny?"

"No." She considered. "Not funny. He just knows, that's all."

"Since when?"

"Since always. Or I could say since last year, or last week, or since yesterday. What does it matter?"

"I shouldn't believe a word you say, should I?"

"I told you before, that's your business. I don't care. Pick and choose, Raphael. Take what you want."

"You mean," he said unsteadily, "you could be anyone. If nothing you say is true. If I pick and choose. You could be anyone."

This sounded incoherent to his own ears, but Ida seemed to understand him. "That's right," she assented calmly. "I could be anyone. You think you know me. You haven't begun. That's because there's nothing to know. No matter how hard you grab, I'll always invent someone else you haven't met. It's no use, sweetheart. It's like trying to pick up a reflection in a lake. When you dip your hands in the water it ripples into little pieces and floats away. That's the way it is."

Raphael licked his lips. "I think. Sometimes." His lips felt heavy. It was hard to talk. "Sometimes I do believe you're crazy."

"Go right ahead. Believe that. But a crazy lady is just one more person that I won't stay for you. That you can't keep."

Raphael felt as if his lungs were filling up with water. This conversation was too much for him, too adult or something. He was only seventeen. This was too liquid to breathe in. Carefully putting one foot in front of the other, he crossed his living room to open a window, leaning out into the cool night air to clear his head.

Yet it went on for the rest of the year. He had to have her. Knowing that Walter knew about their affair, Raphael grew brazen and would sometimes stand under their bedroom window and call for her. She usually ran downstairs, to go with him or dismiss him, but once Walter himself came to the window.

"It's two in the morning," said Walter from the second floor. "What is your problem?"

"I want to fuck your wife."

"Is that so?" said Walter, perhaps at last a little incredulous. They'd never spoken before. "She's asleep, Sarasola. How about you get that way, too. I'm tired."

Raphael said, "I don't care," a phrase he'd heard so often from Ida that he was beginning to use it himself. "I want to fuck your wife. Now."

"Son, why do you have to become a part of my life every time you get a hard-on? Seems like you should have figured out by now how to take care of that little business yourself."

"Walter," said Raphael, "don't call me 'son.' And, Walter, I didn't say I wanted to jerk off tonight or I wouldn't have involved you, right? I want Ida. Wake her up. Wake her up so I can fuck her. Now." Raphael was beginning to feel an anger and a directness of an intensity he had never known. He felt possessed, vertical, on fire.

Walter worked his jaw back and forth. "I'm just curious, *son*, whether this is some generational thing, like a fad, or whether you, personally, are out of your mind."

"I'm not out of my mind. Your wife is. She set this up. These are her rules. See—" He was breathing too deeply but couldn't stop, and the oxygen made his head float higher, his body shoot taller. "I know this is crazy, Walter. But that's the way it is. We're both in Ida's nut house, *Walter*. We're in her Looney Tunes cartoon, Walt, my buddy, understand? So I don't have any choice but to stand here under your fucking window and you don't have any choice but to wake her up, or I'm coming in to get her."

"You poor schmuck," said Walter softly. And the odd thing was, he sounded sincerely sympathetic.

Walter pulled back into the house, and a minute later Ida appeared at the front door in a light robe. It was March, and still cold; she wrapped her arms around her. "Raphael," she whispered, "go home and go to sleep."

He walked up the porch stairs. He slid his hand between the flaps of her robe and took hold of her hip firmly. "No, Ida. I'm not going home."

Her hip pulled at his hand. "It's late. And cold. Walter's home."

"Since when are you so practical?" He took his other hand

and swept back the robe, holding her in front of him by both hips. She was naked underneath, and her small angular pelvis squirmed. "Right now, Ida."

He pushed her against a post of the porch; holding her with one hand, he loosened his jeans with the other, and slipped them over his buttocks to the floorboards.

"Raphael, not here," she said, and squeezed out from between his prick and the post, only to be caught again by his left arm. She pulled him down the steps, but Raphael swung her to the side against the edge of the porch. Her robe fell open, and the moonlight hit her body along its full length, which was now white from winter. He lifted her up so she was half sitting on the porch and shoved inside her all the way up. She was wet, extremely, but she thrashed from side to side until she worked her way off him and ran toward the lawn.

Toward the lawn. Not into the house to lock the door, but onto the lawn, where he overtook her at just the place Ida sunbathed in summer. He swung her onto the grass, wet with dew, and stretched her out on her back, pinning her arms down. Just as he urged into her he saw a shadow on the porch out of the corner of his eye, and turned to find a figure standing at the front door. Walter.

The moon was out, and surely the view was good, of Ida pinned, her robe splayed on either side, his buttocks catching blue light over this man's wife. At last Raphael did feel a little demented, for the image of what he was doing became so strong that it floated more clearly in front of him than Ida's face as it reeled from side to side on the wet grass. The picture of the two of them from that porch overtook even the sensation of his prick pushing rapidly into her. For a moment he slowed down and took longer, keener, more meditative slices of her insides. He shook his head over her and laughed until tears rolled down his cheeks. "Oh, Walter," he shouted, looking up at the sky, "I'm so glad you could join us."

The stars glimmered and fattened and doubled. He wondered fleetingly if he was raping her, but he knew as he felt the walls of her vagina spasm and contract, and looked down to see her lips fall open and flush, her eyes blur and go liquid, that it was entirely the other way around. *She* had set this up. She had somehow made him do this, in front of her husband on the lawn, and it was Raphael who was being raped, not Ida. With anger, a sense of his own abuse, he racked against her, and their pelvises met bone against bone. "I'm coming, Walter," he shouted. "I thought she'd want you to know that." Raphael felt used and sick, and came like spit. He rolled off her onto his back and wept. Ida stood up and pulled her robe around her, facing away from both men.

"Ida," said a tired voice on the porch. "Come inside, sweetheart. It's too cold."

He heard her take one breath, a single breath, a sigh of some sort, he supposed. That was all he got: his reward, his punishment, he wasn't sure which. She strode numbly back to the porch. Raphael heard the screen door creak, bang shut, and rattle. It was coming off its hinges, and he lay on his back with only a shirt on, listening to that door creak and waver in the wind for a long time.

I don't believe this," said Dave.

"I do not have such a sick mind," said Errol, "that I would make this up."

"He fucked her in the front yard, with her husband watching."

"So I understand," said Errol.

"And I thought *I* was a wild kid."

"So what happened?" asked Gabe.

"I've got it," said Nathan. "She divorced her husband and married Raphael, and now they have three kids and a cocker spaniel."

"Right," said Errol wanly, feeling the same perverse sympathy for Raphael that Walter had from that window. "That's the way these stories always end up, isn't it?"

Errol shivered; the sky was scarlet. Regretfully, he pulled on his pants and drew on his shirt.

"You're not going?"

"No, but what do you say we go get a couple of drinks indoors? It's getting cool."

So the four of them drove off to a nearby bar, where there were only a few other customers; as Errol told the end of his story, strangers switched stools to sit nearby. It was such a familiar and predictable ending, Errol wondered that they were interested. A boy, a married woman who was a lunatic—what would happen, really? Errol was saddened there weren't more surprises in the world.

All through those high-school summers Raphael and his crew had regularly made trips to Cape Cod, so he knew the feeling of riding the crest of a wave, keeping his board just inside the curl, and surveying the whole beach as he rode forward. He knew how to cut a fine figure and stand high on liquid with a balance as on solid earth. He reminded himself that March that he knew this feeling, and tried to remember the light spray in his face, the feel of his hair whipping back, the keen cut of the board as it shore its way into the water. All he could recall, though, were earlier trips to the beach, family vacations when he was five or six. He had forged into the water then, too, but with no board and no height and no exhilaration either, only that stoic bravery that had gotten him through his entire childhood. At five he had trudged dutifully into the surf, stumbling at first in knee-deep foam, but walking on, even quickly and easily as the water drew back, until suddenly he faced a wave three times his height. He'd stand straight before it and wait, as he did in front of his father when Frank was going to hit him. In sickening slow motion the wave drew up and crumbled him under. The boy rolled and hit against the stony bottom and saw nothing. As he tried to stand up and stumble back, he'd no sooner get the water away from his eyes than the undertow sucked his legs out from under him and tucked him under the next wave, and the next—it wouldn't have been so bad, he remembered, just one wave, some salt in his eyes, a few swallows of brine—just one wave, and the others saved for another time, he could have taken that. But it never stopped. Over and over the water broke and pulled and dragged him down, and little by little Raphael swallowed too much water and not enough air, until he could no longer stand between waves and he gave over to his life as being lived below the surface of the ocean. Finally, and always a little too late, Frank would wade out and drag his son, coughing and limping and blinded by salt, back to shore.

But Raphael had left his father behind, and the steady crush of his affair with Ida was unrelenting. No one was pulling him out for air. Gradually his lungs were filling with water. Gradually his balance was less steady; there was no resting, no shore. The breakers from across the street bore down on him, and little by little he was being plowed under. With the same terrifying slow motion of a wave about to break, April and May curled over his head.

So much had changed. He did his homework with insane eagerness, and was frightened when it was through and he no longer had a sure distraction. He began to lose weight, for he wasn't very good about stringing girls along for pies lately; besides, at eighteen they expected more than a kiss at the door. Louis and the crew were loyal and brought him what they could, but at the end of senior year all their lives were widening and speeding up; Cleveland Cottons seemed smaller now, and behind them. And Raphael did not reliably deliver what he'd always traded for food: stature, silence, live black eyes. There were times his tensile strength failed, and he had trouble keeping his height; he could be heard to mumble; his eyes would deaden and go white.

Of course, there was always Ida if he got hungry enough, and sometimes he did. One weekend in late April, though, she insisted on sitting him down to eat a sandwich she'd prepared for him. Walter was there, naturally. Raphael was ravenous, but he could hardly swallow the bunches of heavy bread, and halfway through the meal decided that even starving to death was better than this: Walter looking dully at him and trying to make conversation, out of either sadism or embarrassment, he couldn't tell which, and Ida, as usual, having the time of her life. Finally, when Walter asked him, "How is school going?" he rolled his eyes and walked out the door.

Raphael continued to give parties, but not because he was in a festive mood. At least it was one sure way of eating something once a week or so; his guests brought provender, and often there were leftovers. He sometimes wondered, though, if the real reason he kept giving dances on his second floor was for the preparations beforehand, taking the cord over the road, pulling it down to Ida's house, and plunging those two prongs of his plug deep into her side socket. He liked the idea of the umbilical wire connecting them those evenings, the electricity tripping from her outlet to his mill, and he would watch out the window late at night to catch sight of the wire waving between poles in the moonlight.

Then it was June. School ended. At his graduation Raphael looked over the audience from the stage to find Ida clapping happily in the front row, in an insanely upstanding way, like a proud aunt. Then he noticed Walter next to her, clapping, but faintly, and looking pale, and he could not believe the man was there, as he could not believe it was June and it was time. He had to bolt from the auditorium to the boys' room to vomit what little food he had eaten that day.

"I cannot *believe*," said Ida, collapsing onto his white couch, "you're asking me to run away with you. I am stunned, I really am."

Raphael stood some distance away from her, tall again, determined. "There's nothing else for me to do. So believe it."

"Well, I'm curious," said Ida. "Where is it you propose to run off to?"

"Boston, for now."

"Pretty high rents."

He had to smile. "So I've heard."

"You're going to find another factory to play in?"

"I'll live somewhere. I'd like running water. I think I've earned running water."

"And how're you going to pay for your flush john?"

"I may go to school."

"That pays?"

"It can."

"Then what?"

"Then I'll travel. With you."

"And I thought *I* lived in a fantasy world."

"You do."

"Raphael baby, sweetheart, my little darling, don't you realize? All I can do is watch movies and get a tan. I cook like shit. I don't have a high-school diploma. I can't even read worth a damn, you idiot—I can't concentrate for more than five pages. I'm unemployable, stupid. And how would you buy me a john and paperbacks and olives? Forget oil-cured, how about the no-frills green ones?"

Raphael raised his hand to his forehead and touched himself between the eyes lightly with two fingertips, with a rare gentleness and sympathy for himself, as if giving himself a blessing or a baptism. "This is all beside the point," he said quietly. "The world is malleable. Ingenious people don't die in it without a fight. I've proved that. At thirteen I proved that. You're thirty-three. You'd think of something."

"If this is all beside the point, what's the point?"

Raphael shook his head. "Why do *I* have to say it?"

"You don't. I told you a long time ago, questions don't have to be answered. But if you don't say something, we're both just going to sit here."

"We are just sitting here. You don't mean that crap about olives. You're just talking. You're not even considering coming with me. You're just saying words. Making yourself feel better."

"I don't need to feel better," she said defiantly. "I feel just fine."

"No, you don't," said Raphael with difficulty. "You'll miss me."

Ida looked down and played with that same black kimono, over the same black bikini, and said nothing.

"Is that true?" he asked. "That you'll miss me?"

Ida mumbled something.

"What?"

"I said yes. Okay?"

Something huge in the boy fell. He turned away from her and exhaled; his shoulders crumbled toward each other. "Yes, okay," he said softly. "But you can only miss me if you're not with me. So we're straight. Thank you."

Behind his back Ida fidgeted in the ensuing silence, and at length jumped up from the couch and took several short, quick steps around the room. "You could stay through the summer," she said. "It was always our best season."

Raphael didn't turn. He said nothing.

Ida looked out the window at her lawn and tapped her fingernails against the pane. The sound was unnervingly loud; she stopped.

"Well, for Christ's sake, what did you expect?"

"I didn't expect anything," said Raphael. "I don't think that way. I'm only eighteen."

"Well, come on. You're a kid. I'm a grown-up."

He laughed.

"Thanks a lot," said Ida. She scuffed along the floor. "And I'm married.—Don't laugh at that, too, 'cause I *am* married."

"I wouldn't laugh at that, Ida. You think your marriage is funny. But I don't."

The next silence was longer.

"—Well, Raphael, it was fun and—"

"It was not fun."

"Come on, you've forgotten, when we used to—"

"Ida." Raphael turned to face her. "If you're going to keep saying things like 'It was fun,' maybe you'd better be out the door. I don't know what movie you last saw, but it seems to have been a comedy, or at least full of clichés. For God's sake, get out of here and go watch something with a little integrity. See *Casablanca* again and listen to the ending. You may not be discriminating, but I am. I don't want your bad movies in my life."

"You condescending son-of-a-bitch." Her eyes flashed as she looked at him; though she was angry, Ida hesitated for a tiny instant before swinging toward the door. No doubt Raphael missed this moment, for he had no mirrors in the mill and so could not now see himself as she saw him for one instant and as the world saw him then and ever after: Raphael Sarasola, hair blazing, lips full and red and drawn together, and most of all, those eyes beginning to burn. They did not look like the eyes of a man on whom any woman would turn her back ever again. Perhaps for some portion of that moment even Ida had second thoughts about walking out, but Ida was Ida and this story was set up from the very beginning to end a certain way. Maybe as much because she was a reader, a moviegoer, and could show some loyalty to form and plot, Ida did, then, turn and let herself out the boarded entranceway, imagining to herself that it was just Raphael. It was just Raphael, the vagabond.

So the next morning Raphael folded a few clothes into the same backpack with which he'd left Frank behind and let himself out of Cleveland Cottons with a hammer and a bag of nails. Slowly he drove nail after nail into the boards of the entranceway. All around the mill he covered the windows with planks, and the sound of his hammer, steady and slow and hard, carried across the street to wake Ida from her sleep. Incredulously she drew herself out of bed and watched from the porch in her robe as Raphael went with a deadly level gaze from window to window. He didn't look at her. Board after board he slapped over the glass, until the building let no light in and no light out and it stood facing Ida wooden and impenetrable. It would stare at her stoically for years this way; that was the idea.

After driving his last nail, he was about to throw the hammer aside, but he paused before he tossed it. You never know, he figured, what you'll have to protect, what you'll have to hit or drive in, where you'll need to board up next, so instead, he tucked the hammer in his pack along with Nora's rolled-up paintings and walked on down the road toward Boston.

He did go to college," said Errol. "When he filled out forms he said his parents were dead, and they gave him financial aid. In school you can bet he burned his way through several dozen women. He was a terror. And, gentlemen," said Errol to the gathering at large, placing his hands flat on the bar, "Raphael Sarasola is still with us. He is only twenty-five. And he is still"—Errol shook his head—"a terror."

chapter sixteen

For the next three evenings running, Errol threw on his corduroys and went slumming in roadside bars with Gabriel Menaker's construction crew, drinking heavily, driving wildly in Gabe's pickup over the same weaving roads that had made him so cautious in the Porsche, embellishing stories of Gray and Raphael and even Charles Corgie. For these few days the crew became Errol's secret underground life, one in which he was loud, expansive, garrulous, and well liked. Errol McEchern was a novelty to them—the anthropologist was, according to Dave, "a hoot."

Errol liked being a hoot. With a curious dread he noticed the light on in the den when he returned to the manse on the third night. So Gray was back from New York; the party was over.

He found Gray stooped by the ferret's cage. She toyed with the animal through the bars, and Solo didn't bite this time.

"Ralphie here?"

"No."

"Ah," said Errol, going over to the pet, "but his emissary is. This animal is a spy."

The ferret bared his teeth at Errol and hissed.

"I thought you'd like to know I've decided to give up anthropology and become a carpenter."

"That's nice, Errol." Gray finally pulled herself away from the ferret and looked at him. "So you're drunk. You don't usually do that. It's cute."

"I am cute. That's another thing I decided today. I am a handsome and entertaining man."

"I could have told you that a long time ago."

"But you didn't. Isn't that the way," said Errol cheerfully. "You know, I told a whole bar the other night about Ralph and that schizo in North Adams. Made quite a sensation, I must say."

Gray wasn't paying enough attention to find this strange. "I was thinking about Ida O'Donnell today. That pattern—I wouldn't want to repeat it."

"What?"

"I don't want to hurt him."

"*You* don't want to hurt *him*?" Errol laughed.

"What's so funny?"

"Our friend Ralph—well, I've never met anyone so impenetrable in my entire life! He's worse than you are."

"Oh?" She took a seat in her chair; the leather creaked stiffly.

Yet Errol felt breezy and somehow, after the raucous nights with Gabe, immune. "So tell me," he said flippantly, lounging onto the couch and propping his feet on the table, "are you fucking him yet?"

Gray looked up sharply.

"Pardon me," said Errol. "Let's give you both the benefit of the doubt: have you two *made love?*"

"It wasn't the wording. It was the question."

"And the answer?"

Gray paused and drew herself farther into the padding of her armchair. "No," she said finally.

"Ah. And has he tried?"

Gray chewed on the inside of her cheek and flipped the edge of her skirt down over her knee.

"Well?"

"Tonight."

"But you said no."

"That's right."

"Why? He's not bad-looking."

Gray just shook her head and said, "Too much," looking away.

Something about the way she said that made Errol stop. He didn't want to be cruel to her. She seemed sad. "Gray, do you want to talk about this? Do you want me to leave you alone?"

Gray looked down at the arm of her chair, her hand against her cheek with that same gentleness with which Errol had imagined Raphael touching himself when Ida wouldn't come with him to Boston. "No. Don't leave me alone. Who else am I going to talk to?"

"You wouldn't rather talk about this with a woman?"

She laughed bleakly. "What woman?"

"A friend."

"Haven't you noticed? I don't have any."

"You do, too—"

"All my friends are men. That is a fact. The women I know are *colleagues*. Errol, women don't like me."

Errol paused.

"See? You can't think of one."

"It's funny, Gray, I can't. That's damned strange."

"No, it's not."

"Why?"

"I don't know why, except that it makes perfect sense that women would have no use for me."

Errol stroked his beard. "You probably make them nervous."

"I make men nervous."

"They feel competitive."

"Men feel competitive."

"You're very critical."

"I'm critical of men, too."

"And I think you make women look bad."

Gray considered this.

"You make men look good, beside them. They want to be seen with you. But next to you other women look short. They look boring. They often look old, even though lately you're older than they are. They look as if they—need something. Want something. They look as if they're waiting. You're not. Other people are waiting for you."

Gray let out a long breath. "You're kind, Errol. Thank you. But we know each other well, so let me tell you." She paused. "And please, I'm a little sheepish admitting this to you. But I am waiting a little bit, and it makes me sick at heart. I don't want to disillusion you, Errol—I don't mean I'm a terrible fake. I keep busy; I love my work and my life and I have very few regrets. Or no regrets, because regrets are stupid. Had I wanted to live a different life I would have lived it—I'm that kind of person."

"You mean you don't regret you never got married."

"Thank you, Errol, you keep doing that. I hate being vague. Yes, I don't regret never having married. But—" She stopped.

"But what?"

"There is a place in me. It's about the size of a half-dollar. Sometimes I feel it right under my ribs. In my throat. Under my breastbone. It moves around. Sometimes it lodges in my lower back, and I slump in my chair. It's an ache. It feels a little bit like having a mobile tumor or blood clot or kidney stone. It's not solid, though. Oh, it feels that way, it feels heavy. But I've had it long enough and it's sunk to enough different places in my body that I've felt it out and I know what it's made of. It's made of nothing. It's my own private black hole. Wherever it goes is cold. If you put your finger in it, you'd feel it sucking at you, like a vacuum-cleaner hose that tunnels off forever. You'd feel all funny inside, Errol, even frightened. You'd take your finger back and hold it in your other hand and breathe on it to get it warm again.

"Don't get me wrong, Errol. I don't mean I feel this way, that my whole body is a gaping vortex. No. I go through my day. I talk to you, and I enjoy that. I do fine work and give lectures. I run off to Africa and make contact with people who will never understand until it's too late that I'm not a very typical representative of the white race. All this is real. It's just this small half-dollar-sized hole. It's not big. But it's there."

As Errol was listening, a particular question bloomed in his mind until it grew overwhelming, and Errol sat up straighter; his eyes opened wide as he sat and watched Gray speak in her chair. "Gray," said Errol, "I'm going to ask you something. You don't have to answer me. And don't take offense. But—"

"No."

"All right. I won't ask, then."

"No, I mean I know your question. The answer is no. No, I haven't."

Errol just sat there.

"You're surprised."

"I am. Astounded."

"I had a feeling from a long way back you assumed . . ."

"I did."

"I even felt guilty, as if I were lying to you."

"But, Gray, it's so unlike you—"

"Mm."

"There's hardly anything you haven't done."

"When I was young it was a culturally complex thing to do when you weren't married. Besides, I was on the lookout for an excuse to get out of it. I always imagined it would destroy me somehow. Obliterate me."

"You overestimate the experience."

"Maybe I'm overestimating *your* experience. But I've read a lot. And I know me. So I know this is a truly dangerous activity. For me."

"Gray, you're a human being—"

"Now, there is a frightening thought. No, Errol, I don't suppose I'd explode or dissolve or die. I never decided, Oh, I won't do that, it would hurt me. I didn't marry and time went on; I was busy. Until after a while and I didn't and I didn't and then finally the opportunity would come along and I still wouldn't because I never had. Stupid, isn't it?"

"But you've gone out with a lot of men—"

"Most men are afraid of me, Errol. They treat me with deference. If I'm to be blunt for a moment—"

"Please do."

"They don't put their hands up my skirt."

Errol looked her in the eye. "All of them except—"

She looked away, rubbed her arms as if she were cold, though it was a warm night, and stood up. She crossed to the window and stared out to the light by the walkway.

"Gray, what happened tonight?"

Her shoulders rose. "He put his hands up my skirt." Her attempt to sound casual was pathetic.

Errol now understood the phrase "treading on thin ice"; each step grew more precarious than the last. "So what did you do?"

"I *froze*."

". . . And?"

"He stopped. He was surprised."

"Does he know about your—historical reluctance?"

Gray shook her head.

"And you didn't tell him."

"I was embarrassed."

"Does he think you're a prude?"

She laughed quickly. "I guess I am."

"I mean, do you think he figures you're, well, cold?"

"Maybe I am cold. One of those sad, stiff women that other women like to write sanctimonious books about. Manuals, with diagrams, that make lots of money."

"No . . ." said Errol. "If you really believe it would be dangerous, you're not cold." Errol's heart was beating hard. "You've always seemed very—sexual to me."

"Well, I don't need a manual," she snapped. Errol was relieved she wasn't listening to him very carefully. "I know what an orgasm is. I'm not a fifty-nine-year-old ice tray."

"No one said you needed a manual," said Errol softly. "You're the only one who thinks there's something wrong with you."

Gray rubbed her forehead. "I'm too old for this. Errol, what have I gotten myself into?"

"Do you want out?"

"No."

"So what are you going to do?"

"What do you mean, what am I going to do?" she asked angrily.

The ice under Errol's feet was extremely thin now, and he heard it crack and rumble as Gray's voice itself gradually shattered with each answer. "I suppose I was asking," said Errol slowly, "whether you're going to sleep with him—or not. And I suppose I was also asking"—Errol spoke so slowly, so carefully now—"whether you ever will. Have sex. With a man. In your life."

Gray covered her eyes with her hand and shook her head in bewilderment. Had Errol been thinking, he would have excused himself to leave her alone, but he wasn't thinking, so instead he rose from his chair and went over to Gray by the window, taking her in his arms and pressing her head to his shoulder. With his other arm around her back he could tell how small she was, how thin her bones were, as he fit each finger of his hand neatly between her ribs.

The following couple of weeks Raphael appeared insistently at Gray's, often with Corgie's red baseball cap on backward at a cocky angle, which grated on Errol more than he could say. Even when the man was absent from the manse, the ferret scrabbled in its cage, hissing and raking its claws over the bars whenever Errol entered the room that used to be his favorite. Bwana would no longer walk near the den, and would use only the back door to go in and out of the house, because the foyer was too close to that sharp, narrow creature.

"I know, Bwana," Errol would confide to the dog. "New regime around here. We're the old guard." He stroked the iron-gray sides, and the dog stood still and looked into Errol's eyes with great trust. "But I've seen revolutions come and go. You take a step back and stay out of trouble, my boy. Lay low. Let the cocky young usurper strut through the halls of the old castle as if he's in for silk shirts and fine cognac and leisurely afternoon sports for the rest of his life. You and I, we pour his wine and take his coat and wait patiently for the new prince to make his first mistake and land smack back in the middle of his textile mill. Got it? The old guard endures. So we're going to cool our heels, doggie. We're going to use the back door and pad around the halls real quiet-like. We're going to keep our toenails tucked in. But when the new order topples, we'll move in for the kill. I'll take care of that ferret, Bwana, if you go for Raphael."

Bwana's tail hit dully against the wall.

"Aw, you're not going to go for Ralph at all, are you? I'm supposed to help you with Solo, but what do you do? What kind of an ally is that?" Errol rumpled Bwana's ears affectionately and shook his head.

In keeping with his own advice, Errol started going back to his own apartment at night. It was a place where he'd stayed more and more rarely through the years and had never put much into, but that didn't matter now—it was his, with some of the original furniture from his bedroom as a boy; the junk mail had his name on it; the clothes he kept here were the ones he never wore, but they still fit. It was a relief to be alone.

Though he hadn't seen her in five years—she was a film editor in Australia and not often in the States—Errol couldn't help but feel a twinge of resentment when in his second week of lying low a cable announced an imminent visit from his sister Kyle. She *would* have to come now, when for the first week in years he was living without a domineering older woman in his home. It was as if the fates had arranged his life in such a way that this particular relationship was his problem, and he was not to try to get away from it, because they would place it in front of him whichever way he fled. Errol was a responsible person, so he shouldered his problem with a sigh, having put it down for only a week, and tried to persevere with the weight of the thing returned to his back without complaining. She-was-his-sister. He-should-be-glad-to-see-her. He-loved-her. It was dreadful to have to hyphenate on the way to her plane.

For the moment before he recognized her, Errol saw his sister as others saw her: a fifty-two-year-old woman, aging gently but not miraculously, a few pounds overweight, with great energy, striding toward him with efficient carry-on luggage. Then she was Kyle. He wouldn't see her so clearly for the rest of her visit.

She was warmer than he remembered, and walked arm in arm with her brother toward the car. When she asked him how he was, Errol didn't know what to tell her. "Fine. Or I've been better. I don't know, Kyle. I thought when you grew up everything got all straightforward. It's not working out. Lately what I thought

I understood one day completely baffles me the next. I don't know if I'm fine. What's fine?"

"Are you in a mood, or did you just get weird these last five years?"

"Okay, Kyle, I'm just fine." Errol slammed the car door.

"Errol, don't pout. It's just I asked you how you were and you went into this long *thing*—"

"You mean you didn't really want to know, you were being polite. So, fine. I-am-fine."

They drove in silence, until Kyle squinted at him. "Are you okay? You do seem weird. Work okay?"

"I read about matriarchies. Of course. But I won't go into it. You were never much interested in what I do."

"Jesus, Errol, I just got off the plane."

Errol looked down to find he was clutching the steering wheel so hard his knuckles were turning white. "I'm sorry, Kyle," he said, not sounding very apologetic. "Please. Why don't you tell me about *your* work. Tell me about the ad you're editing and how well it's going and what awards it's going to win. Tell me how much money you're making and how everyone in Australia thinks you're the best, and tell me how happily married you are. Then I'll tell you that I'm distracted and screwed-up and that I work for someone else, that I'm second-rate, or at least second-fiddle, permanently, and that would be sad except that I don't give a damn about my profession right now. I'll tell you that I haven't slept with a woman for three years, but that I have a sick relationship with my large foam-rubber pillow that I hope to keep up through old age, as we crumble and yellow together in the coming years. I'll tell you I'm tired and confused and angry and jealous, and this is a strange time for you of all people to walk into my life."

Errol was glad he was driving and had an excuse not to look at his sister, who he could see in his periphery had bent her head down and was staring at her hands in her lap. He shouldn't have said any of this, Errol knew, but something had given way in him, as if he'd been holding his breath for months like *The Man Who Swallowed the Sea* and suddenly couldn't hold it in any longer. All the water he'd swallowed spewed back out, drowning his sister because she was there.

"Errol," asked Kyle quietly, "do you want me to stay somewhere else? I didn't know this was a bad time. Maybe I should see you on another visit."

As she said this, Errol felt a peculiar panic, and pulled over to a gas station as if by stopping the car he could also halt the progress of this conversation. She was his *sister*. Errol had a sudden visceral understanding too rare for an anthropologist of the importance of blood ties. At long last, you idiot, someone to talk to besides a dog. "I feel bad," said Errol. "I'm lonely. I feel betrayed, but I don't have any right to feel that way. I haven't been betrayed. No one has broken any promise to me that they actually made. So I can't even be angry. I'm just sick. I walk around, Kyle, and I feel sick. That's the answer to your question. I'm not fine at all. I don't want you to leave. I need someone around now. I'm glad you're here."

Kyle reached for Errol's hand and stroked it the way Errol petted Bwana when the ferret was making noises in the den.

"She's famous, Kyle. I can't talk to anyone about it."

"I assume this all has to do with Gray Kaiser."

"You said it." Errol took a deep breath and started driving again. "She's gotten into a—relationship. With a man."

"Well, you two are just friends, aren't you? Or are you?"

"Oh, we are just Friends, with a capital F. We should have T-shirts printed up: *Just Friends*. Lapel buttons. Paperweights for our desks. I feel as if I'm working on a goddamned merit badge."

"So who's the man?"

"For one thing, he's only twenty-five."

"You're kidding."

"I wish."

"She is too much."

"People are beginning to notice, too. It makes her look bad."

"I think it's a kick! That takes guts, Errol. What's he like?"

"Gorgeous. Savvy. *Opaque*. I don't trust him."

"You think he's looking for a Sugar Mommy?"

"Possibly."

"Even if he is, Gray Kaiser can take care of herself."

"That's what she thinks."

"Well, if it turns out he's in it for side benefits, she can throw him out on his ear, right? Meanwhile, she's having a good time. What a riot. I cannot believe this."

"I don't know how to explain it, but somehow it's not that simple."

"You have explained it. You're jealous, you said so."

"No, beyond that. She's seen men before. They've come and gone. This is different."

"Come on, baby brother. You don't expect this to last, do you? Just wait for it to blow over."

"It's not like that."

"What, they're going to get married?"

"No . . ."

"Well, then."

Errol liked this point of view. "So I should just wait, as always."

"Sure . . ." Kyle's brow rumpled, and she added uneasily, "Though for what?"

"Nothing," said Errol warily. "We'll go back to the way we were."

"You liked the way you were? Wearing T-shirts?"

"I'd rather be friends with Gray than married to any other woman."

"My God! What do you do, masturbate furiously every night?"

"That's none of your business."

"In all this time, have you seen other women?"

"Plenty."

"For how long?"

"It's varied."

"The longest."

"Couple months."

"You're forty-eight years old and the longest relationship you've sustained lasted a couple of months?"

"I've seen Gray Kaiser for twenty-five years!"

"As a friend!"

"Who cares?"

"You do!"

"You don't understand. All right, I'm frustrated, I admitted that. But I don't care that much about sex—"

"My brother doesn't care about sex. No wonder you get in the car and explode the first time I open my mouth."

"Our culture blows sexuality way out of proportion."

"Every culture does! There are only so many experiences of

consequence: getting born, having sex, having children, and dying. There you go. Everything else is just icing on the cake. You're the anthropologist; you should be telling me this! Art and work and friends, possessions, education—all just little extras."

Errol sighed.

"I'm right. You know I'm right."

"I don't want you to be right. I see her, talk to her, work with her, eat with her. I have everything, or almost. It shouldn't matter. It should be small."

"It couldn't be bigger."

"I don't understand it."

"That's just one of those mysteries you'll have to puzzle out nights sitting up awake in bed by yourself. But let me save you the trouble. Know how it works? You see a woman and you like her and you go for her. It doesn't work and you move on until something does, not move in and be 'friends' for the rest of your life and lock the bathroom door a lot. God, why do I have to tell you this? When can I give up on being your Big Sister? When are you going to give me advice for a change?"

"I'll give you some," said Errol. "Lay off and shut up."

Kyle laughed. But she did shut up.

E rrol showed Kyle his apartment; they had dinner; after an evening of talking about food and how to decorate Errol's flat, Gray snuck back into the conversation.

"I see articles by her from time to time," said Kyle. "I like to read them, as a way of keeping up with you."

It depressed Errol that to keep up with Gray's articles was in fact to follow his own work. "Yes," he said, trying to be mature about it, "she sometimes lists me as a consultant on her publications, which I appreciate."

"She writes some interesting stuff. But she can be—oh, how should I say it?—not very compassionate. A little hard."

"I'd think you'd like that."

"Why? You think of me that way?"

"Well. Yes."

Kyle shook her head and laughed. "Errol, you never have forgiven me for locking you in that cabinet, have you?"

He smiled. "No, I haven't. I'm still angry. And that was forty years ago. What would my Freudian friends call me? Retentive. That's it."

"Errol, I've raised four children, and I'm a regular sweetheart, a softie. A pushover even. I give them too much money. I let them come home and loll around the house eating sandwiches and watching TV when the poor confused darlings are between marriages. I brake for animals, Errol. I feed strays and give bums my quarters. I'm sorry, but I'm not who you think at all. And I feel so bad about that cabinet, yes, even forty years later, you sweet boy—" She reached over and tousled Errol's hair as if he were still eight years old. "So please, let me apologize. I'm sorry. I'm sorry, I'm sorry, I'm sorry."

They laughed, and finally at forty-eight Errol forgave her for locking him in that stupid cabinet.

K yle wanted to see Gray. They had liked each other before, if with a certain wariness; besides, Kyle had a taste for gossip, and Errol could let her in on the ground floor of this one.

Sure enough, when they drove up to the manse, the white Porsche was gleaming out in front, pulled up to the bumper of the gray coupe. Errol rang the doorbell.

"Come in!" cried a strained voice inside.

Errol walked in with Kyle to find Gray and Raphael in their tennis clothes arm wrestling in the den. Gray didn't look up as Errol entered the room; her gaze was locked with Raphael's. The tendons stood out on Gray's metacarpus all the way down her forearm; veins were beginning to rise. She had a pretty shoulder. There were hollows that formed at this degree of flex that Errol had never seen before, just about the size of a thumb; Errol had to resist the urge to touch them in the same way he had to stop himself from plumbing depressions of marble sculptures in museums.

While the look on Gray's face was one of pleasure, amuse-ment, the muscles over her eyes were curdling and her head began gradually to lower toward the table.

"Don't get this wrong," said Gray in a tight whisper. "This is a joke, Errol."

It was a joke. Errol looked at Raphael. There was no tension in his face, no pain, just an absurd gentleness. A small smile played over his lips. His own arm appeared firm, but not swollen. His shoulder was low; its lines were simple. He held her long, thin palm in his and seemed less inclined to defeat it, to press it down onto the table, than to keep it held in front of him indefinitely, balanced, force against force.

He nodded at Gray. "I'm pleased," he said. "I can feel it."

Gray rolled her eyes and with her mouth set in a wry contor-tion increased the pressure against his hand; the edges of her palm went white; small bulges of purple bloomed along her arm;

the hollows in her shoulder deepened. Her neck bent, bowed. Her elbow smeared on the mahogany table. Her forehead kneaded and the muscles stood out on her jaw.

At last a single indentation showed on his forearm. Yet the peak of their arms remained still. Gray did not push his hand one millimeter lower, so that the only movement in the pyramid was the rise and swell of muscles, the trickle of sweat from the crook of Gray's elbow, the tremble of her grip.

His eyes warmed from black to brown. "It saddens me to win. You know that."

Gray, whose head was now so low that she was staring into the wood grain, nodded with difficulty.

"However, I don't know how else to end this. You'll tire. Eventually you'll pass out." His voice was low, even, easy. "So here," he said, "let me help you."

Slowly, gracefully, the pyramid fell. Yet at no point did Gray relinquish her pressure, give in to defeat. When her arm was an inch from the table, Raphael looked regretful. In this last inch the two hands slowed and hovered, until they carefully lowered to the wood like a helicopter landing. Only then did Gray's arm relax, but gradually, the way big engines die.

Gray leaned back in her chair. Raphael spread her hand out on the table and traced her fingers. "You're strong," he said. "It's magnificent to see."

Gray smiled. "It feels good. That complete resistance. You know the feeling? Sometimes I try to move furniture by myself—a couch, a filing cabinet, something ridiculous, two or three hundred pounds. I can't do it, but I like to try. I like the feeling of applying more and more force, and meeting absolute resistance, absolute refusal. Watching the filing cabinet just sit there.

The only reason I don't pass out is that I always start laughing."
Finally, Gray took her hand back and swung around to her guests.
"Errol, I'm terrible. How are you? It's been so long. And, Kyle,
I didn't know you were in town. You've stolen your brother away!
I've missed him."

"Actually, I've only been here a day."

"Quite the recluse, then, Errol. Was it something I said?"

Errol mumbled something about work and could see that
Gray understood perfectly well.

"Who won your tennis game?" asked Kyle.

"The master," said Raphael. It was unclear to whom he
referred.

"So, Kyle, how long are you in town?"

"A week."

"We're getting tickets to see Hard Cheese on Tony next
Thursday. Would you two like to come along?"

"A new play?" asked Errol.

"They're a new-wave band," said Kyle.

"Oh, of course," said Errol. "I guess with all the other new-
wave bands we listen to day and night it's easy for Hard Cheese
on Tony to get lost in the shuffle."

"I've been to my share of symphonies," said Gray. "I thought
I'd try something different."

"Seems to me," Errol attempted to say casually, "you've tried
plenty that was different lately."

"I'd love to go," said Kyle.

"How do you know who they are?" asked Errol.

"They're from Australia. I helped edit their video for
'Marjorie and Her Filthy Dog.'"

"Oh, *they're* the ones who did 'Marjorie and Her Filthy Dog.'

There's only one thing you need to clarify, then, Gray," said Errol. "Are you serious?"

"Why wouldn't I be?"

"Well, what's the average age of the audience at one of these things? Twelve?"

"You mean I'm too old for this."

"I'm suspicious of your impulse."

"What is it you suspect?"

"Maybe we should wait to discuss this in private."

"Maybe we shouldn't. I'm curious now. What is it you suspect?"

Errol had the distinct sense of all three of them ganging up on him, but he took a deep breath and persevered. "The will to please . . ." he said steadily. "An effort to be youthful . . ."

"I am fifty-nine years old. I'll tell anyone who asks me. As for pleasure, I please myself, but I do sometimes try to please other people. If I didn't, I'd be a totally inconsiderate, self-absorbed woman. Isn't that so?"

Errol said nothing, pressing his lips together.

"When we go into the bush," Gray continued, "do we tell tribesmen, 'No, we don't want to hear drums and crude wind instruments. We don't want to pretend we're something we're not. But if you have a recording of Mahler's Sixth Symphony, we haven't heard that in a while'?"

"The parallel eludes me."

"Raphael is, effectively, from another tribe. It's simple graciousness to discover what his culture has to offer. It seems to me that our profession has a great deal wrong with it, a great many pitfalls, but I do embrace some aspects of our work: distaste for provincialism; reservation of judgment. When we're weak in our work it's when we fail to embody these qualities, never when we take them too far. Your suspicion, Errol, is *bad anthropology*."

Errol had the strangest experience. For a moment he didn't know what was happening to him. The skin on his face prickled and grew hot. His eyes burned. His chest tightened, and it was hard to take a full breath. This feeling was so unexpected and inappropriate that Errol didn't realize until it was almost too late that he was about to cry.

He stopped it just in time. "Gray, I'd really like to speak to you alone for a moment."

She inspected Errol carefully and at last nodded. They went upstairs to her study, and Errol closed the door.

"My sister is here," he said with effort.

"Raphael is here."

"All the worse, then."

"For both of us."

Time went by.

"Why did you do that?"

"Do what?"

"Make me look—" Errol ran his hand through the air, looking for an adjective. He could not come up with an interesting one. "Bad."

"To shut you up, frankly."

"Why?"

"You only remember what I said, don't you?"

"What did I say?" He honestly couldn't remember.

"That I was only interested in going to this concert to impress Raphael, and that I was trying to act younger than my age."

"You made me spell it out."

"I'd rather there had been nothing to spell."

"I didn't mean—" He did mean, Errol remembered. He meant everything, and more.

"You're my closest friend, Errol." She spoke now with steadiness and care. "But you can't say anything to me. I can't say anything to you. Our loyalty isn't that perfect; no loyalty is. I'm sorry I did that to you in front of Kyle. But likewise, you watch what you say in front of Raphael. Though we're close, we're both capable of the unforgivable. We're good anthropologists, Errol, but it's a shame to waste all our tact, deference, and respect on total strangers."

Errol stood.

"I'm apologizing," said Gray. "What are you doing?"

Errol found gradually he could breathe again. "Just now. You weren't threatening me, were you?"

"NO!" She stamped her foot. "It's just I don't want you to be cutting in front of that man downstairs when you know very well that you're right, that I do want to impress him, so if you care about me you keep your mouth shut, or I will humiliate you right back, and probably better. Is that clear?"

"Ever so clear." Errol sighed. Everything suddenly appeared simple. "And you won't accuse me of being a bad anthropologist in front of my sister, who is only too eager to believe that. And you will stop accusing me of being fusty."

"I won't stop accusing you of being fusty if you don't stop acting that way. For God's sake, what is wrong with seeing what a rock concert is like? I'd like to find out."

"Nothing. Nothing is wrong with it."

"All right. All right, then." Gray seemed confused that there was suddenly no argument. "So will you go?"

"I don't know."

"I want you to go."

"You're not just saying that?"

"How often do I say things because I should?"

"Not often enough."

"All right, then."

"You want me to go."

"I've missed you, Errol."

"It's not the same, with Ralph here."

"I know. But I like having you with me. I feel"—Gray had a hard time saying the word—"protected."

"Well, have you two . . ."

"No."

"Have you told him?"

"No. I have to, soon. It keeps coming up." She smiled. "So to speak."

"I'll come, if that's what you want."

Gray took Errol's hand. "Splendid."

When they returned downstairs, everyone was absurdly relaxed. Raphael acted like a human being, and seemed to have had a personable conversation in their absence. Kyle said she knew the members of Hard Cheese and could call to get good seats. She told stories of editing rock videos, but actually listened (a little pointedly, Errol thought) when Errol described their matriarchy study coming up in February. Never having been to Africa, she didn't react strongly when Errol told her about the Lone-luk, but she seemed excited when he mentioned they were arranging parallel interviews the following week in the South Bronx. Kyle had lived in New York for several years, and the idea of forging through those burned-out buildings and junkie-strewn streets seemed braver and more exotic to her than going on safari through Africa.

When the four of them went out to dinner, they had a wonderful time, again in this absurd way, as if the odds against such an evening being civil, much less a joy, were so great that it struck them all as a challenging project. In fact, the time went so fast and they got so drunk and the conversation was so rapid-fire that Errol actually found himself looking forward to the concert later that week. Then Errol realized he was looking forward to a rock concert with Raphael Sarasola and felt, inescapably, a little crazy.

chapter seventeen

I know you don't want to hear this, Errol," said Kyle as they were both recovering from mild hangovers the next morning, "but I think the two of them are pretty amazing together. I've never seen Gray around anyone who was her match before."

"Thanks," said Errol.

Kyle reddened. "I mean, except you—"

"I know what you mean," said Errol curtly.

"Gray obviously thinks a whole lot of you," said Kyle with care. "But there's a way you don't see people anymore when they're too familiar."

"Swell. So Errol the Invisible Brother doesn't measure up to the incomparably visible Sarasola."

"Well, frankly—"

"Frankly what?"

Kyle squirmed. "You're a good-looking man, Errol. And you're intelligent and funny; you're sweet. In fact, you're tremendous, I'm proud of you."

"I get the feeling there's a big 'but' coming that I'm not going to like."

"But."

"Go ahead."

Finally Kyle blurted, "But Raphael Sarasola is the most handsome man I've ever seen." She looked into her coffee. "Sorry."

"Don't apologize. Mr. Sarasola's looks are a matter of record."

"You're up against one heck of a thing, Errol."

"In some ways I always have been."

"Errol, how can you stand it?"

"I'm either a man of great character and endurance, or I'm an idiot. And don't tell me which, because I think after twenty-five years I'd rather not know."

Impulsively, Errol called Gabriel Menaker.

"Gabe, you like Hard Cheese on Tony?"

"Sure. They're a little after my time. But for new wave they're top-flight. The drummer's sharp. And the lyrics are nasty. Why'd you ask?"

"I wondered if you wanted to see them in concert with me and some friends this week."

"Errol, my boy, are you going through midlife crisis?"

"I told you to stop thinking that way, Gabe. Besides, this wasn't my idea; it was Sarasola's."

Gabriel's voice perked up. "You mean Ralph's coming? The lady killer?"

"Yes. So if you have a woman you're interested in, don't bring her along."

"Well, you've sparked my curiosity, McEchern. Count me in. Maybe I'll bring the boys."

G abe, it's Errol again."

"Eight o'clock, right?"

"Yes, but listen." Errol felt as if he were back in seventh grade. "What do I wear?"

He laughed. "I think: designer jeans, a silk shirt open to your navel, and a lot of gold chains . . . or is it spiked hair, black boots, and a dog collar? Honest to God, McEchern, I'm not sure. I think I should warn you, my boy, *I'm* gonna look old there. Most guys like me are still listening to their scratched-up Grateful Dead albums."

"The good old Grateful Dead."

"You've never heard of them, either."

"Sorry."

"You have been living in this country the last twenty years?"

"Much of the time. Same country as you. Different tribe."

"My man, you do have a way of putting things."

"So does a friend of mine."

"What's that?"

"I want you to meet that woman."

"Can do."

"But something about middle-aged men in jeans has always annoyed me."

"Khaki."

"Good idea. Thanks, Gabe. And listen. Did you mean we're going to be surrounded by teenagers?"

"Pre-cisely."

"This whole thing is crazy."

"My man, McEchern. What d'ya say. This could be a riot. You're right, it's crazy. That's why I'm going. There's no sign at Ticketron says you gotta be under seventeen to get a seat. So, fuck it. I like their music, I like you, I like my crew. Fuck it. Maybe we'll get high, that'd help."

"Terrific. I'll get high, the way I always do before a rock concert."

"You ever smoked?"

"I've smoked concoctions you and your friends have never dreamed of, but the lowly marijuana plant, never."

"Then we'll get you stoned out of your mind, my man. I've got some sinse that'll shave hairs off your head."

"I'd like to keep my hair for as long as possible."

"I've hit a sensitive area, McEchern?"

"I have middle-aged spread, but a full head of hair, Menaker. Don't take shots."

"Got it. But I am bringing some smoke. And you will be one relaxed boy, let me tell you."

"Good enough," said Errol, surprised at himself. "I could stand to be relaxed. I don't think I've been relaxed in twenty-five years."

As their party collected on Gray's front lawn before the concert, Errol noted that Raphael had hardly decked himself out. He was wearing faded jeans, old off-white long underwear, and ratty Converse All Stars; but he looked fantastic, and he knew it. Errol looked down at his own deliberate khaki slacks, the shirt which was "casual" but brand-new and never washed, still showing the creases from its folding in the original package, stiff with sizing from the factory. He'd kept his new desert boots carefully out of puddles for a month now, and why had he bothered? When Ralphie Sarasola hadn't even combed his hair?

"So what are we waiting for?" asked Gabe.

"Madame Kaiser."

"You mean the old lady. She, like, caking on the makeup in there?"

"No, the Wise One doesn't do that. She's probably finishing just one more paragraph of an article. I haven't figured out whether Gray actually enjoys making people wait, but she definitely considers it her privilege."

"Hey, your sister's all right," said Nathan. "She knows more about rock and roll than *I* do. And she's been all over the place!"

Errol gritted his teeth and did not say, "So have I," but, "Yes, all over the world." Adulthood could be so taxing.

Gray appeared at the door with that little pause of people who know how to make an entrance before she turned to lock it behind her. Then she looked at Raphael. Something was changing. Lately when the two were present at the same time the air hummed like a transformer, the voltage went up a few watts. When Gray drew toward Raphael, Errol could hear the creak of those porch boards like the crackle of a Jacob's ladder.

Errol retreated quickly to Gabe's pickup with the crew; as they drove over to the hall, Gabriel lit up a joint and passed it around. As instructed, Errol pulled in the smoke and held his breath. Its acid, basil flavor was tangy and lasting, like a good Italian tomato sauce, and Errol savored this bitterness with his tongue.

Their party had good seats, right in the pathway of two

ten-foot speakers. Errol sat between Gabe and Gray. He watched intently as Raphael leaned over and kissed her. They both kept their eyes open. Can you focus on someone's face that close up?

I can't remember. I haven't kissed a woman for three years, and she wasn't even important. Funny how crucial Julia has become simply for being the last one, the last paltry effort at having Relationships with Women. What a farce they were. So I could answer Kyle correctly, Yes, I have seen other women. Remember "going out," dressing, usually at Gray's, making a show of it. Putting on cologne. Fridays like this one, finally there being nothing more to do, no more restaurant reservations to call in, and I'd have to be sure I had the keys to my apartment—Gray always cracking some joke about "Don't stay out too late," and me trying to decide whether to drop the woman off and come back to Gray's or take the woman back to my place and do it.

Raphael's arm was around her back. Errol moved over so that those fingers grazed his own shoulder. They had pretty nails, clean, trimmed.

It was always hard to walk out that door. I always wanted to stay in the manse, even if I only read all night in the den. Then I could still hear the clack of the typewriter upstairs, the sound of her feet overhead, the flush of the toilet, running water; besides, it was her house. But duty called. So I'd spend the evening with some pretty, intelligent, witty woman, someone plausible—I was good at casting. And I usually did take them home and take off their clothes the way I was supposed to. I made sure I was a man. I know what this thing feels like, what Kyle thinks is so important. Then Gray said—Gray said I didn't, or something. What did she say? "Maybe I'm overestimating your experience." Well, maybe so, but that's your fault, Gray Kaiser. So it hasn't been so great. So my mind has even wandered, okay? I've thought about appointments; I've thought about . . . You know what I've thought about, damn it.

Errol moved his shoulder away from Raphael's fingertips.

My mind has wandered, and it's your fault, Kaiser.

The warm-up band began to play. They were loud, and Errol had to admit he liked them. The bass vibrated his diaphragm as if he were talking in a low voice. The guitar trembled in his bones; the synthesizer sent the smoke in his lungs into turgid, acrid little circles. The seat, too, shook from the drums, and Errol could feel the tom-toms hollow out his bowels.

Hard Cheese on Tony were even better, but they frightened him. Somehow the music and the performance didn't jibe; Errol had the feeling he was watching the picture from one channel and the sound from another. The music was tense; the musicians were languid. Loudly as he played, the lead singer moved calmly and bonelessly about the stage as if he were deaf. Yet the more dispassionate his delivery, the more the lyrics rippled with disdain. Errol shifted in his seat, feeling uneasy, disconnected, mistrustful.

The band began with "Earnest Couples Sitting Alone," "Queasy and Despondent," "Muffins Stand for So Much," "Two More Chaps in Gas Ovens," "Mother Has Got Rather a Cold," and "The Art of Being Shown over Houses." In their second set they played "A Trip to the Bonesetters," "When Father Papered the Parlor," "Sheila Shrub," "The Pudding without Protein Was Unattractive," and "Nursie Panting at the Bridle." As Errol listened to the words, he was overcome by a burdensome irony. He was sure Hard Cheese could write a perfectly hilarious song about his shirts with the factory sizing and his Hush Puppies and his little handful of fat upstairs in the bathroom mirror. So close to the front, Errol became convinced that the vocalist was mocking him in particular; he slumped inconspicuously in his chair.

For their encore Hard Cheese on Tony returned for "Marjorie and Her Filthy Dog" and "Two Is a Crowd." Errol braved a look to his right. Raphael had pulled Gray's head to rest on his shoulder. His eyes were open and soft. Slowly Raphael turned to look straight back at Errol over Gray's head. His eyes did not change but remained wide and furred. The white lights on stage flecked in his pupils and flashed in the oily surface of his skin. Errol looked back. Raphael did not blink. *Here*, the man seemed to say. *Swallow this. Hold it in. I am your after-dinner smoke. I am the sting in your lungs, the heat in your eyes. It is I who make the flap of your diaphragm quiver, who make your bones tremble, your bowels grumble, your chair loosen in its bolts on the floor. You breathe me in. You inhale my arm around this woman. Here is your bitterness. And you are a sucker, Errol. You are a fool. You ask for pain and you get it. I will not pity you, for a moment. You feel the bass? I am the power of those chords. You feel the drums in your skull? I am sitting at those traps. I am on that throne, with my foot on the pedal. I am younger and this is my music. I play it at you. It overtakes you. You have been overtaken. You have been overtaken and you could have prevented it, so you are a fool. The only thing you could not prevent, though, was being a fool. That is what you were born and the rest follows from that and that is what is so pathetic.*

chapter eighteen

I told him."

"What?" Errol didn't care. Such an awful morning. When he moved his hand to reach for his cup, it seemed it would never get there. Finally, the porcelain on his finger was smooth and warm. Please, Gray, shut up. I am not a hero.

"You know," said Gray.

It seemed minutes before her words slurred into his head. Oh, I know, do I? And why do I know so goddamned much? I want to be a carpenter. Jesus was a carpenter, right? So what's wrong with that? I could be Jesus, but skip the parables on the hillside, and *please* skip the crucifixion. I mean, it's clear to me lately that I'm a saint; I wouldn't dismiss the possibility out of hand that I'm the son of God. However, I think I'll be Jesus the Carpenter. I'll skip the stuff about beams in people's eyes and stick to the ones on the roof. I will redeem the sins of the world by constructing a series of perfect mortise-and-tenon joints. I think this tack will make me more popular than the cross gambit in the long run. It wouldn't make everyone feel so guilty. Gabe, how about it? Set me up. Sit me in front of a red-and-white-checked oilcloth every morning. I don't have to have Gray's fresh-ground coffee; instant would do, bad instant, old, crusty, STALE instant—just get me out of here.

"Errol, are you still asleep?"

"I wish."

"What's wrong?"

Somehow the question struck Errol as hysterical, and he laughed.

"You're acting very strange lately."

Errol sighed and leaned back in his chair. "I spend a lot of time living other people's lives, Gray. You know that about me, don't you? Well, once in a while I live my own life. It's not fun, but somebody's got to do it. Whenever I do that, you see, whenever I'm not completely focused on what's happening in your life, you think I'm distracted."

"Now, what did I say to deserve that?"

"Nothing. I'm so sorry. I'm a terrible person."

"You are not, but would you snap out of this?"

"You mean, would I please go back to living your life."

"Errol, did something happen to you I don't know about?"

"Oh no. You know everything, or just about. That's actually what makes this whole thing interesting."

She paused. "I hope you're enjoying this, because I'm not."

"Don't worry, I'll stop. I'll go back to being 'normal,' and everyone will be happy, or whatever it was they were. Besides, Gray, honest to God, I'm not doing anything. I'm just talking."

"You were pretty strange last night, too."

"I was stoned."

"And you give me a hard time about going to a rock concert."

"You said we were investigating the culture. I was participating in the full ritual, that's all. However, I must say I don't remember the end of the evening. Did we go somewhere?"

"We went out for drinks. And you were incredibly nice to Raphael. You paid him compliments, made conversation, bought him vodka, top-shelf."

"I was nice to him?"

"You acted like his long-lost friend."

Errol smiled. "Splendid."

"Frankly, he started to avoid you after a while." Gray paused, and inserted casually, "You don't happen to recall what Arabella was bending your ear over, do you? After talking to Raphael, she spoke to you for quite a while."

"I do, come to think of it. She's upset with you. She's done all that work for you on matriarchies, but according to Arabella, you have yet to ask her to go with us in February to study the Lone-luk. Granted, it's still only August, but she claims you've avoided the subject whenever she's brought it up. And she's really put herself out setting up the interviews in the South Bronx next week, but evidently you're not even asking her to go with us to New York. You've asked Ralph."

Gray grunted.

"Why not ask both of them to New York?"

"Absolutely not."

"Why?"

Gray drummed her fingers on the table. "She answers the phone a lot."

"She's supposed to."

"Fast. Within one or two rings."

"So?"

"Then she chats."

"What's wrong with that? And you think I'm strange."

"She stays late."

"What are you getting at?"

"More than she ever has, she stays and works late into the evening. She eats here more often than she used to. She gets the door."

Errol waited. Gray tapped the table with the pads of her fingers now in a slow, heavy rhythm. "She hurries to get the door. I've seen her."

"Uh-huh."

"And then she chats."

"Uh-huh."

The tapping got slower and heavier.

"*She plays with my ferret.*" She stopped tapping; her eyes blackened and narrowed and she sounded for all the world like an angry little girl.

"Ah," said Errol.

"Yes," said Gray. "Ah."

"I think maybe," said Errol delicately, "you're getting paranoid."

"I've always been a rational person."

Errol almost added, "Before February," but bit his lip. "Did something happen last night?"

"Nothing I could point to."

"Your evidence isn't very persuasive."

Gray sighed. "I suppose not. I'll try to stop being ridiculous." She brushed the crumbs of coffee cake off her hands and began cleaning the kitchen.

"Sorry I came back here. I should have gone home and left you alone with the protégé."

"It was fine. You walked inside and you were out. Raphael and I stayed on the porch. I was glad you were inside. I told him, but that was all I intended to do."

"What did he say?"

Gray slowly wiped her hands with a damp dishcloth. She smiled shyly. "It was nice out last night. Lots of stars." She stroked each finger with the cloth separately. "There's a way he has, of smiling." She wiped her forearms one at a time.

"He doesn't smile very much," said Errol, watching. "Have you noticed?"

"No, but when he does . . ." Gray wiped across the counters with her cloth. She swabbed down the canisters of sugar and flour. She took her damp forefinger and pressed it onto stray coffee grounds, picking them up one by one. She examined the grounds closely and rolled them around between her thumb and forefinger. "There's a passage in Mahler's Sixth. In the *Andante*. You know that symphony well?"

"Since it's one of *your* favorites, of course I've heard it performed ten or twelve times."

"The Tragic Symphony. There's a moment when a flute rises, and a high, lyrical cadenza pulls out from nowhere. It's the single place in that symphony where you can breathe; where the clouds break; where for a few measures everything doesn't seem so terrible. Well, Raphael's smile is like that, this particular smile. It pulls out of nowhere. It raises the hair on my arms."

She seemed happy, purling around that kitchen as if a cool, secret creek burbled quickly and serenely at her feet. Errol yearned to be hateful. He wanted to stay a stolid black lump in her kitchen, disgruntled and charred. It wouldn't work. Gray seemed light this morning, and every move she made with that damp cloth was graceful. Her ankles were so slim. The water ran beneath the muscles in her face, and her voice spilled from her mouth as a stream through a sluice. Listening to her was like going for a swim. He could not maintain his anger, so he gave up and dissolved the soot of his disgust into the brook of her pleasure. Bits of black grain by grain trickled away from him as he watched Gray pick up grounds with her finger, run the faucet over her hand, and wash the dark specks down the drain.

"So you told him," said Errol, "and he smiled."

"Yes," she said. "That way."

"And?" Errol felt immersed in a horrible reservoir of understanding.

"He was delighted."

"Why do you suppose?"

"I don't know. No reason. Just that it was the most charming and wonderful thing he'd ever heard."

"God, I hope he's for real," said Errol quietly.

Gray's face dropped. The water drained away. The sluice ran dry. "What do you mean?"

"Nothing."

"*What* do you mean?"

"Nothing," said Errol staunchly. "I shouldn't have said that. I'm sorry."

Having pulled the plug on such a clear, cheerful spring, Errol slunk away to his work for the day.

* * *

That Sunday Errol drove Kyle to the airport, and when she said "Take care of yourself" in parting, Errol had a funny feeling he probably wouldn't.

I've always felt bad about missing out on World War II," said Errol. "It looks as if I'm going to get my chance. This looks like Dresden."

They were driving up Melrose Avenue in the South Bronx. "What's the story here?" asked Raphael.

Gray explained. "Landlords hire arsonists to burn their buildings for the insurance money."

"Can we leave a sign? I don't want the insurance for my Porsche."

As they parked, Gray suggested they stay together for the first interview so Raphael could get an idea of the kinds of questions to ask; later she'd send him on a separate mission.

Once they got out, Raphael shot his car a wistful look. He picked a dried piece of mud affectionately off the body, and checked twice that the doors were locked. He had set the alarms, all three of them. Then he paid a boy on the corner ten dollars to watch the car, with the promise of another ten if the car was intact on his return. Raphael might never have been here before, but he immediately seemed to understand how the place worked. Errol found himself thinking that maybe Raphael wouldn't make such a bad anthropologist at that.

The lobby had once been ornate, though its mahogany trim was slapped over thickly with dour green paint and the fireplace was filled with garbage. They picked their way upstairs. Roaches rustled through the trash. Shadows darted down the halls; Raphael shuddered on the landings. The stairwell smelled of old fat; Errol breathed through his mouth. The lights were out. The grating of their shoes was loud.

Outside 6B Gray spoke to someone through the door; the woman who opened it held out her large hand to Gray and pumped it once, hard. "Leonia Harris; real pleased to make your acquaintance." Her voice was deep, her vowels round.

"Gray Kaiser. My colleague Errol McEchern. My assistant Raphael Sarasola."

"Lord," said Leonia, looking Raphael up and down. "Do come in, honey. You'll brighten up this place in no time."

Errol sat on the couch. The springs were broken, and Errol found he had either to perch on the edge or sink so far back it would be hard to get out.

"Where'd you get an assistant like that is all I'd like to know," said Leonia. "Wouldn't mind that kind of assistance myself! So tell me, darlin'," she said to Raphael. "You talk?"

"Not much." Of course, he'd found the one comfortable chair in the whole living room.

"Smart, honey. Boys like you open your mouth, it most always be terrible disappointing. Now, can I get you folks a cup of coffee?"

"Yes, I'd love a cup," said Gray.

While Leonia was in the kitchen Errol looked around the room. It was neat and clean. While much of the furniture looked like curbside salvage, the wood was polished and rips were repaired. Travel posters covered the walls.

Leonia returned; her wide arms didn't jiggle as she set down the tray. Though not fat, she had breadth. Her shoulders stretched her cotton dress taut. Her calves swelled as big around as Gray's thighs. If Errol were ever in a fire and needed saving, this is the kind of woman he'd want to pull him out.

"You a professor?" she asked Gray.

"I'm an anthropologist," said Gray. "I study people and the way they live."

"So what can I do for you, Missus Kaiser?"

"Miss."

Leonia raised her eyebrows. "Too smart for 'em, huh?"

"Oh, I don't know," said Gray softly. "If you end up by yourself after fifty-nine years, how smart is that?"

"'Pends on what you pass up. Sometimes pretty damn smart. Sometimes not."

"And you're married."

"More or less. You ask Raymond that same question, I wonder what he'd tell you. That is, if you could find him."

"Your husband has taken a—leave of absence."

"That's a real sweet way of putting it."

"How long ago did he leave?"

"Six years. But he be back. Ray be back. I just waitin'. I ain't in no big hurry, neither. But he be back."

"Why?" asked Raphael.

She turned to him and pointed her finger. "You boys think you so precious. You thinkin' you don't need nobody. I look at you, I see right through your little head. I's a hundred years ahead of you. You got a big surprise comin'. Time come and you get in on it, but I's already in on it. I got this big secret, an' every man in the world gotta take so long gettin' to it, something I knowed when I's fourteen."

"What's the secret?" Raphael seemed to really want to know.

"All these men afraid of bein' crowded, ain't they? They need all this room, they afraid some woman gonna crawl in their head and take over. Well, surprise, surprise. Ain't nobody crawlin' in there 'cept *you*, honey, and you get older and older and it get stuffy in there. Let me tell you, you afraid of other folks takin' away your elbow room, well, just relax. You born alone, you die alone, and you get any *kind* of company in between, you one lucky boy. Bein' by yourself ain't no accomplishment. Ain't like being no kind of hero. Ray, see, Ray sho 'nough figures he gettin' away with somethin', understand me? He think he a clever boy, runnin' round with whores, gettin' diseases, drinkin' his heart out till five in the a.m. Lucky Ray, huh? Well, what Raymond Harris gettin' away with is not see his kids grow up, and when he do come back they call him Mr. Harris 'steada Daddy, and they shake his hand 'steada kiss his cheek, and they spit when he turn his back. And I spit, too, though I'll take him in again and love him, 'cause that's what I's here to do. But I spit anyways, 'cause he such a dumb sucker, understand me? 'Less stupid ole Ray Harris die by hisself in some alleyway. Sho, run away. Best way in the world to be nothin'. Risk endin' up croaked by garbage cans, when he could die in my arms?" Leonia put her coffee cup in its saucer, and it rattled softly. "That no way to be the big man, baby. That just be dumb and sad. You got me?"

Raphael's brow creased ever so little. "There's something missing," he said after some consideration.

"'Course you think so. You a baby. A pretty baby at that, so you think you extra precious."

Raphael seemed actually to be thinking. Errol had never seen this. "Yes, something is precious. Maybe Raymond is keeping it. I'm keeping it."

"And what's that, baby?"

"He means," said Gray slowly, "he never stays home for even ten extra minutes to see if the phone will ring. That even if he is home and it rings, he can choose not to answer it. That he goes to movies by himself and has a wonderful time." Gray leaned back heavily in her chair, as if the exertion of these last statements had been exhausting.

"You're waiting," said Raphael. "I wouldn't do that."

"Waitin'?"

"For Raymond."

She shrugged. "It's somethin' to do."

"I'm alive," said Raphael. "That's enough to do."

"So you happy by yoself?"

"Happy. Unhappy. I don't make those distinctions. I can remain as I am."

"How lucky for the world." Errol couldn't restrain himself.

Leonia cocked her head, her eyes moving between her three guests. They were not just colleagues.

"How do you make a living, Mrs. Harris?"

"I work for the Water Department, filin', answerin' phones. It's part-time, but I'm goin' to school now down the way, at College of New Rochelle, South Bronx campus? I'm learnin' computers."

"How many children do you have?"

"Four."

"And you support the family?"

"Best I can."

"You mentioned you'd be willing to take your husband back."

"That's right."

"Would you support him?"

"Honey, I'd have to. Ray can't do nothin' but drink. I hear that don't pay so good."

"You'd call yourself the head of the family now?"

"I spose."

"If your husband returned, who would be the head of the family then? Or would there be one?"

"Oh sho. Ray'd be head. He the man, ain't he?"

"Yes," said Gray slowly, with professional lack of irritation. "But you'd consider him your superior even if you were supporting the whole family?"

"Superior. I don't mean he better than me. But a man gotta be top dog in his own castle, don't he?"

"Even if—"

"Maybe you don't understand, Miz Kaiser," Leonia interrupted. "Out there on the street Ray Harris get treated no better than a wad of gum stuck on somebody shoe. One of the reasons Ray don't come back home is he embarrassed. He don't have no job. He losin' his muscle, gettin' a belly. Where else but here he gonna get treated like somebody?"

"Have you seen him since he left here?"

"Oh . . ." Leonia resettled in her chair, perhaps none too comfortable with her memories. "Couple times he show up. Stewed, as usual. I gots to send the kids next door . . ."

"Why?"

"Ray can get a little—charged up when he drinkin'."

"Did he hit you?"

"I spose that what I's gettin' at."

"But you'd still take him back, and as the head of your household."

"Yep."

"Would you do what he told you to do?"

"'Pends on what it was, maybe," she said warily.

"First, in general."

". . . Yes."

"Would you go somewhere he wanted to go, even if you wanted to go somewhere else?"

"Yes."

"What if he told you to quit school?"

"Why he do that?"

"You never know. Maybe he'd be afraid you were getting smarter than he is."

"I already smarter than him."

"All the worse, then. Would you quit?"

"If it mean he stay—yes."

"Mrs. Harris, what if he continued to beat you?"

". . . Yes . . ." Her yeses were getting harder, and so more important. Having taken a certain tack, though, Leonia seemed doggedly determined to see it through.

"Mrs. Harris, what if Raymond threatened to kill you? Would you still keep him in your home?"

"I kick him out, he so much as touch my children."

"That wasn't my question."

"To kill me?"

"Yes."

Leonia was struck with a peculiar paralysis. "I got a lot to say, or somethin' anyway. It not too clear."

"Take your time."

"I'd—die for that man, Miz Kaiser. Not 'cause he so special. I know he a drunk, and gettin' old, and surly. He not so smart, nor handsome, nor nothin', really. But I's a bit heavy myself, and doin' awful in my English class . . . That not what I mean." She seemed flustered.

"Relax. We'll listen. Some things are difficult to say."

"I can see from the questions you been askin', Miz Kaiser, you think I's some kind of a—"

"These are simply the questions of my study. I don't intend—"

"You think I's a duck."

"I'm not familiar—"

"An easy mark," Raphael interpreted. "A pushover."

"I don't—"

"A duck. You a lady don't let no man tell you what's what, that right?"

"Yes, that's right," said Errol.

"But see," Leonia went on, "I could tell Ray at my door, I go to school, I earn the green, you do what I say. And Ray say, Woman, look at my back. There his back be, lower and lower down the stairs. Bye, Ray. And then I got my school. I got my kids. I got my say. I got everything I got now. Well, that ain't enough, Miz Kaiser. My bed big and messy and lonely. If I gotta say, Ray, you the head, and he say, You bet, all right. If I gotta do this, I gotta do that, all right. 'Cause the main thing is, Ray Harris in my house. If I gotta convince him he the boss, all right, 'cause in the end I still gettin' my say. I got a man in my bed. I got somebody to cry over if he dead. I got somebody who, wherever he be, don't hear the name Leonia Harris without perkin' up his ears and feelin' funny inside. That what I say—I want. All that other stuff, movin' and followin' orders and even gettin' hit around once in a while— that be nothin'. And if he threaten to kill me, or even if he kill me—well, he crazy, but he still gonna hear 'Leonia Harris' and feel real funny. But you think *I's* crazy, doncha, Miz Kaiser?"

"I don't know." Gray shook her head. "I don't know what's crazy anymore.—I'm sorry," she said, trying to pull herself out of whatever she'd gotten herself into. "I don't understand what I'm studying. That's why I study anything, because I don't understand it. Otherwise there'd be no point. Thank you so much. You've been most helpful."

On the way out the door, Gray turned resolutely to Leonia and told her, "We've located your husband, Mrs. Harris."

"Oh?" she asked in a small voice.

"He's in a city shelter a few blocks from here. Mr. Sarasola is going to interview him after leaving here."

"Well—tell him hey," she said limply.

"Anything else?"

She suddenly seemed plunged into despondency, and for all her romanticism, her real situation must have presented itself in all its unpleasant complexity. "No," she said. "Don't even say hey. Don't bother."

Errol turned from the door with a general feeling that everything was impossible and oppressive and bound for no good.

Downstairs, Gray sighed and told them, "For every Leonia Harris, there are five other women who would meet their husbands at the door with a Colt .44. Errol, you're right, this place does feel like a war zone." Gray gave Raphael directions to the shelter where Raymond Harris had been found; she and Errol would do the next two interviews and they'd all meet back at the car. Once Raphael had launched down the dusty streets, Gray suggested she and Errol split up and do the two interviews separately.

"Well . . ." Errol scanned the old men with bottles in doorways and the group of teenage boys on the corner kicking the parking sign and smoking pot. "Maybe we should stick together."

"Oh, Errol, this whole place is beginning to get to me. I want to get this over with; 182nd is right up there. Don't forget to record everything. I'll meet you at the car."

Errol paused, and thought of calling her back as he watched her stride with that characteristic lope down the crumbling sidewalk. The men in the nearest doorway, too, watched her swing by, the gray silk skirt rippling, her white blouse blazing in the hard sun of early afternoon. But Errol could never call her back from anywhere, *'l-oo-lubo, ol-changito, ol-murani*, and he shook his head at the picture of this striking woman ranging so casually through burned-out streets and past junkies with swollen arms. Errol turned to do as she'd told him.

The woman Errol was supposed to interview was not home. Par for the course. Standing at her doorway, Errol kept hearing sounds in the hallway and looking over his shoulder. Quickly he left the building. This area was unnerving. So far he had yet to see another white person in the whole neighborhood. As an anthropologist he was used to standing out, but somehow, in his own country he felt far more uncomfortable as an outsider. When he walked back to the car he was conscious of being watched, and strode briskly and efficiently, as if he were an important person who was running late, though he had nothing to do once he reached the Porsche but wait. While Errol leaned on the hood, their hired guard eyed him suspiciously and clanged his metal pipe against a bus stop, as if Errol would somehow try to gyp him out of his second ten.

Half an hour later Raphael showed up, disgusted. "He was

drunk," said Raphael. "Incoherent. Smelled bad." Suddenly Raphael froze. "Where is Gray K.?"

"She went to do an interview on her own. Mine was a no-show. Gray's not back yet."

Raphael looked at Errol with angry incredulity. "Look around you," he ordered distinctly. "We are now in one of the most dangerous neighborhoods in the United States of America. You let her walk by herself through *this*?"

"I don't *let* her do anything. She does what she likes."

"She has to be controlled."

"You haven't been paying attention to her angle on this study, then, have you?"

"I don't care about her study. That woman needs babysitting. Especially here. You are obviously not up to the job."

"Gray can take care of herself," said Errol through his teeth.

"She *cannot*! Give me that address.—That's straight down this street, six blocks. Six blocks! In this? McEchern, are you out of your mind? We're going to pick her up."

Errol trailed angrily behind Raphael. Errol was almost twice this man's age, and here Ralph was ordering him about like a child. What was particularly irritating, as they walked double-time past the black carcasses of apartment buildings, many of them shooting galleries where heroin addicts would warm their spoons, was that Raphael was right. This place was worse than Belfast, or the villages of the Lone-luk. Errol felt like an idiot. Gray had no business by herself here.

Errol waited on the street as Raphael went up to the apartment. He returned more quickly than Errol expected, running, and without Gray. His eyes were blazing.

Raphael's fist came down furiously on Errol's shoulder. "*She never made it there!*" Errol was left aching on the sidewalk as Raphael took off down the block, ducking into each lobby and every burned-out cavity, and running out again.

"Gray!" Errol called. Her name echoed between the deserted buildings.

Errol started running toward where Raphael had last disappeared. But there is a simple and stupid explanation for this. We'll laugh about it later. Ha-ha. Errol didn't see her anywhere. Raphael reappeared, ducked into an alleyway and out again. He crossed the street and started up the other side, in and out. Errol tried to concentrate. There was a pay phone two blocks away, he could see it. Call the police.

As Errol ran toward the phone, the sun shone through polluted air with parodic cheer. The cold white light gleamed in the broken green glass under his feet. The buildings rose harsh and mocking, staring down at Errol with chary eyes.

When Errol got to the phone he found the receiver had been ripped off the cord. He could see there was another phone down the next block. Breathing hard, he bolted for that one. The receiver was on the cord this time, but there was no dial tone. He jiggled the cradle; nothing. Again, Errol ran a couple of blocks and spotted another phone; his side hurt, and he had to slow down. He kicked an empty bottle of Thunderbird as he went, and it splattered against the curb beside him as two old men in a doorway laughed dryly.

Errol wheeled around and went back to the doorway. "Have you seen a woman—white—older—"

"Maybe," one of them said nonchalantly. "Maybe not."

"Please—" Errol took out five dollars. "If you've seen anything."

The man reached out quickly and took the bill, slipped it in his pocket, then swigged his beer.

"Well? Tall, handsome, fifty-nine but doesn't look it—"

The man smiled grimly through a chin full of stubble showing yellow, crumbling teeth. "Nobody round here never see nothin', don' you know that?"

"That's right," said Errol, feeling the pressure build behind his eyes. "I'm an anthropologist. I do know that. Now, for five dollars can you tell me where there's a phone that works?"

"Another five?"

"Sure. But tell me first."

The man's eyes narrowed as if he was afraid of being cheated.

"Come on!" Errol shouted. "Five dollars for where the phone is?"

"Round the corner. At the sto'."

Errol ran. They weren't sober enough to chase him. The phone by the liquor store did have a dial tone.

Yet just as he picked it up, Errol heard a long scream from a couple of blocks away. He dropped the receiver and ran. Gray had a deep voice, but not that deep. The scream hadn't been a woman's, but a man's.

This was the block. Errol jogged down, scanning into gaping doorways. At last, just as he passed by one more, he caught a flash of motion in the corner of his eye. Quietly Errol picked his way inside. He didn't know what he would do. On the way through the door he picked up a charred two-by-four and, gripping it, felt better.

When Errol reached the main interior of the building he froze. He was standing at the entrance to what had once been a first-floor apartment. A few beams of the living-room walls remained. The floor was a sooty rubble. Gray light from the airshaft filtered into the room. The only thing that moved in this picture was black dust, shifting through the air in slow, eddying swirls.

Gray was standing to Errol's left, in profile. She was erect, but slack, as if hung from the roofbeams like a marionette. Her blouse was lying at her stocking feet; the exposed bodice of her slip was torn, and the belt of her skirt was missing. Her hair was poised wildly as if blown by the wind, though not a strand shifted in the slowly curling air.

Errol stared at her face. It was ashen, streaked with soot; her eyes were dead. Her brows had lost their peak. He'd never seen her face so washed of expression, for its muscles never collapsed that way even when she was asleep. The only bright thing about her, starting just under her chin and running down her neck to her breasts as Errol was used to seeing sweat seek the folds of her tennis dress, was a thin trickle of blood.

Errol turned his head a few degrees to the right. A man crouched there; taut as bronze, he might have made a fine war memorial for any state park. The switchblade in his hand glistened red, but didn't drip.

There was another man on the other side of the knife. He held his hands out from his sides with the fingers extended, as if keeping his balance. Only the sound of his breathing marked the passing of time.

Yet there was another figure in this tableau, more still than the others. He lay draped over the stone and burned wood and broken bottles, the tips of his fingers pointed toward Gray; they almost reached her toes.

Errol looked down at his two-by-four and felt dizzy. When

he looked up again the tableau unfroze. The man with the knife turned toward him, and Errol breathed deeply. The man at Gray's feet was a stranger. The man with the switchblade was Raphael.

"I thought that scream, that it was you," said Errol.

"Are you disappointed?"

Errol smiled wanly. "No, Ralph. You and I—it's not like that."

"No," said Raphael, his eyebrows raised, "I suppose it's not."

"Gray, are you okay?" asked Errol.

She nodded dully.

Errol stooped to the man in the rubble and felt his pulse; there were hard scabs on his wrist. Errol superstitiously wiped his hand on his shirt when he stood back up. "He's out, but he's alive. What are you going to do with that one?" Errol gestured to the man at knife point, a Hispanic in his mid-twenties, and a strikingly good-looking boy—in fact, he and Raphael eerily resembled each other.

"What do you suggest?" asked Raphael.

"We could call the police—"

"McEchern, you have no imagination."

"Hey, man," said the Hispanic. "We didn't touch her—"

"You obviously *touched* her, Paco," said Raphael. "Dr. Kaiser doesn't undress in public routinely."

"We was just messin' around. Nothin' serious, Joe."

"Don't call me Joe."

The Hispanic must have been tempted to say, "Don't call me Paco," but instead told Raphael, "I call you Jesus, you put that blade in your pocket. Why don't we call it, mister? Just fun an' games, you know? No big deal. You know how some ladies, they walk down the street like they so hot, like they somebody—"

"She is somebody. That's why she walks that way."

"She got some mouth," said Paco, changing his tack and presumably trying to pay her a compliment. "Man, she 'most get us to take her out and buy her a big steak and, like, send her home in a limo—"

"I don't see any limousine, Paco."

"I mean, like, she broke our hearts, you know? Like, we was gettin' to be friends—"

"Is this a friend of yours, Gray K.?"

Gray said nothing.

"Your friend isn't sticking behind you, Paco."

"Ralph, why don't you let me call the police. It's clear-cut self-defense—"

"No, this is clear-cut. Right now."

"Hey, mister," braved Paco. "Is it true? Is she really a *virgin*?"

"Cut him up." The voice was quiet and dry. Errol turned to Gray and wondered if he'd heard right. Even Raphael looked at her quizzically. "Don't kill him," she explained. "Cut him."

"Gray, think about it," said Errol. "Are you going to regret this later?"

"Not for a minute."

"Gray—"

"Later, Errol."

Raphael didn't stalk his victim. He took his time. Backing up, the Hispanic tripped over fallen beams as he was angled up against a wall of brick. Raphael took slow, peaceful steps, holding the knife close to his body. His eyes were clear and without anger. The man seemed disconcerted. For a moment the fear in his face fell away to a peculiar admiration.

Then he bolted for the door. Raphael's hand shot out, the

knife flashed in the sun and came down—though Errol knew the boy was running and that Raphael's motion must have been quick, still the moment seemed extended, languorous; later Errol would be able to play it back to himself in exquisite detail. The slash seemed so studied, as if Raphael had had the leisure to calculate exactly where to start—at the corner of the boy's eye; how deeply to cut; and where to stop—just below the corner of his mouth. Perfect.

Raphael understood pretty faces. With queer clarity Errol could imagine how even years from now the hardened scar tissue would draw the boy's eye into a permanently leering wink and pucker his mouth into an old man's scowl. That face, minutes before fresh, open, and smooth, was forever more surly and cynical. In a stroke Raphael had made Paco into a very ugly boy. The resemblance between the two was over.

The Hispanic wheeled around and whipped his hand to his face. Blood leaking between his fingers, he lurched out of the building, and no one stopped him now. Gray watched him stumble past her with a mechanical lack of sympathy.

Once he was gone, she told Errol quietly, "I'm sorry to disappoint you. I'm not the liberal altruist you always wish I were. I've spent a lot of time in Africa. I've evolved a tribal mind. Justice and power aren't abstractions to me but matters of great practicality."

At last, heavily, she picked up her blouse and put it back on. She found her shoes. She held out both her hands and took Raphael's in one, Errol's in the other. Errol felt her palm cold and dry as she gripped his tightly. They walked to the Porsche. Only when she had to in order to duck into the car did she let go of either hand.

Raphael handed their watchman his ten and said quietly, "It seems I hired you to guard the wrong thing."

Once in the car, Errol was relieved to be back in his regular life, though he couldn't help but feel that it would never be the same again. No doubt untrue, this was a feeling he sometimes had.

"It's a long drive back," said Raphael. "Do you want to stay in New York?"

"I want to go home," said Gray, like a child.

Raphael pulled over to the liquor store; Errol called an ambulance for the man in the airshaft and canceled the other interviews for the day.

The ride back was long and quiet. Raphael drove carefully at fifty-five. He kept his right hand gently joined with Gray's left, and didn't let go to shift gears.

At last Errol inquired discreetly about the incident. Raphael answered his questions. It seems the cut on Gray's throat was shallow, from being rustled off the street with a knife at her throat.

"Did they . . ." Errol approached, "succeed in . . ."

"No. Not quite."

"How did you get their knife?"

"I didn't."

"So where did the switchblade come from?"

"I always carry a knife. I have since I was thirteen."

"You're such a sweetheart, Ralph."

"No, I'm not." With that he closed the subject.

After an hour on the road Raphael pulled over to a restaurant. Gray ordered soup. She took a wide spoon and filled it carefully with broth, avoiding the vegetables. She looked at the steam rising from the stainless steel and finally slipped the spoon into her mouth. She did this five times, each time with no solid food, then put the spoon down. Raphael watched her, then nodded to Errol, and they stood to go.

They rode most of the way in silence. Though it was warm, they kept the windows closed. When Raphael put on the air conditioning, Gray shook her head. The car was hot but quiet and enclosed. The sun was steady. The leaves by the road didn't stir.

Errol could have ridden like this for days, held in a state of transport. He'd never had less of a desire to arrive anywhere. It was fine to feel the gentle glide of the sports car as it took rare bumps with good shocks, to hear the thrum of the motor and the chock of gears.

Regretfully Errol noted that they were drawing close to home. The sun was low and cast warm, even shafts of amber into the car. Wistfully Errol watched Raphael ease the wheel around each increasingly familiar corner. The shade fluttered as they passed under the mottled shadow of leafy hardwoods. The colors of the neighborhood he knew so well were unusually brilliant. It was August, but there'd been plenty of rain—lawns were thick and a deep tropical green. Red flags on mailboxes looked newly painted. Clothes on playing children were the fantastic blues and flaming yellows of detergent advertisements. Each brick on passing Tudors flushed as if just fired; shutters and doors and window trim flashed so brightly in the setting sun that they seemed to loom forward from their houses, floating above the smooth slate walkways and gardens in full flower.

When Raphael pulled up in front of the manse, Gray waited, uncharacteristically, for Raphael to open the door for her and lift her out by three fingers. Errol stretched. No one spoke. The air was cooler now, moist, and smelled of cut grass. Oxygen wafted from overhanging branches.

In single file they padded to the front door. Inside the foyer, squares of saffron sunlight angled toward the stairs. The rows of small panes on either side of the door were thick glass, and their beveled edges bent the light and sent prismatic shimmers over the banister and onto the polished wooden floor. In one such shaft Raphael stood facing Gray Kaiser. Errol hung back by the door. Her color had returned, and in this light she looked young, perhaps twenty, tan and blond at the end of summer. The expression on her face was young, too—open, her eyes bright but not clever, her lips parted with naïve expectation, her face suffused with shy joy. She looked as if she'd just returned, not from being accosted in the South Bronx, but from an afternoon at the beach, where she'd finally held hands with this boy in front of her. Maybe he'd lent her his towel when hers got wet, his jacket when the beach got chilly.

Raphael stroked her cheek with the back of his forefinger. He himself looked older and darker and more tired than Errol had ever seen him. His clothes were sooty, rumpled, and damp with sweat; his shirt was spattered with blood; his hair tangled back from his forehead. His beard was beginning to rise, and darkened his chin. The man still looked handsome, though for once without *style*.

Simply, Raphael picked Gray up in his arms and carried her through the rippled rainbow of the beveled glass into the soft shadow of the stairwell. Slowly he rose stair by stair, while Errol stood at the bottom looking up. Gray seemed small and light, with her head leaning on his shoulder. She shot Errol a single look as they turned on the landing, a look of terrific complexity—a mixture of fear and trust and the most peculiar request that Errol stay with her.

Errol did so as best he could. Raphael rounded the bend and started the next flight, disappearing from sight, but Errol still saw him. Standing at the bottom of the stairs, gripping a banister in each hand, Errol stared up at the ceiling. Raphael was gliding down the hall with his charge. Errol could hear the footsteps stop at the entrance to Gray's bedroom. The door creaked overhead and closed with a soft click.

He closed the door by leaning against it with his back. He has not yet put you down. He will wait as long as possible before he puts you down, who knows when he will carry you again. Yes, he is standing by the bed, but he is still holding you.

That room has a western exposure. The sun is more orange than before. That is clear to me from the squares at my feet, the color of marigolds. The curtains are gauze; they let light in untampered. The room is fully flushed. I've seen it this time of day. I don't go in there often, though I don't suppose you'd mind—there isn't much to find. Still, I always feel I'm intruding. I walk inside only when you're not home. I've stood there now, about six-thirty. There are a lot of mementos around this house, gifts—animal heads, walking sticks, and all those weapons—they aren't the kind of thing you throw away or toss down the basement stairs, but I know from your room what you really love. There are no mementos there, no detritus from the past, no clutter. It's a clean room, the floor is bare. I like to stand there when you're out and breathe, get my bearings. I like the straight-backed chair by your bed. I've sat there and thought of being you sitting there, taking the pins out of your hair, the stockings off your feet, closing your eyes and feeling your spine fully erect against its back, the ridges of the dowel massaging the muscles that have surely tightened during such a long day. I like to scan the dark, steady mahogany bureau and notice, as he is doing now, that there are no age-spot-fading salves or hair-coloring preparations; no foundations or blushes or eyelash boxes; only one square of white cloth, and a tiny white porcelain saucer for those hairpins. He's pleased; I always have been. Finally he puts you down on the bed. It's a small bed; it's never needed to be large. Four tall posts rise at each corner, like spears to defend you. They will do you no good this evening.

He takes off your shoes. He places them side by side on the floor, neatly, with the fringe of the spread grazing their toes. Your arms are lying straight at your sides. You are insanely relaxed; you can't explain why. He opens your thin white blouse. The slip underneath is torn, I remember. He slides the silk over your shoulders. You have to turn to the side for him to slip your arm out of the sleeve. He's very patient. You know you have plenty of time. His fingers work deftly, like a man who is used to dressing and undressing small children. His gaze is steady. He doesn't smile; his eyes are live, though. He sees you. He's aware of what he's doing. There, the other sleeve. You've had to turn on the other side. Any motion you make now seems large. He takes your blouse and drapes it over that straight-backed chair; though it's sooty and crumpled, he still takes care that the corners of the back poke perfectly into the padded shoulders. It hangs there on the chair and makes a pretty picture. All the clothes you own hang in handsome folds, have you noticed? You always choose fabrics that drape well.

From now on, he will proceed even more slowly. His own shirt is half unbuttoned. You take a look at his chest. It is dark and strong; shadows well in his collarbone. You shake your head slightly in amazement. He pretends not to notice, but at the corners of his mouth there is the suggestion, just barely, of a smile. He pulls down the short zipper on the side of your skirt. Gradually he slides his hands on either side of your narrow hips, and as he pulls your skirt down his fingers trace the edge of your legs. He notes that your toes are long; your feet are narrow, double A.

He shakes out the skirt. He drapes it flat over the seat of the wooden chair.

You are beginning to get anxious. There is only the slip, and . . . You don't like "lingerie," even the word. All you are able to buy has lace, ribbons, flowers. None of this is your style. The hose, too: you like the way they feel, you admit that. You like the slightly rough, regular mat of their surface, and the way they darken at the edges and show the shape of your calves. But having them taken off seems vulgar to you. You wish fleetingly that this were over, that you could lie under the sheet.

He sees your impatience. He stands up straight. He looks down at you, his face stern. You turn your head to the side; your cheek nestles into the pillow. He doesn't move. Finally you look back. He will wait. You're not sure exactly for what. Your forehead gathers. He looks at you long and hard. You take a deep breath, and when you exhale you discover that many of the muscles in your arms and shoulders had tightened. You release them. You feel your face soften. You bow your head. You are now willing to rest here for hours, if need be. That would not be so bad. Now that you feel this way, though, that will not be necessary.

You have imagined that getting your slip over your head will be awkward, but you have been told clearly that is not your problem. Actually, it comes off easily enough. The secret is time, and pleasure. Working it by the inch up your thighs, he feels the material between his fingers as it gathers together in his hands. It is smooth and slippery and, as it folds up your body, compact. Now it drapes between your hipbones—you've lost weight. You arch your back to make it easier, but the stretch feels good; you raise your hands over your head and draw yourself long. Your hips and shoulders pull at their sockets; your rib cage fills high; your chin reaches for the ceiling and pulls each tendon in your neck taut. Now he draws the slip over your head, and you feel the slick material glide over your arms and the wisps of the straps trail over your fingertips.

You know that what you want is not to be wearing what remains. This is no longer embarrassment or impatience. You simply want to feel your full body without division. He understands this, and works more quickly. You sit up now; he unhooks the bra behind your back, lingering a moment as his arms draw a circle about you. When he pulls them away he has the hooks in one hand, the eyes in the other; even this garment you have no love for gets folded on the chair. He turns back to you. Your breasts are small. You've had no children, so the nipples are round but not long. You're surprised not to be shy, but then you've always liked them. They are tight to your chest, with a single burst of fullness near the armpits, but never with enough weight to pull them down. They go well with your body. They belong to your body. They aren't separate, to be revealed in a special way. They make you no more shy than your upper arms or your rib cage. They are your body.

For some reason, this is enough tending. You will take off the rest yourself. You drop your legs over the side of the bed and roll down your hose, slipping your fingers under the nylon and running them down each leg to the toe. Oh, you're not in a hurry; you enjoy this. You're proud of your legs—you think I don't know? You've never had to say so. From way back in photographs, even when skirts were long, you've had a way of getting them before the camera. There's one picture in which you're turning quickly and the skirt swirls above the knee; the pose by Corgie's ladder, with his parachute silk slit all the way up the thigh; or sitting on that pier? In Ghana? You remember? With a brightly colored dress gathered in your lap and your ankles crossed and gleaming, for you'd dangled your feet in the water a moment before.

Even in that very first film I saw of you, I remember those long legs angling into the camera. I'm sure you haven't watched it in years, but I'll never forget it: New Guinea: Land of the Hidden Peoples. *It was a bad film technically, and the text was hideous. I'm sure you didn't produce it, but there you were, wading through the river with your skirts held high again, the water rippling over those high, full calves of yours, your narrow ankles flashing their small white bones as you lifted each foot from the water. You weren't yet thirty years old, but at the time you looked older. I thought you were beautiful. I'd never met you. It was for this first film, not for your reputation, that I swore to take that seminar with you, no matter how long I had to remain on the waiting list. I remembered your laughter. I remembered seeing, even though the filmmakers had tried to disguise anything true, that you weren't just working—you were having a wonderful time. It was clear, too, from the eyes around you: they were not simpering or awed. The people of that tribe liked you. This time you had come to them as ordinary. You showed them your ten fingers and ten toes, like theirs; you showed them your long, strong legs and how far you could hike with them into the mountains without complaint. You offered, too, to carry bundles, and they tried to keep them from you—a woman—a white woman—but you insisted and carried your load. You washed your own clothes on stones. Your hair was tawny then; you kept it back, and it went bright blond in the sun—how often I've watched it do that, until now it remains this gray-gold, a wistful color, fine and nostalgic and soft to the touch.*

Errol looked down. The squares of sun had elongated at his feet into rectangles and deepened to vermilion, the color of persimmons. Errol rubbed the smooth wooden banister. It was oily from so many hands. He looked at the pearly grain under his fingers. Splinters of blond wood caught the light under the dark stain. The banister was warm. The foyer was elaborately quiet. He could hear nothing from upstairs. Gray, it's so brilliant here. Your room must be on fire.

Your room is on fire. No longer do you lie passive on the spread. Huge spans of flaming orange sun are thrown against the walls behind you as you pull back the blankets and extend on the bed. He undresses swiftly and with that lithe animal grace he uses on tennis courts and in the living rooms of burned-out buildings. The sun cuts a wide diagonal across your body. You are at home in your body. It is long and strong and thin, and takes up the bed from head to foot. That sunlight is hitting his pupils now. The lines of his irises catch the red in splinters like the grains of this banister. There is a naked man in your room. There is an animal in your room. He has climbed in beside you. He is over your neck. His eyes are burrowing and flecked with red. His mouth is overhead, and now that tongue is sunk into your throat, lower and deeper than you thought it could go. This has all been so chaste, Gray, I know—it must be a relief to feel the full length of his body all at once against yours; to feel his arms around your back; to feel the skim of sweat between your skins, the lubrication that makes moving parts function smoothly. The knobs of your shoulders meet and roll against each other, neat and quiet like bearings packed in oil.

You feel it against your stomach. You'd always thought it would frighten you; instead, it's a great comfort, even a thrill, like a new and exotic animal you might find in the bush that means you no harm. You fit it neatly into the socket of your hipbone, as if to make it feel at home. The surprise is how reasonable this feels. The surprise is that your body takes to this simply, and that you don't have to think. You look in his eyes, and they undulate—they've become larger and their perimeters are no longer defined. The pupils shift like deep black water lapping up against the bright sand of their whites. He is no longer an exact, precise person, with traits, idiosyncrasies, things to say. He has become wider and more vague. Every observation you could make of him would be both true and a lie.

It is against your thigh. Its nose nudges forward. It is between both thighs. Why does it seem you have done this always? How can this be at once so new and so familiar? You think, Why is the rhythm of his body as it builds against me so easy, so understandable? Why is this a code I don't need to decipher? His body moves like waves pushing forward, washing back. You feel the breaking, you feel the undertow.

You have been on your side. He shifts you onto your back. Wash forward. Pull back. It is time. You can't help but smile. On his face is the look of falling into a cavern, plunging from a great height when you want to, throwing yourself into a dark distance with great joy.

You open, and fill. You pour, and fill. For so long you have expected this to make you regretful: how terrible I haven't done this before; how wonderful; how deprived I've been. In the oddest way, though, it is fine that you've waited. This is the correct time. Just. Now. You are full of him. There is no regret. It is best now.

The procedure is even and simple and brilliant. Why did you ever think there was anything to learn? Why did you think there was something wrong with you? Yes, it has taken fifty-nine years for you to be ready. But that's quite different from never being ready.

Yet all this thinking is disappearing. Ideas of what you are doing float off into the warm golden air—you can almost see them rise like balloons and pop at the ceiling. There is only color left, and breathing. There is only motion left, like music. Nothing remains to think, so it doesn't even occur to you that your mind has risen to the ceiling and popped. Who you are is gone. What you are doing, the idea, is gone. The light in the room pulses; the squares of vermilion on the wall brighten when you inhale, blacken when you breathe out. Gradually they lift from the wall and pull forward, wrap around you. What has happened is that diagonal across your body has moved—the sun has set a few more degrees and is striking your two bodies in full now. The shifting of the sun does not occur to you, though. Stars and orbits no longer exist. You are not even aware that this is sunlight. It is hot color you create. If you were thinking, you'd imagine you were hallucinating. But you have no more ideas. And if you were thinking, you'd know it's a relief to have no more ideas.

Yet Errol had to stop. He himself felt giddy, and the squares of sun at his own feet loomed off the floor. He held on to the banister now just to keep his balance. When he looked at the ceiling it seemed to throb. Sweat was running in streams down his neck, and he noticed his shirt was drenched now. His breathing was strained. He was leaving something out. It was best, he supposed, to face things. There was a fact missing in his projection overhead. Errol would try to insert it, and then see if the banister was enough to keep him standing.

The man. Errol took a breath. The man upstairs—Sorry,

but overhead it's not only rhythm and sunlight, color and mind-lessness. A great deal is blurry now and floating and wildly colored over the width of that room, but one thing remains utterly clear. Oh, Errol. Must you have it put to you so bluntly? Upstairs. There is a man. There is a man, Errol, and *it is Ralph*, Errol, *it is Ralph and not you.*

The banister was not enough. Errol crumpled onto the first stair. It was as if someone had punched him in the solar plexus and knocked all the air from his lungs. Errol leaned his head up against the railing and wrapped his arms around his chest. He stroked his sides up and down, nestling his fingers lovingly into the depressions of his own ribs. Then he drew his knees to his chest and held his legs tightly. He put his cheek to his knee. Held in his own embrace, Errol felt comforted, as if by a different person. The man who offered him succor was not a stranger; indeed, he knew Errol well. Yet he was distant and, even in his consolation, cold. He could see Errol's peril but not sanction it. It was all very sad that Errol was crumpled at the foot of these stairs, but not admirable. The man who held him there was strong and stoic and did not accept excuses. He was, of course, Errol himself—the Errol that endured, that would endure all of this and absolutely anything else Errol chose to subject himself to. Errol felt his double, then, extend a hand and lift him, with kindness but also with severity, from his crouch on the stairs and help him over to the den, where he collapsed weakly into the couch. Errol's head fell back. His face felt white. His arms went cold. He would no longer think about Gray just now. They would have to finish without him. No doubt they would manage just fine.

The air was cooler than before, and darker. The dim light

in the room was relaxing; Errol was relieved to be away from the vermilion patches rising at him from the floor. The colors in this room tonight were even and kind, as if seen through gray-tinted lenses. The tick of the large clock at his side soothed Errol into the cushions of the couch. Errol knew he would fix himself a cool glass of white wine soon, but not just yet. The clock chimed eight times. The rhythm of the bells was careful and slow. The room filled with round, low sound. The upholstery vibrated under Errol's fingertips. It was over. It was over, and Errol was all right. *You are all right*, said the man. *You can take anything. Now, sit there. Open your collar. There's a book you're in the middle of, and within the hour you'll be able to read it, with concentration. I'll get you that glass of wine. You'll be fine. Sometimes a comfortable sofa and a book and a glass of wine are enough. Sometimes a quiet evening as it gets dark is enough. And you're lucky for that, too. For tonight, you mustn't expect more.*

Errol got up and went to the kitchen and felt his own mouth smile with a wan tenderness, the kind of smile a physician might use with a formerly brilliant patient who had lost his mind.

chapter nineteen

Errol spent the night at Gray's. The worst was over, and to go back to his own apartment would not have spared him anything but simply have forced him to make a drive on an evening when he had no desire to make an effort of any kind.

He woke the next morning to the sound of the shower. Errol felt every muscle in his body tense one by one as it woke. Rigidly he lay in bed listening to the water, to the moan of pipes.

Gray took her showers at night.

Errol remained in bed, though no longer sleepy. It was childish to think he could avoid this upcoming breakfast scene by hiding under the sheet, but still he stayed there as long as he could stand it. Finally, like a good soldier, Errol rose, dressed efficiently, and trooped downstairs. Lieutenant McEchern, reporting for heartbreak, sir.

Raphael was already in the kitchen, with Gray nowhere in sight. Stiff as his upper lip had been, Errol had to pause with a faint wave of nausea from what he found at the counter: Raphael was wearing a towel tucked around his waist. The hair on his chest was curling from his shower; the hair on his head was slicked back in an unpleasant Valentino style. He was making coffee, and seemed to know where the beans and filters were kept. His gestures were blithe. One night and the guy comes down in a goddamned towel and makes coffee as if he's done it a hundred times before. *He acts as if he lives here.*

Masochistically curious, Errol hung back from the doorway and watched Raphael glide over to the refrigerator and survey its contents, picking at this and that until he found something of interest. Gray had recently been given a whole Scotch salmon by a visiting dignitary; he pulled it out. Errol bristled. Sealed in cellophane, the fish would have kept for several weeks, but the unopened package didn't intimidate Raphael. He sliced into the plastic and cut himself a generous slab, then rolled it around a hunk of cream cheese. He munched on this handful distractedly as he studied the various international utensils hanging on the walls. He didn't look very interested, and returned to the refrigerator to drag out a few more expensive snacks. Errol felt like a Roman whose city has just been overrun by Visigoths. Welcome to the Dark Ages.

"Morning, McEchern," said Raphael, still pawing through the refrigerator.

"I didn't mean to spy," said Errol, flustered. "But I don't usually find a naked man in this kitchen. It gives me pause."

"Well, get used to it."

"I don't bother to habituate myself to singular occurrences."

Raphael smiled to himself, and returned to his salmon.

"Sarasola," said Errol with exasperation, "you're butchering that fish."

"I'm a brute, McEchern, what can I tell you?" Raphael went on sawing away at the salmon.

"It's pre-sliced!"

"Ask me how much I care."

"The point is, I care."

"This is your fish?"

Errol squirmed. "No."

"Well then."

Raphael had already lost interest in the salmon, anyway, and turned to the crab salad. Errol poured himself a cup of coffee and took it upstairs to his office, remembering with a pang that the Dark Ages had lasted a hideously long time.

A bout midmorning Errol could no longer pretend to be working, so he wandered into Gray's office. Gray wasn't even pretending to work but was standing by her window humming, keeping time to her tune by tapping her fingers against the windowpane. This whole house was becoming an anthropological farce.

"Earth to Kaiser."

"We read you, base station."

When she turned around, Errol started. For a moment Errol could have sworn she'd just stepped out of *New Guinea: Land of the Hidden Peoples* at the very beginning of her career.

"I was going to ask you if you were all right," said Errol. "I guess I don't have to. You're aglow."

"Radioactive."

It was true. She pulsed. Errol was careful not to get too close. "Where's the young barbarian?"

"He drove to the beach. He'll be back tonight."

"I'm surprised you didn't go with him. You don't seem to be getting a lot done here."

"I didn't stay to work," said Gray, taking slow, buoyant steps around the room. "I stayed to think and sing little songs and talk to myself a lot. Sometimes I enjoy things more when I'm not actually in them."

"You like to bask."

"Exactly. Raphael can do that on the beach. I don't need the beach."

"I can see that. I think I could get a tan by lying out in this office this morning. Do you want me to leave you alone?"

"Soon. But not now. I don't even care. I feel amenable."

"If you don't care—"

"No; stay, Errol. I didn't mean it that way. I'm happy to see you. You look wonderful this morning."

"I look dreadful. But you . . . Do you want to talk about it? Or not?"

"I don't know." She considered. "We could try. I'll tell you if we have to stop."

"I don't want to pry, Gray. I just wondered if you were right. If it was dangerous."

She paused. "Yes," she said at last. "Very."

"Even after the South Bronx?"

"It was all—of a piece. Yesterday was one big dangerous day. What was in peril was—my life. In the Bronx; in my room."

"But you came through."

She laughed. "Barely."

"Did it hurt?"

"Well, the whole thing was—wrenching, somehow. And I

am a little sore this morning. But whether it hurt at the time I couldn't tell you." Gray smiled. "Now, why doesn't it embarrass me to talk about this with you? Should I be shy? Would you feel better?"

"I think I can generate enough embarrassment for both of us."

"Good. I'm not in the mood."

"Since you're not shy this morning, there was one thing I was wondering. Are you still fertile?"

"Funny you should ask that. I think I am, which is odd. It's as if my body were waiting. In fact, I suppose I took a risk last night. But the chances against pregnancy must be astronomical." She sounded wistful.

"Do you regret not having children?"

"I've always been too—behind for children."

"Well, it's obviously too late. I just wondered."

"I mean I couldn't have had them at thirty, don't you see? I'm barely ready for a man now; I'll be ready for children in three or four years. I'm stunted, Errol, slow. The kind of person who goes to a special school until she's thirty-five. Sometimes I'm surprised I get articles published and lectures engaged, when it's amazing I can tie my own shoes or go to a grocery store." She looked concerned for a moment, but couldn't keep it up. "If I stay inside any longer, I'm going to jump out this window. I'm going for a walk. I'll work this afternoon, I promise."

"You don't have to report to me, Gray. Take the whole day off if you want."

"No, I do have to report to you, Errol. That's one of the things you're for." With that she slipped on her shoes and tripped out the door.

That afternoon Gray worked on editing a scene of Charles Corgie footage, and lines of dialogue drifted through her door over and over: "We'll see if he knows the words 'Hand it over' and 'Say your prayers'" "When there's only one of them and it makes you a god, there's no such thing as *only* a tape recorder" "I don't know for a fact you took it, so I'm not going to shoot you. But you're going to watch." Watch. Watch. The words were Corgie's, but the voice was Raphael's.

Errol shot his own afternoon. Whenever he started to read something, images of shattered green glass and disfiguring gashes would loom between his eyes and the page. Errol found that as the afternoon progressed, the events of the day before were shifting weight, changing places.

Gray worked through dinnertime. At about eight o'clock she poked her head in Errol's door. "I wanted to tell you—those interviews you canceled yesterday? See if you can set them up again for next week."

"You're joking."

"We'll be more careful."

"I'm not going back there."

"Don't, then. I'll get another bodyguard."

"Well, you can use Ralph to protect you from the locals. You need someone else to protect the locals from Ralph."

Gray watched Errol from the doorway. "Are you getting at something, or are you just being amusing?"

"I guess I'm trying to accustom myself to the fact that he knifed two people yesterday. I wonder how hard it was for him, frankly."

"Have you forgotten what they were going to do to me?"

"No, but—The second man—"

"I told him to."

"You were—under stress."

"I was perfectly in my right mind."

"I'd prefer not to believe that, Gray. Because the whole thing gives me the willies."

"Life is harder-edged than you give it credit for, Errol. You've been on the veldt almost as often as I have. I can't understand how you maintain this sentimental attitude when any number of lions have noshed on hartebeests right under your nose."

"Life isn't hard-edged, it's what we make it. That's the kind of wobbly generalization you used to stay clear of: Life is. And I suppose happiness is a warm puppy? Love means never having to say you're sorry?—Not that you don't have a point. Because people can be hard-edged, that's for sure."

"Errol." Gray rubbed her forehead and looked away. "You really can't stand it, can you?"

"Stand what?" Errol pushed back his chair.

"That man saved my life! And you want to make that out as an act of cruelty. You can't stand anyone else's heroics, can you?"

"I didn't think cutting that boy's face was heroic. It wasn't necessary—"

"Errol, what did you do?"

"When?"

"When you couldn't find me, what did you do?"

Errol faltered. "I—tried to call the police."

"Uh-huh."

"It seemed reasonable at the time," Errol snapped. "*I* wasn't carrying a knife."

"That's half the point, Errol! I admire someone who carries a knife!"

"Fine." He stood up from his chair and walked over to Gray. He tapped her chest with his forefinger. "You like someone who carries a knife. Well, just see how much you admire it when he points it at *you*." Errol turned on his heel and left the room.

He marched downstairs to the front door; he needed some air. He opened it to find Raphael Sarasola squarely in front of him, a towel over his shoulder.

"Telepathic," said Raphael. "I hadn't rung."

Errol did not have a snappy reply. He felt cut off at the pass. In front of him was a man who carried a knife. Behind him was a woman who told him to use it.

"Don't fall all over yourself," said Raphael. "I don't need a drink, dinner. You don't even have to kiss me. But I would like to come in."

Errol realized he'd just been standing there for a good minute or so. Sometimes Errol hated Raphael most, not because he knifed Hispanics or even because he was Gray Kaiser's lover, but because he could make Errol feel so stupid.

Gray trotted down the stairs with a bubbly demeanor that suggested she'd already shrugged off her fight with Errol with an ease that hurt him in some ways more than the fight itself. She left to pull out some cold cuts and a bottle of wine, and Raphael sauntered into the den. She'd asked Errol to join them, and Errol was still fashioning a stinging, brittle declination when the door-bell rang.

Errol answered it, and found, for once, someone on his side. "I am delighted to see you."

Ellen Friedman looked at him in surprise. "Why, you sound as if you mean that." She seemed pleased, but when she came in and saw Raphael in the den, her color blanched. "Mr. Sarasola," she said gravely.

Raphael looked at Ellen quizzically. "Have we met?"

"Not formally. But I recognize you, from pictures." Her voice sounded unusually hard.

"My fame has spread more widely than I imagined."

"We don't call people like you famous, we call them assholes."

"Mm," said Raphael, unaffected. "I don't like that word nearly as well. Especially from such a lady. It doesn't suit you."

"You must have heard the word 'asshole' from women pretty often. You must be used to it."

"I'm not a very curious person, but I'm beginning to wonder what I did to deserve this."

Just then Gray returned with a tray, but pulled up short. Something was going on.

"In a word: Anita Katrakis. Unfortunately, she still remembers you. Errol, would you like to go for a walk? It's gotten stuffy in here."

They turned to go, but Raphael spoke up behind them. "It's cowardly to make accusations and run away."

Ellen turned back. "Interesting you hear her name as an accusation."

"Aren't you old enough," said Raphael, "to have noticed how often things between men and women don't end well? They want different things; there are misunderstandings. Surely this isn't news to you."

"Couples split, yes. But when one person flagrantly uses the other for his own gain—"

Raphael raised his hand. "I'm not finished. Sometimes things end worse for one side than the other. These 'injured parties' always seem to see themselves as the victims of a moral outrage. They never feel simply rejected, but also abused. I've known many women who were great believers in the curative powers of indignation."

"You have it all worked out, don't you?" Ellen seemed genuinely amazed. "You really sound as if you don't think you did anything wrong. Do you practice in the mirror?"

Raphael sank into the couch, leaned his head back, and closed his eyes. "Oh, go ahead. You're having such a good time reviling me, and there's very little joy in the world. I'd hate to deprive you of yours." Once more he looked tired and older. In the last couple of days he had aged at an incredible rate. He took the glass of wine Gray offered him and held her fingers lightly in his other hand. He didn't give Errol or Ellen another glance. They'd been dismissed.

"Ellen, this is pointless," said Errol. "Let's go."

"That," she said outside, "is a horrible man."

"You think so?"

"Don't you?"

Errol said nothing.

"What's going on between those two?"

"Oh," said Errol vaguely, "they're friends."

"Come on."

"Close friends," Errol conceded.

Ellen rolled her eyes. "You don't trust me."

"My position . . ."

"Do you talk to anyone?"

"Every five years to my sister from Australia. And to a construction worker in Boxford."

"A construction worker."

"He's a nice guy."

"Errol, what do you think you're keeping secret? I didn't know it was Raphael, but I already knew she was having an affair with a much younger man."

"Where'd you get that idea?"

"Summer's a slow season, Errol. Not much happening. It gets around."

"So what's the consensus?"

"A lot of people have been waiting for thirty years for Gray Kaiser to make a mistake. I think she's just made it. The comments I hear aren't—kind."

"What are yours like?"

"I've defended her. After all, if she were a man everyone would be titillated, even envious. That macho-Picasso sort of thing. But for a woman it looks—"

"Pathetic. In the words of Herself."

"But now that I know who he is, it looks worse than pathetic. It looks ugly. Gray has a lot of power, and I'd hate to see that man get his hands on it. Is there anything immediate she can do for him? Something tangible?"

"There is the Ford Fellowship," Errol admitted. "I'm sure she has final say on it."

"I'm sure she does, too. Those foundations don't know zip about anthropology, just Gray Kaiser."

"You sound a little bitter," said Errol edgily.

"I'm sorry, I know she's your idol. And she is good, but so are a lot of people."

"Has something in particular set you off?"

"I suppose. I talked to Bob Johanas. He had everything lined up to direct a film project in New Guinea. Lots of money, NEA,

NET. For a two-hour documentary. It was his baby, Errol. And suddenly, zip. Oh, the project's going to go. Bob isn't."

"Mm."

"He was *quashed*, Errol."

"Uh-huh."

"He put months into this, and bang! Nothing! It took very little probing to turn up Gray's name."

Errol shrugged.

"And do you know why?"

"I'm not sure, but I do remember a while back Bob wasn't very—diplomatic."

"And over what?"

"Ralph."

"Who?" She looked at him queerly.

"I mean Raphael."

"You have to do something. That boy is dangerous and Gray's being irrational. You know that was no reason to get Bob dismissed from that project. It wasn't even like her. She's usually fair. You've got to get her away from him."

"How am I supposed to do that?"

"You're closer to her than anybody. Get her to take a look at this thing. Why would a man that good-looking go for a woman her age?"

"There are things I'm not at liberty to say."

"Someone's got to say them! What's going to happen? He'll get his money and she'll never see him again, and then she's going to feel pretty stupid."

"She might feel worse than stupid," said Errol quietly.

"Listen. Take her to see Anita Katrakis."

"You're kidding."

"No, I'm not. It would be better than shock therapy. Here." She scribbled on a piece of paper from her purse. "This is her address. Feel free to use my name."

"We'll see," said Errol uncomfortably. "I don't drag Gray many places. She drags me."

"Errol," said Ellen with exasperation, "you're a wonderful guy, but sometimes—"

"I'm a dishrag."

"You said it, I didn't."

"No, you did say it."

They walked a couple of blocks in silence. The bugs were bad.

"At least make sure she doesn't give him that damn fellowship," said Ellen at last.

"No problem," said Errol. "I'll say, 'Gray, don't give the kid the fellowship,' and she'll say, 'Oh, I was going to give it to him, but I certainly won't now. I didn't realize you disapproved. Why didn't you tell me before?' Then I'll tell her, 'Well, I wasn't going to mention it until Ellen Friedman pointed out to me how weak and ineffectual I was, so I decided to start being more forceful.' Then she'll tell me, 'What a good idea, Errol. While you're at it, is there anything else you'd like me to do?' Then I'll make her give that documentary back to Bob Johanas. I'll order her to fund your projects. I'll tell her to stop eating so much sugar. Any other edicts I should deliver?"

"Very funny."

"The problem isn't that I'm a spineless jellyfish, Ellen. The problem is Gray Kaiser."

Ellen stopped walking. "Errol, you're right. I'm angry for Anita, and I'm old-fashioned—I like to see people get what they deserve. But they don't, and that's not your fault. You should probably steer clear of this whole business. In fact, I was thinking: Errol, you've worked in New Guinea, haven't you?"

"Yes, why?"

"Why don't you apply for that position? It's wide open now."

"I have some other projects lined up."

"But, Errol, you're qualified, you'd be away from all this, on your own—"

"Ellen, I don't want it, period, and I don't want to talk about it, either."

"But, Errol—"

"I'm serious. Drop it."

"Okay." She shrugged.

There wasn't much more to say.

W hen Errol returned by himself, Gray and Raphael were still in the den and the bottle of wine was gone. They were talking; Errol went into the next room to pick up his book. He paused to listen.

"Do you keep up with your father at all?"

"We haven't spoken since I was thirteen."

"All that time in the mill you never ran into him? North Adams is a small town."

"It was a dance. We walked on opposite sides of the street. We shopped down opposite aisles of the grocery store. He went to one pool hall; I went to the one across town. And I went home occasionally, when he wasn't there. I'd sneak in for a shower. Once, he came home early and must have heard water running. I poked my head out and heard the front door close again. Very softly. Not a bad guy, *Dad*."

Gray didn't say anything. After a minute or so, Raphael went on. "Sometimes I was hungry. I'd warm up a can of ravioli. I cleaned it up, put everything back. But he must have noticed the cans missing. Still, he didn't change the lock. When I first came back the pantry was still full from my mother's shopping trips—she loved a full pantry. I used up all the ravioli, my regular lunch. Later that year, though, a whole new stock of these cans showed up—wall-to-wall Chef Boy-ar-dee. It struck me that he threw a shit fit whenever my mother put that stuff in front of him. My father hated ravioli." Raphael laughed dryly. "Now, you can't say the guy didn't care.

"So I did my part. I went by the house once a month. Every time, I'd eat a can of ravioli. I started leaving the pan in the sink. By the time I got older I didn't even like the shit anymore. I ate it, anyway. He kept a huge stock. After a while I'd stop by the house even when I wasn't hungry. I figured as long as he found a pan in the sink he knew I was all right."

"Why don't we go back?"

"What?"

"Why don't we go back to North Adams? I want to meet your father."

"You're serious."

"I am."

"*I* don't want to meet my father."

"Coward."

"This is easy for you."

"You only do things that are easy?"

"I prefer them."

"Then why are you with me and not with Pamela Rose?"

"She bores me."

"Easy bores you."

"Is this a dare?"

"Yes."

"Actually—" Raphael stopped. "Actually, there is one person I'd love to give my regards."

Gray didn't ask whom. Nor did Errol wonder. They both knew perfectly well. "Regards" wasn't quite the right word was all.

chapter twenty

W hy?"

"It's anthropologically important to me."

"I'd thought about asking you, but I assumed you wouldn't be interested."

"I'm desperately interested."

"You won't carp about the speed limit and get out of the car?"

"He can do 130 and I'll keep my mouth shut like an absolute idiot."

Gray sighed. "All right. But, Errol, don't bait him."

"Me, bait Ralph?"

"Don't even call him Ralph for once. This is hard for him. For me, please? Be nice, and quiet."

"Sounds as if we're going to church."

"If you expand your idea of the sacred, then yes, this is a sort of pilgrimage. Don't profane it. That's all I'm asking."

Braced as Errol was for gripping the seat with both hands

all the way to North Adams, Raphael obeyed the speed limit. He braked at yellow lights. He pulled over to a gas station when the tank was still half full. In their last leg off the main highway Errol watched Raphael closely as he eased ever more slowly through the Berkshire foothills. He held the steering wheel, ten and two. Errol was incredulous: *Raphael Sarasola was nervous.*

Raphael pulled into town and stopped the car. They were on the main street, lined with a series of limping commercial projects. Errol knew this kind of lineup: the diner would be overpriced; the hardware store poorly stocked; the styles in the department stores outdated. It was hot and the sun was out, but the street still managed to look gray.

"Are we there?" asked Gray.

"Not quite."

"Well?"

Raphael leaned back in the seat. "This is crazy. I'm going back."

"To Boston? Now?"

"Yes."

Errol was looking around in amazement. This was it. This was the place. Down at the bottom of the hill, that must be the grocery store. That was where the olives were, and Ida's five-dollar smoked abalone, and Frank's cans of ravioli.

Gray put her hand on Raphael's neck. "What are you afraid of?"

"I'm afraid of this place," he said simply.

"Why?"

"It's small."

"So?"

"I don't feel small."

"You're not."

"I am, here. And it's ugly."

"That makes you ugly, too?"

"Places are important. They rub off on you. I left here. On purpose."

Gray shrugged. "You can leave again. This very afternoon."

"That's right. I can leave right now."

"If you go now, you will feel small."

Raphael said nothing. He glanced out the window, but when someone passed by the car, he looked down at his lap. He did not drive to his father's. He did not drive to Boston.

"You are from North Adams? You were born here."

"Yes, but I don't have to wallow in it."

"I think you do."

"What."

"I was born in Racine, Wisconsin," said Gray, leaning back. "Bigger than here, but only numerically. I stayed away for years. Now I go back sometimes. Buy shampoo at the same Squabbs Drugstore. Run my hands along the fence of Lincoln Elementary School. Notice that the Silas A. Jacobs Memorial Hospital, where I was born, has a new parking lot. I walk down the sidewalk of Bentnor Avenue, where I used to draw hopscotch squares. I go back and eat red-hots and nonpareils. I order a 'suicide' at the fountain, with a pump of every flavor syrup they have. I sing songs. I learned a lot of radio jingles as a child." Gray started to sing, and Raphael looked at her as if she were crazy. "Pepsi-Cola hits the spot. Twelve full ounces, that's a lot. Twice as much for a nickel, too! Pep!-si Cola is the drink for you . . ." Gray raised her eyebrows and smiled.

Raphael looked at Gray for a long time. Then he looked

out the window. He looked at the diner. He looked at the grocery store. "There," he pointed, "is my billiards parlor. Rudy's." He smiled to himself as he started the car. "My movie theater"—he nodded as they rode down the block. "I saw *Casablanca* twelve times there."

Raphael parked his car out in front of a surprisingly well-kept clapboard. The yard was full of weeds, but pretty ones—Queen Anne's lace, goldenrod. The screen door hinges appeared to be in good repair. He paused once more before getting out of the car. "I hope he's not dead," he said casually, then swung out of the seat with resolution.

The man who opened the door also surprised Errol a little. Errol had imagined an overweight, dismal character with blunt features. The real Frank was burly but solid, and only forty-five, younger than Errol, with hair still thick and dark. And while there was no comparison between his son's radical looks and Frank's acceptable ones, there was something about the sharp ridge of his brow and the black flash of his eyes that was eerily familiar. Errol had always assumed Raphael had gotten his eyes from Nora; now he wasn't so sure. Frank didn't immediately appear to be a dull, stupid man. He had an edge about him, so that when he saw Raphael on his doorstep he didn't reel or catch his breath, but raised his thick eyebrows with a sophisticated understatement Errol admired.

"Hi, Dad," said Raphael, almost blandly.

"Hi, son."

"This is Gray and Errol."

"Let me guess: they're your parole officers."

"No, I haven't been caught yet."

"At what?"

He shrugged. "Assault. Breach of promise. Not being a nice guy."

"You came for a visit?"

". . . Yeah."

Frank stepped aside and let them in. Errol had expected a hovel—deserted husband floundering in shambles. But Nora had been gone twelve years, and Frank seemed to be managing nicely. The living room was orderly and militantly male. Couch. Chair. Table. Not a trinket, a vase, a plant, and, God, not a picture. Errol wondered if he'd ever been in someone's house before where there was absolutely nothing on the walls.

Frank didn't speak to Errol or Gray. Perversely, Raphael didn't explain who they were. With return perversity, Frank didn't ask, either. Errol was beginning to pick up an old game: I will withhold information from you; so what—I don't care about your information. It was a game that encouraged two people to sit in a room saying nothing, forever.

"I figured you'd be back," said Frank.

"That's surprising."

"I see it on TV all the time. Kids always turn back up, looking for their roots or something."

"I wouldn't know. I don't watch TV."

"No electricity?"

"I've got electricity. But brains, too."

Frank just smiled affably. "Trouble is, I don't think we're doing this right, Ralph boy. I think we're supposed to hug and kiss."

"You want to kiss me?"

"I'd rather smack you, to tell the truth." Frank looked immediately as if he regretted saying this, and added moderately, "'Course, best we just stick a good ten feet apart."

"Or ten miles or ten states."

"What we've been doing."

Errol and Gray sat down on the couch and positioned themselves so they had a good view. Until now Errol had been pretending not to listen, politely looking out the window, but the other two were so oblivious that there was no reason not to watch the show. Neither of them would sit down and so show his weakness or seem to commit himself to a whole conversation. But Errol would take the weight off his feet. He was beginning to feel invisible. He imagined if he were to get up and fix himself a cup of coffee, the father and son would see only a cup and saucer floating over the couch.

"Found another factory yet?" asked Frank.

"I live in a room in a nice part of Boston. Near school."

"My my. College boy."

"Graduate student. Anthropology."

"Anthropology. You thought that'd impress me, I bet."

"Sure, I did. You were always intimidated by big words."

"Sounds like a load of crap, actually."

"It is. But it suits my purposes."

"You always were a good little student. That was never my idea of smart, though."

"Nor mine. I mean, Dad, I learned all the important things I know from you."

Frank looked skeptical. "Like what?"

"I learned to carry this, for example." A soft snap. Gray jumped. Raphael ran his finger up and down his switchblade.

Frank smiled too widely. "Come to revenge yourself on your old father?"

"Now, what have you ever done that might require revenge?"

The gleam on the blade was also in his eyes. Errol sat forward on the couch. He wouldn't. To his father? Yet Errol wasn't going to watch for a second time, and he perched, coiled, watching the knife as Raphael turned it in his hand. Gray, too, seemed on edge. See, there were stories of Frank. Frank and his little boy. Everyone in that room knew them.

"Beats me." Frank shrugged.

"Think hard."

"Kids don't realize what's for their own good. It's hard to discipline a child."

"You seemed to manage."

"You're holding a grudge, Ralphie, I swear. I thought I taught you to take it. But here you come back to sniffle and feel sorry for yourself. You make me wonder if I hit you around enough. How'd you turn out so soft?"

Raphael's back snapped straight; his eyes went to coal. Surely it must have struck Frank just then that Raphael was taller than he was, in better shape, and fully a man at twenty-five. That must have been a great deal to learn all at once, for the circuits in Frank's face were overloading. He could not maintain a single clear expression of any kind.

"Soft," said Raphael quietly. "Do you want me to do something hard for you? Walking out of here was hard. Sleeping with rats was hard. Washing in a polluted river at five in the morning was hard. Stealing students' jackets from their lockers. Eating the hamburgers thrown out in the back of Arby's because they were too stiff and dry from the heat lamp to sell to normal kids with normal fathers who bought them something to eat. And that's not enough for you? I didn't come back here to prove anything. I proved all I needed to at thirteen. So don't force me to do something to show what you've done to me. I'm not sure you want to know what I'm like. I might frighten you." Raphael held the knife up to his father. "Revenge myself? No, I want you to stay alive as long as possible, because I want to put off indefinitely finding out how little your death will affect me. Maybe that makes me soft, but I'd like to preserve a few illusions."

He retracted the blade and slipped the knife back in his pocket.

Yet it was interesting to see: Raphael's height fazed Frank; his son's age and strength fazed Frank; the hatred didn't faze him. Frank was at home with hatred. He looked comfortable now. Frank put his hands in his pockets and shifted back on his heels. He seemed to be toying with a smile, but thought better of it; the boy did have a knife, just like last time. "I figured this from you. Oh, you never said much. But you were always spiteful. You'd cruise through the streets in those tight jeans with your head in the air—"

"At least it wasn't up my ass—"

"Passing me by like I was some kind of telephone pole—"

"Instead of responding to your own warm greetings, is that right?"

"It's a son's responsibility to acknowledge his father, not the other way around—"

"What do you know about sons? How can you remember what it's like to have one?"

"But no"—Frank plowed ahead—"you were too much of a pretty face to bother with your ugly old father. You were so hot and so smart that you didn't need anybody—"

"That's right, I didn't. I didn't need you, that's for sure, and that ate you up, didn't it? I started warming up your goddamned ravioli as a favor to you, understand? I figured it made you feel useful."

Frank came up short, opened his mouth, and closed it again. "You shouldn't have bothered being so considerate. It was a dollar a can."

"You did put yourself out."

"I did something!"

"You did jack shit!"

"What an ungrateful kid—"

"I should be *grateful*? For *ravioli*?"

"Yeah," said Frank staunchly.

Raphael laughed and looked at the ceiling. "The sick thing is—" He shook his head. "The sick thing is that I was. Grateful. For ravioli."

This struck Errol as one of the more convincing indictments of a parent he had ever heard.

"I've still got some," Frank admitted.

"You're kidding."

"You know I can't stand that shit. Must be seven or eight years old, but I've still got a few cans. Breaks your heart, don't it?"

"My heart doesn't break very easily anymore."

Frank nodded. "I can see that. You take after your daddy. I was never the sort to go to movies and bawl."

"So those TV programs when children come back home don't make you cry?"

"I change the channel."

"To what?"

"Wrestling. Hey, listen. It's lunch. You want some? Chef Boy-ar-dee. Like old times. I'm not going to eat it."

Raphael laughed. "You've still got a sense of humor."

"How often you gonna be here, Ralphie? I gotta get in all the jokes I can. You want some?"

Raphael's eyes glittered. "I'll take it to go."

Frank went into the kitchen and returned to throw Raphael a can from across the room. Raphael caught it and examined the label with an interesting combination of fondness and distaste.

Frank walked slowly across the room, eyeing his son. At last he said slyly, "I know where your mother is."

"Is that so?" said Raphael coolly.

"Yeah, that's so." Frank kept looking at his son and waited.

"Well, that must be nice for you."

"It doesn't matter to me."

"Then why did you mention it?"

Frank shrugged. "Just making conversation."

"We've made enough conversation."

Frank looked at Raphael intently, and for the first time that afternoon seemed to be genuinely admiring his son. Perhaps as a reward for this behavior Frank said simply as the four of them filed outside, "I like your car."

"Thanks," said Raphael, climbing in and closing the door. "Bye." He started the car and then placed the can of ravioli on the dashboard, like a trophy.

"So long, Ralphie."

"Just one more thing." He revved the motor and put on his sunglasses.

"You want money."

"No. Just don't call me Ralphie."

"Whatever you say, Ralphie. You're never here; I can not call you whatever you want."

"No, I'm here right now. Go ahead. Say goodbye. But use

my real name." Raphael used his best smile on his father. Frank recoiled slightly in its wake.

"I never liked the name, Ralphie . . ."

"What did you call me?"

"I said I never liked that name. Your mother—"

"Do you address people by their correct name only if you happen to like it?"

Frank looked at his feet. "You're not just anybody."

"God, I'd like a recording of that."

"Bye, son."

"I'm not moving this car until you say it."

"That's a hell of a threat."

"I thought it would get to you."

Frank took a breath, and must have felt old—his own son was beating him. "Bye, Ra-fee-ell."

"Good start, but needs practice. Maybe I'll come back in ten years to see how you're coming. So long, Vincent." With that Raphael accelerated swiftly away from the curb to leave his father in a cloud of exhaust.

"You wanted to know where your mother is, didn't you?" asked Gray when they'd pulled away.

"Of course."

"But you didn't ask."

"I wouldn't give him the satisfaction."

"Was it worth it?"

"Absolutely."

Gray looked despairingly out the side window. Errol for once wasn't listening. He was in shock. Frank's name wasn't Frank. Errol had made Frank up. His name was Vincent. Errol found this disturbing, but also funny, and he laughed.

"You all right back there?" asked Raphael.

"You wouldn't understand, Ralph."

"Watch it, McEchern. You're next." Raphael accelerated to the next light with a peculiar jauntiness considering what a largely venomous scene he had just left behind. He turned the radio on, loud. He nodded in time to "Under My Thumb," and an odd little smile crept onto his face. Errol couldn't actually hear the words for the music, but he saw Raphael turn to Gray and mouth it clearly enough: "He liked my car." Then he shifted into gear and tore off gleefully around the next corner.

When Raphael pulled up in front of Cleveland Cottons, he said nothing. He got out of the car and went to the trunk. Errol scanned the mill. The windows were still boarded up, the grounds overgrown. The CLEVELAND COTTONS sign was completely rusted, and squealed in the breeze. The building was even bigger than Errol had imagined; to have renovated and exterminated such a place must have been an enormous task.

Raphael returned with a hammer.

"Is that the same one?" asked Errol.

"How do you know about my hammer?"

Errol smiled and said, "I'm a romantic," and didn't explain.

Raphael went first to one of the front windows and pried off the boards one by one. He piled them on the ground with quiet care, like stacking hymnals; he dropped nails with a deliberate *ping* on the broken bottles at his feet, like coins into offering plates full of change. Halfway through he started to sweat and pulled off his T-shirt, draping it around his neck like a vestment.

Yet when he stepped away from the window he looked wistful. Each pane had been individually shattered. No, he shouldn't have been surprised, as he shouldn't have been when he made his way to the side entrance of the mill to find the boards he had pounded over it pulled away again. The cathedral had been overrun, there could be no doubt now. Still, Raphael gestured for the two of them to come with him; he waited for Gray's hand before he ducked down and stepped into his old sanctuary.

It took a few minutes for Errol's eyes to adjust; the only light in the mill was from the window Raphael had uncovered. The way the sun caught shifting clouds of dust reminded Errol of the South Bronx, and he felt a chill. There was a scuttering in the shadows. As he began to make out the room around him, Errol was disappointed. Why did he expect a well-swept expanse with high ceilings and long white sheets hanging spare and graceful like Gray's clothes? Why did he expect homemade lanterns still burning in their sconces? Why did he even expect Ida O'Donnell to be lingering with her pink-tinted wineglass in the middle of the room, eyes flickering with mischief in the lantern light, her kimono falling away to show the delicate mound of her stomach and the single angling pubic hairs crooking out from her black bikini? They were all adults here; it had been seven years; why the big surprise? All three of them knew about mildew and decay, about the boredom and maliciousness of little boys. Of course there were beer cans underfoot, and bottles of Yago Sangria. Of course every single pane of glass was broken, hadn't they been before Raphael moved in? And of course married women did not remain standing in the middle of old factories and drink and smile and wait.

Raphael picked his way silently through the first-floor living room. Once in a while he would reach out and touch something, then pull away—an old sheet would crumble in his fingers; a dish sticking out of the rubble would turn out to be a shard.

"It's odd," said Gray, "what we choose to put ourselves through, isn't it?"

Yet in the midst of the decimated trash heap the mill had become, there was a turn—even Errol felt it. Subtly their focus shifted from what had changed to what was the same; from what was gone to what remained. Certainly this did not look like the Cleveland Cottons of Raphael's adolescence, but everywhere it was evident that he'd been there. The cotton was crumbling, but sheets still hung on the occasional window. Raphael pointed to bits of wood and metal on the walls where his lanterns had been fixed. And though damp and rank-smelling, the trunk was still there, even if Ida was not on top of it now. He touched the leather with the springy deference of incredulity.

The trunk had a padlock on it, never cracked; Raphael spun the dial; Errol was amused that he still remembered the combination. When he opened the chest it creaked; the leather hinges broke, and the whole top fell off with a *poof* onto the floor. Raphael peered inside. He lifted, one by one, carefully wrapped in plastic: a caulking gun, a drill, a ten-inch carving knife. Then: a corkscrew and two bundles of felt. He unwrapped these and walked over to set two fluted, pink-tinted wineglasses gently on the sill of the window he'd unboarded. Just then the sun came out from behind a cloud and the glasses glowed.

"Who's there?"

Raphael froze.

"I told you assholes to stay out of here! You're gonna get hurt, you hear!" It was a woman's voice, and sounded nervous.

Raphael took a breath so deep that Errol could see his chest expand from fifteen feet away. "Don't worry, I know my way around here!" he shouted back.

"I don't give a damn! This place is about to collapse. I've got a kid across the street, and I don't want him to see people going in and out of here. I'm trying to keep this place boarded up!"

Raphael looked down at the pink glasses and ran his finger pensively around the rims. "A child," he said, no longer shouting.

"Listen, I mean it, get out of here or I'm calling the police!"

"No, you won't."

"Oh yeah?" Someone was scuffling through the entrance. A bottle skittered away and a board tumbled. Suddenly a woman stepped into the light. "And why wouldn't I call the police?"

Raphael turned toward her. He was right by the window, and the sun lit his one side brilliantly, leaving the other half in full shadow. "Because that's not like you," he said quietly. "You might board this place back up with me inside and bury me alive. Or forget the whole thing and go back to your towel, because you've gotten bored, or whatever it is you get now. But the police? Sedentary Ida. That's not your style."

Ida stared. "You son-of-a-bitch," she said slowly.

Errol was surprised to be looking at a stranger—he had expected, ridiculously, to recognize her. She was wearing a faded denim shirt and cutoffs and heeled sandals that didn't function well in this rubble. Errol noticed her legs. Her knees were a little knobby, but the legs were still long and thin and imperious-looking. Her face, though, was disappointing. That sharpness that Errol had imagined was there, but while at thirty it had possibly been insolent, provocative, now her skin had tightened and her weight was too low, so what remained was a look of strain, even harshness. Perhaps it was the light, the severity of shadow, but she didn't look pretty.

"Kind of depressing here, huh?"

"No," said Raphael. "Complex. Interesting."

"Kids stayed away from here for a long time. They thought you'd be back and do something terrible. They'd take a board and run away. It wore off, but you had a reputation."

"Funny, and I was never violent. Then."

"Reputation has nothing to do with what you've actually done. Only with what you seem like you've done. For example, you look right now like you could've just run somebody through with your carving knife."

"I have."

"Trying to scare me?"

"I've always scared you."

"You've gotten uppity."

"You've gotten older," said Raphael sadly.

"What did you expect?" she snapped. "So have you. Time marches on, right? I'm not superhuman."

"Why so angry?"

"I'm tired of being told I'm older like some accusation. Like I've done something wrong."

"Be easy on me, Ida. I've never watched people age before."

"You'll get bored with it soon enough."

"I'm afraid you may be right."

Gray walked into the light and looked Raphael in the eye. Ida started. Gray and Errol had been in the shadows, as they'd been, in a sense, all afternoon.

The startling thing was that now, with both of them in the light, Gray looked by far the younger of the two women. Gray was on the soft edge of sunlight; with the dust rising and flecking around her, she seemed at her most hauntingly timeless, looking both kind and grave, like a seraph who has come to deliver tidings which are not exactly bad but which will require mortals to make painful choices.

Ida, by comparison, looked ancient, and entirely of this earth. The lines in her face seemed to deepen, the veins on her legs to rise.

Yet side by side they were also joined by an odd commonality. Not only were they both tall and thin and physically strong; their resemblance had more to do with the way they held themselves, which was, more than inches, what made them tall. Each head lengthened so far over each set of shoulders. Simply, they both stood as if they were somebody. The difference was that Gray seemed to believe it; Ida was no longer sure, and stood that way out of habit, and anger. They both burned tall in that sunlight, but Ida from fury, Gray from something else, and something, Errol had to admit, new. By Gray's fire you could warm yourself, put out wet clothes to dry, go to sleep in the surety that she would keep wolves away through the night. Ida's fire would burn down your house.

"Gray," said Raphael, "Ida."

"This is the kind of scene you like, isn't it?" Gray observed.

"Don't act like you know me. I've never met you."

"I do know you. I know you well."

"You can't believe anything he tells you. I never told him anything."

"You told him everything."

"Are you kidding? I lied my head off."

"That's what you think. But you can't lie, Ida. You don't know how. Every time you lie you tell the truth. How old are you?"

"What do you care?"

"I'm just curious."

"Thirty-five," said Ida warily.

"See? Now, I know you're at least forty. It always intrigues me that it's the people who think they keep secrets who are so transparent."

"You're going to invite us to your house," said Raphael.

"Oh, am I?"

Now, as Errol emerged from the shadows, Ida must have felt a little invaded. She took a step back. "Well, we've got enough for a regular party, don't we?"

"That's right," said Raphael.

Ida's chin rose. "What if I'm not in a party mood?"

"Ida," said Gray, "admit it. You can't resist. Is Walter home?"

"Yes . . ." she said, not getting Gray's drift.

"All the better," Gray went on. "It would be twisted, wouldn't it? Gnarled, even impossible. Think how awkward it would be, Ida—how pointless and painful."

"You think you know so much," snapped Ida. "You don't. You predict what I'll do, I do the opposite."

"Maybe I know that," said Gray evenly. "Maybe I don't want to go to your house. Maybe I was just getting out of it."

Ida looked confused.

Raphael stepped toward her and looked down; he could now make her look short. "You're afraid of me, aren't you? You're afraid to take me home with you."

"You must be joking," she said bravely. "You're a kid."

"Not anymore."

"I'm supposed to be so impressed you grew up? That happens to everybody, you know. It's not some kind of accomplishment."

"I'm not so sure," said Raphael. "I regard every year as a trophy, won at some risk."

"I guess by that way of thinking you've got yourself a regular award winner there."

"She's better than you are," said Raphael, as if realizing this for the first time himself.

Ida smiled. "So. I still get to you, don't I?"

"How do you figure that?"

"You came here to show off, didn't you? Look how old I am. Look, I have another woman, even older than you are. Though God knows why you think that's so impressive. And you took your shirt off. So you've got more chest hair! Did you go to college? Are you going to show me your report card?"

Raphael stared at her steadily. "I came to see if you'd changed. Somehow that was important."

"Yeah? So what's the verdict?"

"I can't decide yet. You put on a very good Ida-act. I'm curious if it's real, or just something you remember."

"You never give up, do you? Why don't you just forget about me? What's your problem?"

Raphael sighed. Errol had, for once, some clear sense of what was going on in his head: a certain tiredness. It must have occurred to him to claim that he'd forgotten her; that, like his father, she wouldn't affect him if she died. To go through this again was boring, though. Sometimes that's what's

wrong with lying, that it's boring, because when you allow
yourself to say anything at all, something convoluted happens
and you can no longer say anything in particular—you get
lost and you're left with only words, or not, and they are too
much trouble; you might as well keep your mouth shut.
Raphael had not come here to bluster, for bravado. He was
not sure why he'd come here exactly, but it wasn't for bravado.
Errol had to grant Raphael this much: he wasn't interested in
fakery. If the man acted cold, he felt cold. That's what was
frightening.

"Ida," said Raphael.

"What?"

He stared down at her and didn't let up until she looked
back at him. "Ida," he repeated. "There are a lot of hours, a
lot of days. Only so much happens. I have to think about
something."

She began to look nervous, and broke their gaze. She looked
down at her feet and tried to pick her way in her sandals a few
steps away. She looked back up, with several boards and bricks
safely between them. "I didn't do anything to you, understand?"

Raphael just looked at her.

"I've got nothing to feel bad about."

There were so many things Raphael was not saying that the
ensuing silence was astounding.

"You had a crush," she went on, but her voice was losing its
bite; it seemed unlike her to explain herself. "It happens all the
time. To kids. What was I supposed to do? I was nice to you."

Raphael smiled, just a little.

"What's so funny?"

"*Nice* is such a strange word to hear from you."

"All right, so I wasn't nice," she said, tossing her hair back with a flick of her head. "Who cares about nice? I don't have to be anything. Who cares about any of this? Just so much small change, I mean, who cares? The whole thing is trivial. Really, who gives one little goddamned fucking shit?"

"Are you all right?" asked Raphael softly.

"Of course I'm all right! I'm fine. I could hardly be better. You come here, you don't come here, big deal either way, okay? It doesn't matter to me. But you walk in, you expect me to get all broken up, don't you? I'm supposed to say, I'm sorry! I'm sorry! Gosh, I was so terrible! You poor baby, what have I done to you—"

"People have just done things to me, that's all," he said steadily. "So I've ended up a certain way. Good or bad, I couldn't tell you. You'd have to ask Gray K." He looked over at Gray. "She's the one who will have to pay for what I'm like."

"Oh?" asked Ida. "And what are you like?"

"I am"—Raphael paused and considered—"like this." At that he turned simply to his left and picked up the pink wine-glasses one by one off the sill and unceremoniously dropped them onto the concrete. The shattering lasted little time and barely reverberated; then it was over and they were broken. Raphael looked at Ida unperturbed.

It took Ida a minute. "Fine," she said. "This is old business. Who needs it. I sure don't."

"You have new business?"

"I don't need any business. I don't need you or your woman or your friend, understand?"

"All you need is Walter."

"Boy, do I not need Walter."

"And you make sure he knows that, don't you?"

"He knows. But he needs me. I put up with it."

"Why?"

"Well, I have a little boy," she said reluctantly.

"I'm going to meet him now."

"What if I say you can't see him?"

Passing Ida as he walked toward the exit, Raphael paused to stare her down. Beside him she looked brittle and small. "A little something I picked up from anthropology: If I'm bigger than you, I do what I like." He walked on out.

"You'd just love to beat the living shit out of me, wouldn't you?" she shouted after him.

Raphael laughed softly from the shadows. "You wish."

"What a big man," Ida muttered to Gray and Errol, and the three of them ducked out of the mill. Raphael was ahead of them, crossing the street toward Ida's bedraggled clapboard. "He thinks he's changed so much."

"And has he?" asked Gray.

"He's the same. He's a baby."

"He can't be the same," said Gray, more to herself than to Ida, "if he thinks he's different. That in and of itself is a change. And maybe if you think you're a certain way long enough and hard enough, you become that way. Maybe, Ida, those wineglasses were a performance. But how many times can a man discard objects of great sentiment and still be sentimental?"

They crossed the street. "You talk pretty weird," said Ida, striding away from them to where Raphael was standing and staring at a boy on the front lawn. The two were facing each other, saying nothing.

"Sasha!" said Ida. "Come here."

The boy didn't move, and continued to look at Raphael with wary curiosity.

Ida knelt by her son and pulled him over to her. Even with her arms around him, though, the boy didn't take his eyes off Raphael. "This is Raphael," said Ida. "He wanted to meet you. This is Sasha." She squeezed his shoulder and stood up. "Okay, you can go off and play now." Sasha didn't move. Ida looked down at her son as if he were broken. "Go on."

"I played," he said.

"Well, do it some more."

"I don't feel like it." He kept looking at Raphael. Raphael kept looking back.

As Errol and Gray drew toward the boy, they gradually understood what Raphael was staring at. Sasha was thin, delicate, and dark. His hair was black and wild, like Ida's, but heavier. His lips were small, sullen, and scarlet. His cheekbones were high. His eyes drove deep to the back of his head.

"How old are you?" asked Raphael.

"He's five," said Ida quickly.

"I didn't ask you. How old are you, little boy?"

Sasha pulled away from his mother. "Six."

"Sasha, how many times have I told you not to lie?"

"I bet not many times," said Raphael. "Do you lie, Sasha?"

Sasha compressed his lips and shrugged his shoulders.

"You don't even know," said Raphael. "I believe that. But tell me—and you can lie if you want—are you five or six?"

Ida turned her son around to face her and knelt so their eyes met. "You shouldn't round up, Sasha. I know you want to be older, but—" She looked sharply at Gray. "There's plenty of time for that later."

"But—"

"You're as old as I say you are. I'm your mother. Now, how old are you?"

"Five," he said reluctantly.

"That's better." She let him go, and Sasha drooped like a humiliated soldier who has just been demoted.

"Reality is so malleable with you, Ida," said Raphael. "It doesn't even exist within several feet of you, does it? Your life is one big multiple-choice problem, and every answer's right. Every answer's wrong. So there's no answer, and finally no problem. I mean, *you* don't exist, do you, Ida? Why don't you just disappear?"

He was right. It was as if Ida were surrounded by a force field. Errol imagined if he reached into it his hand would shimmer and split into several translucent images; it would be impossible to tell which were his real fingers. In fact, he might no longer have "real" fingers. Ida's game was like shyster threecard monte: the ace was not on the table at all.

"Why don't *you* disappear, buddy?" A tall, massive, middle-aged man with a beard had trooped down the stairs of the front porch.

"Because I choose to be someone in particular," said Raphael mildly, turning. "So I exist. If I keep a secret, at least I know what it is."

"You're not making sense, boy, and I don't care. I'm used to nonsense. All that matters to me is that you're gone in two minutes, and then I'm going back inside to have another beer and I'm going to pretend you never showed up here."

"*Walter*," said Raphael, with a melting fondness that stopped Walter in his tracks. "Don't you get tired of pretending? Pretending to have a wife. Pretending to have a son."

"We're not talking."

"What an imagination. I could swear we were."

"Get out of here."

"Walter, we used to have such fine times. I'm beginning to think you don't love me anymore."

"You're leaving *now*."

Walter started to reach for Raphael's arm, but Raphael quickly pointed his finger at him and said, "No." Walter froze. Raphael didn't need a switchblade. That finger did just as well; it held Walter at bay.

Ida's husband took a different tack. "Listen," he said quietly. "It's been a long time. We've got a kid. She's all right, or as all right as she's going to get. Maybe this is just a joke to you. But I've gotta live with her, and we've worked stuff out. You're a man now, so maybe you know women—if you do, you know they're bugged out and anything can send them into a tailspin. So please just say goodbye nicely and get in your car. You've done enough damage already. Leave me to take care of her."

"Oh, Walter, you're breaking my heart."

Walter punched Raphael in the stomach. Raphael doubled over. As he pulled himself upright again, he was laughing, but he didn't make much sound because the air had been forced from his lungs. "Too late, Walt," he rasped. "You missed your chance seven years ago. You're wasting your time."

In fact, Walter did not look as if the punch had given him much satisfaction. After all, there's nothing to do after you hit someone but to hit him again. Yet Walter's hands hung at his sides now, with boredom. "I could waste a lot more time like that if you stick around."

"No," said Raphael wearily, "you won't do that again."

Errol cased the two side by side. Walter had the weight over the younger man, but that was the end of it. It was so obvious that Raphael could decimate the man in a few blows that the fight was over already. They were back to an adult way of settling things: tally and verdict. When in one set of figures each number is larger than in the other set, there isn't even any point in taking out pencil and paper.

"See, it doesn't matter if I go or stay," Raphael explained patiently. "It wouldn't matter if I never came. I have no effect on your wife, Walt. Neither do you. If she doesn't like the way this afternoon turned out, she'll change it. If she didn't like what I said, I'll have said something else. I wouldn't flatter myself that I could damage her. You shouldn't flatter yourself that you can protect her. We're putty, Walt. Maybe she isn't married to you at all. Maybe she's married to me."

Walter may have been used to nonsense, but he still shifted uncomfortably from one foot to the other. He looked at the sky. "Not a beer," he said. "Jack Daniel's."

During all this Gray and Errol had been teaching Sasha to throw a Frisbee.

"Sasha," said Raphael, perhaps tired of Walter already, "throw it here."

The Frisbee came dutifully wobbling over to Raphael. He picked it up and threw it high enough that the gleaming of the sun obscured it at its peak; Sasha squinted. Gently it came banking back down and returned to Raphael, who caught it by reaching behind his back. Sasha smiled. "Teach me to do that." Raphael gave him some tips; Sasha tried and got the Frisbee a few feet up; it did return to him. "Teach me more."

Raphael showed him how to spin the disk on the tip of his

finger. The Frisbee hovered, whirring, over Raphael's hand, and with his forefinger pointing up and his face gentler than usual, he looked like Da Vinci's *St. John the Baptist* gesturing heavenward. Errol apologized to himself for the analogy, but Raphael had Renaissance features, and sometimes these images were overwhelming.

Sasha tried and dropped it several times, intently.

"Sasha," said Walter, "toss it over."

Sasha looked at his father warily, then threw the Frisbee to Raphael. Again the two hardly stopped looking at each other. Raphael returned the Frisbee to Sasha and told him generously, "Throw it to your *father*." Only then would Sasha toss it to Walter. When Walter threw it back, though, it curled on its side and dropped to the ground. Sasha rolled his eyes and retrieved it; he wouldn't send it to his father again.

"Raphael is good with that thing, isn't he?" said Ida to Walter.

"Just swell."

"He's gotten rather nice-looking, hasn't he?"

Walter licked his lips. "He always looked all right, Ida. You pointed that out a number of times."

Ida sidled closer to her husband. "They have the same eyes."

"Yes, Ida. I noticed that a long time ago."

The incredible patience! Errol was astounded. Casually Errol walked closer. What was Walter's secret? How did he do it? Ida could say anything and Walter would breathe and shake his head and say something understated. Then, this murmur of indefatigable suffering had a weirdly familiar ring to it. Errol recognized with a chill that it was the sound of his own voice.

"He hasn't gotten over me," said Ida, with a grim little smile.

"He never will," said Walter. "That's the way those things go, when you're a kid."

"It's not 'those things.' It's me."

"It's those things, Ida. You're not exactly Elizabeth Taylor anymore."

"Elizabeth Taylor isn't Elizabeth Taylor anymore," said Ida, sulking. "She's fat. At least I'm not fat." Ida tapped her foot. "He might still go away with me."

"Go ahead, Ida."

"No, really."

"Go ahead, really." Walter sounded so tired. In Errol's head everything Walter had ever said sounded tired.

"I can't believe he's running around with that old bag," said Ida, rather loudly.

"She seems like a pretty interesting character to me."

"I bet she can't do anything with him in bed besides tuck him in and sing 'Rock-a-bye-baby.'"

"She's got a lot of getup and go with a Frisbee."

"A man and a little piece of plastic are hardly the same thing."

"You mean all this time you knew there was a difference between objects and people and you never let on," said Walter. "You're a sly dog, Ida."

"She acts so high and mighty—"

"All she's doing is playing Frisbee."

"She's showing off."

"The kid is showing off. She's just throwing the thing."

Walter stopped to watch. The Frisbee had rolled across the street, and Gray threw it from the mill. It was true she never twirled it or caught it under her leg, but her tosses were always long and low and smooth. The Frisbee was white and caught the sun; it made a sleek picture hovering gradually across the road and skimming a few inches over the roof of Raphael's Porsche.

"In fact, she's pretty well preserved, Ida. Maybe you should find out her secret."

"I bet she sleeps in a coffin and sucks blood."

"That's your trick, sweetheart," said Walter softly. "It's not working."

But Ida didn't listen. She was watching her son with satisfaction. "He's going to be pretty," she said, "I made sure of that."

Errol had had enough, and walked away. There was something sickening about that last statement of hers. Errol would hate to be around this happy family in ten years. It would be the kind of trio about which movies are made: a damning retrospective on a man's early life which explained why he later became the second Boston Strangler. By the end of the movie you'd be entirely sympathetic, too, and when he stepped into the electric chair you might even cry, because you'd know very well who should really get strapped into that thing, even though *technically* she hadn't strangled anyone.

Diving for a toss, Sasha fell hard on the walkway. Everyone stopped. Ida and Gray started toward the boy, but Raphael shot them both looks and they hung back. Raphael approached the child, but didn't reach to pick him up. Sasha looked up from the concrete at the man who was not helping him. Slowly, not taking his eyes off Raphael, he drew himself upright. His hands and knees were bleeding, but the boy didn't cry.

"You know you'll be all right, don't you?" said Raphael.

Sasha nodded.

"And you know you'll always be all right, don't you?"

Sasha nodded again.

"I'm going to have to go. I'm going to give you some advice first. You're going to remember it for the rest of your life. Are you listening?"

"Uh-huh."

"Ready?"

"Uh-huh."

"This is serious."

Ida hovered a few feet away, and looked ready to whip her son out from under Raphael at the first opportunity. Even Errol had an odd feeling of wanting to save the boy from some terrible spell that was being cast on him, a curse that would follow him until someone shot him with a silver bullet or ran a stake through his heart or burned down his entire castle. Sasha should have run off to his mother by now, and for God's sake, he should certainly be crying. Blood was beginning to run down his leg in streams.

"First," said Raphael, "keep quiet."

"Okay."

"That's harder than you think."

"Uh-huh."

"There's only one other thing. Ready?"

"Uh-huh."

"Don't count on anyone."

Sasha looked back.

"Do you understand?"

He shrugged.

"Say it."

"What?"

"What I told you."

"Keep quiet."

"Good. What else?"

Sasha thought a minute. "Don't count . . ."

"Go on."

"Don't count on anyone."

It was a truly bizarre experience to hear a child of five or six repeat this advice. It gave Errol the same shiver as photographs of children with progeria. Errol would have comforted himself that the boy didn't know what he was saying, but when Ida came up to him to help him with his cuts, Errol could only conclude that Sasha understood Raphael's advice perfectly well.

"Let's go inside," she said. "I'll clean those hands and knees right up."

When she took him by the hand he pulled away. "I'm okay."

"Sweetheart, we've got to get the dirt out or you'll get infected."

Again Sasha shook her off. "I'll do it." Shooting a conspiratorial glance at his mentor, he marched inside by himself. Raphael smiled.

"Well, you've created a regular little hero, haven't you?" said Ida.

"Being your son is heroic by definition." He watched the screen door bang behind the boy.

Errol had followed all this standing by Walter. "You like having a kid?" Errol asked, making conversation.

"I don't know. I don't really have one."

"No?"

"He steers clear of me. She tells him stories, see. I reach for him, he flinches. And I've never hit him once."

"That's odd."

"No. Nothing's odd. Not anymore."

Errol knew it wasn't polite, but he had to ask, "Do you ever think about leaving her?"

"Think, sure. Do it, never. Then what would I do, go marry a nice girl? I'd probably flip out. I'd end up beating the crap out of her just to get her to say something with a little sting in it, you know?"

"I'd think you'd get tired of sting."

"You think I'm some sort of henpecked asshole, don't you?"

"Well," said Errol amenably, "if there are going to be people like Ida, I suppose there have to be people to put up with them."

Walter nodded to Ida and Raphael. "She's coming on to him."

It was true. She was standing right up against Raphael; he didn't step away, either, though Errol looked up to find Gray seated on the porch with an excellent view. Gray looked worn out and increasingly annoyed; Errol was sure she'd gotten all the amusement she was going to out of this escapade, and was now waiting for it to be over.

But it didn't stop. It wasn't just a passing moment. Ida didn't move away. Raphael leaned closer. He must have felt her breath on his chin. Errol stopped talking to Walter and craned his neck. Gray uncrossed her legs on the porch. Only Walter was not incredulous. It was a fact, then, that nothing was odd to him anymore.

Raphael reached up and placed his hand gently on Ida's cheek. Errol decided: Great. Do us this favor. Kiss her and we will dispense with you quickly. Kiss her and Gray will stand and lift the keys from your pocket as she strides down the walkway, and the two of us will take your car back to Boston and leave you stranded here where you started: back with this mess, and a hovel across the street that has rats again, and Ida older and worse than ever, Walter harder to entertain, at last impossible to surprise, until you screw her in broad daylight on the grass and he yawns and goes for his beer. Not even Jack Daniel's, he won't need it, but Rolling Rock, Bud, something cheap. Fine. Do us all that tremendous favor.

A sound cracked across the lawn. Raphael had slapped her. Only once, but so hard that Ida almost fell over.

"Now don't tell me," he said tenderly, "I never did you a favor."

Ida looked up at him and rubbed her cheek. She looked wary, but amused also; pleased. "How do you figure that?"

"You've been dying to have someone smack you for twenty years. You beg them and beg them and they just won't do it. I hate to see you suffer, Ida. Maybe I came all this way just to help you out."

"That's real smart. You tell yourself that everything you do to people they're asking for. Then you can do whatever you want."

"'People put themselves in the situations they put themselves.' I've never forgotten that. A miracle cure for responsibility. One of the most useful things you ever gave me, dear." And now he did kiss her, lightly, on the forehead. Then he turned and reached toward the porch, and Gray came down the stairs to take his hand. The two walked across the street to the car, saying nothing, not looking back.

Errol shook Walter's hand. "So long, Walt," he said warmly. "Enjoy."

"Endure, maybe. That's all I ask."

"I admire you," said Errol.

"Then you're the only living human being who does."

"No, I do. I should put you in touch with someone. Seriously, you two should write. Her name is Leonia Harris, and she's a big black woman in the South Bronx. She's in for the duration, regardless. You'd understand each other. Here." On this odd impulse, Errol reached for a scrap of paper and a pen. The first piece he found had Anita Katrakis's address on it, which he put wryly back in his pocket. He scribbled Leonia's address and gave it to Walter. Errol slapped him lightly on the shoulder and walked away, waving goodbye to Ida. The funny thing was, stranded there, getting older on that same front lawn, her black hair lank, her face red on one side and white on the other, her knees knobby, her perch unstable in those high-heeled shoes, she seemed actually grateful to Errol, and waved back, though they hadn't spoken that whole afternoon. Errol would always remember her left alone there on that lawn, squeezing out that one drop of niceness like water from a stone.

Once they were in the car, Raphael reached for the ignition, but Gray put her hands over the keys. "Before we go, kiss me."

Raphael looked at her.

"I'm serious. Now. Just once."

Raphael turned back to the steering wheel. "I don't feel like it." He started the car. As he revved the engine, Gray reached over simply and took the key back out again. The motor died.

"I said now." She held the keys in her lap.

Raphael looked at her incredulously. "You're not giving me my keys unless I kiss you?"

"That's right. On the lips."

"If we were sixteen this would be funny."

"If we were sixteen this would be a joke."

Raphael looked into her face. Actually, for someone who had just begged to be kissed, her expression was quite dispassionate. He looked down at the keys in her lap. With an air of clinical curiosity, he did kiss her lightly on the lips. Gray raised her eyebrows calmly and dangled the car keys in his outstretched hand.

"You're going to explain what that was about?" asked Raphael as they started toward Boston.

"I needed to experience human emotion for a change."

"There were plenty of emotions back there."

"They weren't my favorites."

"No?" Raphael chided. "Hatred is exhilarating. I can get high on it."

"You hate her?"

Raphael considered. "No."

"You hate Walter?"

"Oh no. Who could hate *Walter*?" Raphael had a way with Walter's name.

"Then Walter hates you."

"Walter likes me. That's one of the reasons he's sick."

"Then I don't understand. Where's all this hatred you're high on?"

"From my father, for one."

"A matter of debate. But from whom else?"

"Ida."

"Ida doesn't hate you. She couldn't if she tried."

"What, you think she loves me?"

"Don't be ridiculous. Ida can't—she isn't—Ida's unplugged. You said it yourself: she doesn't exist."

After they rode a while, Gray told Raphael, "I didn't like it when you dropped those glasses. It was chilling."

"No? I loved it. I haven't enjoyed anything more in weeks."

"Thanks."

"You're touchy today," said Raphael with irritation. "It's unattractive."

Gray said nothing. The word "unattractive" hung in the air for a long time.

chapter twenty-one

Things were beginning to happen. Little things, Errol told himself. Everything's fine, Errol told himself. Errol even told the dog: Bwana, relax. We'll wait this out. She'll get bored, right? How much can a guy that age have to say to her? She'll wake up one day with that man taking more than his share of the bed and feel crowded. Or she'll look out the window and find him once again waxing that stupid car, and she'll roll her eyes and decide she'd like someone around with a little more maturity. Or better yet, Bwana: she'll go off to Ghana in February—we can wait five months, can't we? and he'll disappear, and in the meantime she'll realize she's a brilliant professional who doesn't need to be jerked around by some little twenty-five-year-old nobody.

Bwana would stare back and hit his tail against the wall skeptically.

Bwana had good reason to be skeptical. Raphael turned up often in the kitchen now with that towel wrapped insolently around his waist, or in the den with the red baseball cap cocked over hundred-dollar cognac. Yet suddenly sometimes three or four days would elapse and no Ralphie. He didn't stop by; he didn't phone. At times like these Errol breathed easier, but Gray paced and stayed up late and listened to Mahler symphonies turned up incredibly loud. Or sometimes she'd be blasting one of her favorites all over the house and then just—turn it off. Then Errol would know not to talk to her, and he'd find himself tiptoeing down the halls and holding the bolt in when he shut doors behind him.

It was September, too early to put on the heat, but on certain evenings a chill would set in; Gray would go about the house closing all the windows. Even with the windows closed, a draft seemed to cut through the upper floor and down the staircase. Gray would put on a sweater, then a jacket, maybe two layers of socks, and still Errol would find her upstairs pacing from her office to her bedroom rubbing her arms. Sometimes her teeth would actually chatter.

"It's not cold," Errol might point out. "It's only September."

"I just can't get warm," she'd claimed more than once. "No matter what I do."

Toward the end of the month, Errol found Gray one such evening huddled in her straight-backed chair wearing her fur coat. It was surely no colder than fifty-five, maybe even sixty degrees, but still Errol went downstairs and built a fire in the den. He fixed hot buttered rum, and placed the two mugs beside a pile of heavy quilts and pillows by the hearth and brought her downstairs. It was absurd, of course, for this was the kind of scene Errol was used to preparing after a long day of skiing in January; but she seemed pleased, and huddled in the quilts, cupping her hands around her mug and breathing in the steam. At last she admitted she was getting warmer, though it had been four days since Raphael had called.

"You know, I've never been to where he lives," Gray confided. "We've never even passed by."

"That's odd. Why don't you stop in sometime, then?"

"I can't. I don't have his address."

"You're kidding."

"I even checked his fellowship application," she admitted sheepishly. "He gives a box number at B.U., no help. He says he lives in a big house in the better section of Belmont. That's all I can get out of him."

"A tony location, for a student."

"Yes." She stared into her rum pensively. "But I don't think he pays rent."

"How does he swing that?"

"The owner is evidently—an older woman."

Errol looked up sharply. "Interesting that he told you that."

"Very interesting." She sighed. "Furthermore—" It seemed she had to talk to someone tonight. "He never makes appointments with me."

"Appointments?"

"Plans, anything. He says he'll call. That's all, or sometimes not even that. Sometimes he just leaves."

"Well, that's his problem, right? You have a busy schedule. People who don't make appointments with you don't get to see you."

"Mmm."

"Then you can always call him."

"I do. But lately I don't. I can't. Sometimes it rings for ages, ten, twelve times, before he finally picks it up. I picture him looking at that phone, watching it tremble. I have to let it ring twenty times before I know he's not home. And even then I can't be sure. He picked it up on nineteen once. I counted."

"Maybe he'd just walked in."

"Oh no. He was there. Imagine watching the phone ring for nineteen times and then picking up the receiver as if nothing were unusual."

"Let it ring six or seven times and hang up."

"If I call him, I want to talk to him, Errol. I'll wait if I have to."

"But if he knows that, then next time it'll be twenty rings, then twenty-one."

"Then I'll wait twenty-one."

"Gray, there are limits."

Gray shook her head and stared into the fire. "No, there aren't. I thought there were, but there aren't."

The phone rang. Gray's eyes widened. Her body went rigid and wavered. She stood and untangled herself from the quilts with uncharacteristic awkwardness. She picked up the receiver and swallowed.

"Hello?" Her voice was thin. Her ears were bright red. "Hello?" She held the receiver away from her, looked at it, held it back to her ear, and hung up the phone. "Nothing," she said, leaning on the desk. "Dial tone."

"Wrong number, I guess."

Gray hung her head and breathed deeply, as if she couldn't get enough air.

"Gray, are you all right?" Errol walked over to the desk. She tried to stand up straight, but immediately had to grab Errol's shoulder for support. Her eyes were glazed and her coloring blotchy. Errol took her hand; it was limp and cold. He held her wrist, and after a moment or two made her sit down. Surely he was making a mistake. He tried again, this time putting his hand around her neck. He placed his fingers over the artery there. There was no mistake. The rate of her pulse was astounding—not only frantic, but uneven: *bu-bum* . . . BUM. BUM. *Bu-bu-bu-bum* . . .

"Gray, your heart—"

"I know."

"Does this happen to you often?"

"Only when the phone rings." She stopped to breathe. She let her head hang over the back of the chair. "When the doorbell rings. I have a problem with bells, I suppose."

"Gray, you should take it easy."

"What am I supposed to do, wear earplugs?"

"Maybe you should lie down."

It rang again. Gray closed her eyes.

"I'll get it," said Errol.

She shook her head, prepared herself however she did that, and picked it up again. "Hello?" She put it back. "Dead."

"It's late. You should go to bed."

"Have you ever tried to sleep with your heart beating like the drums in 'Marjorie and Her Filthy Dog'?"

"I'll take the phone off the hook." Errol started for the receiver.

"NO!"

Errol withdrew his hand. "All right," he said quietly, the way he would talk to a child who had just gone wild-eyed when he reached for her bedroom light switch.

Gray fell asleep in front of the fire that night. Errol stayed to watch it die to embers, until in the glow of the last red coals he wrapped a quilt around Gray's thin frame. She was still breathing too fast and whimpering in her sleep. He picked her up and carried her up the stairs to her bedroom with her head on his shoulder. As he climbed he had a clear picture of this ascent from the foyer floor. When he left her on the bed with the four posts, by the straight-backed chair and the bureau with the small white cloth and the porcelain dish for pins, he had to leave the room quickly and shut the door. He was sure that when she woke in the morning she would not understand that her sleeping upstairs that night had cost him some pain.

S omething was happening. Errol had to admit it even to the dog. Something was happening, and it was serious.

"Did you know she's impossible to see?" Ellen asked Errol. "No one can make an appointment with her. Is she too busy getting ready for this next project?"

"I wish she were," said Errol. "She spends most of her time obsessing over the Charles Corgie documentary. But what do you mean, no one can see her? She's home all the time. More than ever, sometimes all day."

"That's strange. Because I've tried. Bob's tried; Tom. No one's seen her in weeks."

"What does she say on the phone?"

"Just that her schedule is completely packed for the next month and I should call later. I got the impression—much later. Like in about five years."

Errol heard this himself: "I couldn't possibly" would come drifting through the cracks of Gray's office door. "Next week is out of this world." "I wish I could." "You would not *believe . . .*"

Because they shouldn't have believed. There was Gray, breakfast, lunch, and dinner. With exceptions, of course. Always the same exception.

"Do you ever tell him," Errol asked one morning, "that you're busy?"

"What do you mean?" She knew exactly what he meant.

"When he wants to get together. Do you ever tell him you have something else you have to do?"

"Not often," she said warily. "If I want to see him, I will. I'll cancel something else if I have to."

"Gray"—Errol spoke slowly and distinctly—"is that wise?"

"Why can't I see him if I want to? No one is looking over my shoulder. Except you."

"That's not true. There is one other person watching you."

Gray glowered at the kitchen table. She did not like this conversation.

"Our buddy Ralph is watching you awfully closely, don't you think? And you're never busy. You never kick him out in the morning so you can get to work."

She hit the table. "I don't want to! I want him to stay as long as he'll stay!"

Errol couldn't tell if she was missing the point; more likely she didn't care about the point. "Is he ever busy?"

"*Sometimes.*"

"Well . . ." Errol was glad that Gray wasn't a man, because it takes a lot longer for a woman to get to the point where she will actually hit you. "Perhaps it would be diplomatic—whether or not you have commitments—to say you do—once in a while."

Gray stood so quickly that she knocked her chair over backward. "Diplomatic! I've been a diplomat my whole life! For once I'm not a representative of my country or my profession, for once it's just me, Errol! Diplo*matic*!" She raged around the kitchen as if looking for something to break, though she didn't do that sort of thing. "I *know*," she said with loathing. "*Don't you think I know?* What I'm supposed to do? Put him off, make it weeks before I see him, let the phone ring two or three times and hang up, forget five or six? Don't you think I know? I WON'T. Errol, I WON'T. I don't want it I don't want it I don't want it." She shook her head back and forth with her hand over her face. There was no helping her, Errol knew that, so there was nothing to do but to give her advice she wouldn't take, in the end just to make Errol himself feel better, for saying the "right thing."

"But you've got it," said Errol softly. "I'm sorry it's a contest, but it is, and you're losing."

"I want," she said, "to lose."

"But do you understand what that means?"

"Not at all, Errol. That's what I intend to find out."

S he started finding out that very week. It was October now. One of the things she discovered was that losing costs you. Costs money.

Gray had seen Raphael the day before. Late that next afternoon Errol was highlighting sections of the transcript of the Leonia Harris interview. Gray came into his office and sank into a chair by his desk. Errol looked up; she was touching her forehead and staring out the window. Errol went back to his transcript. It was too bad such a fine woman as Leonia was pinning so much on some lousy drunk. Gray sighed several times. Each time Errol looked up, she looked away. After five or six bouts of this, Errol put down the paper and sat back in his chair. "All right. What has he done now?"

"Nothing much, I suppose," she said, chewing her lip. "It's little, actually."

"Anything to do with Ralphie at this point is not going to be little."

"It shouldn't matter."

"Which means it does."

"Well, I have plenty of money, don't I?"

"Didn't you just skip over something? Like the whole story?"

"It's not much of a story."

"Gray!" said Errol impatiently. "What?"

"All right. We went to lunch down at the wharf." She stopped.

"And—"

"They brought me the check, as usual."

"Right."

"It wasn't that much, compared to sometimes . . ."

"Gray, this is like pulling teeth."

"Well, Raphael has always paid for lunches. I pay for dinners, and a lot of other expenses, too—play and concert tickets, gas and tolls, even his clothes. It's seemed fair he should pay for something."

"Doesn't sound unreasonable."

"I put the check by his plate. He looked at it and handed it back."

"What did you do?"

"I said, 'What am I supposed to do with that?' He said, 'What wealthy people do with lunch checks.' I said, 'I'm a wealthy person, and what I do with lunch checks is give them to you.' He said, 'Then maybe you should learn a new trick.' All this time he's holding out the check across the table waiting for me to take it, and people are looking over at us. I said, 'I'm an old dog if there ever was one. I don't care for new tricks.' Then he said, 'You can't screw twenty-five-year-old men and still claim the benefits of old age.' That last line made me shudder."

"And?"

"And I knew what I had to do."

"Walk out."

"Exactly. Stand up, say something very biting and very clever, and stride coolly out of the restaurant."

"So did you?"

Gray looked down at her lap and ran her fingers over the back of her other hand.

"You didn't."

"I'm sorry, Errol."

"I am, too, Gray."

"If I'd left, I'd have gotten a taxi. I'd have come back here and worked, maybe grabbing a sandwich for dinner, if that. Then I'd have gone to bed. By myself. That's how I would have ended up paying for that lunch: lying there wide awake by myself. I'd have won, Errol. Terrific. I didn't want it."

"But you know what this means, don't you?"

"It means every check."

"So bringing him home with you last night cost you a good deal."

"I can afford it."

"I wonder."

She stood up. "I just had to tell you. Errol. To confess, I suppose."

Errol pushed the interview aside. "Listen. It's getting late." He took her hand. "I'll take you out. My treat."

She smiled wanly. "Only if you understand that it won't make much difference."

"Unfortunately, I do understand that." Yet despite her glumness and his inability to relieve it, Errol led her out the door and proceeded to buy her the most expensive dinner he'd ever paid for in his entire life.

T he one appointment Raphael rarely canceled was his weekly tennis game with Gray. Errol couldn't play her anymore. Playing Raphael she'd gotten too good. Was this just fine with Errol? Well, on Thursdays he got a little *edgy*.

One Thursday afternoon in November, Gray called. "Errol," she said, "please come pick me up."

"You're at the courts?"

"That is correct."

"Why can't Ralphie give you a lift?"

"I have sent him home."

"You're kidding."

"I am not in a joking mood. Now hang up the phone and get in your car."

"Well, Gray, I'm in the middle of something here. Why don't you get a taxi?"

"I do not wish to take a taxi. Please come take me home."

Errol listened carefully. There was something about her voice. Something about the way she wasn't using contractions. "All right. But give me half an hour."

"Come right this minute."

"Don't be unreasonable—"

"Right this minute. Goodbye." She hung up.

Well. Where did she get off? Come right this minute. Who did she think he was, her valet?

Errol got in the car.

When he arrived, Gray was standing against the front wall, her racket at her side. Her expression was composed. So she'd sent Ralphie home. Maybe something wonderful had happened. She looked powerful, even serene, against that wall. Tennis did that to her. Winning anything did that to her.

Yet when Errol walked closer to his mentor he noticed something overly balanced about her face, excessively careful about the set of her bones against one another, and the fine lines in her skin looked suddenly as if they went all the way through her to the wall. She was deceptively assembled, perched. Someone had left her against that wall as an irresponsible dinner guest might leave a broken glass at his setting, delicately resting it against the edge of his plate so that his host will find the thing in pieces only after reaching for it to clear the table.

Errol reached for Gray, and she fell apart. Her arms broke over his shoulders; her head cracked at the neck and fell against his cheek. Errol picked up her tennis racket and half carried her to the car. He lifted her into the bucket seat, collecting the pieces of her body like shards in a pail. She shook her head from side to side. Tears leaked down her cheeks in a steady stream.

"Tell me it didn't happen."

"It happened." She could only whisper.

"Maybe it was just a bad day—"

"No, it was a good day, Errol. I played—" She put her fingers over her eyelids and pressed, but the tears still found their way out the corners; some of them trailed down her fingers and trickled down her arm. "I played the best game—I have ever played—in my life. And he played—"

"Sh-sh—"

"*Better.*"

When they got home the phone rang as Gray walked upstairs; she froze. "No," she instructed Errol. "I can't."

Errol picked up the phone. "I think you'd better take it, Gray," he shouted up. "It's one of your contacts in Ghana. He says it's important."

"All right," she said leadenly. "I'll take it upstairs."

Half an hour later, as Errol had a drink earlier in the day then he usually allowed himself, Gray wandered into the den and fell into the leather armchair. She looked dazed, even disoriented. She wasn't blinking. Her mouth fell a little open.

"Gray?"

Her eyes darted around the room, fixing on stray objects, until they found the soapstone lion on the desk. She stared at it as if waiting for it to talk, as if it could explain something.

"What was that about?" asked Errol.

"The Lone-luk," she told the lion. "The women—have been overrun."

"By whom?"

"Whom do you think? By the men. Yesterday. They took the villages by force, with guns. The Lone-luk," she said quizzically, "are no longer . . . matriarchal."

The lion grinned.

Much as Errol would have liked to suggest to her that the Lone-luk were only a society for study, and had nothing to do with this manse in Boston and Gray in her chair, he could not shake the feeling that everything had to do with everything and that this was bad in that everything-being-bad way. He said nothing. They stayed like this, until Errol decided that the best therapy was to proceed, and he picked up the phone.

"Lenny, this is Errol McEchern. I want you to book us a couple of tickets to Ghana. I know this is the last minute, but something's come up. Money's no object. We have to get over there *tout de suite*.—Just a second." He covered the receiver. "Gray, how soon can we get out of here? You need a day, maybe? Try for Saturday?"

"What?"

"Do you want to wait until Saturday," he said impatiently, "or do you want to go tomorrow if there's a flight?"

"What?"

Errol rolled his eyes. "Lenny, I'm going to have to get back to you. Meanwhile, see what you can scavenge for tomorrow. We're miracle packers when we have to be. Otherwise, as soon as possible. Thanks."

He hung up and turned to Gray, tired of humoring her. He was a sympathetic person, but he wished she would snap out of this and do her job. "I know this is a blow, Gray. And one of several lately. But you're going to have to get into gear. We'll have to move fast the next few days."

"Why?"

Errol felt as if he were talking to a retarded child. "It's bad enough we weren't there yesterday. This next week is going to be incredible. We should bring the movie cameras. Frankly, if Lenny can swing it, I think we should fly tomorrow."

"Nnno."

Somehow they weren't communicating.

"What can't you wrap up? Leave the documentary. The world has waited all these years, it can live without Charles Corgie for a few months more."

"But I can't," she said quietly.

"What?"

She got up and paced aimlessly about the den. "It would be months, wouldn't it?"

"Yes, but it was going to be months originally, so just move the whole project up. Cancel what you have to. You haven't been making appointments with anyone, anyway—"

Gray picked up the phone. "Lenny? Gray. Make that a booking for three. And Lenny? Don't pay for them until you hear from me, understand?—Definitely not before Saturday. Errol is a little optimistic about our ability to extricate ourselves so easily. Yes. I'll call. Thanks. Goodbye."

"Three?" Errol inquired sourly.

"We always bring an assistant."

"Oh? Arabella will be delighted you thought of her."

"Arabella will not be delighted."

Errol made another drink, very stiff. With his back to her he was thinking an unpleasant question, and by the time he asked it he was furious, for there was a time not long ago when such a question would have insulted her.

He turned around. "*And what if he says no?*"

She shrank back. "Why would he do that?"

"Why would he do anything? Do you know him? Can you ever predict what he'll do?"

Her nostrils quivered.

"How many orders has he been taking lately, Gray? He wasn't much of a soldier even in Toroto, as I remember."

"Not orders. The opportunity—with Gray Kaiser—" She seemed to have trouble delivering her own name with the proper sense of importance.

"Ralph has his own plans, doesn't he? He's going to the Pacific. To lie in the sun and avoid difficult vocabulary. In February, when the weather's so unpleasant here. Had you forgotten? *You're funding him.*"

"Not yet I haven't. My recommendations aren't due for two months."

"So would you hold that over his head? To get him to go to Ghana?"

Errol really did seem to be driving her toward despair; this gave him some sadistic satisfaction. "I don't care for that kind of leverage," said Gray. "I'd want him to come to Ghana because he wanted to be with me."

"Too bad. With Ralph that's the kind of leverage that works, and you know it."

"No," she said feebly. "Not only."

"It's November. The Lone-luk is a six-month project, maybe more. You're asking him to put off his trip for yours. Is he likely to do that, Gray? Really."

"I'll simply ask him," she said faintly, "tomorrow."

"You didn't answer my question: What if he says no?"

She bowed her head. "I won't go."

The den swallowed her admission into a vast silence. The heat came on; the furnace purred below them, throaty and luxurious. Hot air wafted from the vents like the bloody breath of a successful predator; the wildebeest bones shone white and bare.

Errol picked up the smug soapstone lion and brought it down on the desk with anger. Gray jumped. "This is the limit," said Errol, and left the room to phone upstairs. He returned to the den to announce, "We're taking a trip, Gray. Right now."

"To Ghana—?"

"A good deal closer. But maybe it will get you to Ghana at that. Put on your coat. Let's go." He actually took her arm and pulled her to the rack in the foyer.

"What are you talking about? Where are you taking me?"

"It's a surprise."

"I'm not going anywhere. I'm tired and have a lot of thinking to do and would like a drink and a fire and some peace and quiet—"

Errol pointed his finger, just the way Raphael had pointed at Walter. It worked. She froze. "You're coming with me, Gray Kaiser. I've put up with a lot from you lately, doing more than my share of the work around here, and you know it. Meanwhile, you waste away lamely pasting together shots of Charles Corgie while you're waiting for the phone to ring. *I'm* the one who's tired. This may be your project, but I've put in a lot of work on this matriarchy study, and I'm not going to have it botched. I don't want to get our most important material secondhand or not at all because you want to be with your boyfriend. You owe me," said Errol. "So are you coming or not?"

Gray looked at him like an outpatient, but she did get her

coat. Errol almost smiled. He hadn't spent all these months around Ralph for nothing.

At the car, though, she insisted on getting out again. "I'll come back," she said, angrily shaking his hand off her arm. "I want to get my ferret."

"Oh, Jesus."

"I'd like some warm companionship. That's obviously not going to come from you at the moment."

So Errol waited for Gray to get Solo; she wrapped him around her neck, and the animal glared at Errol with his usual hostility. All the way there he hissed when Errol changed gears.

D r. Katrakis?"

"Anita. And may I call you Errol? Ellen's spoken so much about you; I feel as if we're old friends."

Errol was surprised that Ellen had mentioned him at all, but pleased, too. He led Gray inside the apartment, which was attractive though dissettlingly clean, like the rooms of the retired. When he introduced Gray, Anita nodded with a small, dense smile.

"Have a seat and let me get tea." Errol watched her go. He'd imagined her as a nervous, fragile character, and Anita was no such thing; yet there was something slightly peculiar about the way she moved. Her timing was off. There was a lag to every gesture that made her motions seem infused with effort.

Reminding himself that this was Ralph's most recent discard, Errol assessed her looks. Though her clothes weren't flattering, she was dark and interesting-looking. If this were his teacher, Errol would definitely come to class.

When she brought in the tea tray, Errol explained, "Gray is on the board to determine who's awarded the Ford Anthropology Fellowships. One of your old students has somehow"—Errol shot Gray a look—"come near the top of the list, and we were hoping you could shed some light on his qualities. He has become the object of some controversy."

"You must mean—Raphael." She said his name with that same lag of hers. She leaned back in her chair and breathed the steam from her tea.

"Did you know him well?" asked Errol deftly.

This time she didn't hesitate, though she spoke to Gray. "I had an affair with him."

Gray looked over at Errol in dull horror; she put her cup down hard in its saucer. Tea slurped over its side.

"You knew that, didn't you?" Anita asked Errol. "That's why you're here."

"True," Errol admitted. "But it's kind of you to be so forthright."

That dense smile again. "Not that kind. Still, everyone knows, Errol. There's no point in pretending." The smile turned to a wan one. "I know all about pretending, so I'm not very keen on it anymore."

"Does it distress you to talk about this?"

"Distress me?" She drew a finger thoughtfully to her chin. "I am distressed." She leaned forward toward Errol as if they shared a secret. "That's all that matters in the end, isn't that right? Just the facts."

She sat back in her chair, a little crooked but relaxed. Errol supposed that the one nice thing about being disappointed about what mattered to you most in the world was that you could not be disappointed anymore; to be immersed in your own pain was perhaps to overcome it. Nothing, after all, was going to come knocking at the door that would fell this woman, for no one could push you down if you were already on the floor.

"We were wondering," said Errol slowly, "did Raphael Sarasola use you in any way?"

"In every way," she returned with a shrug. "For my sailboat. My money. My connections. You name it. Up to the very end." She added wistfully, "Beyond the end, even."

"How do you mean?"

"This last February Raphael hadn't called me for a long time. I'd lost my job, and was still unemployed. Out of the blue he showed up at my door. With no apology—he doesn't do that— he told me he'd read a passage that had struck his eye. Funny, he wasn't at all well read, but single sentences could have more impact on him than whole books on other people."

"What had so struck him?" asked Gray.

"Some story about a man in Africa. He told me a last-minute assistantship had been posted for fieldwork in Kenya. He was dying to go. I know it's difficult to imagine Raphael dying to do anything, but he had an urgency I'd never seen—I certainly never saw it in his arrangements to see me . . ." She took a sip of her tea. "Anyway, he knew I had some close friends in anthropology, and asked me to do what I could."

"And you did?" asked Errol incredulously.

"I can't explain if you don't understand."

"He used your connections to go to Kenya? He used you to leave you."

"That's right," she agreed without heat. "He left the continent within a few days, and I haven't heard from him since."

Errol was getting frustrated with her mildness. "Doesn't this make you angry?"

"No. He used me. I allowed it. It was my fault. Or my choice, anyway. Why should I be angry?"

"That sounds to me as if you're taking too much responsibility."

"Raphael was responsible," she responded reasonably. "He was faithfully the person I knew he was from the moment I met him. When you know someone, you know what they'll do to you. You accept that, or not."

So Anita had refined responsibility, just as Ida (people put themselves in the situations they put themselves in) had refined blame. Ida would say: "You asked for it." Anita would say: "Yes, I did." Ida would hit her; Anita would say: "I knew you would do that." Ida would say: "Yes, you did." They would get along famously.

"By that way of thinking," Errol pointed out, "the behavior of everyone in your life is your fault."

"Maybe it is," said Anita, as if the assertion weren't the least farfetched. "But especially Raphael's. It's easy to know what he'll do, because he doesn't even lie. He never told me he loved me, not once."

Gray squirmed on the couch. "Maybe he has a hard time saying such a thing."

Anita looked at Gray sympathetically. "Or maybe it wasn't true. I knew that. I also knew," she went on with a sigh, "that maybe he couldn't ever say that to anyone. So if I still insisted on believing that he loved me anyway, that was my own weakness. He was hardly to blame for that."

"Errol," said Gray, in a funny, strangled voice, "maybe we should go, please?"

"Before you leave," said Anita, "what is that?"

"A ferret," said Gray heavily.

"May I hold it?"

"Well," said Gray reluctantly. "He's very fond of me, and well behaved. With other people he can be unpredictable. He sometimes bites."

"I'll brave it," said Anita. She reached for the pet with hunger, as if she hadn't touched anything warm and animate for a long time. Gray looked disappointed when Solo acted with Anita exactly as he did with Gray—he was tolerant of being fondled and rested placidly in her hands. Anita stroked him, purring, "There. I'm not so different from your master, am I? I'm not so bad." She looked up. "These can be vicious. You've got him well tamed."

"I hope so," said Gray, taking Solo back and walking toward the door.

"I was glad to finally meet you, Errol. And Dr. Kaiser—"

"Yes?"

"I just wanted to extend my—congratulations, in a way. He's a hard catch."

"Pardon?" asked Gray coldly.

"But you also have my sympathy."

"I don't need your sympathy."

"You will. You're already suffering. I can see it around your eyes. Why are you here, after all? You shouldn't have had to ask me if Raphael used me. He would tell you himself. It's one of the things that's most appalling, isn't it? He answers questions. But you can't afford to ask him something like that anymore, can you?" She pressed Gray's hand. "I'll pray for you tonight."

Errol had the strange sensation as they parted that she hadn't always been a religious woman.

Gray ran down the stairs; Errol had trouble catching up with her. "Gray!" he called. "The car's right here!"

She kept walking. The ferret was sitting on her shoulder and stared back at Errol with black, mocking eyes. Errol ran up and stopped her with a hand on her arm. She wouldn't look at him. "Why did you do that to me?" she asked, looking straight ahead.

"I didn't do it to you. I did it for you."

"You lost me."

Tact was beside the point now. "The sooner you get away from the man, the better, and you know it."

"I know it? That sounds strangely like your opinion."

"And the opinion of anyone who's ever known him or seen you two together. The man is poison, and even Dr. Impervious can't swill that kind of arsenic week after week without getting a little woozy."

"I was wondering when you'd pull this."

"I'm your best friend. To keep quiet any longer would be to do you a disservice—"

"That's very considerate, but I can live without your little revelations, thank you."

"He's doing you in!"

"But I want him to!" Gray stood and breathed.

Errol's hands fell to his sides. She wanted to be done in? Gray had no idea what she was talking about, but Errol did. He wanted to save her. He wanted to save her from what his own life was like.

"The point is," he explained practically, "especially knowing what kind of man he is—"

"You have no idea what kind of man he is, and neither does she."

"—*You cannot allow him to affect your work.*"

"So that's it. Work. The great sacred icon, isn't it? The untouchable Work. The one real God in Gray Kaiser's life, isn't that right?" For someone who didn't believe in regret, she sounded awfully bitter. "Imagine a mere man interfering with the study of man. Let me ask you this," she said, with an almost ugly insight. "What if I asked you to go live with the Lone-luk by yourself? What if I told you to go ahead and fly there tomorrow? Since Work is so hallowed, so all-important?"

Errol drew himself up. "I would say," he said icily, "absolutely not. This is your project, and I've done plenty more than my share already. If you think you can shove me off to Africa so you can ruin your life and your career with total abandon—"

"I wouldn't be ditching you, Errol. You and that sister of yours!"

"You would, too! But you're not packing your only conscience off to do your work for you just because Ralphie isn't up to Ghana this month—"

"We may all be packing off to Ghana if you would just give me a chance to ask the man to go."

"What if I told you that if he goes, I'm staying here?"

"Is that what you're telling me?"

Errol stopped, frightened of his own ultimatum. He stammered, "I have to think about it."

"You do that, Errol. I'm going for a walk. Goodbye." She wrapped the ferret around her neck and turned on her heel. Errol turned on his, and they both walked militantly in opposite directions back to back, as if marking off paces in a duel. Yet neither turned around and fired; instead, Gray rounded a corner and did not return home until late at night. As for Errol, he drove to his office and spent the whole evening typing letters.

chapter twenty-two

There was a mirror in the foyer that reflected a panoramic view of the den. Errol had noticed this before, but because information so frequently bounded over him uninvited, he'd rarely resorted to this wide screen. As Errol walked downstairs that next Friday evening, though, the mirror had the same enticing quality of drive-in movies that one passes on the highway; of big, unbidden human anguish splashed up beside the road. Errol paused.

"Frankly, I'm surprised you asked," said Raphael, leaning back on the couch.

"You shouldn't be. What else was I to do?" Gray had that brave look. She faced Raphael on the couch with her head high, the way Barbara Stanwyck might face into a stiff prairie wind.

"But you must know the answer," said Raphael.

"I don't presume anything with you."

"What would I do?"

"Collect data. Talk to people. Live as they do and take notes. Find out what it's like, how the power structure has shifted."

"Why would it make any difference that I was there?"

"You're younger," said Gray, in a passable imitation of her most professional voice. "You could make contact more easily with the young adult and adolescent population. And—" She shrugged.

"And what?"

"Why do I always have to spell things out?"

"We don't have to do anything. We could both"—Raphael smiled—"just sit here."

"We are just sitting here," said Gray with difficulty, turning away. "Aren't we? It would make so much difference to me, but you aren't even considering going for an instant, are you? What are we doing. We're just passing time."

"Nothing wrong with that," said Raphael mildly. "What else is there to do with it?"

"Plenty else. Love each other. Set people like the Lone-luk a good example. Work hard. Go somewhere else and suffer and return and have a whole new appreciation for a gin-and-tonic in a tall glass with lots of ice and a twist of lime. Otherwise tall drinks go to nothing."

"I still have a taste for them. I've already suffered. I've gone and returned. I've had enough."

"You're too young to make a statement like that. I don't care what you went through as a child. You're only twenty-five, and hardly ready for permanent sun and fun in the Pacific and early retirement."

"Gray K.," he said, now sounding almost wistful, "I'm older than you, by far. You know that. That's why this has been possible. You—" He shook his head. "You're a little girl."

"You say something like that," said Gray, "and I get lost.

The whole meaning of age falls apart. Why talk about it? Why say anything?"

Raphael shrugged. "You're the one who likes to talk."

Gray raised her hand to her forehead and touched herself between the eyes lightly with two fingertips. "This is all beside the point."

"The point is, you said they live in squalor. But I already know what it's like to live without running water, to sleep with rats, to scavenge. I don't need a wilderness camping trip as a refresher course. I also know what it's like to live with people who hate each other, and beat each other—I grew up with it. I learn something and move on."

"No, that's not the point. And what you'd have to learn you haven't learned yet, not at all."

"What's that?"

"To do something hard," said Gray simply, "for me."

Raphael said nothing.

"Then I will leave when I originally planned to," said Gray heavily. "In February."

"That's good timing. I'm leaving then myself."

"Oh?"

"To study the Goji," he said without question. "Where they have plumbing and small, clean houses and a beautiful beach. You're paying for it, remember?"

"We'll see," she said weakly. "Until then we'll have some time together. In February we'll go our separate ways." She paused, and gathered courage. "Will you miss me?"

"I don't know."

Gray looked at the ceiling. "You won't even do anything easy for me, will you?"

"Like what?"

"Even say you'll miss me."

"Gray K., you're wrong. That's not easy at all." Raphael got up off the couch and walked to the window.

"I'm begging you," said Gray at his back in a strange, flat voice. "I'm begging you to go with me."

"I would never have thought," said Raphael, "when I first saw you by that fire—so tall, so commanding, so wry—that you would ever beg anyone to do anything."

"Are you disappointed?"

"It's either odious or admirable. I can't say which. So let's just say that it doesn't make any difference."

"It does to me."

"How?"

"I would hate to think," said Gray, "sitting in a tin hut with only Errol at my side, that I hadn't tried everything." She turned away. Raphael left the room and quietly picked up his coat in the foyer. Before he left he looked up at Errol on the stairs with no particular surprise. They looked each other in the eye for a long time before Raphael turned to the door and softly let himself out.

From then on, Errol could only admire her. She did not, as he feared, cancel the Lone-luk project altogether but advanced toward its due date with fatalistic resignation, the way an inmate on death row might approach his upcoming execution when there was little hope of pardon. Somehow it didn't help matters that a few days before they were to fly to Ghana, Gray would turn sixty years old.

Yet she persevered. At length Errol could almost approve of letting the Lone-luk wait, for she'd started another project she had to finish: the project of being done in. She went at it with the commitment, tenacity, and abandon with which she attacked all the other projects of her life; in fact, he'd never seen her do a better job. She continued, for example, to play tennis at least once a week, though ever since that game in early November she'd lost every single game they played. She said she tried, too, tried hard; Errol believed her, for he remembered the picture of her arm at full tension when she wrestled Raphael in July, the way it remained taut and tendonous until it lay absolutely flat against the table. She continued, too, to dine with Raphael, lunch and dinner, though the bills landed with regular humiliation in her hands. Perhaps most surprising and lovely of all, she continued to have a good time. She laughed a lot. Sometimes she laughed until she cried.

Gray managed to plant two colleagues with the Lone-luk— no substitute for being there herself, of course, and they would want more than their share of credit later. Still, at least someone was keeping track of this fragile society, and regular reports were wired to Boston. These telexes did not present a pretty picture. The new patriarchy was harsh. Women were often beaten; girls were no longer allowed to go to school. Women had been divested of property and had few legal rights. The men drank to excess, and children were hungry. As he read these reports, Errol was in some ways relieved Gray was spared this unpleasant drama. The anthropologists on location, a man and a woman, were being treated badly, and after two weeks the woman returned abruptly to the United States. The man remained, but certainly out of determined professional ambition rather than pleasure or even interest. His wires were bleak, spare, and dutiful. By week three he confessed that he disliked his subjects, and that he had lice.

In spite of the fact that she was about to turn sixty years old, Gray arrived one afternoon in early December with, she said, a Christmas present for herself. The package was not large, but she was out of breath by the time she got it upstairs.

"Errol! Come see!"

Errol followed her into her bedroom. When she laid the bag on the bed, it pressed into the mattress. One by one she lifted out two short red-and-black iron barbells and two sand-filled ankle weights with Velcro closures.

"What's all this for?" asked Errol, as politely as he could.

"What does it look like? Lifting weights."

"These are for you?"

"Of course."

"Why?"

"Tennis isn't enough lately. I feel weak."

"That's understandable. You always lose."

"Now go away. I want to play with my new toys."

Gray came downstairs later with a purple cast to her face and a glaze of sweat over her body.

"Are you sure you can handle that stuff?" asked Errol.

"Come on, I've always been in fine shape. This is one more exercise. It's wonderful!"

"Gray, don't overdo it."

"There's a burn—"

"You're really making me nervous."

"And afterward the muscles sear. You could have fried an egg on my upper arm."

"Just take it easy, will you?"

Gray never took it easy. Through the month of December, from behind Gray's door nights, Errol heard all kinds of grunting, breathing, and heavy thuds as she barely got the barbells back to the floor without dropping them.

Errol tried to leave her alone on such evenings, but when Raphael called one night near Christmas, Errol decided she would want to be interrupted. He knocked.

"Come in!" came a thin voice from inside.

Errol opened the door. "Ralph's on the phone."

To Errol's surprise she shook her head. Gray was sitting on her straight-backed chair with one arm across her knees, the other braced above the elbow in the crook of her wrist. Leaning over, she lifted the barbell from the floor toward her face.

"You'll call him back?"

She nodded. Her ears were a brilliant red. The muscles around her mouth were twitching. Errol paused before he left. It was interesting to watch her. He noted that the muscles in her arms were getting better defined; the faces of her forearms were rumpled with a series of small lumps; the dent of her biceps had deepened, though Errol couldn't help but wonder what difference any of this made to anyone, even to Gray herself. So much effort, and for what? Why was she doing this?

"Somehow this seems unlike you," Errol ventured.

"Why?"

"It's so—narcissistic."

"I'm not in love with *myself*," she said, abruptly pulling one more curl. Just then Errol felt the heaviness of those barbells in his own chest, the dullness and burden of the iron, and dragged himself out of her bedroom lifting his feet with difficulty, as if his own ankles were strapped with pounds of sand.

Christmas was a strangely quiet and simple time. Although it was a season when many people stopped by, Gray frequently cloistered herself upstairs and pretended she wasn't home. Gray, Raphael, and Errol decided to exchange gifts on Christmas Eve, just the three of them. Errol built a fire in the den. At midnight Gray set out three globular snifters and poured a generous round of expensive cognac. Raphael leaned back in the leather armchair and held his glass before him, watching the flames flash in the amber brandy and lick up the curves of crystal. As Errol brought his glass to his lips, the fumes rose and his eyes smarted. He held the cognac in his mouth until his tongue went numb. Gray stood by the fire and stared down into the liquor, swirling it around and watching the eddies curl and die, as if there were a fortune to be read there. The quality of the gathering was subdued, like a Christmas when a member of the family has been hospitalized with a terminal illness.

Still, the evening had a quiet humor. When Errol handed Raphael his present in an envelope, Raphael said, "Don't tell me: a one-way ticket to Elba." He opened it to find a two-hundred-dollar gift certificate to Gray's favorite restaurant by the wharf.

"That's to take the guest of your choice out to dinner," Errol explained. "Or lunch."

"Maybe you and I should go out, McEchern."

"We're actually exchanging gifts, Ralph. Let's not push it."

It was hard to understand later why most of this evening

was so even-tempered and mildly amusing, but it seemed natural at the time.

Raphael reached beside his chair and handed Errol a long, flat box. "I couldn't think of anything you needed more, McEchern."

Errol pulled the ribbon. As he lifted the top, fire flashed inside the box. Errol withdrew a ten-inch carving knife of fine Solingen steel.

"I sharpened it myself," said Raphael. "Here." He reached for the knife and ran the edge lightly over Errol's forearm. He raised the blade for Errol's inspection—several dark hairs lay on the steel. "You can shave with it."

"I think I'll stick to vegetables," said Errol.

"At least use it on meat. Just for me."

"All right," Errol agreed. "As long as you don't make me use it on my father. He's a nice man."

"There's one more thing there," Raphael pointed out. "The travel version."

Errol picked the second object out of the box. Though smaller, this one caught the light more fiercely than the first gift. Errol snapped it open: a switchblade. Exactly the same design as Raphael's, all steel and chrome.

"I wouldn't shave with that one, though," Raphael advised. "It might be dangerous."

Errol ran his thumb over the bevel; it made a chilling, sheer, scraping sound as it traced over the whorls of his skin. "What am I going to do with this?"

"Carry it. That's usually enough."

Errol found Raphael's presents disturbing, but also flattering somehow, and though he thought of any number of barbs as a response, Errol simply said, "Thanks, Ralph," and held his tongue. "Gray." Errol pointed. "Those two are for you."

Gray opened the smaller package first, and stood before the fire dangling the present critically. "Unless Bwana has lost some weight," she said, "I think we have a problem here."

"It's not for Bwana. I had it specially designed. It's a ferret leash."

Gray laughed.

"See, this strap goes under the belly, this one around the neck."

"I'll try it. But he won't like it."

"That occurred to me. But that's the lesser of the two. Try the bigger box."

Gray tore it open with appealing impatience. "Errol!" She held it up. This, too, caught the firelight; flames whipped around its rim, shot down its throat, and cross-hatched across its tight new strings. "It's beautiful."

"I wasn't sure you'd be open to a new one," said Errol. "I know you've had that same wooden one for twenty years. But they're making better rackets now. This is graphite; it absorbs more shock. A larger head means you get more shots, and these strings should give you more power."

Gray kissed him lightly on the lips. "Thank you. You know the racket won't make any difference. But at this point I'll try anything."

It was an evening of gestures and sentiments; a very O. Henry Christmas. When Errol thought back on every gift they gave one another, not one of them was something that anyone would actually use.

Errol unwrapped his present from Gray. "I'm not sure you

want this, Errol. You made a remark once. You were drunk. I don't know if you were serious."

Inside the box Errol found a complete array of wood-working tools. "I was half serious. I've got some work to do on my apartment."

"Yes," said Gray, "I thought you might want to make it nicer there. I'll—help you if you like." Errol wasn't sure—was he being unfair?—but he could swear this was the first time Gray had offered to help him with anything.

Errol pawed around in the box. When he found the hammer and nails he smiled. Between this and the two knives, he'd been given a nearly complete Raphael Sarasola kit. He wondered, Would he get the cheekbones and the chest hair and the eyes? Maybe next year. He'd ask for a cape, too, with a big *S* on the back. He'd seen them around.

Silently Raphael handed Gray a large rectangular package. Errol could see her eyes calculating its contents, but she wasn't doing very well.

The face that stared out at that company when Gray tore back the paper made Errol's heart skip a beat.

"Are you sure you want to give this to me?" asked Gray. Raphael nodded. "But it's your mother's."

"I have other canvases. And I've looked at this one more than enough for one lifetime."

There it was, Nora's portrait of her husband. Errol had to admit she wasn't a bad painter. Especially around the eyes and mouth the portrait had an amazing softness and delicacy. It had a Renaissance quality, in browns and reds, with sudden lighting on the cheekbones, gentle shadows around the lips, and of course a cavernous blackness in those eyes. While this was clearly a picture of Frank—Vincent—it brought out the resemblance between father and son.

"I almost hate to take this from you," said Gray. "God, he's changed. This portrait is so trusting, so open. So naïve."

"And who needs that?"

"I do," said Gray.

"That's why you're going to keep it, then. I'm outgrowing this picture."

"I'm sorry to hear that," said Gray. "Here." She handed him her box. "One last thing."

Raphael lifted out Gray's presents and set them on the table. The flames rippled in the pink-tinted fluting. Raphael stared and said nothing.

"They weren't at all expensive," Gray explained nervously. "Just hard to find. It took a lot of combing. I finally found them in a Salvation Army . . . after I'd almost given up . . ."

Raphael kept staring at the glasses. "They're like ghosts," he said at last.

It was true. There was something eerie about the way these two glasses hovered now before the fire, bubbles in the cheap glass glinting in their stems. All three had watched these destroyed, and now they were back, exactly the same. It was like being haunted.

Raphael's breathing grew labored. The muscles in his jaw popped in and out. Errol hardly ever saw Raphael disturbed, but something was mounting as he leaned forward in that chair eyeing those pink glasses. "You can't," he said, "do this, Gray. You aren't divinity, Gray K. You can't resurrect whatever you like."

"I'm sorry . . ." she said, "if you don't like them. I tried—and there's champagne to go with them for later. Domaine Chandon. A good year . . ."

Gray saw what he was about to do just in time, and stepped quickly out of the way. Raphael picked up the glasses and flung them both into the fire. They smashed against the back brick.

He stood with his back to her. "Think of something else, Gray," he said hoarsely. "Save the champagne for something smooth and cold and brand-new. Do that, get me new glasses. Sheer and modern and uncomplicated. Got that?" He picked up his coat and looked at neither Errol nor Gray. "Good night. I'll call."

They didn't hear from him for a week, and then it was as if nothing had happened. Nothing at all.

T he happy trio went to Tom Argon's for New Year's Eve. Errol drank too much. He spent most of the party with Ellen Friedman. Having to tell someone at last, he confided to Ellen what had happened in the South Bronx. She was appropriately appalled, and for once wasn't disappointed in him for not being more forceful.

Raphael was perfect this evening. Reserved, urbane, amusing. Errol knew his buddy Ralph better now, though, so he could see that the man was on autopilot. Ralph could steer his way through parties this smoothly in his sleep.

Gray, however, was hyperactive. Again, for someone who knew her less well, she must have seemed exuberant, charming. Errol saw her as more on the edge of hysteria. Her coloring was fantastically high and her movements quick, angular. She didn't talk to anyone long; she didn't talk to Errol or Raphael at all. Her laughter was slicing, and in the middle of talking with Ellen,

Errol would hear it cut across the crowded room to his ear. The sound pierced him, and he would turn aside and lose his train of thought. As the evening progressed, Errol would continually imagine he heard someone sobbing. Hearty laughter sounded like throes of distress. Likewise, the glaze of alcohol over everyone's eyes looked for all the world like tears. Grins turned to grimaces, expressions of surprise or pleasure to contortions of pain. Errol began to feel unwell, and led Ellen onto the porch for air.

As Tom's grandfather clock struck midnight, Errol kissed Ellen Friedman, and was surprised by the heat in her lips, at the lingering after. He looked at her quickly and noticed she was pretty. Prettier than he remembered.

Yet Errol had to turn to the big picture window. Many mouths were at each other. It was a strange cultural ritual: one minute for giving away secrets, grabbing other men's wives, slipping in the tongue. Normally Errol enjoyed watching this gathering jockey for position before the bell, but tonight it gave him no pleasure. For on either side of this brief bacchanalia stood two pillars. Stalwart and austere, Gray and Raphael stared at each other from opposite ends of the room. The hysteria fell from Gray's figure, the sleep from Raphael's eyes. The grappling crowd looked grotesque between them. Errol shivered. Ellen, beside him, seemed disappointed, but he would not kiss her again, or touch anyone else tonight, and having been taught some time ago to take his own car, he left five minutes later. He did not leave in time, though, to miss Bob Johanas planting a big kiss, wet and sardonic, on Gray's cheek, which broke her line of contact with Raphael, and struck Errol, skeptical as he was of Gray's alliance, as a regrettable defilement.

*   *   *

New Year's Day Gray came to Errol looking haggard. "I want you to escort me somewhere," she said. Only a couple of days later, on the way, did she explain. "We're going to my gynecologist. I didn't want to go alone."

"Routine, or anything special?"

"Since I was thirteen you could set your calendar by my periods. I've missed two."

"Jesus. Well, have you two been using any—"

"No, nothing."

"But the chances—at your age—"

"There are medical anomalies."

"Would an abortion be difficult for you? Dangerous?"

"I've thought about it. I wouldn't have one."

"Woman, you are out to lunch!"

"So? I'm paying the check, as usual."

"Pregnancy could kill you."

"I could die from worse."

Errol sighed. "God, I hope there's nothing to this. Have you experienced any symptoms?"

"I have felt odd lately. Food often makes me ill. I can't sleep. I run fevers. We'll see." She sounded oddly hopeful.

In the outer office they were surrounded by pregnant women of reasonable child-bearing age and young, nervous girls. Gray sat calmly with her urine sample perched on her knee. "I've never done this before, you know. I never knew how the test was performed before this week."

"Gray, why did you want to come here with me instead of Ralph?"

Gray looked meditatively at her jar and swirled the yellow liquid against the sides like brandy in a snifter. She raised her eyebrows and took a breath as if to say something, but let it go, and swirled.

"Sorry," said Errol. He wasn't sure what he was apologizing for, but somehow that hadn't been a nice thing to ask.

Gray surrendered her jar to a nurse, who shot her a quizzical glance, and fifteen minutes later she was ushered into the doctor's office. She took Errol with her, gripping his hand like a talisman. They sat down before his desk to await the verdict.

Dr. Denton swung genially in his chair. "Well, Gray, it's negative. Now, while you're here, I've looked at your records. It's been a couple of years since your last Pap smear, and at your age—"

"Negative?" said Gray.

"Yes, relax, Gray. You're not pregnant. Now, if you've got the time, I could get that Pap in five minutes . . ."

Gray did relax, but not, it seemed, with relief. She compressed her lips in what she must have hoped to pass off as a smile. She wasn't looking at Denton but was staring fixedly at the photographs of his family behind him on the wall.

"Gray, are you feeling all right?" asked Denton. "Is there some other problem?"

"I suppose I'm wondering," she said, pronouncing each word carefully, "why I've missed two periods. I've always been quite regular."

"Well, Gray," said Denton, seeming a little embarrassed, "you're almost sixty. It's surprising you didn't shut down a few years ago."

"Shut down?"

"Well, excuse my language. But you know."

"Of course," said Gray, and she had to clear her throat.

"This whole thing was silly, I suppose. I'm sorry I wasted your time." She stood to leave.

"You didn't waste my time, Gray, that's what I'm here for—" Denton rose and seemed apologetic, though he surely had no idea what he'd said wrong. "But if you could let us take that Pap—"

"I really can't do that today, thank you. Errol?"

"For some women," said Denton after her, "this is a difficult period. If you have any questions—"

"I have plenty of questions," she said crisply. "You can't answer them." Looking at neither Denton nor Errol, she clipped out the office door.

Gray wouldn't talk on the way home.

"It's a big relief to me," said Errol. "Really."

She said nothing; she changed gears stiffly and kept her eyes on the road. When she got home she walked upstairs without a word. Errol heard the door to her bedroom close and shortly afterward the sound of strained breathing and an occasional thump against wood. Errol stayed upstairs, pausing nervously when he passed her door, hovering nearby when he heard her suck air through her teeth a little too audibly. After about an hour of this, a heavy thud shook his office floor.

Errol rushed into Gray's bedroom to find her splayed on the floor, her chair tipped over and a barbell beside her sitting in a dent it had made in the wood. Gray's eyes were closed; her face was splotched purple and white. He touched her cheek, finding it moist and cold. He patted it lightly; she didn't move. Errol collected her carefully in his arms and lifted her onto the bed. He went to get a warm washcloth, and a few minutes later as he was wiping her forehead she came to.

"What?" she asked feebly.

"Sh-sh," said Errol, swabbing her long neck.

"I'm cold."

Errol pulled out several blankets. "Gray," he said after she looked more awake, with her head propped up on pillows. "There's something we haven't talked about much, and I think it's time, all right? Today's a big day for reality; we might as well get it all over with at once."

"I'm not sure I'm ready for this."

"You'll never be ready. That's why I'm not going to wait any longer. Because we're going to talk about how old you are, Gray—"

"Errol, please—"

"And," Errol overrode, "we're going to talk about Ralph."

"It seems to me both those subjects have come up before."

"Yes, but certain things we've never said out loud, and I think it's time. You're almost sixty and—"

"How many times do I have to hear that today?"

"Be quiet and listen to me. Remember? Gray Kaiser, anthropologist, grows more astute. Gray Kaiser, animal—"

"Disintegrates."

"Basically. And that's true no matter how much tennis you play or how much weight you lift. You're going to kill yourself one of these days with those crazy barbells of yours—"

"They're not crazy. I simply pushed it too far today."

"Sh-sh. Now listen." Errol wiped her forehead again with the wet cloth. "This is going to hurt, but you're a grown-up. Ralph is a handsome man of twenty-five. Do you really expect him to stick around for years and years? Do you expect him to marry you?"

"I would marry him," said Gray.

It pained Errol to hear this, but he persevered. "That's not the question I asked."

"I've never said that, Errol, about anyone. Don't pass over that so lightly."

"I have to, because you're avoiding the subject, and we *are* going to discuss it, I don't care if you don't want to. Now, you know I've got my problems with our friend Ralph. He's not my favorite person in the world."

"You have a positively British gift for understatement."

"But the point is, even with Ralph I can be sympathetic. I wonder if you're asking him to be too much of a hero. You're going to get old, Gray, and you're going to die. You're asking him to watch all of that."

"I'm in tremendous condition. I could live to be a hundred."

"But what are hundred-year-old people like?"

"They're wizened and funny and smart, and they eats lots of yogurt," she said sulkily.

Errol stood up from the bed and sighed. "Do you ever think how you'd feel if Ralph were sixty and you were twenty-five?"

"Raphael will never be sixty. He won't live that long." She said this quickly and with certainty.

"You say the oddest things sometimes."

"I know the oddest things sometimes."

"If you're so perceptive, why can't you hear what I'm telling you? You're asking him to make a tremendous sacrifice, and one that I'm not sure anyone has a right to expect."

"It's a sacrifice of which he's entirely capable. If he'll choose to make it."

"But, Gray," said Errol in exasperation, "a man like that doesn't have to make a sacrifice! He'll have plenty of opportunities."

"There's where you're wrong," said Gray, sitting up and letting the blankets fall away. "A man like that has very few opportunities. This may well be his last. And he knows it."

Errol suddenly had a sense of something large in that house he'd been quite left out of. He had the humbling impression that she knew far more than he did about all of this. Still, with the residue of his original surge of paternalism, he kept her weights away from her for the rest of the afternoon.

chapter twenty-three

Errol went to the screening of Gray's documentary about Charles Corgie, *King of Toys*, with trepidation. He had stayed away from the project through its editing, and had every intention of following through on his threat to take his name off the credits should the movie turn out the adulatory eulogy to the great white ruler that he feared. Whether or not the gesture meant anything to the rest of the world, it would at least mean something to Gray.

Errol grew particularly concerned when, on the way to the auditorium, Gray prefaced the screening with a nervous defense: "There have been plenty of critical treatments of white imperialism done by now" halfway there: "Charles was always asking me to give him a break" and as they got out of the car: "Try to understand that this material is too close to me to be used politically." Errol held his tongue and waited to see the film.

It was not like watching Errol's own version. The plot was censored—there was no kiss in the cathedral, no scrambling on Corgie's bed, none of Corgie's insults, and no Gray marching away from the ladder, hurtling them back. No tennis game, no war. Yet in spite of her scrupulous G-rated cleanup job, there was still a suggestion of a romance. Those "wet green eyes" of Arabella's gave it away. Because of Arabella's warm performance, then, Corgie seemed to be the one holding out. He was daily tempted by a beautiful, affectionate redhead, and he did nothing.

However, more than the plot had changed. Gray slumped in her chair next to Errol. Halfway through she said, "Something is wrong." Errol understood. Whatever intentions she might have had, they'd been subverted. It was as if someone had crept into her office late at night while she slept and changed frames, shifted cuts, revised inflections. Charles Corgie had been perverted.

First, Errol couldn't help but notice that the movie was now more Raphael's. It seemed less as if Raphael had stepped in to imitate Charles than that Charles had been standing in for Raphael until his successor was born and old enough to play his rightful part. The movie now read as some grotesque, enigmatic parable about Raphael's current relationship with Gray. Errol found himself looking around the audience nervously. He was embarrassed for Gray that all these people were watching. It was too intimate.

Second, and most surprising to Errol, was that as he watched the movie he did not feel the admiration for Charles Corgie that he had feared. He felt *pity*.

In the last close-up of Raphael on top of the plane, the frame held: Raphael in that strange ecstasy, the flames framing his face, the credits rolling in silence. Errol was double-billed with Gray for production and direction; he felt flattered; his name would stay. The houselights went up much too quickly. No one talked. Gray dragged herself to the podium to lead the discussion.

A man in front spoke up. "In comparison with your previous work, Dr. Kaiser, do you really believe this film represents a professional treatment of your subject? I have to confess I was surprised at the amount of obvious editorializing here. You've traditionally been so—restrained and—objective."

"Objectivity, in film and in our profession, is often a cultivated illusion," Gray explained. "In some ways it's more honest to admit our biases than to cover them up unsuccessfully. As for the contrast with my other work, at this point in my career I am interested in a—departure."

"To what degree this film holds up as anthropology I don't know," another man commented, "but as a character study I think it's outstanding."

"Yes," the man next to him agreed, "I saw it more as an art film. It may imply too much about Charles Corgie to constitute a serious academic work. Why, the inferences one can make are almost fictional—"

"I had intended," Gray interrupted with difficulty, "to create an enigmatic portrait."

"I wonder if you succeeded, then," the man went on. "The point of view seems clear enough."

"And how would you characterize that?" asked Gray, but without any eagerness, as if she didn't really want to know.

"Well, he's completely lost," said the man easily.

"Not even contemptible," a woman joined in. "More pathetic. Desperate—"

"But not egomaniacal," a young man added enthusiastically.

"That's what interested me. Like Il-Ororen, who thought they were the only people in the world, our Lieutenant Corgie thought he was the only person in the world. So he could be great or nothing. It didn't even matter. Without comparison there's no such thing as scale, isn't that part of your point? There was no difference between the models and the real buildings, because he wasn't sure that either one of them existed outside his head. A fascinating study of the mind in isolation. Of a different kind of African starvation than we're used to."

"I thought the presence of the young woman made him particularly poignant," commented a woman. "Someone who so obviously cared about the man and for whom he seemed to have some feelings if he were to allow them—"

"The ending, too, I thought was *tremendous*," joined her companion. "His *embrace* of his own death. As if he'd arranged it; his *joy* in it. That scene sent chills down my spine, Dr. Kaiser, really."

"Yes," said Gray quietly, "mine, too."

Raphael sat in the very back row, his eyes burning.

"Mr. Sarasola," said Gray bravely, "you played this part. Do you have anything to add?"

Raphael cocked his head. "One thing."

"Yes?"

The gathering turned and craned toward Raphael. He waited until they were silent, all rustling of programs stilled. Then he reminded Gray quietly, "He couldn't be any other way."

That was it.

"Would you care to elucidate?" asked another audience member.

"No."

The audience breathed, turned frontward, and rubbed their arms; the hall suddenly felt cold.

"In Charles's defense," said Gray, looking at Raphael as she spoke, "he had his moment of salvation. I meant it to be clear: he could have used the anthropologist to cover his own retreat. He refused. He granted the existence of one person. Perhaps that's enough."

"Yes." Raphael pronounced this with difficulty, as if speaking his first few words in a foreign language. "That's everything." He licked his lips. "It's not always possible."

Gray looked down at her lectern, and announced abruptly and much too soon that the discussion was closed.

Errol understood that Gray needed to be gotten home. He threaded through the crowd to pull her away, for he could see she was fending off questions, keeping her head down and shuffling papers in a manila folder. Before he could retrieve her, though, "'L-oo-lubo!" resounded through the room. Gray looked up with sudden recognition and smiled for the first time that whole afternoon.

The crowd parted for a tall, aging African with splendid bone structure. He and Gray clasped each other's hands.

"So veddy good to see this feelm!" He smiled, his teeth rich. The man seemed large and booming and ingenuous. "This was the Corgie as Hassatti see him in the head."

"I had to leave him with his gun, Hassatti," said Gray, "so I couldn't bring it back to you. I could only bring it back on film."

"I hear of 'L-oo-lubo other times before now. She return from this puddle with one barrel of Corgie's gun in each eye."

Yet suddenly those gun-barrel eyes of hers constricted. Gray craned over Hassatti's shoulder to follow a certain young man as he skirted the auditorium and walked out the door. Gray's eyes went bare, casting over the carpet, rumpling over Hassatti's feet.

"*L-oo-lubo,*" said Hassatti affectionately, raising her chin back up with his forefinger. "The eyes of the impala have spent their bullets, yez? So tall? So strong? So—brilliant, yez?" He rolled the *r* in "brilliant" with relish. "*Ol-changito* has changed a small bit? *Ol-murani?*"

"Not so much—*ol-murani,*" Gray faltered.

"Ah." Hassatti nodded, and Errol could see that, though the man might not have seen Gray Kaiser for nearly thirty-eight years, he came to her with the warmth of a great friend, and would do her any favor in his power. "Perhaps—*e-ngoroyoni?*"

"*E-ngoroyoni na-nana,*" said Gray with a sigh. Errol knew Masai, and knew Gray, and so understood her concession was a great one. She'd admitted to being a woman. *Na-nana,* a gentle one. "And maybe," she added, "wise."

"You like?"

"Wisdom—this kind." She was having difficulty. "It must be necessary. But I don't think it's the sort of thing one likes."

She smiled weakly, and Hassatti helped her out of the auditorium. She rested a hand on his shoulder and he kept a hand lightly at her back, as if she were an old woman whose strength was failing and whose balance was poor. Errol walked after her, and had to admit that she was very nearly hobbling out the door. Time was going fast now. Errol, Raphael, and Gray were aging, tangibly, by the day.

chapter twenty-four

The next week Errol was awakened in the middle of the night by a loud cry from down the hall. He sat up in bed. Errol was reminded of nights on the veldt, when he would come out of a deep sleep to hear a lion far away, or the shriek of a wildebeest the lion had discovered.

As he woke, though, Errol had to revise this impression. That was not the sound of an animal, if there were distinctions to be made between animals and men. Coming from down the hall was a quintessentially human sound, and it was powerful enough to fill Errol's bedroom even with the door closed. Errol rose and put on his robe, and stepped tentatively out of his room. There the sound was louder, and echoed down the staircase to well in the foyer. Errol tiptoed down the hall. It was coming from Gray's bedroom, yet her voice, deep as it was for a woman's, loud as he'd heard it when she shouted over a crowd or across a plain, was not that deep or quite that forceful. Errol heard that night the unmistakable suffering of his same sex.

As Errol approached the door to her room, the sound grew louder and more terrible. He imagined at first that Raphael was having a nightmare, but the body didn't sleep and exert itself so.

Something had happened to Gray. Errol remembered her uneven heartbeat when the phone rang, her pasty complexion when she passed out lifting weights, and put his hand on the doorknob. He opened his mouth to ask what was wrong. Just as he was about to shout and force his way in, though, he detected the steady, rhythmic creak of Gray's old box spring. He closed his mouth and took his hand off the doorknob and went back to bed. After a time the cries peaked and subsided. Though he was relieved not to have barged in, after all, Errol knew he would never forget that sound, the open-throated anguish raking through the halls of that house, nor would he ever look at Raphael after that night in quite the same way again, knowing, incredibly, that this was the man who had made it.

chapter twenty-five

The following morning Errol got up at six, for he wasn't sleeping well. No one, it seemed, was sleeping well that night, for as he walked toward the stairs he noticed the hall light was on and Gray's door was open. Intending to glance in and keep going, instead Errol paused.

Raphael was lying on his stomach, with one arm dangling over the side of the bed. Somnambulant as Raphael so often seemed during the waking day, Errol had rarely seen him asleep. Certain edges of his face were rounded; as a result, he looked not only gentler, but sad—sad in a large, exhausted, world-weary way. His hair lay wild on the pillow, splayed and tangled as if during the night he'd run a great distance. The blankets were drawn up only to his lower back, so with his other hand over his head the muscles along his spine were drawn into soft, velvety ripples.

Gray stood beside him in her dressing gown. She was being very quiet. Only a series of tiny clicks came from the open door.

She would take a step away, a step toward, a step to the side. Each time she put her foot down gradually, to keep the wooden floor from creaking. When she moved in only a foot from his face, the soft shuttering sound was close enough to his ear to make him stir. Gray started guiltily and quickly focused one more time before hiding her camera back in its drawer and slipping back to bed.

E rrol was out all that day. When he returned to the manse that evening, all the lights were out on the first floor. In a pensive mood, Errol enjoyed the dark, and walked softly into the den to stare out his usual window. There was no moon or walkside lamp tonight, only shadow and deeper shadow. The wind whistled through the bare trees on the lawn. There was a heaviness in this house now such as there had never been. Gray was keeping the heat up extraordinarily high; the air was thick and sooty, exhausting to take in, difficult to expel. Errol sighed a couple of times and tried to empty his lungs completely of the black air, but he felt its tarry residue remain. He said out loud, "God, when is this going to be over?"

"Soon."

Errol jumped. He turned to find a shape at his elbow, in an adjacent chair. There was a small red light floating over the shape. It glowed brighter, then died. The smoke in the air got thicker.

"Ralph?" asked Errol tentatively.

"That's right," said the voice. "This is Ralph. Good old Ralph."

"Since when do you smoke?"

"Since about an hour ago."

"And what moved you to cigarettes?"

"I just felt like it. Funny. I've never felt like smoking before. Isn't life just jam-packed with new and exciting experiences."

"Gray won't like it."

"Gray K. won't like a lot of things. What's one more?"

Raphael took another hit, and the glow of the cigarette reflected oddly around his eyes.

"Ralph, are you wearing dark glasses?"

"That's right."

"It's nine o'clock at night, Ralph."

"Sometimes," said Raphael, "it doesn't get dark enough for me. Like now. Even with these glasses. It's too light out. Some kids were afraid of the dark. I liked it. I used to climb into closets. The line of light under the door drove me insane. I'd stuff a towel in the crack. But there was always light from somewhere. I hardly ever got myself real dark. But I tried. It gets tiring, McEchern, looking at shit all the time."

"Looking isn't what tires me," said Errol. "It's thinking. And talking. Between the two of them, whole days become one incessant yammer. I don't care so much about dark. But I'm big on quiet."

"I've disturbed your quiet, then."

"Yes. But it doesn't matter. My head won't shut up. It's been clamoring all night."

"You think in words, McEchern?"

"I suppose. Mostly."

Raphael took another drag and blew the smoke out slowly. "I don't so much. I look out this window: nothing. Too much light. But no words. I just look. If I could stop seeing I could become a complete cipher."

"Even blind I don't think you'd make a very good nonentity, Ralph."

"That's a compliment?"

"Almost."

"Well, you're wrong. I'd make a great one. I go blank sometimes. Like on those medical shows when the patient's on the operating table and there's a *blip blip blip* sound. And suddenly the EKG goes flat. There's a solid straight line on the machine. No more blips. Just a hum. I can get like that. The doctors on the program go crazy, but I always look at the guy on the table. He doesn't seem to have any problem with it at all."

"So you like it?"

"I don't like it; I don't dislike it. When you're blank you don't like or dislike anything. In that way, sure, it's nice."

"Are you blank now?"

"No. This place isn't good for blankness. Too many words, for one. That's why I asked you that, about thinking. Since I've come here I think more in words than I used to."

"That bothers you?"

"Nothing bothers me, McEchern. It's just a change, that's all."

"If you're not blank," said Errol cautiously, "what have you been sitting here thinking about?"

"Darkness. And some practical matters."

"Such as."

"Tomorrow her recommendations for that Ford Fellowship are due. She's filling out the forms tonight."

"Are you worried that because the grant would send you to the Pacific she'll withhold your name?"

"No. She's threatened to go with me."

"Uh-huh." This was news to Errol. "Do you have any other reason to think she wouldn't select you?"

"Oh no. She'll select me."

"So what's there to think about?"

"I'm just thinking," said Raphael with an edge. "Do I have to think something about it?"

"So what else," asked Errol, after a pause, "have you been thinking?"

"Let's see. My mother. I was thinking about trying to find my mother."

"Are you going to do that?"

"No."

"Would she be hard to locate?"

"Not at all."

"So why not find her?"

"Because I don't want to."

"I thought you were thinking about it."

"I was. What I was thinking was that I didn't want to."

"Why not?"

"Because I don't care."

"That's hard to believe."

"Then don't strain yourself, McEchern."

"—You're going through that whole pack."

"That's right."

Raphael sat and smoked. Errol stared out the window for two or three minutes, until just as he was about to make a casual exit Raphael said, "You're not going to ask me anything more?"

"What else should I ask you?"

"About what I was thinking. Ask me what else."

"What else were you thinking, Ralph?" asked Errol obediently.

"I was thinking," said Raphael, "about you. And about her. About my mother and father and Ida and *Walter*. About a lot of women you don't know. I was thinking about me, even. I was thinking about practically everyone I've ever met, McEchern—it's been one of those evenings."

"Did you think anything in particular about these people, or did your mind simply get crowded?"

"I was wondering," said Raphael, "why nothing works out."

"Nothing works out?"

"Nothing."

"You mean between men and women?"

"Between anyone and anyone. But that, too."

"And what did you conclude?"

"Nothing."

"Well, let me know what you decide," said Errol. "I'm curious myself."

"I won't decide anything," said Raphael. "I don't like to think like this. I won't soon."

"Back to blankness?"

"That's right."

"Well, good luck, Ralph."

"You, too, McEchern."

Errol had the strangest feeling of saying goodbye in some large way, though no doubt they would see each other later that night. Still, when Errol began to walk out of the room Raphael called after him, "McEchern!" and Errol turned around as if to receive a final blessing or parting advice. They stood facing each other in the dark for a moment or two, Errol waiting, Raphael silent, until finally Raphael seemed to think better of it and said, "Nothing," a word which had come out of his mouth in the last two minutes with curious frequency.

Errol went upstairs to Gray's office and found her surrounded by fellowship applications. She'd done a number of interviews that fall, narrowing the stack down to fifty, but there were only five awards to give out. She'd started four stacks: yes, no, maybe, and Raphael.

"Looks as if you're going to be up late," said Errol.

"Arabella agreed to stay and type up my final recommendations in case you're worried this will land on you."

"Still pulling all-nighters like a freshman in college."

"Irresponsibility keeps me young."

Errol wandered over and picked Raphael's application off her desk. "Well."

She shook her head and spread her hands.

"You really haven't decided?"

"What do you think I should do?"

"It amuses me you even ask."

"You're short on amusement lately. You're due."

"You're going to let me lambaste him. As a favor."

"Go ahead."

Errol felt a peculiar reluctance, and stalled, flapping the pages in his hand. "I've seen better," he said weakly.

"I've seen much better."

"This project any good?"

"Depends on the execution."

"How would he execute it?"

"With me, splendidly. Alone, maybe he'd take the check and no one would ever see him again. Who knows."

"A really solid investment."

She shrugged. "He has great capacity. He won't necessarily choose to use it."

"But all in all, how does he stack up against the other applicants?"

"How does anyone stack up against anyone else?" said Gray with exasperation. "A whole array of these people aren't better or worse, just different. Maybe Raphael's is the one recommendation I can make with any confidence at all."

"Professional confidence?"

"Professionalism is a myth. If we aren't paying back favors, we're at least rewarding people we like."

"A convenient theory tonight." Errol fingered the application in his hand. "But people know about your liaison by now, Gray. For your own sake—"

"I'm Gray Kaiser. I can get away with whatever I like. They'll give the money to whomever I say—to my lover, my nephew, my *dog*. So I'm asking what you think I should do."

Errol opened his mouth. Nothing came out. All the acid invective he'd been storing for months seemed to have been oddly neutralized. All he could see was Ralph standing before Ida in Cleveland Cottons with his finger between his eyes; boarding up those windows and prying them open again; setting those glasses gently on the table, on the sill, even if he'd later thrown them twice against masonry.

"Do what you want," said Errol. "This has nothing to do with anthropology."

Gray got up and roamed around the room. "I have an idea—we could go to that island and work together. Do interviews, take pictures, film a documentary. On our off hours shoot takes of each other, swim. Stay lean and tan and salty, with sand in our scalps. Eat fruit. Learn local dances. Run down long beaches at the foam line . . . At night we could build fires and roast meat on a spit and say absolutely nothing, which always makes him happy. Maybe we'd send in the film, and then I'd take off, Errol. I'd quit for a while. A whole year, maybe, and see no one from Boston. I'd write a book about what it's like to be a regular person—just to eat and sleep and run and make love and think tiny little thoughts, about dinner and tides and seedpods. I'd like to play games with children. I'd like to read nothing but fairy tales and science fiction. I'd like to talk about strong winds and the price of papayas; to use clichés and say things like 'That boy favors his father.' I wouldn't really mind getting old. I'd sit on porches. I could take up weaving baskets or dyeing rugs. Oh, Errol!" She turned to him with her eyes shining. "I'd live a long time. I'd support him if he wanted, travel wherever he wanted to go, just as long as I could watch him walk off down the beach and smile and catch the sun in his teeth. I'm sorry, I know this sounds weak, but I'd give anything, lose any game, just to watch him fall asleep in the sand every day, with water beading on his chest and the hair curling as it dries . . ."

"You don't want to go to Ghana, do you?" asked Errol heavily. "With me. And do what we've always done."

"I don't want squalor! I don't want conflict and hatred and divisiveness. I just want to be around healthy, vibrant people, and not as their observer, either. I think I could give up anthropology altogether. Because I've missed out, Errol. I've watched the way people love and have families and resolve differences, and it's time I did it myself and stopped taking notes. Only now, Errol, am I ready to live my life. I'm tired of being *strong*. If someone says something mean to me, I want to *weep*. And I don't want power unless I can use it to help people I care about."

"So go ahead," said Errol sadly. "Give him the money. Then you can comb beaches and give the Goji a vocabulary lesson. I can be a carpenter with a checked tablecloth and read tabloids. And Ralph—Ralph can watch medical shows on TV and go blank."

"What are you talking about?"

"Nothing. It's just odd to me that while Ralph's the one applying for the island paradise fellowship, he's downstairs in sunglasses in a dark room and you're the one up here raving about sea foam and sand dollars, you know? It's just odd."

"What are you getting at? Doesn't he want to go?"

"I don't know what he wants."

"What did he tell you?" she asked urgently.

"Just that nothing 'works out.' He seemed distressed about it."

"He's nervous about this fellowship," she said, rubbing her hands. "I haven't told him what I'll do."

Something hissed in the corner.

"That ferret hates me," said Errol.

"Lately Solo hates everybody," said Gray. She stooped down and called for the animal as it huddled under a chair. It scrabbled. She reached for it and pulled it out; the ferret squirmed. There was a look in its eyes that Errol had never seen before—like the wide, reflective glare of Raphael's sunglasses. "Ow!" She dropped him and held her hand. "He bit me, Errol. Solo hasn't done that since I first got him."

"I'll take him down to his cage." Errol grabbed the ferret

quickly by the back of the neck. It pawed at the air, wriggling and gurgling, but Errol held fast. "There's one thing that occurs to me, Gray," said Errol before he left, dangling the struggling ferret out in front of him. "All this 'regular life' business. I mean, it's fine if you want to live on a beach or if I want to take up interior carpentry. We can both do that. But this is regular life, isn't it? Already? We eat; we drink; we talk. We buy things—we've probably already discussed the price of papayas, even if sometimes they were imported. I know how you're thinking. I've thought that way, too. Live like the People. Don't agonize, don't analyze, don't be tense. But these are our lives, Gray. Maybe even in regular life there's agony and analysis and tension. It seems to me that to pretend to have lived outside of all this is a conceit, maybe even a pretension. We're in it as much as the next guy, whether we read journals or science fiction, whether we use long words or short ones. Sure, Gray, go to the beach. But there you'll be, on the beach. There's no getting away. That whole fantasy about being a normal person seems like running away, doesn't it? It's as if to say there's an island somewhere where there aren't any real problems—"

"Where everything works out," said Gray softly.

"Exactly. You don't need fairy tales; you just came up with a great one. Here we are. In our lives. Certain things happen, just the way they do to everyone else. Your ferret is acting weird. You have to decide to whom to award these fellowships. Ralph has taken up smoking. There you have it. You're stuck with it, Gray, and I can't blame you for wishing you could get out from under. You can't. Welcome to your life. You've already lived fifty-nine years of it. Fifty-nine regular years."

"I just want to be with him, that's all," said Gray, looking at the floor.

"I know," said Errol. "It's actually pretty simple, isn't it." Errol walked downstairs holding the ferret before him and watching the saliva burble between its teeth.

E rrol returned to her office an hour later to announce that there was a bat in the kitchen.

"Is that what Arabella is screeching about?"

"Of course."

"You know that girls are taught to squeal like that. It isn't an inherent sexual trait that the female of the species gets up on chairs and makes piercing sounds in the presence of small animals."

"Anyway, the Big Brave Men will take care of it. Thought you'd want to know what was going on."

Errol returned to the kitchen to find Arabella crouching behind Raphael, her sharp, polished nails clutching his shirt. "Is it flying again?" she squeaked.

"You have eyes, don't you?" asked Raphael, sounding tired. "I saved him for you, McEchern. I figured you could use some practice smashing something. Today we start your not-so-nice-a-guy lessons."

Errol picked up a broom. Raphael shook his head. "No style. Do you have that blade on you?"

"No, but—"

"I told you to carry it."

"Sorry. *Ralph II* isn't ready for release yet."

"Get it."

"What am I—"

"Get it."

Out of curiosity, Errol did as he was told. Raphael took the knife, held it by the blade, and pointed at a knothole in the paneling of the breakfast room; when released, the knife turned through the air to land squarely in the center of the knot.

"That's wonderful!" Arabella cooed.

Raphael turned to Arabella and looked into her eyes with the torches turned up full. "You think so?"

Arabella took an involuntary step back. Her face turned red. "Y-yes," she stuttered. "Where did you learn that?"

Raphael wouldn't stop looking at her; his eyes had her pinned against the wall as surely as any switchblade. "As a kid I used to lie in bed picking off rats before I went to sleep. Better than counting sheep." At last he eased his eyes off Arabella kindly, as if she were an animal he'd caught by the tail and decided to let go. This time.

"McEchern. Try it."

Errol pulled the knife out of the wood and held it by the blade. It was a fine knife, well weighted. He tested it in his hand, then aimed for the same knot. He missed, by a few inches, but the motion felt good, and the knife stuck well into the paneling.

"A natural," said Raphael, and gave Errol some pointers. With a few more tries, Errol was getting closer to the knothole.

The bat flashed by and landed in the upper corner of the room.

"Now," Raphael whispered.

Errol pitched the switchblade; the knife sunk into the wall with a small brown animal between the handle and the paneling.

Raphael smiled, and stopped Errol from retrieving the knife. "Leave it there," he said. "Let her see it. Tell her you did that. She'll be pleased."

"Since when do you look out for what Gray Kaiser thinks of me?" asked Errol suspiciously.

"She's an appreciative woman," Raphael explained. "It would be good for her if she still thought well of someone."

"She still thinks well of you . . ." said Errol warily.

"For now."

Errol looked at Raphael and felt the house's heaviness again; he remembered Gray upstairs dreaming of beaches and chest hair. "Oh, *Raphael*," said Errol, perhaps for the first time in six months using the man's real name, as a plea, a concession, a final resort.

"Watch it," said Raphael coldly. "You forget who I am. What do you expect from me, McEchern? Really?"

There was a look on Raphael's face. He was right. Errol had forgotten it briefly, but Errol had seen it often enough: when he turned on Pamela Rose and called her unattractive; when he bore down all the more on the accelerator, with Errol imploring him for a little consideration from the back seat; when at the concert he kissed Gray without mercy, with Errol in the next chair; when he drew a knife on his own father; when he found two fragile, sentimental objects that had survived winters and trouble-making adolescents for seven years, only to throw them onto cement, and again when he was willing to pitch them once more, even though Gray had spent days trying to replace them. How could Errol have forgotten? More important, how could Gray? Because she had forgotten. She was upstairs with her papayas and cockleshells and basket weaving and a $45,000 fellowship about which Errol suddenly did have an opinion, a strong one.

Errol turned on his heel and headed upstairs, leaving a speared bat on the wall behind him, not to impress Gray, but rather to leave behind a scene in which slaughter "with style" was a route to impressing anyone.

Errol walked in without knocking. "Gray, before you give him that money, you should know he has absolutely no intention of your going with him."

She stood up. "What has he told you?"

"I'm not his emissary. But I've watched enough. If he walks out of here with $45,000, his back and little wads of green in his fists may be the last you ever see of him."

Gray grabbed Errol's arm. "*What* has he told you?"

"You're an anthropologist," said Errol, pulling away from her hand coldly. "Remember *human beings*, Gray? Remember what they're like?"

Gray pushed past him and toward the stairs. Errol followed behind her. Just before the landing her arm shot out to stop him.

Raphael was on the second stair. Arabella faced him. Her belt and heels were red patent leather and glistened like newly wet lips. Her hair rippled. Freckles spattered across her breasts. The torches were blazing, but this time she didn't step back.

Raphael reached for Arabella's soft white neck and kissed her. She buried her long fingernails in his hair.

Gray waited respectfully until they were finished. Their lips parted; she took two more steps to the landing, where she could be clearly seen.

"Vandal," said Gray softly. That was all.

Raphael did not start but looked smoothly up at his lover: *I am like this*. Shards of pink glass shattered all over the foyer floor.

Gray turned and went back upstairs. It seemed she no longer had any questions to ask Raphael about his project, after all. She seemed to understand his project only too well.

Errol remained a moment longer to overhear Arabella tell Raphael quietly, "We can talk later."

Raphael looked back at her as if she were a used paper towel. "Whatever for?" he asked, and passed Errol casually on his way upstairs.

It was not necessary to spy on the ensuing conversation, for Raphael spoke clearly enough for the whole household to hear, as if his statements were a matter of public record. Gray was furious, and couldn't have been inaudible if she'd tried.

"Don't apologize," said Gray through her teeth.

"I wouldn't dream of it," said Raphael. "You should know better."

"Why don't *you*?"

"You're not going to give me that fellowship now, are you?"

"*What else can I do to you?*" Gray screamed.

"Well," said Raphael calmly, "I suppose that means I've wasted several months of time and effort."

"You mean to tell me—"

"Now, Gray K.," he said fondly, "why else would I seduce a woman more than twice my age?"

"Get out!"

"I was concerned at first that you were canny. But you're like the rest of them. A pity, really."

"I told you to get out of this house."

"Why certainly," said Raphael genteelly. "I was just leaving."

Holding himself erect, his face relaxed and imperturbable as ever, Raphael walked casually downstairs and picked up his coat. Without a glance at Errol or Arabella, he swung it over his shoulder and left the house.

E rrol went into Gray's office and sat. Gray sat. They said nothing. It was like a wake, though no one cried. Gray stared at the wall, at a space where nothing hung. Errol didn't feel anything. Gray, too, looked turned off. She didn't move but sat in her chair with her hands curled before her the way he'd seen old women sit for hours in nursing-home wheelchairs. The silence in the room was wide. Errol wondered, Is this blankness? Hey, Ralph, is this what it's like?

Time passed; Errol had no idea how much, until Arabella slipped in the door. "I'm sorry, Dr. Kaiser, I—"

"Leave me alone."

"I'm in love with him," said Arabella staunchly.

"Don't make me laugh."

"It's just, if I didn't feel so strongly—"

"What did I tell you?"

"To go—but I feel we really have to discuss this, because if I start seeing him, this could get really awkward if we don't have an understanding—"

"Good, let's arrive at a understanding. Did you hear what he said to me?"

"Some of it."

"I'm like the rest of them, you heard that?"

"Yes . . ."

"So what makes you so special?"

"Dr. Kaiser, I think you should know that there have been some strong feelings between Raphael and me for a while now, but we haven't acted on them for your sake, all right? It's just after a certain point, when you're young, and human, it's impossible to resist any longer—"

"You're trying to tell me that he's been passionately in love with you for months, but that he hasn't done anything about it for my sake?"

"That's right."

"Now, that is truly incredible."

"Dr. Kaiser, give me a break. You're fifty-nine and I—"

"Arabella," said Errol. "Later."

Arabella sighed and left the room.

"You, too, Errol," said Gray wearily. "I have work to do."

"It's three in the morning."

"I have to get these recommendations in. Leave me alone now."

"If that's what you want."

"And—thanks for sitting with me."

"Sure."

Errol was not about to sleep; he had a sense that Gray bore watching, though he wasn't sure for what. He roamed the house. He threw out the bat, and contemplated chucking the switchblade, too. Symbolism seemed beside the point now, though, and it was a nice knife; he slipped it in his pocket. As he walked into the den Solo raked his claws against the bars, raving back and forth in the small space, hissing and burbling as if the house were on fire and he'd been left shut up in his cage to fry cruelly by himself.

"If you behaved better," Errol advised the ferret, "we'd let you out. But if you're going to be nasty, there you are. All by your little lonesome. Suit yourself."

Errol found Raphael had left his sunglasses. Just to see what it looked like, Errol turned out the light and stared out the window with them on. Raphael was right. Even with sunglasses he wasn't looking into complete darkness, not quite. Errol looked beside him to find Raphael had left one cigarette in the pack; he lit it. The smoke burned his throat and made him cough once or twice, but he could see the appeal of the things, the relaxation. The nicotine made him lightheaded. Late as it was, Errol thought about calling Gabriel Menaker. It would be nice to get stoned.

Errol was trying to decide how he felt. He was trying to decide if he was pleased, if he was gloating. Yet he felt more disconcerted. Standing there in Raphael's dark glasses, breathing the same smoke, Errol heard bits of the evening's earlier conversation at this window come back to him. Funny, that already seemed such a long time ago.

Errol snuffed out the cigarette and walked up to the exact spot where Gray had stopped him before the landing. Then he walked down to the second stair and looked up. Yes. Certainly it was possible. Especially in the corner of his eye.

"A vandal," Errol could hear softly in his ear, "is someone who destroys things of value on purpose."

"And for what, Ralph?" asked Errol.

"Nothing."

"I don't understand you." Errol listened for more, but the foyer only echoed with that even, EKG hum of someone finally at peace. "There's plenty of time for that," said Errol, just as Ida had warned Sasha about oldness. "There's plenty of time for that later."

Errol's voice shuddered in the foyer and died on the stairs.

All night the light burned in the crack under Gray's office door. Though Errol urged Arabella to go home, she insisted that she'd promised to type up a finished copy of Gray's fellowship recommendations; she finally fell into a fitful sleep on the couch. Errol knew better than to sleep himself. Not that he couldn't have. Rather, this was one of those evenings that had become so particular that to sleep through them would be to waste a certain richness his life afforded him only once in a while. There was a feeling in this house he wanted to experience— something outside the realm of ordinary time, as if the manse had spun high into the air in the middle of a tornado and would soon land in Oz.

Or perhaps it would land somewhere more bleak. Errol watched the sun rise at six, but the sky was overcast and the dawn grudging. There were no brilliant colors; the front walkway was no yellow brick road. Instead, dim gray light leaked reluctantly into the house, as if, yes, it's true, no matter what happened the night before, the sun will always come up the next day; but there are days and days, you know. Just because it's light outside doesn't mean everything suddenly becomes so great. This was not the sort of sunrise, then, that would be of any comfort to Gray upstairs.

Massive clouds lodged themselves around the house steadily through early morning, stacking against one another like sand-bags in a seawall, mounting high in the air to form a heavy gray bulwark on all sides of the manse, as if the house were hunkering down for the duration of winter, preparing itself for a long, monotonous siege. There was a dull white glow outside; it might snow.

At eight o'clock Gray emerged from her office drawn and exhausted, as if she'd undergone a test or feat of skill in there, and passed, perhaps, but if so, just barely. Errol made coffee. He heard Arabella stir and rise in the living room, but she didn't come into the kitchen.

"Did you finish?" asked Errol.

Gray nodded. "I did the final copies, too. Arabella can go home if she likes." Gray stared into her coffee. Though her head wavered slightly from side to side, she spoke with an interesting steadiness. "Errol, I ask you to do a lot for me, but I'm going to ask you to do one thing more. For the next couple of weeks, I want you to take care of me."

"Gray, I'll do whatever—"

"Let me explain. First, my weight is low right now—"

"Too low."

"That's right. I may have trouble eating, but you're to make sure that I do so and that I eat well. Also: put me to bed at midnight every night, and get me up at seven. Don't listen if I tell you I'm not tired, and don't let me sleep late. Pour me a stiff cognac at eleven-thirty, that usually helps."

"Have you ever tried to put a woman to bed who's six feet tall?"

"Be resourceful. Furthermore, take me for a long walk every afternoon. That will be my exercise. Hide my barbells and ankle weights where I can't find them. Put my tennis racket where I don't have to look at it. Take the phone off the hook at midnight, and take it back off the hook even if I sneak out of my room to hang it up. Back at seven, not before."

"Got it."

"Remember, this is only for two weeks. You don't have to babysit me all day, but you do have to be around for meals. Just leaving something for me to eat won't be good enough. You can go out during the day, but always leave a number where you can be reached. Try to be here evenings, and don't sleep at your apartment. There's just one more thing.".

"Certainly."

"My birthday is fifteen days away. Under no circumstances are you to plan a celebration of any kind. Is that clear?"

"If you say so. Now, what would you like—two eggs, toast, bacon—"

Gray blanched. "Maybe we can skip this first one."

"Not a chance. How do you want your eggs?"

Gray turned away. "Errol, I really can't."

Errol was getting up loyally to crack two eggs in a bowl when Arabella shrieked from the den.

"A mouse, or just a spider?" Gray wondered.

Arabella came into the kitchen. "Why didn't someone tell me there was something wrong with Solo? I just opened the door to play with him and he went crazy and shot out of the cage."

"Did you put him back?" asked Gray.

"How could I? I have no idea where he went."

"Well, don't just stand there. Go find him."

"He'll turn up. But what's wrong with him? He made the most horrible little noise. Is he sick?"

"I don't know what's wrong with Solo, but you know I like to keep the ferret away from Bwana. Go find him and put him back in his cage."

"You think Bwana would kill him?"

"On the contrary, Bwana's terrified of that animal. I'm more nervous about the dog. Errol, would you please take care of it? I'm exhausted."

It wasn't until Gray went upstairs that it struck Errol she was already getting on a skewed sleeping schedule and she'd just escaped her first meal. These next two weeks were going to be a challenge.

When Gray got up that afternoon, Errol and Arabella had still not found the ferret.

Gray left briefly to send her recommendations to Ford by Federal Express. When both Errol and Arabella offered to do it for her, Gray held the folder to her chest with a funny possessiveness and claimed she could stand to get out of the house.

"Any calls?" asked Gray wearily on her return. Errol shook his head.

It was Bwana who found the ferret. Or rather, the ferret found Bwana. Errol was just corraling Gray for dinner in her office when hysterical barking came from the staircase landing. They both arrived to find Solo hissing with bared teeth and wild black eyes at the dog. Bwana was wedged into the corner of the landing, pressed against the wall. His pink-gray eyes were shot with red. His whole body was trembling, and his bark was high and raspy.

"Solo," Gray called down. She whistled. "Solo!"

The ferret didn't respond, but made slashing forays at the dog, which was unusually brave for such a small animal—there was something wrong with this standoff; surely the dog should be cornering the ferret, not the other way around. As he and Gray approached the two pets, Errol looked more closely at the ferret. Its eyes were wider and wilder and blacker than ever, and saliva was dripping from its teeth. Its motions were jerky and frantic, though it was usually a graceful creature. Gray was walking down to pull the ferret away, but Errol stopped her. "I think there's something wrong with him, Gray, stay away. I swear he looks rabid. I wouldn't touch him."

Bwana's bark had thinned into a high, wheezy whine; he kept trying to back up farther and pressing up against the wall.

"Errol, I've got to get him away from Bwana. He's an old dog. It's not good for him to get so upset."

"Listen, if that ferret is rabid, he could give it to Bwana, and that's it for the dog."

"Solo!" Gray whistled again. Yet to appeal to the pet as an affectionate creature with normal loyalties at this point was clearly a waste of breath. Solo was raking the floor with his claws, and his charges at the dog were getting closer. For a moment or two Errol was stumped, for he had no interest in being bitten by a rabid weasel himself, even for his favorite weimaraner. However, Errol had been in training, hadn't he? Carrying it was enough. Though he could no longer remember putting it there, the bright chrome switchblade was lying smoothly against his thigh.

"Gray, I'm sorry, but I don't know what else to do." Errol pulled the knife out and flicked it open.

"Errol, you don't know what you're doing with that thing—"

"You'd be surprised."

She was. Perhaps she was even impressed, as Raphael had promised. Errol held the knife by the blade, and just as the ferret made a particularly ferocious jab at the dog, he flipped the knife toward the flurry of brown fur. The blade turned through the air and pinned the weasel against the floor.

Errol walked down a few steps and looked at the ferret,

which was still alive. He'd stabbed it just above one of its front legs, and it was struggling against the switchblade, its head and neck pressed down to the floor. As Errol looked straight into the animal's eyes, the wildness and raving behind them slowly died; the piercing black beads gradually glazed over, and that sense Errol had always had of perception there, of cleverness and treachery, gave way—their glimmer grew dim, their pupils shrank, until finally the sharp, keen-edged face looking up at him went completely blank. Though Errol had never really liked the ferret, to see such edge and brilliance fade and flatten saddened him, and he imagined he would actually miss the flash of those eyes, the litheness of its body, even its wicked hiss as Errol walked into the den. Though hostile, at least the hiss was acknowledgment, and since the ferret had reserved this particular acid sound for Errol alone, it had always made him feel singled out in an almost pleasant way. He had enjoyed, as Walter would say, the sting.

Gray, however, had gone to the dog. Perhaps Errol had done the right thing with Solo, but too late. Bwana had collapsed in the corner with a quiet, choking sound. Gray sat on the floor next to him and pulled his head into her lap. His mouth fell open and his tongue lolled; his breathing was labored and clogged. "Sh-sh," said Gray. "He's gone, Bwana. You're okay now. Bwana, come on now. You're in great shape." She stroked the dog's head and smoothed down his flanks as they rose and fell with difficulty. His eyes were bright red now, and full of pain. "Sh-sh," she crooned, "he's just an old ferret, a sly, spiteful little rat. He can't hurt you anymore. Just relax, Bwana. You'll be all right. Just take it easy, you'll be fine."

Yet Bwana coughed twice; his body convulsed and lay still.

After a couple of abrupt twinges, as if Gray had applied electric shocks, his body relaxed into her lap. For the first time since Raphael had walked down the stairs and out the door, Gray let her head fall back against the wall and, running her hand over and over down the length of the long gray body, cried with a surrender such as Errol had never seen.

chapter twenty-six

The house seemed quieter by far without Bwana, though that was strange, since the dog had hardly made a sound when he was alive. At best in a given day Errol might have heard his toenails click down the stairs, his tail rap once or twice against a wall, or a low throaty purr, like a cat, when he was waiting to be fed. The silence had less to do with sound, then, than with the sensation when Errol and Gray returned from their afternoon walks that they were the only animate creatures in the house; unfortunately, Bwana's absence helped accentuate that not only were there no toenails clicking across the floorboards but there was no young man lolling in the den, either, clinking his ice cubes, drinking up Gray's liquor, sitting in her chair.

These walks were hard work. The night of Bwana's heart attack it had begun to snow, and the following blizzard left Boston buried in drifts several feet deep. That was all right, though; bundling up and pulling on snow gear gave Gray something to do, and slogging along the white sidewalks leaning into a stiff wind made their strolls seem more eventful. The spareness of their conversation fit this landscape well, and Gray's complexion blended nicely with the snow.

Errol followed Gray's instructions as loyally as he could, though he succeeded in getting her to eat only about half the time, and then little. Still, she lost weight more slowly than if he hadn't been there threatening to feed her by the spoonful like an invalid if she didn't swallow something. She admitted, too, that there were nights after he put her to bed when she lay staring at the shadows on the ceiling through to morning, or looking out the window at the moonlight on the snow, but at least it was better for her to rest than to roam about the house all night. Also, as he'd been told, Errol took the phone off the hook at midnight and replaced it at seven, though after a few days of this they both knew this was nothing but ritual or conceit. During the day Gray received routine business calls, and into the second week her pulse would only mildly quicken when the phone rang.

Most poignant for Errol were the afternoons when he walked in on her and she was sitting by the phone, meditatively tapping the black plastic. While he'd seen her dial numbers, she never picked up the receiver; she'd only listen to the dial purr on its return and smile sadly. Errol supposed this was safe enough, though it chilled him; it was a little bit like watching someone play with an unloaded gun.

The ferret had tested positively for rabies; since it had bitten her the night before it went wild, Errol had to take Gray for several shots. They were painful, and Errol regretted they couldn't vaccinate her against the disease from which she was really suffering. However, it seemed that the only antidote to the kind of poison she had swallowed was this gradual flushing out with the days, weeks, maybe months of her life. With Gray now approaching sixty, this struck Errol as a costly cure.

As for Arabella, after the first week she, too, must have stopped waiting for the phone to ring and a certain languorous voice to ask her out to dinner, and in her disappointment she was capable of giving Gray a sincere apology. Errol was surprised, too, how graciously Gray accepted it, given that crude "tribal justice" of hers. Yet there were no tangible repercussions for Arabella's transgression. She kept her position as Gray's graduate assistant, and they even seemed to be getting along better than before. Gray finally told Arabella to stop calling her Dr. Kaiser.

As for Errol, he realized now how he'd imagined this time, and how often he'd imagined it, too: Gray would be crushed for a while, of course, but in her upheaval she would lean on him—and certainly she was doing that. And then . . . There was no "And then . . ." Gray was his friend, and he would help her—feed her, walk with her, put her to bed. Errol didn't feel inclined to expect more.

It was, all in all, incredible that this lasted only fifteen days. Evenings were especially interminable, and Gray would reach for magazines she'd already read cover to cover; Errol roamed the house desperately, looking for trash to take out or something to repair. A few nights they even resorted to TV.

T he day before her birthday Gray got extremely edgy. There was no feeding her, and she paced upstairs all night. She placed all receivers solidly in their cradles.

"Gray," said Errol carefully, "I know tomorrow's your birthday. But he's not a very sentimental guy."

"We'll see," Gray snapped. Errol left her alone.

That morning they agreed to have an "acknowledgment" in the evening—Gray wouldn't call it a party. She told him she wanted to spend the day in the house by herself. What she'd be doing, they both understood, was waiting.

It suited Errol to get away, even if it was her birthday, for he anticipated that, whatever happened with that doorbell, with that telephone, the evening would be difficult.

That morning he went shopping for her present. He had excellent luck finding just the right thing.

Errol took his gift back to his own apartment and picked up the mail. Most of his mail went to Gray's, but he directed a few things to this address. In a stack of special offers, an Audubon solicitation, and a SANE newsletter, Errol found a letter with a curiously illiterate address and one envelope that he was half hoping, half dreading would be there today. To put off reading it, he opened the envelope addressed with the big block letters, "Arol McEkern, Boston, Mass.," confirming that miracles do happen, even in the post office:

Dere Mr. profeser McEkern,

I here from yor frend Waltar. He write a nice letter. For all intensive perpos he my pen pal now. My english teacher say writing letters be good practis.

I tell Waltar about Ray. He seem like he understand. He write he sad sometime. I send him my pitcher I had took at Woolworth.

It cold here in New york, yesterday it 15 degree but below zero with the windshield factor.

Say hay to yor frend mis gray. She seem sad some to. I

have a nice time when you was here. I tell all my frend
profeserrs come see me, they think I fooling.
  Hope you rember me.

                                                    Yor frend,
                                                    Leonia Harris

Errol smiled. He read it several times. Then he went on
to actually open the mailing from the Audubon Society and
thought about sending them money; he glanced over the SANE
newsletter and noted that, according to several names he
respected, he had ten more years to worry about the compara-
tively trivial decision with which this upcoming envelope might
present him before the entire planet was ravaged by nuclear
winter. Errol wondered what kind of comfort that was.
Unfortunately, Errol did not need a set of vinyl suitcases or
matching his 'n' hers terry-cloth jumpsuits, so there was nothing
left to do but open the last piece of mail.

Errol went to fix himself a cup of coffee, but found he had
no milk. Closing the refrigerator, he walked deliberately back to
the table and made himself open the flap and unfold the letter.
In a single moment he knew what it said; though lackadaisically
he went on to read the entire text, it was only for one more
distraction, for as of that moment the decision was imbedded in
his life.

Errol watched his own reaction to this piece of paper with
interest. The letter said what, presumably, he'd wanted it to. Yet
something had just happened in his stomach; he finally understood why Gray had so much trouble eating.

Errol went for a long walk that did him no good. He returned
to his apartment and called Ellen Friedman. She was excited by

his news, though with a slight backwash of disappointment. He told her he had plans for the evening but that he'd love to have a drink with her late that afternoon. He needed desperately to talk, and not to Gray.

It was a day of more than one piece of information, however. When Ellen arrived at his apartment she'd lost the energy and enthusiasm he'd heard over the phone. She seemed wistful. He fixed her a drink, and she sat at the table playing with the ice cubes. Errol found himself doing all the talking. Ellen said "Uh-huh" a lot. He imagined he was depressing her or burdening her or even making her jealous, but when he looked at her more closely, he noticed that she wasn't even paying attention.

Errol waved his hand between Ellen and her glass. "Ellen?"

"I'm sorry. It's just, you know, the thing this afternoon. I suppose I should be happy, or at least unaffected. But when you get older it's harder to brush these things off, no matter who it is."

"What do you mean, exactly?"

Ellen cocked her head. "You haven't heard, then?"

"Heard what?"

Then she told him, and more quickly and casually than Errol would have preferred, but then she didn't really understand; there was no reason she should have.

Errol sat down dully. He told himself it didn't matter. That it was the same without this. Still, his chest ached; he felt physically heavy.

"Errol, are you all right?"

Errol sighed. "Has anyone told Gray Kaiser?"

"Not that I know of, but she may have heard; I couldn't say."

Errol asked Ellen one more question, because he had to, because he'd later be responsible for answering the same question himself. Then he stood abruptly and felt the blood rush from his head; he felt momentarily dizzy. "I have to go immediately."

"Okay. And good luck deciding, Errol. I'm sorry I wasn't attentive. We can talk later. And I don't envy you if you're the one to tell Gray."

"No. You shouldn't."

Ellen kissed him goodbye, long and sexually on the mouth. She was a surprisingly aggressive woman. He liked that. And he had never more keenly needed the luck anyone had wished him in his entire life.

chapter twenty-seven

Errol arrived at the manse with his present for Gray and two pieces of information. He wished desperately to divest himself of all three at once, but after he rang the doorbell with the formality the occasion demanded and Gray opened the door with a ravaged expression, Errol knew that he could give her the present now but he'd have to hold on to the information a while longer. He would have to wait to tell her until the time was right, and Errol knew very well that the time would never be right.

"Happy birthday," said Errol, kissing her cheek and handing her a leash.

"Errol, thank you. He's lovely."

"It's a she."

Gray stooped in the foyer and stroked the new dog. It licked her face lavishly and pawed at her dress. Unlike Bwana, this dog was affectionate and seemed warmly disposed toward everyone she met. "What kind is she?"

"Probably a mutt. I know Bwana was pure-bred. Does it matter?"

"Not at all. She's beautiful."

"My guess is part-retriever, part-Dane, maybe a little collie."

She was a large dog, almost as big as Bwana, but with longer hair, and gold rather than gray. She was old, too, and as a result not stiff and reserved but soft and ungainly, and inclined, Errol had noticed, to romp, as she might have as a puppy, but less successfully. When Errol had taken her with him to the park that afternoon, the dog had leaped at squirrels and jumped over drifts, but often ended up plowed into the snow. She was a good-natured animal, though, and these difficulties didn't seem to disturb her; she'd roll right back up and bound heavily off toward one more drift.

"I got her at the SPCA," Errol explained. "They were going to put her to sleep when the place closed tonight. It seems they took the dog away from some lout who beat her all the time. The man at the kennel said most abused animals get either surly or spooked, but not this one. She's a forgiving animal, he said."

Errol took off the leash and let the dog explore the house. They both looked wistfully after it; eager for distraction of any kind, Errol hoped it would return soon. Errol could talk about that dog for hours.

"How's your day been?" asked Errol.

"How do you think?" said Gray, watching her new pet flounder on the staircase.

"Difficult, perhaps." He wanted badly to add, "But this is nothing," instead asking her, "So how's sixty?" as casually as he could.

"I feel like a carton of milk on its expiration date," said

Gray. "Sour. Everything has the strange quality of being abruptly over."

"I thought you were going to live to a hundred."

"Frankly, I can't imagine as far as tomorrow morning."

Errol couldn't imagine her tomorrow, either. Gray turned to him with a look of quizzical interest when he declined to say something boisterous. Errol could only smile weakly and shrug his shoulders. "You'll manage somehow." Errol wandered into the den. He needed to sit down.

Unsettlingly, Nora's portrait of Vincent Sarasola had been hung next to the leopards on the wall during the day. Errol tried to avoid looking over in that corner once he noticed it, but whenever his discipline waned, he'd find his eyes fixed on the portrait. Determinedly, he'd look away again.

There was so much for them to talk about, but they couldn't talk about these things, so that Errol felt, for the first time in years, awkward here, needing to make conversation. Gray sat down in her leather chair next to Errol on the couch, with the clear understanding that they were to talk now; their silence quickly became odd.

"It's supposed to snow more tonight," said Errol feebly.

Gray turned to Errol with incredulity. "You want to talk about the *weather*?"

"Not really."

"Then why are you?"

"To spare you."—No, he didn't say that. He spared her even that. "It's your birthday," he said instead. "We can talk about whatever you like."

"We could talk about," she said, looking dully over at the desk, "how when you're sixty the phone rarely disturbs your peaceful old age."

"You should know that there was a lot of talk about getting together a big wingding for you today—Tom was going to do it, those guys down at the museum. I stopped it all. You told me to. I told people to leave you alone today. No doubt you'll get a lot of calls tomorrow."

"So you told everyone to leave me alone today, did you?"

"No," said Errol, shooting another glance at Vincent, "not everyone." Errol kept wondering if there was some way of making this easier or better. He experimented. "Listen. Really . . ." This wasn't going very well. "Why did you expect him to call today?"

"You're right, I shouldn't. He's probably too busy packing."

"Why packing?"

"You know. Packing. Swimming trunks. Tennis racket. Deck chairs. And little bamboo umbrellas to stick in tall gin-and-tonics with a twist of lime."

Errol sat and stared. "You didn't!"

"I did."

Errol leaned back into the couch and tried to work this piece of the puzzle into the larger picture, but it didn't fit anywhere. "Whatever happened to justice and power? I thought they were so practical."

"They are." Gray couldn't look him in the eye. "But other things are practical, too. Love is practical."

"Would he have known by today?"

Gray nodded.

"How did you expect him to react?"

"You mean, did I think he'd come back? I spent hours upstairs deciding, Errol. I promised myself right off that if all I was doing was enticing him to return here I wouldn't do it. No, I just gave him what he wanted. That was in my power, so I did that."

"If you didn't expect anything back, why did you think he'd contact you today?"

"Because I'm not perfect. I thought he might at least call. To thank me."

"And then what?"

"I'd say, 'You're welcome.'"

"Pretty marginal expectations."

"They were all I could afford." She glanced at the phone. "Of course, it is early yet—"

"Gray." There was a stone in Errol's stomach. "He's not going to call."

Gray recoiled into her armchair and traced the veins on her hand. She took this as a reprimand. It was not. It was the truth. It was information.

Errol rose from the couch and ambled around the den, treasuring the few moments now before he'd have to tell her. It was her birthday; they were together; he'd spare her a minute or two more, as a favor. He turned back to Gray and caught an image of her: tall and angular and almost cocky, her chin in her palm; thinking, he wondered what. It was incredible she was sixty years old.

"You're a real character, you know that?" said Errol softly. "I forget sometimes. I take you for granted. But we've traveled a lot, and I swear I've still never met anyone like you in the entire world."

That was when she'd said, "Errol, I'm tired of being a character," and leaned back in her chair. They'd talked about age and tiredness. They'd remembered their first meeting twenty-five years before. And Errol had studied the obscure object of this last year.

He'd been about to ask Gray to explain it to him, when suddenly the story seemed simple, after all. She was sixty. She'd fallen in love for the first time in her life, and not with Errol. It hadn't "worked out." That was the story. Errol had only to add the last few lines and it was done.

"I've wondered," said Gray, just as Errol was opening his mouth, "whether he'll come back to visit. I don't mean now, but in ten years, even twenty. I'm not sure I want him to see me at eighty, but I'd love to know what happens to him. Wouldn't you?"

"I know already."

"So do you think he'll get by living off older women, or will he be something?"

"That depends on your point of view. Maybe snagging a woman like you he did get to be something. He got you to lose a game, pay a check, even cry. Maybe that's enough of an accomplishment for anyone's lifetime. I couldn't say."

There must have been a tenor to Errol's voice that made Gray look up at him in that fantastically focused way she had sometimes; Errol averted his eyes and took a restless step or two from her chair. "I told you he wouldn't call tonight—"

"And clearly you were right."

"But not because I'm a good guesser. In the same way I know he won't grow up to be anything he wasn't already when he last walked out of this house." Errol looked her in the eye, and she looked away, over toward the wildebeest. He wouldn't proceed until she looked back at him, and even then it was a struggle, getting her to keep seeing what he was telling her, watch his mouth form certain words. Finally her pupils stopped darting around the room, and he held her gaze steadily, wrapping his eyes around her like arms in an embrace.

They were little words. Now they were over.

Errol kept looking at his mentor and best friend. Absolutely nothing in her face changed. She stared back at him. She said nothing. Maybe the little words hadn't worked. All that had happened since Errol had said them was that the hairs on his arms had risen and a funny cold feeling had crawled up the back of his neck. His heart beat in his teeth. But Gray sat stonily in her chair; not a muscle moved; time passed. She seemed to be waiting for something—waiting for him to take it *back*.

Gray looked down at her lap and picked a pill off her wool skirt. "But Raphael," she said slowly, "is a very good driver."

"Was."

"What?"

"*Was* a good driver." He would start with verbs. Assembling reality was sometimes a difficult project. You turned your back on it for a moment and it slipped, pieces fell away; it was a mess a minute later. Doggedly you had to keep stacking it back up, like a tower of blocks before a defiant child.

Gray's forehead creased. "Of course. Was."

"It was probably icy."

"Yes," she said. "Icy." At last she looked up. "Are you sure of this?"

Errol looked back at her, almost smiling because she actually needed him to repeat it. Yet he tried to keep any tenderness out of his expression, tried to keep it hard and clear and relentless. All he wanted in his eyes was a car accident.

Gray leaned her head back, her eyes at sea, watery and pale. *You remember how Ida made him repeat things? Three times.*

I remember.

That was some story, wasn't it?

Yes, Gray. That was some story.

Gray closed her eyes. "Where did this happen?"

Errol named a road a couple of miles away.

Does this make you happy?

Come on.

I know you didn't like him. But you did like him as a boy, didn't you? At least?

Yes, Gray. He was a fine boy. And how I felt about him later? Well, that's my secret.

You never understood, you see. It was as if he had a disease, like hardening of the arteries. Hardening of something, anyway. He contracted it young; it was terminal. He was calcifying at a tremendous rate. Could you blame him?

Sure I could. I did.

"Errol. Which direction was he driving?"

Errol pretended not to understand. "What difference does that make?"

"Do you know?"

Errol thought about lying, and about telling the truth. And then he realized that she was right: Raphael was a very good driver. All Errol's concern in the Porsche that morning on the way to New York had been his own histrionics, nothing more. So that it really didn't matter what he answered, after all.

"He was driving toward here," said Errol kindly.

Yet when she heard, Gray, too, understood how little that mattered. Had he been in flight, he had not allowed himself to leave; had he been driving here, he had not allowed himself to arrive. Either way, there was a gesture and a cancellation paired. Together they made nothing. He wanted her; he did not. He loved her; he did not. He was, as Ida had said, a baby; he was a grown man, older, as he'd said himself, than Gray. He would come for her birthday; he would not. In the end they made nothing. In which direction was he driving? Whichever way he'd headed, he'd also stopped, abruptly, around a telephone pole. In the room that night were Errol and Gray. That was all.

"Gray," said Errol, groping at something that had troubled him for weeks now, "it didn't have to be this way, did it? Sometimes it does work out, doesn't it? Sometimes you fall for someone and they fall for you and you live in the same house and spend a lot of time together. Tell me that sometimes happens."

She didn't answer.

"Gray," Errol went on, "why did you choose someone who couldn't do it?"

She took a deep breath. "Choose? Do you choose? But that is a very good question." She rubbed the arm of the chair. "Maybe I was still afraid, like those Masai, that a man would take my soul away. Maybe I was stupid, or misjudged him. Maybe I hate myself and love pain. Who's to say?"

But, Errol, why did you choose someone who couldn't do it? That, too, was a very good question.

"Maybe I'm being punished," Gray added, "for admiring the wrong things."

"What things?"

"All my life I've admired people who didn't need anybody— Charles, Raphael, myself. So there's a funny sort of justice in this, don't you think? If you admire people who don't need anybody, then they're not going to need *you*, are they?"

Her question hung in the air for a long time.

"There's one more thing," Errol made himself say at last.

"What's that?"

"I've been asked to head that documentary project in New Guinea. I have to tell them yes or no this week."

"Oh?" said Gray in a small, tight voice.

"Yes." Errol spoke rapidly. "The money's good, and it's a great opportunity. Lots of leeway. And I'd be near Kyle. It's probably a year's worth of work, and if it went well I could pick up more NET grants. You know I like film . . ."

"Yes, you certainly do." Her throat seemed clogged; she cleared it. "When would this start?"

"The project's already behind schedule. As soon as I could wrap up my—other affairs."

"So you wouldn't be going to Ghana."

"Are you?"

"I don't know. Especially if you didn't go, I might not. According to a wire today, the women have started a hunger strike. The whole business is so depressing . . . Maybe I'd only follow through with the project to be with you. To do one more trip together."

"You mean that?"

"Of course I do. When have you known me to be politely warm?"

"When have I known you to be warm?"

She looked down. "Not often enough."

"What do you think I should do?" asked Errol softly. "Should I take the job or not?"

Errol looked at her imploringly. It would take nothing. She had almost said enough already. About wanting to travel with him. Gray, go ahead. Tell me that you need help; that the Porsche coiled around a telephone pole may be conversation now, unbelievable, but that later you'll climb into your gray coupe, tomorrow morning or even tonight, and find the car down the road before they tow it away and drape yourself over the crinkled windshield of that car—tell me that you'll need someone to lift you up and carry you away, someone to pick the bits of glass out of your hair and wipe away the smears of brown that would have dried onto your cheek and remove from your possession all the stray bits of shrapnel and that dented can of ravioli you'd collected from the wreckage as morbid souvenirs. Tell me, Gray, that you won't eat without me, and I'll stay. Tell me you won't sleep well. Just say, Errol, I'd miss you horribly, please don't go.

In fact, Errol realized, she needn't say any of these things at all. She need only say, Stay. She need only say, Errol, I don't think you should take that job, and he would walk upstairs and write out his regrets this very evening, and then he would never leave, he knew that. He'd always have his office here, and he'd watch Gray finally give in year by year to being an old woman; Errol himself would gray and slow; until she didn't publish as much and was mostly a figurehead, invited to many functions, given lots of awards and honorary degrees, but perhaps invited to speak less, and asked her opinion more out of deference than out of real concern over what she thought. This was all much, much later, when she was ninety, say, which she would be—Errol had little doubt she'd live to a hundred, after all. That would make Errol eighty-eight, and he'd wear a hat more and use a cane, and they would finally get a maid for this place, still over

Gray's protest, because she didn't like them, where they came from. The maid would have to be white. They might, too, move the bedrooms downstairs to save climbing all those stairs day after day. The bedrooms, there would be two of them, as always, though in his old age Errol would finally forget why that ever mattered in the first place. When she died, at a hundred and two or three, he'd spend the final years of his own life working out his grief by writing her biography, and he'd be sure to live through to its publication, though after that he wouldn't much care. She'd have left the house to him, and he'd totter in here evenings to light the crimson lamps, eye the dry bones of the wildebeest skeleton, and say hello to Ralph's father. In his dotage, he'd talk to her sometimes as if she were still alive, forgetting in moments of senility that she was no longer perched in that leather chair, where Errol himself would still refuse to sit.

"Gray," he might say, and Errol imagined he would smoke a pipe by this time, "you remember the time I almost left? When I almost went to New Guinea? But you said stay, and by God that was enough for me. I always took your word on just about everything. Oh, I had my problems when you got involved with young Ralph. We came awfully close, you'll remember, to snapping things off. But I guess that was just something you had to go through, to get out of your system. He was certainly a pretty boy. You know, I've still got those pictures you took of him early that morning? You never knew I saw you take them. I didn't find them until after you died—" Errol would pause here and take a puff on his pipe and shoot the wildebeest a look; so she was dead, well past ninety you were so much closer to being a dead person than a live one that it was naturally easier to talk to the dead ones if you had a choice. "I found them tucked away under some papers when I was going through your drawers. You hid them pretty well. I noticed they were soft, though, and wrinkled; you must have found them yourself often enough. Even in those crumpled photos, though, he looks pretty sweet. Asleep, of course. And you sure captured it—he looks real sad, absolutely. Tragic, I'd say. I've never seen so much despair in someone's face while they were asleep. He had one beautiful body, though. You did have taste. And I'm old now, but I remember the guy pretty well. The tone of his voice, you know? It haunts me sometimes—sharp, slow, hollow. I don't know if I ever told you of that conversation we had about blankness. Sent chills up my spine. He could be nasty sometimes, but tear your heart out others, I'm telling you. Well, I guess I don't have to tell you, at that. You're dead, and anyway, you probably knew that better than anybody."

Errol would pour himself a cognac, though the money would be getting tight and he'd buy the cheaper stuff now; Gray would be appalled—the bottle actually said *Brandy*. And that wasn't the only thing that had changed around the house—thank God, he didn't have to eat all those brownies and eclairs anymore. He had Gray to thank for one plate of false teeth, and he was going to hang on to the ones he had left.

"One more thing before I turn in, Gray." He'd take long drags and blow rings aimlessly into the air; the leopards on the wall would still be gnawing on the same meat, and he'd salute them with his pipe. "There was one incident a way long time ago we never talked about since. I swear that's pretty incredible, since out of desperation you'd think we'd have covered everything, even if it embarrassed us a little. But we always managed to come up with something else to talk about, even if by the end there it actually was the weather and what birds came to the feeder and the fact that, though all that tennis and what have you had been good for your heart, it had wrecked your joints something awful. Well, you're dead, so we're safe—don't worry, I won't touch you now, and I never did again, did I? Oh, a comforting hug, a pat on the shoulder, a hand when you got too imbedded in that chair, but I never put my arms around you again and pressed you against my chest until I pushed all the breath out of your lungs. I only kissed you that one night. We'd drunk an awful lot, you were anxious to point that out the next morning. And I was only twenty-six, full of energy; we could pretend, you and I, the next day that I was like that with any woman after two bottles of wine—it's natural, right? But I'll never forget that morning, Gray, just as I'll never forget the night before. I've never been so happy in my life. I didn't tell you that, but you must have known, the way I bounced downstairs to breakfast so jauntily, really wanting to take you out to champagne and pastries, in spite of the hangover. You looked so severe, though, sitting at the table. You looked concerned. You said we had to talk and then *we wouldn't discuss it again*. You made that awfully clear. You said it wasn't 'that way,' that it couldn't be. You said if I felt that way about you, then you'd have to find another assistant, since that situation was untenable. You actually used the word 'untenable.' So what was I supposed to do? This famous woman in my field wants to fire me because I've got a crush? I swallowed hard, and I lied so furiously I broke into a sweat, and then I said I had things to do. I skipped the champagne that morning, if I recall correctly.

"I guess what I was wondering, Gray, was this, see: were you glad I kept my promise? Did you ever wish I had tried one more time? And were you proud of me? Because you asked me once whether I thought you were pathetic. I never asked you whether

I was. Was I, Gray? Are we all pathetic? Is that the secret? We're all desperate? Or was it just me?"

The leopards on the wall would purr. The wildebeest bones would rattle softly. The eyes of Frank Sarasola (in Errol's senility, Vincent would return to Frank) would stare back, clear and trusting. The brandy would swirl in Errol's glass and the fumes would sting his eyes when he raised the liquor to his lips and he would listen for an answer. Yet there would be nothing. Nothing, Ralph. I always think of you when I hear that word.

Maybe then Errol would shuffle off to bed. Or, no. Maybe at that moment Errol would suddenly curl over from a stroke. That would be appropriate, having finally approached the big taboo, as if he could rest in peace only after having addressed it. Errol had always felt, too, that were he to bring it up, something terrible would happen: lightning would strike, a flash of blinding white would fell him in the middle of this den. So then Errol would ask his questions and lie on the crimson carpet with the globe of brandy shattered after all these years and the smell of the stuff rising from the red pile. When you had a stroke, did you bleed? Errol wondered. Did it hurt? Could you think clearly? And would he, maybe, in the end there on the carpet, not even talk to Gray, but reach deeper and keep asking questions, but of someone dead much longer than Gray and therefore, perhaps, better informed on these matters?

Ralph, my buddy. I hated you, I did. I always got the feeling you enjoyed that. Gray was right, Ida didn't hate you, to your regret. I did, though. You seemed to savor walking into a room where I would glare at you and you could say things to needle me. We worked it out, you and I; we had a pact. But you didn't hate me, did you? Did you, Ralph? No, I think I was one of your closest friends. Isn't that appalling.

You admired me. I know that for a fact. I may be laid out here on the carpet, but I'm still the one who's alive; I have the upper hand at last, so I can make my accusations to my heart's content. I accuse you of admiring me. I watched you listen to Leonia Harris. I know you thought she was a sucker. I know you thought Walter and I were suckers. Absolutely, Ralph. We were. Across the board, we'd capitulated. And you were so eaten up with envy I could smell it in the air.

As for me: I worshipped you, Ralph. I would have given anything to be you, Ralph. But of course I could only want to be you being me. If I were you, I wouldn't want to be you one bit. Funny how that works. You'd hate being me, too—toadying and groveling all these years, writing some woman's biography.

But you disappointed me. I've looked at those pictures of you, I've looked down your magnificent back, I've watched the way the early-morning light shone on your cheekbones, the way that amazingly thick black hair of yours flamed out on the pillow, and I remember that number you pulled with your Porsche. Ralph, such a pretty car—how could you? I thought you had it over on her, I really did. I envied that so badly—I thought you had her in the palm of your hand. But she plowed you straight into a telephone pole. Is that what people do over whom we have complete *control*? She destroyed you with only $45,000, with that grotesque generosity of hers, and where did that come from, anyway? She was never like that before, Ralph. She was never like that with me.

But Errol wasn't dead yet, neither was Gray; she was sixty, Errol was only forty-eight, and when she finally spoke and returned him to this particular February day well before he had a stroke and lay mumbling on the carpet, Errol felt suddenly very young at that, and full of possibilities.

"By all means, Errol, you should accept that position. As you said, it's a wonderful opportunity."

Incredulously Errol looked at her in that chair, and suddenly remembered his earlier fear last summer—that vision he'd had of her with all the pins out, the terrible deflated old woman he'd seen her become. He'd imagined Ralph would do this to her, and he stared at her hard as she sat there looking him bravely in the eye and trying, though Errol didn't want to flatter himself, not to cry. Was she withering before his eyes? Were the pins falling from her face? Was the skin hanging sadly from her bones as he'd seen so clearly that one summer night as he drove faster and faster to get home?

Before him sat a beautiful woman. Her bones were slender. Her skin had acquired a slight translucence Errol had never noticed before. With the lamplight welling in her collarbone and shining through the tendons in her high neck, she seemed to glow there, more than ever. No pins fell from her face, for there didn't seem to be any pins, after all. Furthermore, her body looked so light and airy and vertical that surely what would happen in the coming years would not be a gradual crumbling and collapse but an extension—he imagined she would finally get so tall that her head would touch the ceiling, like Alice after she'd eaten too much mushroom, and she might have grown so weightless by that time that when she took a step her whole body would rise from the floor and she'd have to wear those ankle weights of hers just to keep from floating away altogether.

"Gray," said Errol, "are you sure you can manage? Because I'd be glad—"

"I'll be fine, Errol, but that's not even the point." Her voice was clear and lovely. "You've served your time. You have to stop worrying about me for a while. Tend to your own life. Your own success."

"I don't mind tending to your life, Gray. I never have."

"I know that. I've admired that, even." Errol felt a flush of blood rise to his cheeks. "But I haven't been fair to you, Errol. Sometimes I think I've used you, just a little bit. So you can use me for a while. I can help you more than I have. I can help you get those NET grants if you want them, and better if you're up for it. Send postcards, Errol. Come back and visit."

"I've thought," said Errol, "about asking Ellen Friedman to go with me." Errol felt a breaking between his ribs, and his voice began to crack. "I've thought I might ask her to marry me."

Gray smiled with difficulty. "I think that's a splendid idea. I'm sure she'll accept. She's a lovely and intelligent woman, a fine choice."

"Gray, what are you going to do now?"

"I might take that time off, as I was threatening. Go somewhere warm. Think. Maybe write a book. Collect shells. Remember. I can't just go right back to work, Errol, not for a little while. I think that might be arrogant."

"You've always liked being arrogant."

"I have. And I've been that way. Maybe I'll try something else for a change.—But I think you'd better go now. You've got a lot to think about, too. You should give Ellen a call, it's before eleven. Tell her the good news. Ask her to marry you. Go out and celebrate, have a piece of chocolate cake on me."

"I don't have to do that tonight, Gray. I can stay. It's your birthday."

"You do have to go now, Errol. You won't always be able to leave here; I won't always be able to tell you to go. Take advantage of a few minutes of grace and intelligence on both our parts and kiss me goodbye."

Gray held out her hands, and without thinking Errol wrapped his arms around her and pressed her against him, kissing her on the mouth with a long, lingering savor he hadn't experienced in twenty-two years.

"I think I've always wanted to kiss you one more time," said Gray, as if she knew what he would ask her at the age of ninety-five. "I'll miss you terribly. Get out of here before I cry."

She hugged him one more time, and Errol would not glance again at the crimson den but walked out of the house and into the cold night air. The wind hit him in the face with all the force of his future, in New Guinea, in Kenya, wherever he might end up, and Errol walked down the familiar pathway to his car no longer able to see himself at ninety-five in any place in particular, nor for that matter all alone or even in separate bedrooms. As he placed his hand on the cold handle of the door, he thought maybe he would call Ellen, after all. When he accelerated into the night air he sped a little faster than usual, spinning the wheel with three fingers. He took a roundabout route home, passing at one point a couple of miles away a set of blinking orange lights that steered him around the scene of an accident. Errol slowed for a moment, but thought better of stopping and, flooring the accelerator, kept on going.

about the book

Looking Back at a Debut Novel

I haven't read *The Female of the Species* in its entirety since its publication in 1986. I don't make a habit of rereading old work, a pastime that surely falls under the heading of "Get a Life." Nevertheless, I'm surprised by how vividly I remember it. I recall the full names of all the characters and exactly what they look like in my head. I can still replay the story in mental Cinemascope, just as Errol McEchern—his imagination inflamed by decades of unrequited love for his august mentor, Gray Kaiser—is able to spool through whole reels of her life that he never witnessed himself. Like first loves, first novels are indelible.

In terms of career trajectory, most first novelists fall into one of two camps. One sort immediately establish themselves as forces to be reckoned with. A debut met by widespread acclaim seems enviable, of course, but it isn't always. Philip Roth was clearly unfazed by the sensation caused by *Goodbye, Columbus*, which he has followed with a long and distinguished literary career. Yet others find the raised expectations of early success a burden, and some writers discover, horribly, that they only had one story to tell. In the worst case, writers praised to the skies for their first novels will spend the rest of their lives trying to regain heights reached back in their twenties, and often end up crafting poor imitations of their own work. Joseph Heller never wrote another novel that was quite as good as *Catch-22*. Jay McInerney has never captured the spirit of his times as well as he did in *Bright Lights, Big City*. Even Richard Yates, whose work I adore, believed that his debut, *Revolutionary Road*, was probably his finest book. Structurally, what an awful arc: all downhill from here.

The second sort of first novelist may garner some appreciative reviews, but they don't hurtle his or her career into the stratosphere. Perhaps the book fell short of genius; perhaps its genius was overlooked—for publishing is capricious, and luck plays as great a role as talent. In either case, as a rule, the second sort of novelist? *Gets better*.

On publication, *The Female of the Species* was critically well received and sold a respectable number of copies. I was encouraged. But my literary life was hardly sewn up, and that made me fortunate. I've always felt sorry for writers who are successful before they know how to handle the stress, before they know their own voice, before they're quite sure what they want to say. While I didn't exactly savor fifteen years of obscurity, not achieving significant commercial success until my seventh novel was good for the books, and good for my character. In retrospect, I wouldn't have wanted *The Female of the Species* to have been hailed as a work of insurmountable genius because I was hoping to surmount it myself in many novels thereafter. I wouldn't have wanted publishers, agents, and magazines breathing down my neck when I was still feeling my way and probably needed most to be left alone.

Of course, were I writing this novel now, there are things I might do differently. I like to think that my prose style has grown quieter and simpler over the years (though it never gets *that* quiet, and simplifying the prose itself is in the service of characters and ideas that grow only more complex). I wonder if nowadays I would have gone on that long riff about Charles Corgie in Africa near the beginning of the book. Such a lengthy early departure is structurally *inadvisable* and could appear to me these days as an indulgence. Nevertheless, maybe it's a good thing I can't get my hands on the novel now; maybe *Female* is better off for that inclusion, which I had enormous fun writing.

Besides, I do think that *The Female of the Species* displays an instinctive feel for narrative structure. The emotional triangle on which the novel is built is classic: Gray Kaiser's becoming smitten with a much younger man, who might merely be using her for her prestige and connections, is all seen through the eyes of her middle-aged assistant, Errol McEchern, who has loved her for years. Errol's sense of insult that his idol exercises such poor romantic judgment enlivens the voice. Errol's exasperation that Gray doesn't love *him* instead also makes his perceptions subtly unreliable, a technique I would also employ in *We Need to Talk About Kevin*. That technical trick I developed in *Female*—getting around the limitations of point of view by hijacking a character's imagination—I would later deploy in *Kevin* as well. The use of quotations from Gray's fictitious anthropology case studies as epigraphs is, I think, a lovely decorative touch, one that helps to shore up the internal reality of the book. Even at this great distance, I still think that the sections about North Adams are inspired and constitute the best parts of the novel. I love the character of Ida, and the way that her manipulative relationship to the adolescent Raphael provides him the model for manipulating Gray Kaiser in his young adulthood. I like the ambiguity of Raphael's relationship to Gray, the suggestion that he is far more taken with her than he pretends—that he is not only fooling her, but himself.

No one enjoys getting worse, so naturally I like to believe that my work following *Female* has improved. Yet despite a few stylistic rough edges, the text teems with an exhilaration distinctive to first novels—an excitement about words, an awe at their power to bring events and people to life from nothing that a veteran fiction writer is less likely to duplicate. In those days, I wrote nonstop for many hours at a go, whereas now I'm much more likely to knock off for a cup of coffee. If (perhaps foolishly) I would cut the Charles Corgie section now, that beginning riff—full of jokes to keep myself entertained, and carrying on in such detail because I was the boss and could do whatever I felt like—is what helps to distinguish the book as formally adventurous, fearless, and playful. Besides, I haven't changed as much as I might think. I didn't obey the rules in my twenties, and I still don't.

Lionel Shriver
2015